THE COMPLETE TALES OF HENRY JAMES
VOLUME TWO 1868–1872

THE COMPLETE TALES OF

HENRY JAMES

EDITED WITH AN

INTRODUCTION BY

LEON EDEL

2

1868–1872

J. B. LIPPINCOTT COMPANY
PHILADELPHIA AND NEW YORK

PRINTED IN THE UNITED STATES OF AMERICA
LIBRARY OF CONGRESS CATALOG CARD NUMBER 62-11335

CONTENTS

INTRODUCTION: 1868–1872

HENRY JAMES'S tales of the late 1860's and the early 1870's, collected in this volume, represent the second phase in his career as a writer of fiction. The first phase belonged to the period of the Civil War and its aftermath. Now the young writer embarks on his study of human types and human behaviour. He examines himself and those around him. He tells himself that it is possible to be mistaken in judging individuals, that even one's closest and best loved may diminish in stature when scrutinised. And then, during these years, he escapes from the oppressive environment of Quincy Street, where the James family lived. He discovers Europe.

"Osborne's Revenge" and "A Light Man" belong to the group in which James explored the paradox of human identity. In later years he was particularly fond of "A Light Man," which he revised and republished; he liked its technical skill; he felt he had successfully carried out his intention. This was to tell an autobiographical tale, in the form of a diary, in which the diarist would provide one picture of himself while the reader would form another. One of James's earliest discoveries had been this double-vision in the old English autobiographical novels: and the fact that very often the "I," as he described himself, and the *kind* of story he told, belonged to two distinct persons, instead of being one. In his twenty-second year, in an unpublished review he had written:

The author not only puts off his own personality, but he assumes that of another, and in proportion as the imaginary hero is different from himself his task becomes difficult. Hence the merit of most fictitious autobiographies is that they give you a tolerably fair reflection of the writer's character. To project yourself into the consciousness of a person essentially your opposite requires the audacity of great genius; and even men of genius are cautious in approaching the problem. Mr Browning, the great master of the art in these days, never assumes the burden of its solution but for a few pages at a time.

James thus foresaw, as far back as 1865, one of the characteristic narrative problems of the twentieth century. When we reflect that the "stream of consciousness" school was not to come for another fifty years and that it was an individual with as much audacity as genius—James Joyce—who was to launch himself into the consciousness of others, we can recognise the closeness with which James was studying his art.

"A Light Man" does not yet show the "audacity of great genius" but it does offer the narrator's self-concept, and asks the reader to keep an eye on his true character. Two of James's greatest tales would exploit the autobiographical form and the double-personality of "hero and historian."

"Gabrielle de Bergerac," an historical tale set in France of the time of the revolution, was written when James was preparing to go abroad: it was as if his imagination had leaped ahead to the bloody history of the Continent. The tale was one of James's rare ventures into this type of fiction, and he regretted writing it almost as soon as he saw it in print. It convinced him that historical fiction—unless written on the panoramic scale of Sir Walter Scott—tends to be factitious and "cheap." A writer can multiply "the little facts that can be got from pictures and documents, relics and prints," but the end result is still "humbug." He felt that "Gabrielle" was "thin and watery." He wrote to his sister that "the present and the future seems to me the best province of fiction." The past was "a grim old deathly reality" he considered little worth his while to describe unless he had a head crammed with facts. And even then! Henceforth he was to remain in his chosen province, and to venture only into a past that could be "visitable," that is within the memory of his time.

There is a charming footnote to "Gabriellè de Bergerac." In his autobiography, *A Small Boy and Others*, written many years later, James describes how, as a schoolboy of fourteen, he had a mate in Boulogne-sur-Mer, the son of the local pastrycook, who had a markedly upturned nose and whose name was Coquelin. In the tale of "Gabrielle" he uses the name of Coquelin, and that of Bergerac for his heroine. He thus anticipates by about three decades a significant conjunction of these names—the writing of Rostand's romantic drama on the life of Cyrano de Bergerac and the casting of the great actor Coquelin—Henry's schoolmate—in the part. For a man of Henry's artistic consciousness to have known the boyish countenance of Coquelin was to have seen—it would appear—the face in French literature that it was designed to match.

The three tales at the centre of this volume reflect James's discovery of Europe. The year he spent abroad—1869–1870 —was to leave its mark deeply on his life. The letters he wrote home at the time are extant. But the record of his emotions may best be read in "Travelling Companions," "A Passionate Pilgrim," and "At Isella." He went into Italy with certain preconceived ideas, and what he found surpassed by far anything he expected. Before that, however, there had been his "passionate" discovery of England—a sentimental journey from Liverpool to Chester, and thence to London. The three tales were written when he was back in Cambridge, trying to measure the effect of his *Wanderjahr*. They show with sufficient clarity the depths of his nostalgia.

Their significance as "early James"—aside from their romantic charm, their excess of sentimentality and their obsession with the European "picturesque"—resides in their foreshadowing of James's major theme. They mark the beginning of the young American's careful observation of travelling Americans, his preoccupation with what he would later call the "Americano-European" legend. "Travelling Companions" contains indeed an excellent sketch of the shrewd practical wealthy American, the predecessor of Christopher Newman or Adam Verver. And the reader is struck also by the extent to which James has mixed up his travel experiences with his fiction; he seems to have written his tales with Murray in one hand and his own travel letters to his family in the other. Of the three tales, he preferred "A Passionate Pilgrim"; he made it the title tale of his first volume of stories published in 1875 and it was the only story of this early time which he resurrected and rewrote for the New York Edition.

James's own feeling about these early European tales was that they possessed a certain "inexpert intensity of art." They are still readable because of this intensity, and thanks to James's faculty for observing and describing. He was essentially a happy and relaxed traveller: and the time was to come when he would either divorce his travelogues from his imaginative writings, or properly combine the two. At this stage of his fictional career however, his travel impressions encroach heavily upon his story-telling. He tends to see foreign places largely in aesthetic and literary terms; the "picturesque" seems to override immediate squalor; and James seems to be able to feel more deeply the blood-soaked past of Europe than any part of its suffering present. On the other hand the old aspect of Europe became identified in Henry's consciousness with his active sense of evil. He possessed this sense with all the intensity of his father's early Calvinism. Europe and evil, America and innocence— this was the simplest equation of his international tales. Later there were to be many subtle variants; for the knowledge of evil also brought wisdom, and innocence, for all its charm, possessed the parochialism and ignorance of Eden. But this is only implicit in these first tales of American adventurers in Europe. What predominates is the atmosphere of the leisurely "grand tour," and a kind of Byronic or Stendhalian communion with the past.

The last two tales in this volume, while they show James's growing skill, reflect also his relapse into the torpor of Cambridge and the flatness (for him) of the home scene. "Master Eustace" can be described as a story of a parochial hero in a perpetual tantrum, although it is psychologically an accurate picture of the dilemma of a young man whose mother has treated him with an excess of seductive charm.

"Guest's Confession" was one of the most unpleasant stories James ever told. His picture of the rivalry between the half-brothers reaches in this tale a degree of morbidity which seldom again appeared in his fiction. What this story seems to be saying is that elder brothers are capable of doing things which make life impossible for their juniors.

These tales are best read in the light of biography. For James is using the short story at this moment of his life—whether consciously or unconsciously—as a vehicle for emotions he cannot elsewhere discharge. He wanted a life of large leisure in which to explore the world; he had long before withdrawn from competing brothers and the competitive forces in American society. And yet for the time he was tied to Cambridge, while his fancy journeyed in England and in Italy. He was conscious that he would have to make a choice: that he could not create in a destiny divided between "home" and the great wide world. The early tales point to the choice that he will make; they show the artist using his art to arrive at personal solutions; and they derive a measure of poignancy from these circumstances.

OSBORNE'S REVENGE

I

PHILIP OSBORNE and Robert Graham were intimate friends. The latter had been spending the summer at certain medicinal springs in New York, the use of which had been recommended by his physician. Osborne, on the other hand—a lawyer by profession, and with a rapidly increasing practice—had been confined to the city, and had suffered June and July to pass, not unheeded, heaven knows, but utterly unhonored. Toward the middle of July he began to feel uneasy at not hearing from his friend, habitually the best of correspondents. Graham had a charming literary talent, and plenty of leisure, being without a family, and without business. Osborne wrote to him, asking the reason of his silence, and demanding an immediate reply. He received in the course of a few days the following letter:

DEAR PHILIP: I am as you conjectured, not well. These infernal waters have done me no good. On the contrary—they have poisoned me. They have poisoned my life, and I wish to God I had never come to them. Do you remember the *White Lady* in *The Monastery*, who used to appear to the hero at the spring? There is such a one here, at this spring—which you know tastes of sulphur. Judge of the quality of the young woman. She has charmed me, and I can't get away. But I mean to try again. Don't think I'm cracked, but expect me next week. Yours always,

R.G.

The day after he received this letter, Osborne met, at the house of a female friend detained in town by the illness of one of her children, a lady who had just come from the region in which Graham had fixed himself. This lady, Mrs Dodd by name, and a widow, had seen a great deal of the young man, and she drew a very long face and threw great expression into her eyes as she spoke of him. Seeing that she was inclined to be confidential, Osborne made it possible that she should converse with him privately. She assured him, behind her fan, that his friend was dying of a broken heart. Something should be done. The story was briefly this. Graham had made the acquaintance, in the early part of the summer, of a young lady, a certain Miss Congreve, who was living in the neighborhood with a married sister. She was not pretty, but she was clever, graceful, and pleasing, and Graham had immediately fallen in love with her. She had encouraged his addresses, to the knowledge of all their friends, and at the end of a month —heart-histories are very rapid at the smaller watering places—their engagement, although not announced, was hourly expected. But at this moment a stranger had effected an entrance into the little society of which Miss Congreve was one of the most brilliant ornaments—a Mr Holland, out of the West—a man of Graham's age, but better favoured in person. Heedless of the circumstance that her affections were notoriously preoccupied, he had immediately begun to be attentive to the young girl. Equally reckless of the same circumstance, Henrietta Congreve had been all smiles—all seduction. In the course of a week, in fact, she had deliberately transferred her favors from the old love to the new. Graham had been turned out into the cold; she had ceased to look at him, to speak to him, to think of him. He nevertheless remained at the springs, as if he found a sort of fascination in the sense of his injury, and in seeing Miss Congreve and Holland together. Besides, he doubtless wished people to fancy that, for good reasons, he had withdrawn his suit, and it was therefore not for him to hide himself. He was proud, reserved, and silent, but his friends had no difficulty in seeing that his pain was intense, and that his wound was

almost mortal. Mrs Dodd declared that unless he was diverted
from his sorrow, and removed from contact with the various
scenes and objects which reminded him of his unhappy
passion—and above all, deprived of the daily chance of
meeting Miss Congreve—she would not answer for his
sanity.

Osborne made all possible allowances for exaggeration. A
woman, he reflected, likes so to round off her story—especially
if it is a dismal one. Nevertheless he felt very anxious, and he
forthwith wrote his friend a long letter, asking him to what
extent Mrs Dodd's little romance was true, and urging him
to come immediately to town, where, if it was substantially
true, he might look for diversion. Graham answered by
arriving in person. At first, Osborne was decidedly relieved.
His friend looked better and stronger than he had looked for
months. But on coming to talk with him, he found him morally, at least, a sad invalid. He was listless, abstracted, and
utterly inactive in mind. Osborne observed with regret that
he made no response to his attempts at interrogation and to
his proffered sympathy. Osborne had by nature no great
respect for sentimental woes. He was not a man to lighten his
tread because his neighbor below stairs was laid up with a
broken heart. But he saw that it would never do to poke fun
at poor Graham, and that he was quite proof against the contagion of gayety. Graham begged him not to think him morbid or indifferent to his kindness, and to allow him not to
speak of his trouble until it was over. He had resolved to
forget it. When he had forgotten it—as one forgets such
things—when he had contrived to push the further end
of it at least into the past—then he would tell him all about
it. For the present he must occupy his thoughts with something else. It was hard to decide what to do. It was hard
to travel without an aim. Yet the intolerable heat made it
impossible that he should stay in New York. He might go
to Newport.

"A moment," said Osborne. "Has Miss Congreve gone to Newport?"

"Not that I know of."

"Does she intend to go?"

Graham was silent. "Good heavens!" he cried, at last, "forbid it then! All I want is to have it forbidden. *I* can't forbid it. Did you ever see a human being so degraded?" he added, with a ghastly smile. "Where *shall* I go?"

Philip went to his table and began to overhaul a mass of papers fastened with red tape. He selected several of these documents and placed them apart. Then, turning to his friend, "You're to go out to Minnesota," he said, looking him in the eyes. The proposal was a grave one, and gravely as it was meant, Osborne would have been glad to have Graham offer some resistance. But he sat looking at him with a solemn stare which (in the light of subsequent events) cast a lugubrious shade over the whole transaction. "The deuce!" thought Osborne. "Has it made him stupid?—What you need," he said aloud, "is to have something else to think about. An idle man can't expect to get over such troubles. I have some business to be done at St Paul, and I know that if you'll give your attention to it, you're as well able to do it as any man. It's a simple matter, but it needs a trustworthy person. So I shall depend upon you."

Graham came and took up the papers and looked over them mechanically.

"Never mind them now," said Osborne; "it's past midnight; you must go to bed. To-morrow morning I'll put you *au fait*, and the day after, if you like, you can start."

The next morning Graham seemed to have recovered a considerable portion of his old cheerfulness. He talked about indifferent matters, laughed, and seemed for a couple of hours to have forgotten Miss Congreve. Osborne began to doubt that the journey was necessary, and he was glad to be able to think, afterwards, that he had expressed his doubts, and that his friend had strongly combatted them and insisted upon having the affair explained to him. He mastered it, to Osborne's satisfaction, and started across the continent.

During the ensuing week Philip was so pressed with business that he had very little time to think of the success of Graham's mission. Within the fortnight he received the following letter:

DEAR PHILIP: Here I am, safe, but anything but sound. I don't know what to think of it, but I have completely forgotten the terms of my embassy. I can't for my life remember what I'm do to or say, and neither the papers nor your notes assist me a whit. 12th—I wrote so much yesterday and then went out to take a walk and collect my thoughts. I *have* collected them once for all. Do you understand, dearest Philip? Don't call me insane, or impious, or anything that merely expresses your own impatience and intolerance, without throwing a ray of light on the state of my own mind. He can only understand it who has felt it, and he who has felt it can do but as I do. Life has lost, I don't say its charm—that I could willingly dispense with—but its meaning. I shall live in your memory and your love, which is a vast deal better than living in my own self-contempt. Farewell.

R.G.

Osborne learned the circumstances of his friend's death three days later, through his correspondent at St Paul—the person to whom Graham had been addressed. The unhappy young man had shot himself through the head in his room at the hotel. He had left money, and written directions for the disposal of his remains—directions which were, of course, observed. As Graham possessed no near relative, the effect of his death was confined to a narrow circle; to the circle, I may say, of Philip Osborne's capacious personality. The two young men had been united by an almost passionate friendship. Now that Graham had ceased to be, Osborne became sensible of the strength of this bond; he felt that he cared more for it than for any human tie. They had known each other ten years, and their intimacy had grown with their growth during the most active period of their lives. It had been strengthened within and without by the common enjoyment of so many pleasures, the experience of so many hazards, the exchange of so much advice, so much confidence, and so many pledges of mutual interest, that each had grown to regard it as the single absolute certainty in life, the one fixed fact in a shifting world. As constantly happens with intimate friends, the two were perfectly diverse in character, tastes and appearance. Graham was three years the elder, slight, undersized, feeble in health, sensitive, indolent, whimsical, generous, and in reality of a far finer clay than his friend, as the latter, moreover, perfectly well knew. Their intimacy was often a puzzle to observers. Disinterested parties were at a loss to discover how Osborne had come to set his heart upon an insignificant, lounging invalid, who, in general company, talked in monosyllables, in a weak voice, and gave himself the airs of one whom nature had endowed with the right to be fastidious, without ever having done a stroke of work. Graham's partisans, on the other hand, who were chiefly women (which, by the way, effectually relieves him from the accusation occasionally brought against him of being "effeminate") were quite unable to penetrate the motives of his interest in a commonplace, hard-working lawyer, who addressed a charming woman as if he were exhorting a jury of grocers and undertakers, and viewed the universe as one vast "case." This account of Osborne's mind and manners would have been too satirical to be wholly just, and yet it would have been excusable as an attempt to depict a figure in striking contrast with poor Graham. Osborne was in all respects a large fellow. He was six feet two in height, with a chest like a boxing-master, and a clear, brown, complexion, which successfully resisted the deleterious action of a sedentary life. He was, in fact, without a particle of vanity, a particularly handsome man. His character corresponded to his person, or, as one may say, continued and completed it, and his mind kept the promise of his character. He was all of one piece—all health and breadth, capacity and energy. Graham had once told his friend somewhat brutally—for in his little, weak voice Graham said things far more brutal than Osborne, just as he said things far more fine—he had told him that he worked like a horse and loved like a dog.

Theoretically, Osborne's remedy for mental trouble was work. He redoubled his attention to his professional affairs, and strove to reconcile himself, once for all, to his loss. But he found his grief far stronger than his will, and felt that it obstinately refused to be pacified without some act of sacrifice or devotion. Osborne had an essentially kind heart and plenty of pity and charity for deserving objects; but at the bottom of his soul there lay a well of bitterness and resentment which, when his nature was strongly shaken by a sense of wrong, was sure to ferment and raise its level, and at last to swamp his conscience. These bitter waters had been stirred, and he felt that they were rising fast. His thoughts travelled back with stubborn iteration from Graham's death to the young girl who figured in the prologue to the tragedy. He felt in his breast a savage need of hating her. Osborne's friends observed in these days that he looked by no means pleasant; and if he had not been such an excellent fellow he might easily have passed for an intolerable brute. He was not softened and mellowed by suffering; he was exasperated. It seemed to him that justice cried aloud that Henrietta Congreve should be confronted with the results of her folly, and made to carry forever in her thoughts, in all the hideousness of suicide, the image of her miserable victim. Osborne was, perhaps, in error, but he was assuredly sincere; and it is strong evidence of the energy of genuine affection that this lusty intellect should have been brought, in the interest of another, to favor a scheme which it would have deemed wholly, ludicrously impotent to assuage the injured dignity of its own possessor. Osborne must have been very fond of his friend not to have pronounced him a drivelling fool. It is true that he had always pitied him as much as he loved him, although Graham's incontestable gifts and virtues had kept this feeling in the background. Now that he was gone, pity came uppermost, and bade fair to drive him to a merciless disallowance of all claims to extenuation on the part of the accused. It was unlikely that, for a long time at least, he would listen to anything but that Graham had been foully wronged, and that the light of his life had been wantonly quenched. He found it impossible to sit down in resignation. The best that he could do, indeed, would not call Graham back to life; but he might at least discharge his gall, and have the comfort of feeling that Miss Congreve was the worse for it. He was quite unable to work. He roamed about for three days in a disconsolate, angry fashion. On the third, he called upon Mrs Dodd, from whom he learned that Miss Congreve had gone to Newport, to stay with a second married sister. He went home and packed up a valise, and—without knowing why, feeling only that to do so was to do something, and to put himself in the way of doing more—drove down to the Newport boat.

II

HIS first inquiry on his arrival, after he had looked up several of his friends and encountered a number of acquaintances, was about Miss Congreve's whereabouts and habits. He found that she was very little known. She lived with her sister, Mrs Wilkes, and as yet had made but a single appearance in company. Mrs Wilkes, moreover, he learned, was an invalid and led a very quiet life. He ascertained the situation of her house and gave himself the satisfaction of walking past it. It was a pretty place, on a secluded by-road, marked by various tokens of wealth and comfort. He heard, as he passed, through the closed shutters of the drawing-room window, the sound of a high, melodious voice, warbling and trilling to the accompaniment of a piano. Osborne had no soul for music, but he stopped and listened, and as he did so, he remembered Graham's passion for the charming art and fancied that these were the very accents that had lured him to his sorrow. Poor Graham! here too, as in all things, he had showed his taste. The singer discharged a magnificent volley of roulades and flourishes and became silent. Osborne, fancying he heard a movement of the lattice of the shutters, slowly walked away. A couple of days later he found himself strolling, alone and disconsolate, upon the long avenue which runs parallel to the Newport cliffs, which, as all the world knows, may be reached by five minutes' walk from any part of it. He had been on the field, now, for nearly a week, and he was no nearer his revenge. His unsatisfied desire haunted his steps and hovered in a ghostly fashion about thoughts which perpetual contact with old friends and new, and the entertaining spectacle of a heterogeneous throng of pleasure seekers and pleasure vendors, might have made free and happy. Osborne was very fond of the world, and while he still clung to his resentment, he yet tacitly felt that it lurked as a skeleton at his banquet. He was fond of nature, too, and betwixt these two predelictions, he grew at moments ashamed of his rancor. At all events, he felt a grateful sense of relief when as he pursued his course along this sacred way of fashion, he caught a glimpse of the deep blue expanse of the ocean, shining at the end of a cross road. He forthwith took his way down to the cliffs. At the point where the road ceased, he found an open barouche whose occupants appeared to have wandered out of sight. Passing this carriage, he reached a spot where the surface of the cliff communicates with the beach, by means of an abrupt footpath. This path he descended and found himself on a level with the broad expanse of sand and the rapidly rising tide. The wind was blowing fresh from the sea and the little breakers tumbling in with their multitudinous liquid clamor. In a very few moments Osborne felt a sensible exhilaration of spirits. He had not advanced many steps under the influence of this joyous feeling, when, on turning a slight projection in the cliff, he descried a sight which caused him to hasten forward. On a broad flat rock, at about a dozen yards from the shore, stood a child of some five years—a handsome boy, fair-haired and well dressed—stamping his feet and wringing his hands in an apparent agony of terror. It was easy to understand the situation. The child had ventured out on the rock while the water was still low, and had become so much absorbed in paddling with his little wooden spade among the rich marine deposits on its surface, that he had failed to observe the advance of the waves, which had now completely covered the intermediate fragments of rock and were foaming and weltering betwixt him and the shore. The poor little fellow stood screaming to the winds and waters, and quite unable to answer Osborne's shouts of interrogation and comfort. Meanwhile, the latter prepared to fetch him ashore. He saw with some disgust that the channel was too wide to warrant a leap, and yet, as the child's companions might at any moment appear, in the shape of distracted importunate women, he judged it imprudent to divest himself of any part of his apparel. He accordingly plunged in without further ado, waded forward, seized the child and finally restored him to *terra firma*. He felt him trembling in his arms like a frightened bird. He set him on his feet, soothed him, and asked him what had become of his guardians.

The boy pointed toward a rock, lying at a certain distance, close under the cliff, and Osborne, following his gesture, distinguished what seemed to be the hat and feather of a lady sitting on the further side of it.

"That's Aunt Henrietta," said the child.

"Aunt Henrietta deserves a scolding," said Osborne. "Come, we'll go and give it to her." And he took the boy's hand and led him toward his culpable relative. They walked along the beach until they came abreast of the rock, and approached the lady in front. At the sound of their feet on the stones, she raised her head. She was a young woman, seated on a boulder, with an album in her lap, apparently absorbed in the act of sketching. Seeing at a glance that something was amiss, she rose to her feet and thrust the album into her pocket. Osborne's wet trousers and the bespattered garments and discomposed physiognomy of the child revealed the nature of the calamity. She held out her arms to her little nephew. He dropped Philip's hand, and ran and threw himself on his aunt's neck. She raised him up and kissed him, and looked interrogatively at Osborne.

"I couldn't help seeing him safely in your hands," said the latter, removing his hat. "He has had a terrific adventure."

"What is it, darling?" cried the young lady, again kissing the little fellow's bloodless face.

"He came into the water after me," cried the boy. "Why did you leave me there?"

"What has happened, sir?" asked the young girl, in a somewhat preemptory tone.

"You had apparently left him on that rock, madame, with a channel betwixt him and the shore deep enough to drown him. I took the liberty of displacing him. But he's more frightened than hurt."

The young girl had a pale face and dark eyes. There was no beauty in her features; but Osborne had already perceived that they were extremely expressive and intelligent. Her face flushed a little, and her eyes flashed; the former, it seemed to Philip, with mortification at her own neglect, and the latter in irritation at the reproach conveyed in his accents. But he may have been wrong. She sat down on the rock, with the child

on her knees, kissing him repeatedly and holding him with a
sort of convulsive pressure. When she looked up, the flashes
in her eyes had melted into a couple of tears. Seeing that
Philip was a gentleman, she offered a few words of self-
justification. She had kept the boy constantly within sight,
and only within a few minutes had allowed her attention to
be drawn away. Her apology was interrupted by the arrival
of a second young woman—apparently a nursery-maid—
who emerged from the concealment of the neighboring
rocks, leading a little girl by the hand. Instinctively, her eyes
fell upon the child's wet clothes.

"Ah, Miss Congreve," she cried, in true nursery-maid
style, "what'll Mrs Wilkes say to that?"

"She will say that she is very thankful to this gentleman,"
said Miss Congreve, with decision.

Philip had been looking at the young girl as she spoke,
forcibly struck by her face and manner. He detected in her
appearance a peculiar union of modesty and frankness, of
youthful freshness and elegant mannerism, which suggested
vague possibilities of further acquaintance. He had already
found it pleasant to observe her. He had been for ten days in
search of a wicked girl, and it was a momentary relief to find
himself suddenly face to face with a charming one. The
nursery-maid's apostrophe was like an electric shock.

It is, nevertheless, to be supposed that he concealed his
surprise, inasmuch as Miss Congreve gave no sign of having
perceived that he was startled. She had come to a tardy
sense of his personal discomfort. She besought him to
make use of her carriage, which he would find on the cliff,
and quickly return home. He thanked her and declined her
offer, declaring that it was better policy to walk. He put
out his hand to his little friend and bade him good-bye.
Miss Congreve liberated the child and he came and put his
hand in Philip's.

"One of these days," said Osborne, "you'll have long

legs, too, and then you'll not mind the water." He spoke
to the boy, but he looked hard at Miss Congreve, who,
perhaps, thought he was asking for some formal expression
of gratitude.

"His mother," she said, "will give herself the pleasure of
thanking you."

"The trouble," said Osborne, "the very unnecessary
trouble. Your best plan," he added, with a smile (for, wonderful to tell, he actually smiled) "is to say nothing about it."

"If I consulted my interests alone," said the young girl,
with a gracious light in her dark eyes, "I should certainly
hold my tongue. But I hope my little victim is not so ungrateful as to promise silence."

Osborne stiffened himself up; for this was more or less of a
compliment. He made his bow in silence and started for home
at a rapid pace. On the following day he received this note by
post:

Mrs Wilkes begs to thank Mr Osborne most warmly for the
prompt and generous relief afforded to her little boy. She regrets
that Mr. Osborne's walk should have been interrupted, and hopes
that his exertions have been attended with no bad effects.

Enclosed in the note was a pocket-handkerchief, bearing
Philip's name, which he remembered to have made the child
take, to wipe his tears. His answer was, of course, brief.

Mr Osborne begs to assure Mrs Wilkes that she exaggerates the
importance of the service rendered to her son, and that he has no
cause to regret his very trifling efforts. He takes the liberty of presenting his compliments to Master Wilkes, and of hoping that he
has recovered from his painful sensations.

The correspondence naturally went no further, and for
some days no additional light was thrown upon Miss Congreve. Now that Philip had met her, face to face, and found
her a commonplace young girl—a clever girl, doubtless, for

she looked it, and an agreeable one—but still a mere young lady, mindful of the proprieties, with a face innocent enough, and even a trifle sad, and a couple of pretty children who called her "aunt," and whom, indeed, in a moment of enthusiastic devotion to nature and art, she left to the mercy of the waves, but whom she finally kissed and comforted and handled with all due tenderness—now that he had met Miss Congreve under these circumstances, he felt his mission sitting more lightly on his conscience. Ideally she had been repulsive; actually, she was a person whom, if he had not been committed to detest her, he would find it very pleasant to like. She had been humanized, to his view, by the mere accidents of her flesh and blood. Philip was by no means prepared to give up his resentment. Poor Graham's ghost sat grim and upright in his memory, and fed the flickering flame. But it was something of a problem to reconcile the heroine of his vengeful longings, with the heroine of the little scene on the beach, and to accommodate this inoffensive figure, in turn, to the color of his retribution. A dozen matters conspired to keep him from coming to the point, and to put him in a comparatively good humor. He was invited to the right and the left; he lounged and bathed, and talked, and smoked, and rode, and dined out, and saw an endless succession of new faces, and in short, reduced the vestments of his outward mood to a suit of very cheerful half-mourning. And all this, moreover, without any sense of being faithless to his friend. Oddly enough, Graham had never seemed so living as now that he was dead. In the flesh, he had possessed but a half-vitality. His spirit had been exquisitely willing, but his flesh had been fatally weak. He was at best a baffled, disappointed man. It was his spirit, his affections, his sympathies and perceptions, that were warm and active, and Osborne knew that he had fallen sole heir to these. He felt his bosom swell with a wholesome sense of the magnitude of the heritage, and he was conscious with each successive day, of less desire to invoke poor

Graham in dark corners, and mourn him in lonely places. By a single solemn, irrevocable aspiration, he had placed his own tough organism and his energetic will at the service of his friend's virtues. So as he found his excursion turning into a holiday, he stretched his long limbs and with the least bit of a yawn whispered *Amen.*

Within a week after his encounter with Miss Congreve, he went with a friend to witness some private theatricals, given in the house of a lady of great social repute. The entertainment consisted of two plays, the first of which was so flat and poor that when the curtain fell Philip prepared to make his escape, thinking he might easily bring the day to some less impotent conclusion. As he passed along the narrow alley between the seats and the wall of the drawing-room, he brushed a printed programme out of a lady's hand. Stooping to pick it up, his eye fell upon the name of Miss Congreve among the performers in the second piece. He immediately retraced his steps. The overture began, the curtain rose again, and several persons appeared on the stage, arrayed in the powder and patches of the last century. Finally, amid loud acclamations, walked on Miss Congreve, as the heroine, powdered and patched in perfection. She represented a young countess—a widow in the most interesting predicament—and for all good histrionic purposes, she was irresistibly beautiful. She was dressed, painted, and equipped with great skill and in the very best taste. She looked as if she had stepped out of the frame of one of those charming full-length pastel portraits of fine ladies in Louis XV's time, which they show you in French palaces. But she was not alone all grace and elegance and *finesse*; she had dignity; she was serious at moments, and severe; she frowned and commanded; and, at the proper time, she wept the most natural tears. It was plain that Miss Congreve was a true artist. Osborne had never seen better acting—never, indeed, any so good; for here was an actress who was at once a perfect young lady and a consummate mistress of dramatic effect. The audience was roused to the highest pitch of enthusiasm, and Miss Congreve's fellow-players were left quite in the lurch. The beautiful Miss Latimer, celebrated in polite society for her face and figure, who had undertaken the second female part, was compelled for the nonce to have neither figure nor face. The play had been marked in the bills as adapted from the French "especially for this occasion"; and when the curtain fell for the last time, the audience, in great good humor, clamoured for the adapter. Some time elapsed before any notice was taken of their call, which they took as a provocation of their curiosity. Finally, a gentleman made his way before the curtain, and proclaimed that the version of the piece which his associates had had the honor of performing was from the accomplished pen of the young lady who had won their applause in the character of the heroine. At this announcement, a dozen enthusiasts lifted their voices and demanded that Miss Congreve should be caused to re-appear; but the gentleman cut short their appeal by saying that she had already left the house. This was not true, as Osborne subsequently learned. Henrietta was sitting on a sofa behind the scenes, waiting for her carriage, fingering an immense bouquet, and listening with a tired smile to compliments—hard by Miss Latimer, who sat eating an ice beside her mother, the latter lady looking in a very grim fashion at that very plain, dreadfully thin Miss Congreve.

Osborne walked home thrilled and excited, but decidedly bewildered. He felt that he had reckoned without his host, and that Graham's fickle mistress was not a person to be snubbed and done for. He was utterly at loss as to what to think of her. She broke men's hearts and turned their heads; whatever she put her hand to she marked with her genius. She was a coquette, a musician, an artist, an actress, and author—a prodigy. Of what stuff was she made? What had she done with her heart and her conscience? She painted her face, and

frolicked among lamps and flowers to the clapping of a
thousand hands, while poor Graham lay imprisoned in eternal
silence. Osborne was put on his mettle. To draw a penitent
tear from those deep and charming eyes was assuredly a task
for a clever man.

The plays had been acted on a Wednesday. On the following Saturday Philip was invited to take part in a picnic,
organized by Mrs Carpenter, the lady who had conducted
the plays, and who had a mania for making up parties. The
persons whom she had now enlisted were to proceed by water
to a certain pastoral spot consecrated by nature to picnics,
and there to have lunch upon the grass, to dance and play
nursery-games. They were carried over in two large sailing
boats, and during the transit Philip talked a while with Mrs
Carpenter, whom he found a very amiable, loquacious person.
At the further end of the boat in which, with his hostess, he
had taken his place, he observed a young girl in a white dress,
with a thick, blue veil drawn over her face. Through the veil,
directed towards his person, he perceived the steady glance
of two fine, dark eyes. For a moment he was at a loss to
recognise their possessor; but his uncertainty was rapidly
dispelled.

"I see you have Miss Congreve," he said to Mrs Carpenter
—"the actress of the other evening."

"Yes," said Mrs Carpenter, "I persuaded her to come. She's
all the fashion since Wednesday."

"Was she unwilling to come?" asked Philip.

"Yes, at first. You see, she's a good, quiet girl; she hates to
have a noise made about her."

"She had enough noise the other night. She has wonderful
talent."

"Wonderful, wonderful. And heaven knows where she
gets it. Do you know her family? The most matter-of-fact,
least dramatic, least imaginative people in the world—people
who are shy of the theatre on moral grounds."

"I see. They won't go to the theatre; the theatre comes to them."

"Exactly. It serves them right. Mrs Wilkes, Henrietta's sister, was in a dreadful state about her attempting to act. But now, since Henrietta's success, she's talking about it to all the world."

When the boat came to shore, a plank was stretched from the prow to an adjacent rock for the accommodation of the ladies. Philip stood at the head of the plank, offering his hand for their assistance. Mrs Carpenter came last, with Miss Congreve, who declined Osborne's aid but gave him a little bow, through her veil. Half an hour later Philip again found himself at the side of his hostess, and again spoke of Miss Congreve. Mrs Carpenter warned him that she was standing close at hand, in a group of young girls.

"Have you heard," he asked, lowering his voice, "of her being engaged to be married—or of her having been?"

"No," said Mrs Carpenter, "I've heard nothing. To whom? —stay. I've heard vaguely of something this summer at Sharon. She had a sort of flirtation with some man, whose name I forget."

"Was it Holland?"

"I think not. He left her for that very silly little Mrs Dodd —who hasn't been a widow six months. I think the name was Graham."

Osborne broke into a peal of laughter so loud and harsh that his companion turned upon him in surprise. "Excuse me," said he. "It's false."

"You ask questions, Mr Osborne," said Mrs Carpenter, "but you seem to know more about Miss Congreve than I do."

"Very likely. You see, I knew Robert Graham." Philip's words were uttered with such emphasis and resonance that two or three of the young girls in the adjoining group turned about and looked at him.

"She heard you," said Mrs Carpenter.

"She didn't turn round," said Philip.

"That proves what I say. I meant to introduce you, and now I can't."

"Thank you," said Philip. "I shall introduce myself." Osborne felt in his bosom all the heat of his old resentment. This perverse and heartless girl, then, his soul cried out, not content with driving poor Graham to impious self-destruction had caused it to be believed that he had killed himself from remorse at his own misconduct. He resolved to strike while the iron was hot. But although he was an avenger, he was still a gentleman, and he approached the young girl with a very civil face.

"If I am not mistaken," he said, removing his hat, "you have already done me the honor of recognising me."

Miss Congreve's bow, as she left the boat, had been so obviously a sign of recognition, that Philip was amazed at the vacant smile with which she received his greeting. Something had happened in the interval to make her change her mind. Philip could think of no other motive than her having overheard his mention of Graham's name.

"I have an impression," she said, "of having met you before; but I confess that I'm unable to place you."

Osborne looked at her a moment. "I can't deny myself," he said, "the pleasure of asking about little Mr Wilkes."

"I remember you now," said Miss Congreve, simply. "You carried my nephew out of the water."

"I hope he has got over his fright."

"He denies, I believe, that he was frightened. Of course, for my credit, I don't contradict him."

Miss Congreve's words were followed by a long pause, by which she seemed in no degree embarrassed. Philip was confounded by her apparent self-possession—to call it by no worse name. Considering that she had Graham's death on her conscience, and that, hearing his name on Osborne's lips, she must have perceived the latter to be identical with that dear friend of whom Graham must often have spoken, she was certainly showing a very brave face. But had she indeed heard of Graham's death? For a moment Osborne gave her the benefit of the doubt. He felt that he would take a grim satisfaction in being bearer of the tidings. In order to confer due honor on the disclosure, he saw that it was needful to detach the young girl from her companions. As, therefore, the latter at this moment began to disperse in clusters and couples along the shore, he proposed that they should stroll further a-field. Miss Congreve looked about at the other young girls as if to call one of them to her side, but none of them seemed available. So she slowly moved forward under Philip's guidance, with a half-suppressed look of reluctance. Philip began by paying her a very substantial compliment upon her acting. It was a most inconsequential speech, in the actual state of his feelings, but he couldn't help it. She was perhaps as wicked a girl as you shall easily meet, but her acting was perfect. Having paid this little tribute to equity, he broke ground for Graham.

"I don't feel, Miss Congreve," he said, "as if you were a new acquaintance. I have heard you a great deal talked about." This was not literally true, the reader will remember. All Philip's information had been acquired in his half hour with Mrs Dodd.

"By whom, pray?" asked Henrietta.

"By Robert Graham."

"Ah yes. I was half prepared to hear you speak of him. I remember hearing him speak of a person of your name."

Philip was puzzled. Did she know, or not? "I believe you knew him quite well yourself," he said, somewhat pre-emptorily.

"As well as he would let me—I doubt if any one knew him well."

"So you've heard of his death," said Philip.

"Yes, from himself."

"How, from himself?"

"He wrote me a letter, in his last hours, leaving his approaching end to be inferred, rather than positively announcing it. I wrote an answer, with the request that if my letter was not immediately called for, it should be returned by the post office. It was returned within a week—And now, Mr Osborne," the young girl added, "let me make a request."

Philip bowed.

"I shall feel particularly obliged if you will say no more about Mr Graham."

This was a stroke for which Osborne was not prepared. It had at least the merit of directness. Osborne looked at his companion. There was a faint flush in her cheeks, and a serious light in her eyes. There was plainly no want of energy in her wish. He felt that he must suspend operations and make his approach from another quarter. But it was some moments before he could bring himself to accede to her request. She looked at him, expecting an answer. and he felt her dark eyes on his face.

"Just as you please," he said, at last, mechanically.

They walked along for some moments in silence. Then, suddenly coming upon a young married woman, whom Mrs Carpenter had pressed into her service as a lieutenant, Miss Congreve took leave of Philip, on a slight pretext, and entered into talk with this lady. Philip strolled away and walked about for an hour alone. He had met with a check, but he was resolved that, though he had fallen back, it would be only to leap the further. During the half-hour that Philip sauntered along by the water, the dark cloud suspended above poor Miss Congreve's head doubled its portentous volume. And, indeed, from Philip's point of view, could anything well be more shameless and more heartless than the young girl's request?

At last Osborne remembered that he was neglecting the duties laid upon him by Mrs Carpenter. He retraced his steps and made his way back to the spot devoted to the banquet. Mrs Carpenter called him to her, said that she had been looking for him for an hour, and, when she learned how he had been spending his time, slapped him with her parasol, called him a horrid creature, and declared that she would never again invite him to anything of hers. She then introduced him to her niece, a somewhat undeveloped young lady, with whom he went and sat down over the water. They found very little to talk about. Osborne was thinking of Miss Congreve, and Mrs Carpenter's niece, who was very timid and fluttering, having but one foot yet, as one may say, in society, was abashed and unnerved at finding herself alone with so very tall and mature and handsome a gentleman as Philip. He gave her a little confidence in the course of time, however, by making little stones skip over the surface of the water for her amusement. But he still kept thinking of Henrietta Congreve, and he at last bethought himself of asking his companion whether she knew her. Yes, she knew her slightly; but she threw no light on the subject. She was evidently not of an analytical turn of mind, and she was too innocent to gossip. She contended herself with saying that she believed Henrietta was wonderfully clever, and that she read Latin and Greek.

"Clever, clever," said Philip, "I hear nothing else. I shall begin to think she's a demon."

"No, Henrietta Congreve is very good," said his companion. "She's very religious. She visits the poor and reads sermons. You know the other night she acted for the poor. She's anything but a demon. I think she's so nice."

Before long the party was summoned to lunch. Straggling couples came wandering into sight, gentlemen assisting young girls out of rocky retreats into which no one would have supposed them capable of penetrating, and to which—more wonderful still—no one had observed them to direct their steps.

The table was laid in the shade, on the grass, and the feasters sat about on rugs and shawls. As Osborne took his place along with Mrs Carpenter's niece, he noticed that Miss Congreve had not yet re-appeared. He called his companion's attention to the circumstance, and she mentioned it to her aunt, who said that the young girl had last been seen in company with Mr Stone—a person unknown to Osborne—and that she would, doubtless, soon turn up.

"I suppose she's quite safe," said Philip's neighbor—innocently or wittily, he hardly knew which; "she's with a clergyman."

In a few moments the missing couple appeared on the crest of an adjacent hill. Osborne watched them as they came down. Mr Stone was a comely-faced young man, in a clerical necktie and garments of an exaggerated sacerdotal cut—a divine, evidently of strong "ritualistic" tendencies. Miss Congreve drew near, pale, graceful, and grave, and Philip, with his eyes fixed on her in the interval, lost not a movement of her person, nor a glance of her eyes. She wore a white muslin dress, short, in the prevailing fashion, with trimmings of yellow ribbon inserted in the skirt; and round her shoulders a shawl of heavy black lace, crossed over her bosom and tied in a big knot behind. In her hand she carried a great bunch of wild flowers, with which, as Philip's neighbor whispered to him, she had "ruined" her gloves. Osborne wondered whether there was any meaning in her having taken up with a clergyman. Had she suddenly felt the tardy pangs of remorse, and been moved to seek spiritual advice? Neither on the countenance of her ecclesiastical gallant, nor on her own, were there any visible traces of pious discourse. On the contrary, poor Mr Stone looked sadly demoralized; their conversation had been wholly of profane things. His white cravat had lost its conservative rigidity, and his hat its unimpassioned equipoise. Worse than all, a little blue forget-me-not had found its way into his button-hole. As for Henrietta, her face wore that look of half-severe serenity which was its wonted expression, but there was no sign of her having seen her lover's ghost.

Osborne went mechanically through the movements of being attentive to the insipid little person at his side. But his thoughts were occupied with Miss Congreve and his eyes constantly turning to her face. From time to time, they met her own. A fierce disgust muttered in his bosom. What Henrietta Congreve needed, he said to himself, was to be used as she used others, as she was evidently now using this poor little parson. He was already over his ears in love—vainly feeling for bottom in midstream, while she sat dry-shod on the brink. She needed a lesson; but who should give it? She knew more than all her teachers. Men approached her only to be dazzled and charmed. If she could only find her equal or her master! one with as clear a head, as lively a fancy, as relentless a will as her own; one who would turn the tables, anticipate her, fascinate her, and then suddenly look at his watch and bid her good morning. Then, perhaps, Graham might settle to sleep in his grave. Then she would feel what it was to play with hearts, for then her own would have been as glass against bronze. Osborne looked about the table, but none of Mrs Carpenter's male guests bore the least resemblance to the hero of his vision—a man with a heart of bronze and a head of crystal. They were, indeed, very proper swains for the young ladies at their sides, but Henrietta Congreve was not one of these. She was not a mere twaddling ball-room flirt. There was in her coquetry something serious and exalted. It was an intellectual joy. She drained honest men's hearts to the last drop, and bloomed white upon the monstrous diet. As Philip glanced around the circle, his eye fell upon a young girl who seemed for a moment to have forgotten her neighbors, her sandwiches and her champagne, and was very innocently contemplating his own person. As soon as she perceived that he had observed her, she of course dropped her eyes on her plate. But Philip had read the meaning of her glance. It seemed to say—this lingering virginal eyebeam—in language easily translated, Thou art the man! It said, in other words, in less transcendental fashion, My dear Mr Osborne, you are a very good looking fellow. Philip felt his pulse quicken; he had received his baptism. Not that good looks were a sufficient outfit for breaking Miss Congreve's heart; but they were the outward signs of his mission.

The feasting at last came to an end. A fiddler, who had been brought along, began to tune his instrument, and Mrs Carpenter proceeded to organize a dance. The *débris* of the collation was cleared away, and the level space thus uncovered converted into a dancing floor. Osborne, not being a dancing man, sat at a distance, with two or three other spectators, among whom was the Rev. Mr Stone. Each of these gentlemen watched with close attention the movements of Henrietta Congreve. Osborne, however, occasionally glanced at his companion, who, on his side, was quite too absorbed in looking at Miss Congreve to think of anything else.

"They look very charming, those young ladies," said Philip, addressing the young clergyman, to whom he had just been introduced. "Some of them dance particularly well."

"Oh, yes!" said Mr Stone, with fervor. And then, as if he feared that he had committed himself to an invidious distinction unbecoming his cloth: "I think they all dance well."

But Philip, as a lawyer, naturally took a different view of the matter from Mr Stone, as a clergyman. "Some of them very much better than others, it seems to me. I had no idea that there could be such a difference. Look at Miss Congreve, for instance."

Mr Stone, whose eyes were fixed on Miss Congreve, obeyed his injunction by moving them away for a moment, and directing them to a very substantial and somewhat heavy-footed young lady, who was figuring beside her. "Oh, yes, she's very graceful," he said, with unction. "So light, so free, so quiet!"

Philip smiled. "You, too, most excellent simpleton," he said to himself—"you, too, shall be avenged." And then—"Miss Congreve is a very remarkable person," he added, aloud.

"Oh, very!"

"She has extraordinary versatility."

"Most extraordinary."

"Have you seen her act?"

"Yes—yes; I infringed upon my usage in regard to entertainments of that nature, and went the other evening. It was a most brilliant performance."

"And you know she wrote the play."

"Ah, not exactly," said Mr Stone, with a little protesting gesture; "she translated it."

"Yes; but she had to write it quite over. Do you know it in French?"—and Philip mentioned the original title.

Mr Stone signified that he was unacquainted with the work.

"It would never have done, you know," said Philip, "to play it as it stands. I saw it in Paris. Miss Congreve eliminated the little difficulties with uncommon skill."

Mr Stone was silent. The violin uttered a long-drawn note, and the ladies curtsied low to their gentlemen. Miss Congreve's partner stood with his back to our two friends, and her own obeisance was, therefore, executed directly in front of them. If Mr Stone's enthusiasm had been damped by Philip's irreverent freedom, it was rekindled by this glance. "I suppose you've heard her sing," he said, after a pause.

"Yes, indeed," said Philip, without hesitation.

"She sings sacred music with the most beautiful fervor."

"Yes, so I'm told. And I'm told, moreover, that she's very learned—that she has a passion for books."

"I think it very likely. In fact, she's quite an accomplished theologian. We had this morning a very lively discussion."

"You differed, then?" said Philip.

"Oh," said Mr Stone, with charming *naïveté*, "*I* didn't differ. It was she!"

"Isn't she a little—the least bit—" and Philip paused, to select his word.

"The least bit?" asked Mr Stone, in a benevolent tone. And then, as Philip still hesitated—"The least bit heterodox?"

"The least bit of a coquette?"

"Oh, Mr Osborne!" cried the young divine—"that's the last thing I should call Miss Congreve."

At this moment, Mrs Carpenter drew nigh. "What is the last thing you should call Miss Congreve?" she asked, overhearing the clergyman's words.

"A coquette."

"It seems to me," said the lady, "that it's the first thing I should call her. You have to come to it, I fancy. You always do, you know. I should get it off my mind at once, and then I should sing her charms."

"Oh, Mrs Carpenter!" said Mr Stone.

"Yes, my dear young man. She's quiet but she's deep—I see Mr Osborne knows," and Mrs Carpenter passed on.

"She's deep—that's what I say," said Mr Stone, with mild firmness—"What do you know, Mr Osborne?"

Philip fancied that the poor fellow had turned pale; he certainly looked grave.

"Oh, I know nothing," said Philip. "I affirmed nothing. I merely inquired."

"Well then, my dear sir"—and the young man's candid visage flushed a little with the intensity of his feelings—"I give you my word for it, that I believe Miss Congreve to be not only the most accomplished, but the most noble-minded, the most truthful, the most truly christian young lady—in this whole assembly."

"I'm sure, I'm much obliged to you for the assurance," said Philip. "I shall value it and remember it."

It would not have been hard for Philip to set down Mr Stone as a mere soft-hearted, philandering parson—a type ready made to his hand. Mrs Carpenter, on the other hand, was a shrewd sagacious woman. But somehow he was impressed by the minister's words, and quite untouched by those of the lady. At last those of the dancers who were tired of the sport, left the circle and wandered back to the shore. The afternoon was drawing to a close, the western sky was beginning to blush crimson and the shadows to grow long on the grass. Only half an hour remained before the moment fixed for the return to Newport. Philip resolved to turn it to account. He followed Miss Congreve to a certain rocky platform, overlooking the water, whither, with a couple of elderly ladies, she had gone to watch the sunset. He found no difficulty in persuading her to wander aside from her companions. There was no distrust in her keen and delicate face. It was incredible that she should have meant defiance; but her very repose and placidity had a strangely irritating action upon Philip. They affected him as the climax of insolence. He drew from his breast-pocket a small portfolio, containing a dozen letters, among which was the last one he had received from Graham.

"I shall take the liberty, for once, Miss Congreve," he said, "of violating the injunction which you laid upon me this morning with regard to Robert Graham. I have here a letter which I should like you to see."

"From Mr Graham himself?"

"From Graham himself—written just before his death." He held it out, but Henrietta made no movement to take it.

"I have no desire to see it," she said. "I had rather not. You know he wrote also to me at that moment."

"I'm sure," said Philip, "I should not refuse to see your letter."

"I can't offer to show it to you. I immediately destroyed it."

"Well, you see I've kept mine—It's not long," Osborne pursued.

Miss Congreve, as if with a strong effort, put out her hand and took the document. She looked at the directions for some moments, in silence, and then raised her eyes toward Osborne. "Do you value it?" she asked. "Does it contain anything you wish to keep?"

"No; I give it to you, for that matter."

"Well then!" said Henrietta. And she tore the letter twice across, and threw the scraps into the sea.

"Ah!" cried Osborne, "what the devil have you done?"

"Don't be violent, Mr Osborne," said the young girl. "I hadn't the slightest intention of reading it. You are properly punished for having disobeyed me."

Philip swallowed his rage at a gulp, and followed her as she turned away.

III

In the middle of September, Mrs Dodd came to Newport, to stay with a friend—somewhat out of humor at having been invited at the fag end of the season, but on the whole very much the same Mrs Dodd as before; or rather not quite the same, for, in her way, she had taken Graham's death very much to heart. A couple of days after her arrival, she met Philip in the street, and stopped him, "I'm glad to find *some one* still here," she said; for she was with her friend, and having introduced Philip to this lady, she begged him to come and see her. On the next day but one, accordingly, Philip presented himself, and saw Mrs Dodd alone. She began to talk about Graham; she became very much affected, and with a little more encouragement from Osborne, she would certainly have shed tears. But, somehow, Philip was loth to countenance her grief; he made short responses. Mrs Dodd struck him as weak and silly and morbidly sentimental. He wondered whether there could have been any truth in the rumor that Graham had cared for her. Not certainly if there was any truth in the story of his passion for Henrietta Congreve. It was impossible that he should have cared for both. Philip made this reflection, but he stopped short of adding that Mrs Dodd failed signally to please him, because during the past three weeks he had constantly enjoyed Henrietta's society.

For Mrs Dodd, of course, the transition was easy from Graham to Miss Congreve. "I'm told Miss Congreve is still here," she said. "Have you made her acquaintance?"

"Perfectly," said Philip.

"You seem to take it very easily. I hope you have brought her to a sense of her iniquities. There's a task, Mr Osborne. You ought to convert her."

"I've not attempted to convert her. I've taken her as she is."

"Does she wear mourning for Mr Graham? It's the least she can do."

"Wear mourning?" said Philip. "Why, she has been going to a party every other night."

"Of course I don't suppose she has put on a black dress. But does she mourn *here*?" And Mrs Dodd laid her hand on her heart.

"You mean in her heart? Well, you know, it's problematical that she has one."

"I suppose she disapproves of suicide," said Mrs Dodd, with a little acrid smile. "Bless my soul, so do I."

"So do I, Mrs Dodd," said Philip. And he remained for a moment thoughtful. "I wish to heaven," he cried, "that Graham were here! It seems to me at moments that he and Miss Congreve might have come to an understanding again."

Mrs Dodd threw out her hands in horror. "Why, has she given up her last lover?"

"Her last lover? Whom do you mean?"

"Why, the man I told you of—Mr Holland."

Philip appeared quite to have forgotten this point in Mrs Dodd's recital. He broke into a loud, nervous laugh. "I'll be hanged," he cried, "if I know! One thing is certain," he pursued, with emphasis, recovering himself; "Mr Holland—whoever he is—has for the past three weeks seen nothing of Miss Congreve."

Mrs Dodd sat silent, with her eyes lowered. At last, looking up, "You, on the other hand, I infer," she said, "have seen a great deal of her."

"Yes, I've seen her constantly."

Mrs Dodd raised her eyebrows and distended her lips in a smile which was emphatically not a smile. "Well, you'll think it an odd question, Mr Osborne," she said, "but how do you reconcile your intimacy with Miss Congreve with your devotion to Mr Graham?"

Philip frowned—quite too severely for good manners. Decidedly, Mrs Dodd was extremely silly. "Oh," he rejoined, "I reconcile the two things perfectly. Moreover, my dear Mrs Dodd, allow me to say that it's my own business. At all events," he added, more gently, "perhaps, one of these days, you'll read the enigma."

"Oh, if it's an enigma," cried the lady, "perhaps I can guess it."

Philip had risen to his feet to take his leave, and Mrs Dodd threw herself back on the sofa, clasped her hands in her lap, and looked up at him with a penetrating smile. She shook her finger at him reproachfully. Philip saw that she had an idea; perhaps it was the right one. At all events, he blushed. Upon this Mrs Dodd cried out.

"I've guessed it," she said. "Oh, Mr Osborne!"

"What have you guessed?" asked Philip, not knowing why in the world he should blush.

"If I've guessed right," said Mrs Dodd, "it's a charming idea. It does you credit. It's quite romantic. It would do in a novel."

"I doubt," said Philip, "whether I know what you're talking about."

"Oh, yes, you do. I wish you good luck. To another man I should say it was a dangerous game. But to you!"—and with an insinuating movement of her head, Mrs Dodd measured with a glance the length and breadth of Philip's fine person.

Osborne was inexpressibly disgusted, and without further delay he took his leave.

The reader will be at a loss to understand why Philip should have been disgusted with the mere foreshadowing on the part of another, of a scheme which, three weeks before, he had thought a very happy invention. For we may as well say outright, that although Mrs Dodd was silly, she was not so silly but that she had divined his original intentions with regard to Henrietta. The fact is that in three weeks Philip's humor had undergone a great change. The reader has gathered for himself that Henrietta Congreve was no ordinary girl, that she was on the contrary, a person of distinguished gifts and remarkable character. Until within a very few months she had seen very little of the world, and her mind and talents had been gradually formed in seclusion, study, and it is not too much to say, meditation. Thanks to her circumscribed life and her long contemplative leisures, she had reached a pitch of rare intellectual perfection. She was educated, one may say, in a sense in which the term may be used of very few young girls, however richly endowed by nature. When at a later period than most girls, owing to domestic circumstances which it is needless to unfold, she made her entrance into society and learned what it was to be in the world and of the world, to talk and listen, to please and be pleased, to be admired, flattered and interested, her admirable faculties and beautiful intellect, ripened in studious solitude, burst into luxuriant bloom and bore the fairest fruit. Miss Congreve was accordingly a person for whom a man of taste and of feeling could not help entertaining a serious regard.

Philip Osborne was emphatically such a man; the manner in which he was affected by his friend's death proves, I think, that he had feeling; and it is ample evidence of his taste that he had chosen such a friend. He had no sooner begun to act in obedience to the impulse mystically bestowed, as it were, at the close of Mrs Carpenter's feast—he had no sooner obtained an introduction at Mrs Wilkes's, and, with excellent tact and discretion, made good his footing there, than he began to feel in his inmost heart that in staking his life upon Miss Congreve's favor, poor Graham had indeed revealed the depths of his exquisite sensibility. For a week at least—a week during which, with unprecedented good fortune, and a degree of assurance worthy of a better cause, Philip contrived in one way and other to talk with his fair victim no less than a dozen times—he was under the empire of a feverish excitement which kept him from seeing the young girl in all her beautiful integrity. He was pre-occupied with his own intentions and the effect of his own manoeuvres. But gradually he quite forgot himself while he was in her presence, and only remembered that he had a sacred part to play, after he had left the house. Then it was that he conceived the intensity of Graham's despair, and then it was that he began to be sadly, wofully puzzled by the idea that a woman could unite so much loveliness with so much treachery, so much light with so much darkness. He was as certain of the bright surface of her nature as of its cold and dark reverse, and he was utterly unable to discover a link of connection between the two. At moments he wondered how in the world he had become saddled with this metaphysical burden: *que diable venait-il faire dans cette galère?* But nevertheless he was afloat; he must row his boat over the current to where the restless spirit of his friend paced the opposite shore.

Henrietta Congreve, after a first movement of apparent aversion, was very well pleased to accept Osborne as a friend and as an *habitué* of her sister's house. Osborne fancied that he might believe without fatuity—for whatever the reader may think, it is needless to say that Philip was very far from supposing his whole course to be a piece of infatuated cox-combry—that she preferred him to most of the young men of her circle. Philip had a just estimate of his own endowments, and he knew that for the finer social purposes, if not for strictly sentimental ones, he contained the stuff of an important personage. He had no taste for trivialities, but trivialities played but a small part in Mrs Wilkes's drawing-room. Mrs Wilkes was a simple woman, but she was neither silly nor frivolous; and Miss Congreve was exempt from these foibles for even better reasons. "Women really care only for men who can tell them something," Osborne remembered once to have heard Graham say, not without bitterness. "They are always famished for news." Philip now reflected with satisfaction that he could give Miss Congreve more news than most of her constituted gossips. He had an admirable memory and a very lively observation. In these respects Henrietta was herself equally well endowed; but Philip's experience of the world had of course been tenfold more extensive, and he was able continually to complete her partial inductions and to rectify her false conjectures. Sometimes they seemed to him wonderfully shrewd, and sometimes delight-fully innocent. He nevertheless frequently found himself in a position to make her acquainted with facts possessing the charm of absolute novelty. He had travelled and seen a great variety of men and women, and of course he had read a number of books which a woman is not expected to read. Philip was keenly sensible of these advantages; but it never-theless seemed to him that if the exhibition of his mental treasures furnished Miss Congreve with a great deal of enter-tainment, her attention, on the other hand, had a most re-freshing effect upon his mind.

At the end of three weeks Philip might, perhaps not un-reasonably, have supposed himself in a position to strike his blow. It is true that, for a woman of sense, there is a long step between thinking a man an excellent friend and a charming talker, and surrendering her heart to him. Philip had every reason to believe that Henrietta thought these good things of himself; but if he had hereupon turned about to make his exit, with the conviction that when he had closed the parlor-door behind him he should, by lending an attentive ear, hear her fall in a swoon on the carpet, he might have been sadly snubbed and disappointed. He longed for an opportunity to test the quality of his empire. If he could only pretend for a week to be charmed by another woman, Miss Congreve might perhaps commit herself. Philip flattered himself that he could read very small signs. But what other woman could decently serve as the object of a passion thus extemporized? The only woman Philip could think of was Mrs Dodd; and to think of Mrs Dodd was to give it up. For a man who was intimate with Miss Congreve to pretend to care for any other woman (except a very old friend) was to act in flagrant contempt of all verisimilitude. Philip had, therefore, to content himself with playing off his own assumed want of heart against Henrietta's cordial regard. But at this rate the game moved very slowly. Work was accumulating at a prodigious rate at his office, and he couldn't dangle about Miss Congreve forever. He bethought himself of a harmless artifice for drawing her out. It seemed to him that his move was not altogether unsuccessful, and that, at a pinch, Henrietta might become jealous of a rival in his affections. Nevertheless, he was strongly tempted to take up his hand and leave the game. It was too confoundedly exciting.

The incident of which I speak happened within a few days after Osborne's visit to Mrs Dodd. Finding it impossible to establish an imaginary passion for an actual, visible young lady, Philip resolved to invent not only the passion, but the young lady, too. One morning, as he was passing the show-case of one of the several photographers who came to Newport

for the season, he was struck by the portrait of a very pretty
young girl. She was fair in color, graceful, well-dressed, well
placed, her face was charming, she was plainly a lady. Philip
went in and asked who she was. The photographer had
destroyed the negative and had kept no register of her name.
He remembered her, however, distinctly. The portrait had
not been taken during the summer; it had been taken during
the preceding winter, in Boston, the photographer's head-
quarters. "I kept it," he said, "because I thought it so very
perfect a picture. And such a charming sitter! We haven't
many like that." He added, however, that it was too good to
please the masses, and that Philip was the first gentleman
who had had the taste to observe it.

"So much the better," thought Philip, and forthwith proposed to the man to part with it. The latter, of course, had
conscientious scruples; it was against his principles to dispose
of the portraits of ladies who came to him in confidence. To
do him justice, he adhered to his principles, and Philip was
unable to persuade him to sell it. He consented, however, to
give it to Mr Osborne, *gratis*. Mr Osborne deserved it, and
he had another for himself. By this time Philip had grown
absolutely fond of the picture; at this latter intelligence he
looked grave, and suggested that if the artist would not sell
one, perhaps he would sell two. The photographer declined,
reiterated his offer, and Philip finally accepted. By way of
compensation, however, he proceeded to sit for his own
portrait. In the course of half an hour the photographer gave
him a dozen reflections of his head and shoulders, distinguished by as many different attitudes and expressions.

"You sit first-rate, sir," said the artist. "You take beautifully. You're quite a match for my young lady."

Philip went off with his dozen prints, promising to examine
them at his leisure, select and give a liberal order.

In the evening he went to Mrs Wilkes's. He found this
lady on her verandah, drinking tea in the open air with a guest,

whom in the darkness he failed to recognize. As Mrs Wilkes
proceeded to introduce him, her companion graciously revealed herself as Mrs Dodd. "How on earth," thought
Philip, "did she get here?" To find Mrs Dodd instead of
Miss Congreve was, of course, a gross discomforture. Philip
sat down, however, with a good grace, to all appearance,
hoping that Henrietta would turn up. Finally, moving his
chair to a line with the drawing-room window, he saw the
young girl within, reading by the lamp. She was alone and
intent upon her book. She wore a dress of white grenadine,
covered with ornaments and arabesques of crimson silk, which
gave her a somewhat fantastical air. For the rest, her expression was grave enough, and her brows contracted, as if she
were completely absorbed in her book. Her right elbow rested
on the table, and with her hand she mechanically twisted the
long curl depending from her *chignon*. Watching his opportunity, Osborne escaped from the ladies on the verandah and
made his way into the drawing-room. Miss Congreve received him as an old friend, without rising from her chair.

Philip began by pretending to scold her for shirking the
society of Mrs Dodd.

"Shirking!" said Henrietta. "You are very polite to Mrs
Dodd."

"It seems to me," rejoined Osborne, "that I'm quite as
polite as you."

"Well, perhaps you are. To tell the truth, I'm not very
polite. At all events, she don't care to see me. She must have
come to see my sister."

"I didn't know she knew Mrs Wilkes."

"It's an acquaintance of a couple of hours' standing. I met
her, you know, at Sharon in July. She was once very impertinent to me, and I fancied she had quite given me up. But this
afternoon, during our drive, as my sister and I got out of the
carriage, on the rocks, who should I see but Mrs Dodd,
wandering about alone, with a bunch of sea-weed as big as

her head. She rushed up to me; I introduced her to Anna, and finding that she had walked quite a distance, Anna made her get into the carriage. It appears that she's staying with a friend, who has no carriage, and she's very miserable. We drove her about for an hour. Mrs Dodd was fascinating, she threw away her sea-weed, and Anna asked her to come home to tea. After tea, having endured her for two mortal hours, I took refuge here."

"If she was fascinating," said Philip, "why do you call it enduring her?"

"It's all the more reason, I assure you."

"I see, you have not forgiven her impertinence."

"No, I confess I have not. The woman was positively revolting."

"She appears, nevertheless, to have forgiven you."

"She has nothing to forgive."

In a few moments Philip took his photographs out of his pocket, handed them to Henrietta, and asked her advice as to which he should choose. Miss Congreve inspected them attentively, and selected but one. "This one is excellent," she said. "All the others are worthless in comparison."

"You advise me then to order that alone?"

"Why, you'll do as you please. I advise you to order that, at any rate. If you do, I shall ask you for one; but I shall care nothing for the rest."

Philip protested that he saw very little difference between this favoured picture and the others, and Miss Congreve declared that there was all the difference in the world. As Philip replaced the specimens in his pocket-book, he dropped on the carpet the portrait of the young lady of Boston.

"Ah," said Henrietta, "a young lady. I suppose I may see it."

"On one condition," said Philip, picking it up. "You'll please not to look at the back of the card."

I am very much ashamed to have to tell such things of poor

Philip; for in point of fact, the back of the card was a most innocent blank. If Miss Congreve had ventured to disobey him, he would have made a very foolish figure. But there was so little that was boisterous in Henrietta's demeanor, that Osborne felt that he ran no risk.

"Who is she?" asked Henrietta, looking at the portrait "She's charming."

"She's a Miss Thompson, of Philadelphia."

"Dear me, not Dora Thompson, assuredly."

"No, indeed," said Philip, a little nervously. "Her name's not Dora—nor anything like it."

"You needn't resent the insinuation, sir. Dora's a very pretty name."

"Yes, but her own is prettier."

"I'm very curious to hear it."

Philip suddenly found himself in deep waters. He struck out blindly and answered at random, "Angelica."

Miss Congreve smiled—somewhat ironically, it seemed to Philip. "Well," she said, "I like her face better than her name."

"Dear me, if you come to that, so do I," cried Philip, with a laugh.

"Tell me about her, Mr Osborne," pursued Henrietta. "She must be, with that face and figure, just the nicest girl in the world."

"Well, well, well," said Philip, leaning back in his chair, and looking at the ceiling—"perhaps she is—or at least, you'll excuse me if I say *I* think she is."

"I should think it inexcusable if you didn't say so," said Henrietta, giving him the card. "I'm sure I've seen her some-where."

"Very likely. She comes to New York," said Philip. And he thought it prudent, on the whole, to divert the conversation to another topic. Miss Congreve remained silent and he fancied pensive. Was she jealous of Angelica Thompson?

It seemed to Philip that, without fatuity, he might infer that she was, and that she was too proud to ask questions.

Mrs Wilkes had enabled Mrs Dodd to send tidings to her hostess of her whereabouts, and had promised to furnish her with an escort on her return. When Mrs Dodd prepared to take her leave, Philip, finding himself also ready to depart, offered to walk home with her.

"Well, sir," said the lady, when they had left the house, "your little game seems to be getting on."

Philip said nothing.

"Ah, Mr Osborne," said Mrs Dodd, with ill-concealed impatience, "I'm afraid you're too good for it."

"Well, I'm afraid I am."

"If you hadn't been in such a hurry to agree with me," said Mrs Dodd, "I should have said that I meant, in other words, that you're too stupid."

"Oh, I agree to that, too," said Philip.

The next day he received a letter from his partner in business, telling him of a great pressure of work, and urging him to return at his earliest convenience. "We are told," added this gentleman, "of a certain Miss ——, I forget the name. If she's essential to your comfort, bring her along; but, at any rate, come yourself. In your absence the office is at a standstill—a fearful case of repletion without digestion."

This appeal came home to Philip's mind, to use a very old metaphor, like the sound of the brazen trumpet to an old cavalry charger. He felt himself overwhelmed with a sudden shame at the thought of the precious hours he had wasted and the long mornings he had consigned to perdition. He had been burning incense to a shadow, and the fumes had effaced it. In the afternoon he walked down toward the cliffs, feeling wofully perplexed, and exasperated in mind, and longing only to take a farewell look at the sea. He was not prepared to admit that he had played with fire and burned his fingers, but it was certain that he had gained nothing at the game;

How the deuce had Henrietta Congreve come to thrust herself into his life—to steal away his time and his energies and to put him into a savage humor with himself? He would have given a great deal to be able to banish her from his thoughts; but she remained, and, while she remained, he hated her. After all, he had not been wholly cheated of his revenge. He had begun by hating her and he hated her still. On his way to the cliffs he met Mrs Wilkes, driving alone. Henrietta's place, vacant beside her, seemed to admonish him that she was at home, and almost, indeed, that she expected him. At all events, instead of going to bid farewell to the sea, he went to bid farewell to Miss Congreve. He felt that his farewell might easily be cold and formal, and indeed bitter.

He was admitted, he passed through the drawing-room to the verandah, and found Henrietta sitting on the grass, in the garden, holding her little nephew on her knee and reading him a fairy tale. She made room for him on the garden bench beside her, but kept the child. Philip felt himself seriously discomposed by this spectacle. In a few moments he took the boy upon his own knees. He then told Miss Congreve briefly that he intended that evening to leave Newport. "And you," he said, "when are you coming?"

"My sister," said Henrietta, "means to stay till Christmas. I hope to be able to remain as long."

Poor Philip bowed his head and heard his illusions tumbling most unmusically about his ears. His blow had smitten but the senseless air. He waited to see her color fade, or to hear her voice tremble. But he waited in vain. When he looked up and his eyes met Henrietta's, she was startled by the expression of his face.

"Tom," she said to the child, "go and ask Jane for my fan."

The child walked off, and Philip rose to his feet. Henrietta, hesitating a moment, also rose. "Must you go?" she asked.

Philip made no answer, but stood looking at her with

blood-shot eyes, and with an intensity which puzzled and frightened the young girl.

"Miss Congreve," he said, abruptly, "I'm a miserable man!"

"Oh, no!" said Henrietta, gently.

"I love a woman who doesn't care a straw for me."

"Are you sure?" said Henrietta, innocently.

"Sure! I adore her!"

"Are you sure she doesn't care for you?"

"Ah, Miss Congreve!" cried Philip. "If I could imagine, if I could hope—" and he put out his hand, as if to take her own.

Henrietta drew back, pale and frowning, carrying her hand to her heart. "Hope for nothing!" she said.

At this moment, little Tom Wilkes re-appeared, issuing from the drawing-room window. "Aunt Henrietta," he cried, "here's a new gentleman!"

Miss Congreve and Philip turned about, and saw a young man step out upon the verandah from the drawing-room. Henrietta, with a little cry, hastened to meet him. Philip stood in his place. Miss Congreve exchanged a cordial greeting with the stranger, and led him down to the lawn. As she came toward him, Philip saw that Henrietta's pallor had made way for a rosy flush. She was beautiful.

"Mr Osborne," she said, "Mr Holland."

Mr Holland bowed graciously; but Philip bowed not at all. "Good-bye, then," he said, to the young girl.

She bowed, without speaking.

"Who's your friend, Henrietta?" asked her companion, when they were alone.

"He's a Mr Osborne, of New York," said Miss Congreve; "a friend of poor Mr Graham."

"By the way, I suppose you've heard of poor Graham's death."

"Oh, yes; Mr Osborne told me. And indeed—what do you think? Mr Graham wrote to me that he expected to die."

"Expected? Is that what he said?"

"I don't remember his words. I destroyed the letter."

"I must say, I think it would have been in better taste not to write."

"Taste! He had long since parted company with taste."

"I don't know. There was a method in his madness; and, as a rule, when a man kills himself, he shouldn't send out circulars."

"Kills himself? Good heavens, George! what do you mean?" Miss Congreve had turned pale, and stood looking at her companion with eyes dilated with horror.

"Why, my dear Henrietta," said the young man, "excuse my abruptness. Didn't you know it?"

"How strange—how fearful!" said Henrietta, slowly. "I wish I had kept his letter."

"I'm glad you didn't," said Holland. "It's a horrible business. Forget it."

"Horrible—horrible," murmured the young girl, in a tremulous tone. Her voice was shaken with irrepressible tears. Poor girl! in the space of five minutes she had been three times surprised. She gave way to her emotion and burst into sobs. George Holland drew her against him, and pressed his arm about her, and kissed her, and whispered comfort in her ear.

In the evening, Philip started for New York. On the steamer he found Mrs Dodd, who had come to an end of her visit. She was accompanied by a certain Major Dodd, of the Army, a brother of her deceased husband, and in addition, as it happened, her cousin. He was an unmarried man, a good-natured man, and a very kind friend to his sister-in-law, who had no family of her own, and who was in a position to be grateful for the services of a gentleman. In spite of a general impression to the contrary, I may affirm that the Major had no desire to make his little services a matter of course. "I'm related to Maria twice over already," he had been known to say, in a moment of expansion. "If I ever

marry, I shall prefer to do it not quite so much in the family."
He had come to Newport to conduct his sister home, who
forthwith introduced him to Philip.

It was a clear, mild night, and, when the steamer had got
under way, Mrs Dodd and the two gentlemen betook themselves to the upper deck, and sat down in the starlight. Philip,
it may be readily imagined, was in no humour for conversation; but he felt that he could not wholly neglect Mrs Dodd.
Under the influence of the beautiful evening, the darkly-
shining sea, the glittering constellations, this lady became
rabidly sentimental. She talked of friendship, and love, and
death, and immortality. Philip saw what was coming. Before
many moments, she had the bad taste (considering the Major's
presence, as it seemed to Philip) to take poor Graham as a
text for a rhapsody. Osborne lost patience, and interrupted
her by asking if she would mind his lighting a cigar. She was
scandalised, and immediately announced that she would go
below. Philip had no wish to be uncivil. He attempted to
restore himself to her favour by offering to see her down to the
cabin. She accepted his escort, and he went with her to the door
of her state-room, where she gave him her hand for good-night.

"Well," she said—"and Miss Congreve?"

Philip positively scowled. "Miss Congreve," he said, "is
engaged to be married."

"To Mr——?"

"To Mr Holland."

"Ah!" cried Mrs Dodd, dropping his hand, "why didn't
you break the engagement?"

"My dear Mrs Dodd," said Philip, "you don't know what
you're talking about."

Mrs Dodd smiled a pitiful smile, shrugged her shoulders,
and turned away. "Poor Graham!" she said.

Her words came to Philip like a blow in the face. "Graham!"
he cried. "Graham was a fool!" He had struck back; he
couldn't help it.

He made his way up stairs again, and came out on the deck, still trembling with the violence of his retort. He walked to the edge of the boat and leaned over the railing, looking down into the black gulfs of water which foamed and swirled in the wake of the vessel. He knocked off the end of his cigar, and watched the red particles fly downward and go out in the darkness. He was a disappointed, saddened man. There in the surging, furious darkness, yawned instant death. Did it tempt him, too? He drew back with a shudder, and returned to his place by Major Dodd.

The Major preserved for some moments a meditative silence. Then, at last, with a half apologetic laugh, "Mrs Dodd," he said, "labours under a singular illusion."

"Ah?" said Philip.

"But you knew Mr Graham yourself?" pursued the Major.

"Oh, yes; I knew him."

"It was a very melancholy case," said Major Dodd.

"A very melancholy case;" and Philip repeated his words.

"I don't know how it is that Mrs Dodd was beguiled into such fanaticism on the subject. I believe she went so far as once to blow out at the young lady."

"The young lady?" said Philip.

"Miss Congreve, you know, the object of his persecutions."

"Oh, yes," said Philip, painfully mystified.

"The fact is," said the Major, leaning over, and lowering his voice confidentially, "Mrs Dodd was in love with him— as far, that is, as a woman can be in love with a man in that state."

"Is it possible?" said Philip, disgusted and revolted at he knew not what; for his companion's allusions were an enigma.

"Oh, I was at Sharon for three weeks," the Major continued; "I went up for my sister-in-law; I saw it all. I wanted to bring poor Graham away, but he wouldn't listen to me— not that he wasn't very quiet. He made no talk, and opened himself only to Mrs Dodd and me—we lived in the same house, you know. Of course I very soon saw through it, and I felt very sorry for poor Miss Congreve. She bore it very well, but it must have been very annoying."

Philip started up from his chair. "For heaven's sake, Major Dodd," he cried, "what are you talking about?"

The Major stared a moment, and then burst into a peal of laughter. "You agree, then, with Mrs Dodd?" he said, recovering himself.

"I understand Mrs Dodd no better than I do you."

"Why, my dear sir," said the Major, rising to his feet and extending his hand. "I beg a hundred pardons. But you must excuse me if I adhere to my opinion."

"First, please, be so good as to inform me of your opinion."

"Why, sir, the whole story is simply bosh."

"Good heavens," cried Philip, "that's no opinion!"

"Well, then, sir, if you will have it: the man was as mad as a March hare."

"Oh!" said Philip. His exclamation said a great many things, but the Major took it as a protest.

"He was a monomaniac."

Philip said nothing.

"The idea is not new to you?"

"Well," said Philip, "to tell the truth, it is."

"Well," said the Major, with a courteous flourish, "there you have it—for nothing."

Philip drew a long breath. "Ah, no!" he said, gravely, "not for nothing." He stood silent for some time, with his eyes fixed on the deck. Major Dodd puffed his cigar and eyed him askance. At last Philip looked up. "And Henrietta Congreve?"

"Henrietta Congreve," said the Major, with military freedom and gallantry, "is the sweetest girl in the world. Don't talk to me! I know her."

"She never became engaged to Graham?"

"Engaged? She never looked at him."

"But he was in love with her."

"Ah, that was his own business. He worried her to death. She tried gentleness and kindness—it made him worse. Then, when she declined to see him, the poor fellow swore that she had jilted him. It was a fixed idea. He got Mrs Dodd to believe it."

Philip's silent reflections—the hushed eloquence of his amazed unburdened heart—we have no space to interpret. But as the Major lightened the load with one hand, he added to it with the other. Philip had never pitied his friend till now. "I knew him very well," he said, aloud. "He was the best of men. She might very well have cared for him."

"Good heavens! my dear sir, how could the woman love a madman?"

"You use strong language. When I parted with him in June, he was sane as you or I."

"Well, then, apparently, he lost his mind in the interval. He was in wretched health."

"But a man doesn't lose his mind without a cause."

"Let us admit, then," said the Major, "that Miss Congreve was the cause. I insist that she was the innocent cause. How should she have trifled with him? She was engaged to another man. The ways of the Lord are inscrutable. Fortunately," continued the Major, "she doesn't know the worst."

"How, the worst?"

"Well, you know he shot himself."

"Bless your soul, Miss Congreve knows it."

"I think you're mistaken. She didn't know it this morning."

Philip was sickened and bewildered by the tissue of horrors in which he found himself entangled. "Oh," he said, bitterly, "she has forgotten it then. She knew it a month ago."

"No, no, no," rejoined the Major, with decision. "I took the liberty, this morning, of calling upon her, and as we had had some conversation upon Mr Graham at Sharon, I touched upon his death. I saw she had heard of it, and I said nothing more—"

"Well, then?" said Philip.

"Well, then, my dear sir, she thinks he died in his bed. May she never think otherwise!"

In the course of that night—he sat out on the deck till two o'clock, alone—Philip, revolving many things, fervently echoed this last wish of Major Dodd.

Aux grands maux les grands remedes. Philip is now a married man; and curious to narrate, his wife bears a striking likeness to the young lady whose photograph he purchased for the price of six dozen of his own. And yet her name is not Angelica Thompson—nor even Dora.

A LIGHT MAN

"And I—what I seem to my friend, you see—
  What I soon shall seem to his love, you guess.
What I seem to myself, do you ask of me?
  No hero, I confess."

A Light Woman—Browning's Men and Women

APRIL 4, 1857—I have changed my sky without changing my mind. I resume these old notes in a new world. I hardly know of what use they are; but it's easier to stick to the habit than to drop it. I have been at home now a week—at home, forsooth! And yet, after all, it is home. I am dejected, I am bored, I am blue. How can a man be more at home than that? Nevertheless, I am the citizen of a great country, and for that matter, of a great city. I walked to-day some ten miles or so along Broadway, and on the whole I don't blush for my native land. We are a capable race and a good-looking withal; and I don't see why we shouldn't prosper as well as another. This, by the way, ought to be a very encouraging reflection. A capable fellow and a good-looking withal; I don't see why he shouldn't die a millionaire. At all events he must do something. When a man has, at thirty-two, a net income of considerably less than nothing, he can scarcely hope to overtake a fortune before he himself is overtaken by age and philosophy—two deplorable obstructions. I am afraid that one of them has already planted itself in my path. What am I? What do I wish? Whither do I tend? What do I believe? I am constantly beset by these impertinent whisperings. Formerly it

61

was enough that I was Maximus Austin; that I was endowed with a cheerful mind and a good digestion; and one day or another, when I had come to the end, I should return to America and begin at the beginning; that, meanwhile, existence was sweet in—in the Rue Tronchet. But now? Has the sweetness really passed out of life? Have I eaten the plums and left nothing but the bread and milk and corn-starch, or whatever the horrible concoction is?—I had it to-day for dinner. Pleasure, at least, I imagine—pleasure pure and simple, pleasure crude, brutal and vulgar—this poor flimsy delusion has lost all its charm. I shall never again care for certain things—and indeed for certain persons. Of such things or such persons, I firmly maintain, however, that I was never an enthusiastic votary. It would be more to my credit, I suppose, if I had been. More would be forgiven me if I had loved a little more, if into all my folly and egotism I had put a little more *naïveté* and sincerity. Well, I did the best I could, I was at once too bad and too good for it all. At present, it's far enough off; I have put the sea between us; I am stranded. I sit high and dry, scanning the horizon for a friendly sail, or waiting for a high tide to set me afloat. The wave of pleasure has deposited me here in the sand. Shall I owe my rescue to the wave of pain? At moments I feel a kind of longing to expiate my stupid little sins. I see, as through a glass, darkly, the beauty of labor and love. Decidedly, I am willing to work. It's written.

7th—My sail is in sight; it's at hand; I have all but boarded the vessel. I received this morning a letter from the best man in the world. Here it is:

DEAR MAX: I see this very moment, in an old newspaper which had already passed through my hands without yielding up its most precious item, the announcement of your arrival in New York. To think of your having perhaps missed the welcome you had a right to expect from me! Here it is dear Max—as cordial as you please.

When I say I have just read of your arrival, I mean that twenty minutes have elapsed by the clock. These have been spent in conversation with my excellent friend Mr Sloane—we having taken the liberty of making you the topic. I haven't time to say more about Frederick Sloane than that he is very anxious to make your acquaintance, and that, if your time is not otherwise engaged, he would like you very much to spend a month with him. He is an excellent host, or I shouldn't be here myself. It appears that he knew your mother very intimately, and he has a taste for visiting the amenities of the parents upon the children; the original ground of my own connection with him was that he had been a particular friend of my father. You may have heard your mother speak of him. He is a very strange old fellow, but you will like him, Whether or no you come for his sake, come for mine.

Yours always,
THEODORE LISLE

Theodore's letter is of course very kind, but it's remarkably obscure. My mother may have had the highest regard for Mr Sloane, but she never mentioned his name in my hearing. Who is he, what is he, and what is the nature of his relations with Theodore? I shall learn betimes. I have written to Theodore that I gladly accept (I believe I suppressed the "gladly" though) his friend's invitation, and that I shall immediately present myself. What can I do that is better? Speaking sordidly, I shall obtain food and lodging while I look about me. I shall have a base of operations. D., it appears, is a long day's journey, but enchanting when you reach it. I am curious to see an enchanting American town. And to stay a month! Mr Frederick Sloane, whoever you are, *vous faites bien les choses*, and the little that I know of you is very much to your credit. You enjoyed the friendship of my dear mother, you possess the esteem of the virtuous Theodore, you commend yourself to my own affection. At this rate, I shall not grudge it.

D—, 14th.—I have been here since Thursday evening—
three days. As we rattled up to the tavern in the village, I
perceived from the top of the coach, in the twilight, Theodore
beneath the porch, scanning the vehicle, with all his amiable
disposition in his eyes. He has grown older, of course, in
these five years, but less so than I had expected. His is one
of those smooth, unwrinkled souls that keep their bodies
fair and fresh. As tall as ever, moreover, and as lean and clean.
How short and fat and dark and debauched he makes one
feel! By nothing he says or means, of course, but merely by
his old unconscious purity and simplicity—that slender
straightness which makes him remind you of the spire of an
English abbey. He greeted me with smiles, and stares, and
alarming blushes. He assures me that he never would have
known me, and that five years have altered me—*sehr!* I asked
him if it were for the better? He looked at me hard for a moment, with his eyes of blue, and then, for an answer, he
blushed again.

On my arrival we agreed to walk over from the village.
He dismissed his wagon with my luggage, and we went arm-
in-arm through the dusk. The town is seated at the foot of
certain mountains, whose names I have yet to learn, and at
the head of a big sheet of water, which, as yet, too, I know
only as "the Lake." The road hitherward soon leaves the
village and wanders in rural loveliness by the margin of this
expanse. Sometimes the water is hidden by clumps of trees,
behind which we heard it lapping and gurgling in the darkness; sometimes it stretches out from your feet in shining
vagueness, as if it were tired of making, all day, a million
little eyes at the great stupid hills. The walk from the tavern
takes some half an hour, and in this interval Theodore made
his position a little more clear. Mr Sloane is a rich old widower;
his age is seventy-two, and as his health is thoroughly broken,
is practically even greater; and his fortune—Theodore,
characteristically, doesn't know anything definite about that.

It's probably about a million. He has lived much in Europe, and in the "great world"; he has had adventures and passions and all that sort of thing; and now, in the evening of his days, like an old French diplomatist, he takes it into his head to write his memoirs. To this end he has lured poor Theodore to his gruesome side, to mend his pens for him. He has been a great scribbler, says Theodore, all his days, and he proposes to incorporate a large amount of promiscuous literary matter into these *souvenirs intimes*. Theodore's principal function seems to be to get him to leave things out. In fact, the poor youth seems troubled in conscience. His patron's lucubrations have taken the turn of many other memoirs, and have ceased to address themselves *virginibus puerisque*. On the whole, he declares they are a very odd mixture—a medley of gold and tinsel, of bad taste and a good sense. I can readily understand it. The old man bores me, puzzles me, and amuses me.

He was in waiting to receive me. We found him in his library—which, by the way, is simply the most delightful apartment that I ever smoked a cigar in—a room arranged for a lifetime. At one end stands a great fireplace, with a florid, fantastic mantelpiece in carved white marble—an importation, of course, and, as one may say, an interpolation; the groundwork of the house, the "fixtures," being throughout plain, solid and domestic. Over the mantel-shelf is a large landscape, a fine Gainsborough, full of the complicated harmonies of an English summer. Beneath it stands a row of bronzes of the Renaissance and potteries of the Orient. Facing the door, as you enter, is an immense window set in a recess, with cushioned seats and large clear panes, stationed as it were at the very apex of the lake (which forms an almost perfect oval) and commanding a view of its whole extent. At the other end, opposite the fireplace, the wall is studded, from floor to ceiling, with choice foreign paintings, placed in relief against the orthodox crimson screen. Elsewhere the walls are covered with books, arranged neither in formal regularity nor quite helter-skelter, but in a sort of genial incongruity, which tells that sooner or later each volume feels sure of leaving the ranks and returning into different company. Mr Sloane makes use of his books. His two passions, according to Theodore, are reading and talking; but to talk he must have a book in his hand. The charm of the room lies in the absence of certain pedantic tones—the browns, blacks and grays—which distinguish most libraries. The apartment is of the feminine gender. There are half a dozen light colors scattered about—pink in the carpet, tender blue in the curtains, yellow in the chairs. The result is a general look of brightness and lightness; it expresses even a certain cynicism. You perceive the place to be the home, not of a man of learning, but of a man of fancy.

He rose from his chair—the man of fancy, to greet me—the man of fact. As I looked at him, in the lamplight, it seemed to me, for the first five minutes, that I had seldom seen an uglier little person. It took me five minutes to get the point of view; then I began to admire. He is diminutive, or at best of my own moderate stature, and bent and contracted with his seventy years; lean and delicate, moreover, and very highly finished. He is curiously pale, with a kind of opaque yellow pallor. Literally, it's a magnificent yellow. His skin is of just the hue and apparent texture of some old crumpled Oriental scroll. I know a dozen painters who would give more than they have to arrive at the exact "tone" of his thick-veined, bloodless hands, his polished ivory knuckles. His eyes are circled with red, but in the battered little setting of their orbits they have the lustre of old sapphires. His nose, owing to the falling away of other portions of his face, has assumed a grotesque, unnatural prominence; it describes an immense arch, gleaming like a piece of parchment stretched on ivory. He has, apparently, all his teeth, but has muffled his cranium in a dead black wig; of course he's clean shaven. In his dress he has a muffled, wadded look and an apparent aversion to linen, inasmuch as none is visible on his person. He seemed neat enough, but not fastidious. At first, as I say, I fancied him monstrously ugly; but on further acquaintance I perceived that what I had taken for ugliness is nothing but the incomplete remains of remarkable good looks. The line of his features is pure; his nose, *cæteris paribus*, would be extremely handsome; his eyes are the oldest eyes I ever saw, and yet they are wonderfully living. He has something remarkably insinuating.

He offered his two hands, as Theodore introduced me; I gave him my own, and he stood smiling at me like some quaint old image in ivory and ebony, scanning my face with a curiosity which he took no pains to conceal. "God bless me," he said, at last, "how much you look like your father!" I sat down, and for half an hour we talked of many things—of my journey, of my impressions of America, of my reminiscences of Europe, and, by implication, of my prospects. His voice is weak and cracked, but he makes it express everything. Mr Sloane is not yet in his dotage—oh no! He nevertheless makes himself out a poor creature. In reply to an inquiry of mine about his health, he favored me with a long list of his infirmities (some of which are very trying, certainly) and assured me that he was quite finished.

"I live out of mere curiosity," he said.

"I have heard of people dying from the same motive."

He looked at me a moment, as if to ascertain whether I were laughing at him. And then, after a pause, "Perhaps you don't know that I disbelieve in a future life," he remarked, blandly.

At these words Theodore got up and walked to the fire.

"Well, we shan't quarrel about that," said I. Theodore turned round, staring.

"Do you mean that you agree with me?" the old man asked.

"I certainly haven't come here to talk theology! Don't ask me to disbelieve, and I'll never ask you to believe."

"Come," cried Mr Sloane, rubbing his hands, "you'll not persuade me you are a Christian—like your friend Theodore there."

"Like Theodore—assuredly not." And then, somehow, I don't know why, at the thought of Theodore's Christianity I burst into a laugh. "Excuse me, my dear fellow," I said, "you know, for the last ten years I have lived in pagan lands."

"What do you call pagans?" asked Theodore, smiling.

I saw the old man, with his hands locked, eyeing me shrewdly, and waiting for my answer. I hesitated a moment, and then I said, "Everything that makes life tolerable!"

Hereupon Mr Sloane began to laugh till he coughed. Verily, I thought, if he lives for curiosity, he's easily satisfied.

We went into dinner, and this repast showed me that some of his curiosity is culinary. I observed, by the way, that for a victim of neuralgia, dyspepsia, and a thousand other ills, Mr Sloane plies a most inconsequential knife and fork. Sauces and spices and condiments seem to be the chief of his diet. After dinner he dismissed us, in consideration of my natural desire to see my friend in private. Theodore has capital quarters—a downy bedroom and a snug little *salon*. We talked till near midnight—of ourselves, of each other, and of the author of the memoirs, down stairs. That is, I spoke of myself, and Theodore listened; and then Theodore descanted upon Mr Sloane, and I listened. His commerce with the old man has sharpened his wits. Sloane has taught him to observe and judge, and Theodore turns round, observes, judges— him! He has become quite the critic and analyst. There is something very pleasant in the discriminations of a con-scientious mind, in which criticism is tempered by an angelic charity. Only, it may easily end by acting on one's nerves. At midnight we repaired to the library, to take leave of our host till the morrow—an attention which, under all circumstances, he rigidly exacts. As I gave him my hand he held it again and looked at me as he had done on my arrival. "Bless my soul," he said, at last, "how much you look like your mother!"

To-night, at the end of my third day, I begin to feel decidedly at home. The fact is, I am remarkably comfortable. The house is pervaded by an indefinable, irresistible love of luxury and privacy. Mr Frederick Sloane is a horribly corrupt old mortal. Already in his relaxing presence I have become heartily reconciled to doing nothing. But with Theodore on one side—standing there like a tall interrogation-point—I honestly believe I can defy Mr Sloane on the other. The former asked me this morning, with visible solicitude, in allusion to the bit of dialogue I have quoted above on matters of faith, whether I am really a materialist—whether I don't believe something? I told him I would believe anything he liked. He looked at me a while, in friendly sadness. "I hardly know whether you are not worse than Mr Sloane," he said.

But Theodore is, after all, in duty bound to give a man a long rope in these matters. His own rope is one of the longest. He reads Voltaire with Mr Sloane, and Emerson in his own room. He is the stronger man of the two; he has the larger stomach. Mr Sloane delights, of course, in Voltaire, but he can't read a line of Emerson. Theodore delights in Emerson, and enjoys Voltaire, though he thinks him superficial. It appears that since we parted in Paris, five years ago, his conscience has dwelt in many lands. *C'est tout une histoire*— which he tells very prettily. He left college determined to enter the church, and came abroad with his mind full of theology and Tübingen. He appears to have studied, not wisely but too well. Instead of faith full-armed and serene, there sprang from the labor of his brain a myriad sickly questions, piping for answers. He went for a winter to Italy, where, I take it, he was not quite so much afflicted as he ought to have been at the sight of the beautiful spiritual repose that he had missed. It was after this that we spent those three months together in Brittany—the best-spent months of my long residence in Europe. Theodore inoculated me, I think, with some of his seriousness, and I just touched him with my profanity; and we agreed together that there were a few good things left—health, friendship, a summer sky, and the lovely byways of an old French province. He came home, searched the Scriptures once more, accepted a "call," and made an attempt to respond to it. But the inner voice failed him. His outlook was cheerless enough. During his absence his married sister, the elder one, had taken the other to live with her, relieving Theodore of the charge of contribution to her support. But suddenly, behold the husband, the brother-in-law, dies, leaving a mere figment of property; and the two ladies, with their two little girls, are afloat in the wide world. Theodore finds himself at twenty-six without an income, without a profession, and with a family of four females to support. Well, in his quiet way he draws on his courage. The history of the two years that passed before he came to Mr Sloane is really absolutely edifying. He rescued his sisters and nieces from the deep waters, placed them high and dry, established them somewhere in decent gentility— and then found at last that his strength had left him—had dropped dead like an overridden horse. In short, he had worked himself to the bone. It was now his sisters' turn. They nursed him with all the added tenderness of gratitude for the past and terror of the future, and brought him safely through a grievous malady. Meanwhile Mr Sloane, having decided to treat himself to a private secretary and suffered dreadful mis- chance in three successive experiments, had heard of Theo- dore's situation and his merits; had furthermore recognized in him the son of an early and intimate friend, and had finally offered him the very comfortable position he now occupies. There is a decided incongruity between Theodore as a man

—as Theodore, in fine—and the dear fellow as the intellectual agent, confidant, complaisant, purveyor, pander—what you will—of a battered old cynic and dilettante—a worldling if there ever was one. There seems at first sight a perfect want of agreement between his character and his function. One is gold and the other brass, or something very like it. But on reflection I can enter into it—his having, under the circumstances, accepted Mr Sloane's offer and been content to do his duties. *Ce que c'est de nous!* Theodore's contentment in such a case is a theme for the moralist—a better moralist than I. The best and purest mortals are an odd mixture, and in none of us does honesty exist on its own terms. Ideally, Theodore hasn't the smallest business *dans cette galère*. It offends my sense of propriety to find him here. I feel that I ought to notify him as a friend that he has knocked at the wrong door, and that he had better retreat before he is brought to the blush. However, I suppose he might as well be here as reading Emerson "evenings" in the back parlor, to those two very plain sisters—judging from their photographs. Practically it hurts no one not to be too much of a prig. Poor Theodore was weak, depressed, out of work. Mr Sloane offers him a lodging and a salary in return for—after all, merely a little tact. All he has to do is to read to the old man, lay down the book a while, with his finger in the place, and let him talk; take it up again, read another dozen pages and submit to another commentary. Then to write a dozen pages under his dictation— to suggest a word, polish off a period, or help him out with a complicated idea or a half-remembered fact. This is all, I say; and yet this is much. Theodore's apparent success proves it to be much, as well as the old man's satisfaction. It is a part; he has to simulate. He has to "make believe" a little—a good deal; he has to put his pride in his pocket and send his conscience to the wash. He has to be accommodating—to listen and pretend and flatter; and he does it as well as many a worse man—does it far better than I. I might bully the old man, but I don't think I could humor him. After all, however, it is not a matter of comparative merit. In every son of woman there are two men—the practical man and the dreamer. We live for our dreams—but, meanwhile, we live by our wits. When the dreamer is a poet, the other fellow is an artist. Theodore, at bottom is only a man of taste. If he were not destined to become a high priest among moralists, he might be a prince among connoisseurs. He plays his part, therefore, artistically, with spirit, with originality, with all his native refinement. How can Mr Sloane fail to believe that he possesses a paragon? He is no such fool as not to appreciate a *nature distinguée* when it comes in his way. He confidentially assured me this morning that Theodore has the most charming mind in the world, but that it's a pity he's so simple as not to suspect it. If he only doesn't ruin him with his flattery!

19th.—I am certainly fortunate among men. This morning when, tentatively, I spoke of going away, Mr Sloane rose from his seat in horror and declared that for the present I must regard his house as my home. "Come, come," he said, "when you leave this place where do you intend to go?" Where, indeed? I graciously allowed Mr Sloane to have the best of the argument. Theodore assures me that he appreciates these and other affabilities, and that I have made what he calls a "conquest" of his venerable heart. Poor, battered, bamboozled old organ! he would have one believe that it has a most tragical record of capture and recapture. At all events, it appears that I am master of the citadel. For the present I have no wish to evacuate. I feel, nevertheless, in some far-off corner of my soul, that I ought to shoulder my victorious banner and advance to more fruitful triumphs.

I blush for my beastly laziness. It isn't that I am willing to stay here a month, but that I am willing to stay here six. Such is the charming, disgusting truth. Have I really outlived the age of energy? Have I survived my ambition, my integrity, my self-respect? Verily, I ought to have survived the habit of asking myself silly questions. I made up my mind long ago to go in for nothing but present success; and I don't care for that sufficiently to secure it at the cost of temporary suffering. I have a passion for nothing—not even for life. I know very well the appearance I make in the world. I pass for a clever, accomplished, capable, good-natured fellow, who can do anything if he would only try. I am supposed to be rather cultivated, to have latent talents. When I was younger I used to find a certain entertainment in the spectacle of human affairs. I liked to see men and women hurrying on each other's heels across the stage. But I am sick and tired of them now; not that I am a misanthrope, God forbid! They are not worth hating. I never knew but one creature who was, and her I went and loved. To be consistent, I ought to have hated my mother, and now I ought to detest Theodore. But I don't —truly, on the whole, I don't—any more than I dote on him. I firmly believe that it makes a difference to him, his idea that I *am* fond of him. He believes in that, as he believes in all the rest of it—in my culture, my latent talents, my underlying "earnestness," my sense of beauty and love of truth. Oh, for a *man* among them all—a fellow with eyes in his head—eyes that would know me for what I am and let me see they had guessed it. Possibly such a fellow as that might get a "rise" out of me.

In the name of bread and butter, what am I to do? (I was obliged this morning to borrow fifty dollars from Theodore, who remembered gleefully that he has been owing me a trifling sum for the past four years, and in fact has preserved a note to this effect.) Within the last week I have hatched a desperate plan: I have made up my mind to take a wife—a rich one, *bien entendu*. Why not accept the goods of the gods? It is not my fault, after all, if I pass for a good fellow. Why not admit that practically, mechanically—as I may say—maritally, I *may* be a good fellow? I warrant myself kind. I should never beat my wife; I don't think I should even contradict her. Assume that her fortune has the proper number of zeros and that she herself is one of them, and I can even imagine her adoring me. I really think this is my only way. Curiously, as I look back upon my brief career, it all seems to tend to this consummation. It has its graceful curves and crooks, indeed, and here and there a passionate tangent; but on the whole, if I were to unfold it here *à la* Hogarth, what better legend could I scrawl beneath the series of pictures than So-and-So's Progress to a Mercenary Marriage?

Coming events do what we all know with their shadows. My noble fate is, perhaps, not far off. I already feel throughout my person a magnificent languor—as from the possession of many dollars. Or is it simply my sense of well-being in this perfectly appointed house? Is it simply the contact of the highest civilization I have known? At all events, the place is of velvet, and my only complaint of Mr Sloane is that, instead of an old widower, he's not an old widow (or a young maid), so that I might marry him, survive him, and dwell forever in this rich and mellow home. As I write here, at my bedroom table, I have only to stretch out an arm and raise the window-curtain to see the thick-planted garden budding and breathing and growing in the silvery silence. Far above in the liquid darkness rolls the brilliant ball of the moon; beneath, in its light, lies the lake, in murmuring, troubled sleep; round about, the mountains, looking strange and blanched, seem to bare their heads and undrape their shoulders. So much for midnight. To-morrow the scene will be lovely with the beauty of day. Under one aspect or another I have it always before me. At the end of the garden is moored a boat, in which Theodore and I have indulged in an immense deal of irregular navigation. What lovely landward coves and bays—what alder-smothered creeks—what lily-sheeted pools —what sheer steep hillsides, making the water dark and quiet where they hang. I confess that in these excursions Theodore looks after the boat and I after the scenery. Mr Sloane avoids the water—on account of the dampness, he says; because he's afraid of drowning, I suspect.

22nd.—Theodore is right. The *bonhomme* has taken me into his favor. I protest I don't see how he was to escape it. *Je l'ai bien soigné*, as they say in Paris. I don't blush for it. In one coin or another I must replay his hospitality—which is certainly very liberal. Theodore dots his *i*'s, crosses his *t*'s, verifies his quotations; while I set traps for that famous "curiosity." This speaks vastly well for my powers. He pretends to be surprised at nothing, and to possess in perfection —poor, pitiable old fop—the art of keeping his countenance; but repeatedly, I know, I have made him stare. As for his corruption, which I spoke of above, it's a very pretty piece of wickedness, but it strikes me as a purely intellectual matter. I imagine him never to have had any real senses. He may have been unclean; morally, he's not very tidy now; but he never can have been what the French call a *viveur*. He's too delicate, he's of a feminine turn; and what woman was ever a *viveur?* He likes to sit in his chair and read scandal, talk scandal, make scandal, so far as he may without catching a cold or bringing on a headache. I already feel as if I had known him a lifetime. I read him as clearly as if I had. I know the type to which he belongs; I have encountered, first and last, a good many specimens of it. He's neither more nor less than a gossip—a gossip flanked by a coxcomb and an egotist. He's shallow, vain, cold, superstitious, timid, pretentious, capricious; a pretty list of foibles! And yet, for all this, he has his good points. His caprices are sometimes generous, and his rebellion against the ugliness of life frequently makes him do kind things. His memory (for trifles) is remarkable, and (where his own performances are not involved) his taste is excellent. He has no courage for evil more than for good. He is the victim, however, of more illusions with regard to himself than I ever knew a single brain to shelter. At the age of twenty, poor, ignorant and remarkably handsome, he married a woman of immense wealth, many years his senior. At the end of three years she very considerately took herself off and left him to the enjoyment of his freedom and riches. If he had remained poor he might from time to time have rubbed at random against the truth, and would be able to recognize the touch of it. But he wraps himself in his money as in a wadded dressing-gown, and goes trundling through life on his little gold wheels. The greater part of his career, from the time of his marriage till about ten years ago, was spent in Europe, which, superficially, he knows very well. He has lived in fifty places, known thousands of people, and spent a very large fortune. At one time, I believe, he spent considerably too much, trembled for an instant on the verge of a pecuniary crash, but recovered himself, and found himself more frightened than hurt, yet audibly recommended to lower his pitch. He passed five years in a species of penitent seclusion on the lake of—I forget what (his genius seems to be partial to lakes), and laid the basis of his present magnificent taste for literature. I can't call him anything but magnificent in this respect, so long as he must have his punctuation done by a *nature distinguée*. At the close of this period, by economy, he had made up his losses. His turning the screw during those relatively impecunious years represents, I am pretty sure, the only act of resolution of his life. It was rendered possible by his morbid, his actually pusillanimous dread of poverty; he doesn't feel safe without half a million between him and starvation. Meanwhile he had turned from a young man into an old man; his health was broken, his spirit was jaded, and I imagine, to do him justice, that he began to feel certain natural, filial longings for this dear American mother of us all. They say the most hopeless truants and triflers have come to it. He came to it, at all events; he packed up his books and pictures and gimcracks, and bade farewell to Europe. This house which he now occupies belonged to his wife's estate.

She had, for sentimental reasons of her own, commended it to his particular care. On his return he came to see it, liked it, turned a parcel of carpenters and upholsterers into it, and by inhabiting it for nine years transformed it into the perfect dwelling which I find it. Here he has spent all his time, with the exception of a usual winter's visit to New York—a practice recently discontinued, owing to the increase of his ailments and the projection of these famous memoirs. His life has finally come to be passed in comparative solitude. He tells of various distant relatives, as well as intimate friends of both sexes, who used formerly to be entertained at his cost; but with each of them, in the course of time, he seems to have succeeded in quarrelling. Throughout life, evidently, he has had capital fingers for plucking off parasites. Rich, lonely, and vain, he must have been fair game for the race of social sycophants and cormorants; and it's much to the credit of his sharpness and that instinct of self-defence which nature bestows even on the weak, that he has not been despoiled and *exploité*. Apparently they have all been bunglers. I maintain that something is to be done with him still. But one must work in obedience to certain definite laws. Doctor Jones, his physician, tells me that in point of fact he has had for the past ten years an unbroken series of favourites, *protégés*, heirs presumptive; but that each, in turn, by some fatally false movement, has spilled his pottage. The doctor declares, moreover, that they were mostly very common people. Gradually the old man seems to have developed a preference for two or three strictly exquisite intimates, over a throng of your vulgar pensioners. His tardy literary schemes, too—fruit of his all but sapless senility—have absorbed more and more of his time and attention. The end of it all is, therefore, that Theodore and I have him quite to ourselves, and that it behooves us to hold our porringers straight.

Poor, pretentious old simpleton! It's not his fault, after all, that he fancies himself a great little man. How are you to judge of the stature of mankind when men have forever addressed you on their knees? Peace and joy to his innocent fatuity! He believes himself the most rational of men; in fact, he's the most superstitious. He fancies himself a philosopher, an inquirer, a discoverer. He has not yet discovered that he is a humbug, that Theodore is a prig, and that I am an adventurer. He prides himself on his good manners, his urbanity, his knowing a rule of conduct for every occasion in life. My private impression is that his skinny old bosom contains unsuspected treasures of impertinence. He takes his stand on his speculative audacity—his direct, undaunted gaze at the universe; in truth, his mind is haunted by a hundred dingy old-world spectres and theological phantasms. He imagines himself one of the most solid of men; he is essentially one of the hollowest. He thinks himself ardent, impulsive, passionate, magnanimous—capable of boundless enthusiasm for an idea or a sentiment. It is clear to me that on no occasion of disinterested action can he ever have done anything in time. He believes, finally, that he has drained the cup of life to the dregs; that he has known, in its bitterest intensity, every emotion of which the human spirit is capable; that he has loved, struggled, suffered. Mere vanity, all of it. He has never loved any one but himself; he has never suffered from anything but an undigested supper or an exploded pretension; he has never touched with the end of his lips the vulgar bowl from which the mass of mankind quaffs its floods of joy and sorrow. Well, the long and short of it all is, that I honestly pity him. He may have given sly knocks in his life, but he can't hurt any one now. I pity his ignorance, his weakness, his pusillanimity. He has tasted the real sweetness of life no more than its bitterness; he has never dreamed, nor experimented, nor dared; he has never known any but mercenary affection; neither men nor women have risked aught for *him*—for his good spirits, his good looks, his empty pockets. How I should like to give him, for once, a real sensation!

26th.—I took a row this morning with Theodore a couple of miles along the lake, to a point where we went ashore and lounged away an hour in the sunshine, which is still very comfortable. Poor Theodore seems troubled about many things. For one, he is troubled about me; he is actually more anxious about my future than I myself; he thinks better of me than I do of myself; he is so deucedly conscientious, so scrupulous, so averse to giving offence or to *brusquer* any situation before it has played itself out, that he shrinks from betraying his apprehensions or asking direct questions. But I know that he would like very much to extract from me some intimation that there is something under the sun I should like to do. I catch myself in the act of taking—heaven forgive me! —a half-malignant joy in confounding his expectations— leading his generous sympathies off the scent by giving him momentary glimpses of my latent wickedness. But in Theodore I have so firm a friend that I shall have a considerable job if I ever find it needful to make him change his mind about me. He admires me—that's absolute; he takes my low moral tone for an eccentricity of genius, and it only imparts an extra flavor—a *haut goût*—to the charm of my intercourse. Nevertheless, I can see that he is disappointed. I have even less to show, after all these years, than he had hoped. Heaven help us! little enough it must strike him as being. What a contradiction there is in our being friends at all! I believe we shall end with hating each other. It's all very well now—our agreeing to differ, for we haven't opposed interests. But if we should *really* clash, the situation would be warm! I wonder, as it is, that Theodore keeps his patience with me. His education since we parted should tend logically to make him despise me. He has studied, thought, suffered, loved— loved those very plain sisters and nieces. Poor me! how should I be virtuous? I have no sisters, plain or pretty!—nothing to love, work for, live for. My dear Theodore, if you are going one of these days to despise me and drop me—in the name of comfort, come to the point at once, and make an end of our state of tension.

He is troubled, too, about Mr Sloane. His attitude toward the *bonhomme* quite passes my comprehension. It's the queerest jumble of contraries. He penetrates him, disapproves of him—yet respects and admires him. It all comes of the poor boy's shrinking New England conscience. He's afraid to give his perceptions a fair chance, lest, forsooth, they should look over his neighbor's wall. He'll not understand that he may as well sacrifice the old reprobate for a lamb as for a sheep. His view of the gentleman, therefore, is a perfect tissue of cobwebs—a jumble of half-way sorrows, and wire-drawn charities, and hair-breadth 'scapes from utter damnation, and sudden platitudes of generosity—fit, all of it, to make an angel curse!

"The man's a perfect egoist and fool," say I, "but I like him." Now Theodore likes him—or rather wants to like him; but he can't reconcile it to his self-respect—fastidious deity! —to like a fool. Why the deuce can't he leave it alone altogether? It's a purely practical matter. He ought to do the duties of his place all the better for having his head clear of officious sentiment. I don't believe in disinterested service; and Theodore is too desperately bent on preserving his disinterestedness. With me it's different. I am perfectly free to love the *bonhomme*—for a fool. I'm neither a scribe nor a Pharisee; I am simply a student of the art of life.

And then, Theodore is troubled about his sisters. He's afraid he's not doing his duty by them. He thinks he ought to be with them—to be getting a larger salary—to be teaching his nieces. I am not versed in such questions. Perhaps he ought.

May 3rd.—This morning Theodore sent me word that he was ill and unable to get up; upon which I immediately went in to see him. He had caught cold, was sick and a little feverish. I urged him to make no attempt to leave his room, and

assured him that I would do what I could to reconcile Mr
Sloane to his absence. This I found an easy matter. I read to
him for a couple of hours, wrote four letters—one in French
—and then talked for a while—a good while. I have done
more talking, by the way, in the last fortnight, than in any
previous twelve months—much of it, too, none of the
wisest, nor, I may add, of the most superstitiously veracious.
In a little discussion, two or three days ago with Theodore,
I came to the point and let him know that in gossiping with
Mr Sloane I made no scruple, for our common satisfaction,
of "coloring" more or less. My confession gave him "that
turn," as Mrs Gamp would say, that his present illness may
be the result of it. Nevertheless, poor dear fellow, I trust he
will be on his legs to-morrow. This afternoon, somehow, I
found myself really in the humour of talking. There was
something propitious in the circumstances; a hard, cold rain
without, a wood-fire in the library, the *bonhomme* puffing
cigarettes in his arm-chair, beside him a portfolio of newly
imported prints and photographs, and—Theodore tucked
safely away in bed. Finally, when I brought our *tête-â-téte* to
a close (taking good care not to overstay my welcome) Mr
Sloane seized me by both hands and honored me with one
of his venerable grins. "Max," he said—"you must let me
call you Max—you are the most delightful man I ever knew."

Verily, there's some virtue left in me yet. I believe I almost
blushed.

"Why didn't I know you ten years ago?" the old man went
on. "There are ten years lost."

"Ten years ago I was not worth your knowing," Max
remarked.

"But I did know you!" cried the *bonhomme*. "I knew you
in knowing your mother."

Ah! my mother again. When the old man begins that
chapter I feel like telling him to blow out his candle and go
to bed.

"At all events," he continued, "we must make the most of the years that remain. I am a rotten old carcass, but I have no intention of dying. You won't get tired of me and want to go away?"

"I am devoted to you, sir," I said. "But I must be looking for some occupation, you know."

"Occupation? bother! I'll give you occupation. I'll give you wages."

"I am afraid that you will want to give me the wages without the work." And then I declared that I must go up and look at poor Theodore.

The *bonhomme* still kept my hands. "I wish very much that I could get you to be as fond of me as you are of poor Theodore."

"Ah, don't talk about fondness, Mr Sloane. I don't deal much in that article."

"Don't you like my secretary?"

"Not as he deserves."

"Nor as he likes you, perhaps?"

"He likes me more than I deserve."

"Well, Max," my host pursued, "we can be good friends all the same. We don't need a hocus-pocus of false sentiment. We are *men*, aren't we?—men of sublime good sense." And just here, as the old man looked at me, the pressure of his hands deepened to a convulsive grasp, and the bloodless mask of his countenance was suddenly distorted with a nameless fear. "Ah, my dear young man!" he cried, "come and be a son to me—the son of my age and desolation! For God's sake, don't leave me to pine and die alone!"

I was greatly surprised—and I may add I was moved. Is it true, then, that this dilapidated organism contains such measureless depths of horror and longing? He has evidently a mortal fear of death. I assured him on my honor that the may henceforth call upon me for any service.

8th.—Theodore's little turn proved more serious than I

expected. He has been confined to his room till to-day. This evening he came down to the library in his dressing-gown. Decidedly, Mr Sloane is an eccentric, but hardly, as Theodore thinks, a "charming" one. There is something extremely curious in his humors and fancies—the incongruous fits and starts, as it were, of his taste. For some reason, best known to himself, he took it into his head to regard it as a want of delicacy, of respect, of *savoir-vivre*—of heaven knows what—that poor Theodore, who is still weak and languid, should enter the sacred precinct of his study in the vulgar drapery of a dressing-gown. The sovereign trouble with the *bonhomme* is an absolute lack of the instinct of justice. He's of the real feminine turn—I believe I have written it before—without the redeeming fidelity of the sex. I honestly believe that I might come into his study in my night-shirt and he would smile at it as a picturesque *déshabillé*. But for poor Theodore to-night there was nothing but scowls and frowns, and barely a civil inquiry about his health. But poor Theodore is not such a fool, either; he will not die of a snubbing; I never said he was a weakling. Once he fairly saw from what quarter the wind blew, he bore the master's brutality with the utmost coolness and gallantry. Can it be that Mr Sloane really wishes to drop him? The delicious old brute! He understands favor and friendship only as a selfish rapture—a reaction, an infatuation, an act of aggressive, exclusive patronage. It's not a bestowal, with him, but a transfer, and half his pleasure in causing his sun to shine is that—being wofully near its setting—it will produce certain long fantastic shadows. He wants to cast my shadow, I suppose, over Theodore; but fortunately I am not altogether an opaque body. Since, Theodore was taken ill he has been into his room but once, and has sent him none but a dry little message or two. I, too have been much less attentive than I should have wished to be; but my time has not been my own. It has been, every moment of it, at the disposal of my host. He actually runs after me; he devours me; he makes a fool of himself, and is trying hard to make one of me. I find that he will bear—that, in fact, he actually enjoys—a sort of unexpected contradiction. He likes anything that will tickle his fancy, give an unusual tone to our relations, remind him of certain historical characters whom he thinks he resembles. I have stepped into Theodore's shoes, and done—with what I feel in my bones to be very inferior skill and taste—all the reading, writing, condensing, transcribing and advising that he has been accustomed to do. I have driven with the *bonhomme*; played chess and cribbage with him; beaten him, bullied him, contradicted him; forced him into going out on the water under my charge. Who shall say, after this, that I haven't done my best to discourage his advances, put myself in a bad light? As yet, my efforts are vain; in fact they quite turn to my own confusion. Mr Sloane is so thankful at having escaped from the lake with his life that he looks upon me as a preserver and protector. Confound it all; it's a bore! But one thing is certain, it can't last forever. Admit that he *has* cast Theodore out and taken me in. He will speedily discover that he has made a pretty mess of it, and he had much better have left well enough alone. He likes my reading and writing now, but in a month he will begin to hate them. He will miss Theodore's better temper and better knowledge—his healthy impersonal judgment. What an advantage that well-regulated youth has over me, after all! I am for days, he is for years; he for the long run, I for the short. I, perhaps, am intended for success, but he is adapted for happiness. He has in his heart a tiny sacred particle which leavens his whole being and keeps it pure and sound—a faculty of admiration and respect. For him human nature is still a wonder and mystery; it bears a divine stamp—Mr Sloane's tawdry composition as well as the rest.

13th.—I have refused, of course, to supplant Theodore further, in the exercise of his functions, and he has resumed his morning labors with Mr Sloane. I, on my side, have spent these morning hours in scouring the country on that capital black mare, the use of which is one of the perquisites of Theodore's place. The days have been magnificent—the heat of the sun tempered by a murmuring, wandering wind, the whole north a mighty ecstasy of sound and verdure, the sky a far-away vault of bended blue. Not far from the mill at M., the other end of the lake, I met, for the third time, that very pretty young girl who reminds me so forcibly of A. L. She makes so lavish a use of her eyes that I ventured to stop and bid her good-morning. She seems nothing loath to an acquaintance. She's a pure barbarian in speech, but her eyes are quite articulate. These rides do me good; I was growing too pensive.

There is something the matter with Theodore; his illness seems to have left him strangely affected. He has fits of silent stiffness, alternating with spasms of extravagant gayety. He avoids me at times for hours together, and then he comes and looks at me with an inscrutable smile, as if he were on the verge of a burst of confidence—which again is swallowed up in the immensity of his dumbness. Is he hatching some astounding benefit to his species? Is he working to bring about my removal to a higher sphere of action? *Nous verrons bien.*

18th.—Theodore threatens departure. He received this morning a letter from one of his sisters—the young widow—announcing her engagement to a clergyman whose acquaintance she has recently made, and intimating her expectation of an immediate union with the gentleman—a ceremony which would require Theodore's attendance. Theodore, in high good humor, read the letter aloud at breakfast—and, to tell the truth, it was a charming epistle. He then spoke of his having to go on to the wedding, a proposition to which Mr Sloane graciously assented—much more than assented. "I shall be sorry to lose you, after so happy a connection," said the old man. Theodore turned pale, stared a moment, and then, recovering his color and his composure, declared that he should have no objection in life to coming back.

"Bless your soul!" cried the *bonhomme*, "you don't mean to say you will leave your other sister all alone?"

To which Theodore replied that he would arrange for her and her little girl to live with the married pair. "It's the only proper thing," he remarked, as if it were quite settled. Has it come to this, then, that Mr Sloane actually wants to turn him out of the house? The shameless old villain! He keeps smiling an uncanny smile, which means, as I read it, that if the poor young man once departs he shall never return on the old footing—for all his impudence!

20th.—This morning, at breakfast, we had a terrific scene. A letter arrives for Theodore; he opens it, turns white and red, frowns, falters, and then informs us that the clever widow has broken off her engagement. No wedding, therefore, and no departure for Theodore. The *bonhomme* was furious. In his fury he took the liberty of calling poor Mrs Parker (the sister) a very uncivil name. Theodore rebuked him, with perfect good taste, and kept his temper.

"If my opinions don't suit you, Mr Lisle," the old man broke out, "and my mode of expressing them displeases you, you know you can easily protect yourself."

"My dear Mr Sloane," said Theodore, "your opinions, as a general thing, interest me deeply, and have never ceased to act beneficially upon the formation of my own. Your mode of expressing them is always brilliant, and I wouldn't for the world, after all our pleasant intercourse, separate from you in bitterness. Only, I repeat, your qualification of my sister's conduct is perfectly uncalled for. If you knew her, you would be the first to admit it."

There was something in Theodore's look and manner, as he said these words, which puzzled me all the morning. After dinner, finding myself alone with him, I told him I was glad he was not obliged to go away. He looked at me with the mysterious smile I have mentioned, thanked me, and fell into meditation. As this bescribbled chronicle is the record of my follies as well of my *hauts faits*, I needn't hesitate to say that for a moment I was a good deal vexed. What business has this angel of candor to deal in signs and portents, to look unutterable things? What right has he to do so with me especially, in whom he has always professed an absolute confidence? Just as I was about to cry out, "Come, my dear fellow, this affectation of mystery has lasted quite long enough —favor me at last with the result of your cogitations!"— as I was on the point of thus expressing my impatience of his ominous behavior, the oracle at last addressed itself to utterance.

"You see, my dear Max," he said, "I can't, in justice to myself, go away in obedience to the sort of notice that was served on me this morning. What do you think of my actual footing here?"

Theodore's actual footing here seems to me impossible; of course I said so.

"No, I assure you it's not," he answered. "I should, on the contrary, feel very uncomfortable to think that I had come away, except by my own choice. You see a man can't afford to cheapen himself. What are you laughing at?"

"I am laughing, in the first place, my dear fellow, to hear on your lips the language of cold calculation; and in the second place, at your odd notion of the process by which a man keeps himself up in the market."

"I assure you it's the correct notion. I came here as a particular favor to Mr Sloane; it was expressly understood so. The sort of work was odious to me; I had regularly to break myself in. I had to trample on my convictions, preferences, prejudices. I don't take such things easily; I take them hard; and when once the effort has been made, I can't consent to have it wasted. If Mr Sloane needed me then, he needs me still. I am ignorant of any change having taken place in his intentions, or in his means of satisfying them. I came, not to amuse him, but to do a certain work; I hope to remain until the work is completed. To go away sooner is to make a confession of incapacity which, I protest, costs me too much. I am too conceited, if you like."

Theodore spoke these words with a face which I have never seen him wear—a fixed, mechanical smile; a hard, dry glitter in his eyes; a harsh, strident tone in his voice—in his whole physiognomy a gleam, as it were, a note of defiance. Now I confess that for defiance I have never been conscious of an especial relish. When I am defied I am beastly. "My dear man," I replied, "your sentiments do you prodigious credit. Your very ingenious theory of your present situation, as well as your extremely pronounced sense of your personal value, are calculated to insure you a degree of practical success which can very well dispense with the furtherance of my poor good wishes." Oh, the grimness of his visage as he listened to this, and, I suppose I may add, the grimness of mine! But I have ceased to be puzzled. Theodore's conduct for the past ten days is suddenly illumined with a backward, lurid ray. I will note down here a few plain truths which it behooves me to take to heart—commit to memory. Theodore is jealous of Maximus Austin. Theodore hates the said Maximus. Theodore has been seeking for the past three months to see his name written, last but not least, in a certain testamentary document: "Finally, I bequeath to my dear young friend, Theodore Lisle, in return for invaluable service and unfailing devotion, the bulk of my property, real and personal, consisting of—" (hereupon follows an exhaustive enumeration of houses, lands, public securities, books, pictures, horses, and dogs). It is for this that he has toiled, and watched, and prayed; submitted to intellectual weariness and spiritual torture; accommodated himself to levity, blasphemy, and insult. For this he sets his teeth and tightens his grasp; for

this he'll fight. Dear me, it's an immense weight off one's
mind! There are nothing, then, but vulgar, common laws;
no sublime exceptions, no transcendent anomalies. Theodore's a knave, a hypo—nay, nay; stay, irreverent hand!—
Theodore's a *man!* Well, that's all I want. *He* wants fight—he
shall have it. Have I got, at last, my simple, natural emotion?

21st.—I have lost no time. This evening, late, after I had
heard Theodore go to his room (I had left the library early,
on the pretext of having letters to write), I repaired to Mr
Sloane, who had not yet gone to bed, and informed him I
should be obliged to leave him at once, and pick up a sub-
sistence somehow in New York. He felt the blow; it brought
him straight down on his marrow-bones. He went through
the whole gamut of his arts and graces; he blustered, whim-
pered, entreated, flattered. He tried to drag in Theodore's
name; but this I, of course, prevented. But, finally, why, *why*,
WHY, after all my promises of fidelity, must I thus cruelly
desert him? Then came my trump card: I have spent my last
penny; while I stay, I'm a beggar. The remainder of this
extraordinary scene I have no power to describe: how the
bonhomme, touched, inflamed, inspired, by the thought of
my destitution, and at the same time annoyed, perplexed,
bewildered at having to commit himself to doing anything
for me, worked himself into a nervous frenzy which deprived
him of a clear sense of the value of his words and his actions;
how I, prompted by the irresistible spirit of my desire to leap
astride of his weakness and ride it hard to the goal of my
dreams, cunningly contrived to keep his spirit at the fever-
point, so that strength and reason and resistance should burn
themselves out. I shall probably never again have such a
sensation as I enjoyed to-night—actually feel a heated human
heart throbbing and turning and struggling in my grasp;
know its pants, its spasms, its convulsions, and its final
senseless quiescence. At half-past one o'clock Mr Sloane got
out of his chair, went to his secretary, opened a private

drawer, and took out a folded paper. "This is my will," he said, "made some seven weeks ago. If you will stay with me I will destroy it."

"Really, Mr Sloane," I said, "if you think my purpose is to exert any pressure upon your testamentary inclinations—"

"I will tear it in pieces," he cried; "I will burn it up! I shall be as sick as a dog to-morrow; but I will do it. A-a-h!"

He clapped his hand to his side, as if in sudden, overwhelming pain, and sank back fainting into his chair. A single glance assured me that he was unconscious. I possessed myself of the paper, opened it, and perceived that he had left everything to his saintly secretary. For an instant a savage, puerile feeling of hate popped up in my bosom, and I came within a hair's-breadth of obeying my foremost impulse—that of stuffing the document into the fire. Fortunately, my reason overtook my passion, though for a moment it was an even race. I put the paper back into the bureau, closed it, and rang the bell for Robert (the old man's servant). Before he came I stood watching the poor, pale remnant of mortality before me, and wondering whether those feeble life-gasps were numbered. He was as white as a sheet, grimacing with pain—horribly ugly. Suddenly he opened his eyes; they met my own; I fell on my knees and took his hands. They closed on mine with a grasp strangely akin to the rigidity of death. Nevertheless, since then he has revived, and has relapsed again into a comparatively healthy sleep. Robert seems to know how to deal with him.

22nd.—Mr Sloane is seriously ill—out of his mind and unconscious of people's identity. The doctor has been here, off and on, all day, but this evening reports improvement. I have kept out of the old man's room, and confined myself to my own, reflecting largely upon the chance of his immediate death. Does Theodore know of the will? Would it occur to him to divide the property? Would it occur to me, in his place? We met at dinner, and talked in a grave, desultory, friendly fashion. After all, he's an excellent fellow. I don't hate him. I don't even dislike him. He jars on me, *il m'agace*; but that's no reason why I should do him an evil turn. Nor shall I. The property is a fixed idea, that's all. I shall get it if I can. We are fairly matched. Before heaven, no, we are not fairly matched! Theodore has a conscience.

23rd.—I am restless and nervous—and for good reasons. Scribbling here keeps me quiet. This morning Mr Sloane is better; feeble and uncertain in mind, but unmistakably on the rise. I may confess now that I feel relieved of a horrid burden. Last night I hardly slept a wink. I lay awake listening to the pendulum of my clock. It seemed to say, "He lives—he dies." I fully expected to hear it stop suddenly at *dies*. But it kept going all the morning, and to a decidedly more lively tune. In the afternoon the old man sent for me. I found him in his great muffled bed, with his face the color of damp chalk, and his eyes glowing faintly, like torches half stamped out. I was forcibly struck with the utter loneliness of his lot. For all human attendance, my villainous self grinning at his bedside and old Robert without, listening, doubtless, at the keyhole. The *bonhomme* stared at me stupidly; then seemed to know me, and greeted me with a sickly smile. It was some moments before he was able to speak. At last he faintly bade me to descend into the library, open the secret drawer of the secretary (which he contrived to direct me how to do so), possess myself of his will, and burn it up. He appears to have forgotten his having taken it out night before last. I told him that I had an insurmountable aversion to any personal dealings with the document. He smiled, patted the back of my hand, and requested me, in that case, to get it, at least, and bring it to him. I couldn't deny him that favor? No, I couldn't indeed. I went down to the library, therefore, and on entering the room found Theodore standing by the fireplace with a bundle of papers. The secretary was open. I stood still, looking from the violated cabinet to the documents in his hand. Among them I recognized, by its shape and size, the paper of which I had intended to possess myself. Without delay I walked straight up to him. He looked surprised, but not confused. "I am afraid I shall have to trouble you to surrender one of those papers," I said.

"Surrender, Maximus? To anything of your own you are perfectly welcome. I didn't know that you made use of Mr Sloane's secretary. I was looking for some pages of notes which I have made myself and in which I conceive I have a property."

"This is what I want, Theodore," I said; and I drew the will, unfolded, from between his hands. As I did so his eyes fell upon the superscription, "Last Will and Testament. March. F.S." He flushed an extraordinary crimson. Our eyes met. Somehow—I don't know how or why, or for that matter why not—I burst into a violent peal of laughter. Theodore stood staring, with two hot, bitter tears in his eyes.

"Of course you think I came to ferret out that thing," he said.

I shrugged my shoulders—those of my body only. I confess, morally, I was on my knees with contrition, but there was a fascination in it—a fatality. I remembered that in the hurry of my movements the other evening I had slipped the will simply into one of the outer drawers of the cabinet, among Theodore's own papers. "Mr Sloane sent me for it," I remarked.

"Very good; I am glad to hear he's well enough to think of such things."

"He means to destroy it."

"I hope, then, he has another made."

"Mentally, I suppose he has."

"Unfortunately, his weakness isn't mental—or exclusively so."

"Oh, he will live to make a dozen more," I said. "Do you know the purport of this one?"

Theodore's color, by this time, had died away into plain white. He shook his head. The doggedness of the movement provoked me, and I wished to arouse his curiosity. "I have his commission to destroy it."

Theodore smiled very grandly. "It's not a task I envy you," he said.

"I should think not—especially if you knew the import of the will." He stood with folded arms, regarding me with cold, detached eyes. I couldn't stand it. "Come, it's your property! You are sole legatee. I give it to you." And I thrust the paper into his hand.

He received it mechanically; but after a pause, bethinking himself, he unfolded it and cast his eyes over the contents. Then he slowly smoothed it together and held it a moment with a tremulous hand. "You say that Mr Sloane directed you to destroy it?" he finally inquired.

"I say so."

"And that you know the contents?"

"Exactly."

"And that you were about to do what he asked you?"

"On the contrary, I declined."

Theodore fixed his eyes for a moment on the superscription and then raised them again to my face. "Thank you, Max," he said. "You have left me a real satisfaction." He tore the sheet across and threw the bits into the fire. We stood watching them burn. "Now he can make another," said Theodore.

"Twenty others," I replied.

"No," said Theodore, "you will take care of that."

"You are very bitter," I said, sharply enough.

"No, I am perfectly indifferent. Farewell." And he put out his hand.

"Are you going away?"

"Of course I am. Good-bye."

"Good-bye, then. But isn't your departure rather sudden?"

"I ought to have gone three weeks ago—three weeks ago." I had taken his hand, he pulled it away; his voice was trembling—there were tears in it.

"Is *that* indifference?" I asked.

"It's something you will never know!" he cried. "It's shame! I am not sorry you should see what I feel. It will suggest to you, perhaps, that my heart had never been in this filthy contest. Let me assure you, at any rate, that it hasn't; that it has had nothing but scorn for the base preversion of my pride and my ambition. I could easily shed tears of joy at their return—the return of the prodigals! Tears of sorrow —sorrow—"

He was unable to go on. He sank into a chair, covering his face with his hands.

"For God's sake, stick to the joy!" I exclaimed.

He rose to his feet again. "Well," he said, "it was for your sake that I parted with my self-respect; with your assistance I recover it."

"How for my sake?"

"For whom but you would I have gone as far as I did? For what other purpose than that of keeping our friendship whole would I have borne your company into this narrow pass? A man whom I cared for less I would long since have parted with. You were needed—you and something you have about you that always takes me so—to bring me to this. You ennobled, exalted, enchanted the struggle. I *did* value my prospect of coming into Mr Sloane's property. I valued it for my poor sister's sake as well as for my own, so long as it was the natural reward of conscientious service, and not the prize of hypocrisy and cunning. With another man than you I never would have contested such a prize. But you fascinated me, even as my rival. You played with me, deceived me, betrayed me. I held my ground, hoping you would see that what you were doing was not fair. But if you have seen it, it has made no difference with you. For Mr Sloane, from the moment that, under your magical influence, he revealed his nasty little nature. I had nothing but contempt."

"And for me now?"

"Don't ask me. I don't trust myself."

"Hate, I suppose."

"Is that the best you can imagine? Farewell."

"Is it a serious farewell—farewell forever?"

"How can there be any other?"

"I am sorry this should be your point of view. It's characteristic. All the more reason then that I should say a word in self-defence. You accuse me of having 'played with you, deceived you, betrayed you.' It seems to me that you are quite beside the mark. You say you were such a friend of mine; if so, you ought to be one still. It was not to my fine sentiments you attached yourself, for I never had any or pretended to any. In anything I have done recently, therefore, there has been no inconsistency. I never pretended to take one's friendship so seriously. I don't understand the word in the sense you attach to it. I don't understand the feeling of affection between men. To me it means quite another thing. You give it a meaning of your own; you enjoy the profit of your invention; it's no more than just that you should pay the penalty. Only it seems to me rather hard that *I* should pay it." Theodore remained silent, but he looked quite sick. "Is it still a 'serious farewell'?" I went on. "It seems a pity. After this clearing up, it appears to me that I shall be on better terms with you. No man can have a deeper appreciation of your excellent parts, a keener enjoyment of your society. I should very much regret the loss of it."

"Have we, then, all this while understood each other so little?" said Theodore.

"Don't say 'we' and 'each other.' I think I have understood you."

"Very likely. It's not for my having kept anything back."

"Well, I do you justice. To me you have always been over-generous. Try now and be just."

Still he stood silent, with his cold, hard frown. It was plain that, if he was to come back to me, it would be from the other world—if there be one! What he was going to answer I know not. The door opened, and Robert appeared, pale, trembling, his eyes starting in his head.

"I verily believe that poor Mr Sloane is dead in his bed!" he cried.

There was a moment's perfect silence. "Amen," said I. "Yes, old boy, try and be just." Mr Sloane had quietly died in my absence.

24th.—Theodore went up to town this morning, having shaken hands with me in silence before he started. Doctor Jones, and Brooks the attorney, have been very officious, and, by their advice, I have telegraphed to a certain Miss Meredith, a maiden lady, by their account the nearest of kin; or, in other words, simply a discarded niece of the defunct. She telegraphs back that she will arrive in person for the funeral. I shall remain till she comes. I have lost a fortune, but have I irretrievably lost a friend? I am sure I can't say. Yes, I shall wait for Miss Meredith.

GABRIELLE DE BERGERAC

I

My good old friend, in his white flannel dressing-gown, with his wig "removed," as they say of the dinner-service, by a crimson nightcap, sat for some moments gazing into the fire. At last he looked up. I knew what was coming. "Apropos, that little debt of mine—"

Not that the debt was really very little. But M. de Bergerac was a man of honor, and I knew I should receive my dues. He told me frankly that he saw no way, either in the present or the future, to reimburse me in cash. His only treasures were his paintings; would I choose one of them? Now I had not spent an hour in M. de Bergerac's little parlor twice a week for three winters, without learning that the Baron's paintings were, with a single exception, of very indifferent merit. On the other hand, I had taken a great fancy to the picture this excepted. Yet, as I knew it was a family portrait, I hesitated to claim it. I refused to make a choice. M. de Bergerac, however, insisted, and I finally laid my finger on the charming image of my friend's aunt. I of course insisted, on my side, that M. de Bergerac should retain it during the remainder of his life, and so it was only after his decease that I came into possession of it. It hangs above my table as I write, and I have only to glance up at the face of my heroine to feel how vain it is to attempt to describe it. The portrait represents, in dimensions several degrees below those of nature, the head and shoulders of a young girl of two-and-twenty. The execution of the work is not especially strong, but it is thoroughly respectable, and one may easily see that the painter deeply appreciated the character of the face. The countenance is interesting rather than beautiful,—the forehead broad and open, the eyes slightly prominent, all the features full and firm and yet replete with gentleness. The head is slightly thrown back, as if in movement, and the lips are parted in a half-smile. And yet, in spite of this tender smile, I always fancy that the eyes are sad. The hair, dressed without powder, is rolled back over a high cushion (as I suppose), and adorned just above the left ear with a single white rose; while, on the other side, a heavy tress from behind hangs upon the neck with a sort of pastoral freedom. The neck is long and full, and the shoulders rather broad. The whole face has a look of mingled softness and decision, and seems to reveal a nature inclined to revery, affection, and repose, but capable of action and even of heroism. Mlle de Bergerac died under the axe of the Terrorists. Now that I had acquired a certain property in this sole memento of her life, I felt a natural curiosity as to her character and history. Had M. de Bergerac known his aunt? Did he remember her? Would it be a tax on his good-nature to suggest that he should favor me with a few reminiscences? The old man fixed his eyes on the fire, and laid his hand on mine, as if his memory were fain to draw from both sources—from the ruddy glow and from my fresh young blood—a certain vital, quickening warmth. A mild, rich smile ran to his lips, and he pressed my hand. Somehow,—I hardly know why,—I felt touched almost to tears. Mlle de Bergerac had been a familiar figure in her nephew's boyhood, and an important event in her life had formed a sort of episode in his younger days. It was a simple enough story; but such as it was, then and there, settling back into his chair, with the fingers of the clock wandering on to the small hours of the night, he told it with a tender, lingering garrulity. Such as it is, I repeat it. I shall give, as far as possible, my friend's words, or the English of them; but the reader will have to do without his inimitable accents. For them there is no English.

*

My father's household at Bergerac (said the Baron) consisted, exclusive of the servants, of five persons—himself, my mother, my aunt (Mlle de Bergerac), M. Coquelin (my preceptor), and M. Coquelin's pupil, the heir of the house. Perhaps, indeed, I should have numbered M. Coquelin among the servants. It is certain that my mother did. Poor little woman! she was a great stickler for the rights of birth. Her own birth was all she had, for she was without health, beauty, or fortune. My father, on his side, had very little of the last; his property of Bergerac yielded only enough to keep us without discredit. We gave no entertainments, and passed the whole year in the country; and as my mother was resolved that her weak health should do her a kindness as well as an injury, it was put forward as an apology for everything. We led at best a simple, somnolent sort of life. There was a terrible amount of leisure for rural gentlefolks in those good old days. We slept a great deal; we slept, you will say, on a volcano. It was a very different world from this patent new world of yours, and I may say that I was born on a different planet. Yes, in 1789, there came a great convulsion; the earth cracked and opened and broke, and this poor old *pays de France* went whirling through space. When I look back at my childhood, I look over a gulf. Three years ago, I spent a week at a country house in the neighborhood of Bergerac, and my hostess drove me over to the site of the château. The house has disappeared, and there's a homœopathic—hydropathic—what do you call it?—establishment erected in its place. But the little town is there, and the bridge on the river, and the church where I was christened, and the double row of lime-trees on the market-place, and the fountain in the middle. There's only one striking difference: the sky is changed. I was born under the old sky. It was black enough, of course, if we had only had eyes to see it; but to me, I confess, it looked divinely blue. And in fact it was very bright,—the little patch under which I cast my juvenile shadow. An odd enough little shadow

you would have thought it. I was promiscuously cuddled
and fondled. I was M. le Chevalier, and prospective master
of Bergerac; and when I walked to church on Sunday, I had
a dozen yards of lace on my coat and a little sword at my side.
My poor mother did her best to make me good for nothing.
She had her maid to curl my hair with the tongs, and she used
with her own fingers to stick little black patches on my face.
And yet I was a good deal neglected too, and I would go for
days with black patches of another sort. I'm afraid I should
have got very little education if a kind Providence hadn't
given me poor M. Coquelin. A kind Providence, that is, and
my father; for with my mother my tutor was no favorite.
She thought him—and, indeed, she called him—a bumpkin,
a clown. There was a very pretty abbé among her friends,
M. Tiblaud by name, whom she wished to install at the
château as my intellectual, and her spiritual, adviser; but my
father, who, without being anything of an *esprit fort*, had an
incurable aversion to a priest out of church, very soon routed
this pious scheme. My poor father was an odd figure of a man.
He belonged to a type as completely obsolete as the biggest
of those big-boned, pre-historic monsters discovered by
M. Cuvier. He was not overburdened with opinions or
principles. The only truth that was absolute to her perception
was that the house of Bergerac was *de bonne noblesse*. His
tastes were not delicate. He was fond of the open air, of long
rides, of the smell of the game-stocked woods in autumn, of
playing at bowls, of a drinking-cup, of a dirty pack of cards,
and a free-spoken tavern Hebe. I have nothing of him but his
name. I strikes you as an old fossil, a relic, a mummy. Good
heavens! you should have seen him,—his good, his bad manners, his arrogance, his *bonhomie*, his stupidity and pluck.

My early years had promised ill for my health; I was listless
and languid, and my father had been content to leave me to
the women, who, on the whole, as I have said, left me a good
deal to myself. But one morning he seemed suddenly to

remember that he had a little son and heir running wild. It was, I remember, in my ninth year, a morning early in June, after breakfast, at eleven o'clock. He took me by the hand and led me out on the terrace, and sat down and made me stand between his knees. I was engaged upon a great piece of bread and butter, which I had brought away from the table. He put his hand into my hair, and for the first time that I could remember, looked me straight in the face. I had seen him take the forelock of a young colt in the same way, when he wished to look at its teeth. What did he want? Was he going to send me for sale? His eyes seemed prodigiously black and his eyebrows terribly thick. They were very much the eyebrows of that portrait. My father passed his other hand over the muscles of my arms and the sinews of my poor little legs.

"Chevalier," he said, "you're dreadfully puny. What's one to do with you?"

I dropped my eyes and said nothing. Heaven knows I felt puny.

"It's time you knew how to read and write. What are you blushing at?"

"I *do* know how to read," said I.

My father stared. "Pray, who taught you?"

"I learned in a book."

"What book?"

I looked up at my father before I answered. His eyes were bright, and there was a little flush in his face,—I hardly knew whether of pleasure or anger. I disengaged myself and went into the drawing-room, where I took from a cupboard in the wall an odd volume of Scarron's *Roman comique*. As I had to go through the house, I was absent some minutes. When I came back I found a stranger on the terrace. A young man in poor clothes, with a walking-stick, had come up from the avenue, and stood before my father, with his hat in his hand. At the farther end of the terrace was my aunt. She was sitting on the parapet, playing with a great black crow, which we kept in a cage in the dining-room window. I betook myself to my father's side with my book, and stood staring at our visitor. He was a dark-eyed, sunburnt young man, of about twenty-eight, of middle height, broad in the shoulders and short in the neck, with a slight lameness in one of his legs. He looked travel-stained and weary and pale. I remember there was something prepossessing in his being pale. I didn't know that the paleness came simply from his being horribly hungry.

"In view of these facts," he said, as I came up, "I have ventured to presume upon the good-will of M. le Baron."

My father sat back in his chair, with his legs apart and hand on each knee and his waistcoat unbuttoned, as was usual after a meal. "Upon my word," he said, "I don't know what I can do for you. There's no place for you in my own household."

The young man was silent a moment. "Has M. le Baron any children?" he asked, after a pause.

"I have my son whom you see here."

"May I inquire if M. de Chevalier is supplied with a preceptor?"

My father glanced down at me. "Indeed, he seems to be," he cried. "What have you got there?" And he took my book. "The little rascal has M. Scarron for a teacher. This is his preceptor!"

I blushed very hard, and the young man smiled. "Is that your only teacher?" he asked.

"My aunt taught me to read," I said, looking round at her.

"And did your aunt recommend this book?" asked my father.

"My aunt gave me M. Plutarque," I said.

My father burst out laughing, and the young man put his hat up to his mouth. But I could see that above it his eyes had a very good-natured look. My aunt, seeing that her name had been mentioned, walked slowly over to where we stood, still holding her crow on her hand. You have her there before you; judge how she looked. I remember that she frequently dressed in blue, my poor aunt, and I know that she must have dressed simply. Fancy her in a light stuff gown, covered with big blue flowers, with a blue ribbon in her dark hair, and the points of her high-heeled blue slippers peeping out under her stiff white petticoat. Imagine her strolling along the terrace of the château with a villainous black crow perched on her wrist. You'll admit it's a picture.

"Is this all true, sister?" said my father. "Is the Chevalier such a scholar?"

"He's a clever boy," said my aunt, putting her hand on my head.

"It seems to me that at a pinch he could do without a preceptor," said my father. "He has such a learned aunt."

"I've taught him all I know. He had begun to ask me questions that I was quite unable to answer."

"I should think he might," cried my father, with a broad laugh, "when once he had got into M. Scarron!"

"Questions out of Plutarch," said Mlle de Bergerac, "which you must know Latin to answer."

"Would you like to know Latin, M. de Chevalier?" said the young man, looking at me with a smile.

"Do you know Latin,—you?" I asked.

"Perfectly," said the young man, with the same smile.

"Do you want to learn Latin, Chevalier?" said my aunt.

"Every gentleman learns Latin," said the young man.

I looked at the poor fellow, his dusty shoes and his rusty clothes. "But you're not a gentleman," said I.

He blushed up to his eyes. "Ah, I only teach it," he said.

In this way it was that Pierre Coquelin came to be my governor. My father, who had a mortal dislike to all kinds of cogitation and inquiry, engaged him on the simple testimony of his face and of his own account of his talents. His history, as he told it, was in three words as follows: He was of our province, and neither more nor less than the son of a village tailor. He is my hero: *tirez-vous de là*. Showing a lively taste for books, instead of being promoted to the paternal bench, he had been put to study with the Jesuits. After a residence of some three years with these gentlemen, he had incurred their displeasure by a foolish breach of discipline, and had been turned out into the world. Here he had endeavored to make capital out of his excellent education, and had gone to Paris with the hope of earning his bread as a scribbler. But in Paris he scribbled himself hungry and nothing more, and was in fact in a fair way to die of starvation. At last he encountered an agent of the Marquis de Rochambeau, who was collecting young men for the little army which the latter was prepared to conduct to the aid of the American insurgents. He had engaged himself among Rochambeau's troops, taken part in several battles, and finally received a wound in his leg of which the effect was still perceptible. At the end of three years he had returned to France, and repaired on foot, with what speed he might, to his native town; but only to find that in his absence his father had died, after a tedious illness, in which he had vainly lavished his small earnings upon the physicians, and that his mother had married again, very little to his taste. Poor Coquelin was friendless, penniless, and homeless. But once back on his native soil, he found himself possessed again by his old passion for letters, and, like all starving members of his craft, he had turned his face to Paris. He longed to make up for his three years in the wilderness. He trudged along, lonely, hungry, and weary, till he came to the gates of Bergerac. Here, sitting down to rest on a stone, he saw us come out on the terrace to digest our breakfast in the sun. Poor Coquelin! he had the stomach of a gentleman. He was filled with an irresistible longing to rest awhile from his struggle with destiny, and it seemed to him that for a mess of smoking pottage he would gladly exchange his vague and dubious future. In obedience to this simple impulse,—an impulse touching in its humility, when you knew the man,—he made his way up the avenue. We looked affable enough,—an honest country gentleman, a young girl playing with a crow, and a little boy eating bread and butter; and it turned out, we were as kindly as we looked.

For me, I soon grew extremely fond of him, and I was glad to think in later days that he had found me a thoroughly docile child. In those days, you know, thanks to Jean Jacques Rousseau, there was a vast stir in men's notions of education, and a hundred theories afloat about the perfect teacher and the perfect pupil. Coquelin was a firm devotee of Jean Jacques, and very possibly applied some of his precepts to my own little person. But of his own nature Coquelin was incapable of anything that was not wise and gentle, and he had no need to learn humanity in books. He was, nevertheless, a great reader, and when he had not a volume in his hand he was sure to have two in his pockets. He had half a dozen little copies of the Greek and Latin poets, bound in yellow parchment, which, as he said, with a second shirt and a pair of white stockings, constituted his whole library. He had carried these books to America, and read them in the wilderness, and by the light of camp-fires, and in crowded, steaming barracks in winter-quarters. He had a passion for Virgil. M. Scarron was very soon dismissed to the cupboard, among the dice-boxes and the old packs of cards, and I was confined for the time to Virgil and Ovid and Plutarch, all of which, with the stimulus of Coquelin's own delight, I found very good reading. But better than any of the stories I read were those stories of his wanderings, and his odd companions and encounters, and charming tales of pure fantasy, which, with the best grace in the world, he would recite by the hour. We took long walks, and he told me the names of the flowers and the various styles of the stars, and I remember that I often had no small trouble to keep them distinct. He wrote a very bad hand, but he made very pretty drawings of the subjects then in vogue,—nymphs and heroes and shepherds and pastoral scenes. I used to fancy that his knowledge and skill were inexhaustible, and I pestered him so for entertainment that I certainly proved that there were no limits to his patience.

When he first came to us he looked haggard and thin and weary; but before the month was out, he had acquired a comfortable rotundity of person, and something of the sleek and polished look which befits the governor of a gentleman's son. And yet he never lost a certain gravity and reserve of demeanor which was nearly akin to a mild melancholy. With me, half the time, he was of course intolerably bored, and he must have had hard work to keep from yawning in my face,—which, as he knew I knew, would have been an unwarrantable liberty. At table, with my parents, he seemed to be constantly observing himself and inwardly regulating his words and gestures. The simple truth, I take it, was that he had never sat at a gentleman's table, and although he must have known himself incapable of a real breach of civility,—essentially delicate as he was in his feelings,—he was too proud to run the risk of violating etiquette. My poor mother was a great stickler for ceremony, and she would have had her major-domo to lift the covers, even if she had had nothing to put into the dishes. I remember a cruel rebuke she bestowed upon Coquelin, shortly after his arrival. She could never be brought to forget that he had been picked up, as she said, on the roads. At dinner one day, in the absence of Mlle de Bergerac, who was indisposed, he inadvertently occupied her seat, taking me as a *vis-à-vis* instead of a neighbor. Shortly afterwards, coming to offer wine to my mother, he received for all response a stare so blank, cold, and insolent as to leave no doubt of her estimate of his presumption. In my mother's simple philosophy, Mlle de Bergerac's seat could be decently occupied only by herself, and in default of her presence should remain conspicuously and sacredly vacant. Dinner at Bergerac was at best, indeed, a cold and dismal ceremony. I see it now,—the great dining-room, with its high windows and their faded curtains, and the tiles upon the floor, and the immense wainscots, and the great white marble chimney-piece, reaching to the ceiling,—a triumph of delicate carving,—and the panels above the doors, with their *galant* mythological paintings. All this had been the work of my grandfather, during the Regency, who had undertaken to renovate and beautify the château; but his funds had suddenly given out, and we could boast but a desultory elegance. Such talk as passed at table was between my mother and the Baron, and consisted for the most part of a series of insidious attempts on my mother's part to extort information which the later had no desire, or at least no faculty, to impart. My father was constitutionally taciturn and apathetic, and he invariably made an end of my mother's interrogation by proclaiming that he hated gossip. He liked to take his pleasure and have done with it, or at best, to ruminate his substantial joys within the conservative recesses of his capacious breast. The Baronne's inquisitive tongue was like a lambent flame, flickering over the sides of a rock. She had a passion for the world, and seclusion had only sharpened the edge of her curiosity. She lived on old memories—shabby, tarnished bits of intellectual finery—and vagrant rumors, anecdotes, and scandals.

Once in a while, however, her curiosity held high revel; for once a week we had the Vicomte de Treuil to dine with us. This gentleman was, although several years my father's junior, his most intimate friend and the only constant visitor at Bergerac. He brought with him a sort of intoxicating perfume of the great world, which I myself was not too young to feel. He had a marvellous fluency of talk; he was polite and elegant; and he was constantly getting letters from Paris, books, newspapers, and prints, and copies of the new songs. When he dined at Bergerac, my mother used to rustle away from table, kissing her hand to him, and actually light-headed from her deep potations of gossip. His conversation was a constant popping of corks. My father and the Vicomte, as I have said, were firm friends,—the firmer for the great diversity of their characters. M. de Bergerac was dark, grave, and taciturn, with a deep, sonorous voice. He had in his nature a touch of melancholy, and, in default of piety, a broad vein of superstition. The foundations of his soul, moreover, I am satisfied, in spite of the somewhat ponderous superstructure, were laid in a soil of rich tenderness and pity. Gaston de Treuil was of a wholly different temper. He was short and slight, without any color, and with eyes as blue and lustrous as sapphires. He was so careless and gracious and mirthful, that to an unenlightened fancy he seemed the model of a joyous, reckless, gallant, impenitent *veneur*. But it sometimes struck me that, as he revolved an idea in his mind, it produced a certain flinty ring, which suggested that his nature was built, as it were, on rock, and that the bottom of his heart was hard. Young as he was, besides, he had a tired, jaded, exhausted look, which told of his having played high at the game of life, and, very possibly, lost. In fact, it was notorious that M. de Treuil had run through his property, and that his actual business in our neighborhood was to repair the breach in his fortunes by constant attendance on a wealthy kinsman, who occupied an adjacent château, and who was dying of age and his infirmities. But while I thus hint at the existence in his composition of these few base particles, I should be sorry to represent him as substantially less fair and clear and lustrous than he appeared to be. He possessed an irresistible charm, and that of itself is a virtue. I feel sure, moreover, that my father would never have reconciled himself to a real scantiness of masculine worth. The Vicomte enjoyed, I fancy, the generous energy of my father's good-fellowship, and the Baron's healthy senses were flattered by the exquisite perfume of the other's infallible *savoir-vivre*. I offer a hundred apologies, at any rate,

to the Vicomte's luminous shade, that I should have ventured
to cast a dingy slur upon his name. History has commemora-
ted it. He perished on the scaffold, and showed that he knew
how to die as well as to live. He was the last relic of the lily-
handed youth of the *bon temps;* and as he looks at me out of
poignant sadness of the past, with a reproachful glitter in his
cold blue eyes, and a scornful smile on his fine lips, I feel that,
elegant and silent as he is, he has the last word in our dispute.
I shall think of him henceforth as he appeared one night, or
rather one morning, when he came home from a ball with my
father, who had brought him to Bergerac to sleep. I had my
bed in a closet out of my mother's room, where I lay in a
most unwholesome fashion among her old gowns and hoops
and cosmetics. My mother slept little; she passed the night in
her dressing-gown, bolstered up in her bed, reading novels.
The two gentlemen came in at four o'clock in the morning
and made their way up to the Baronne's little sitting-room,
next to her chamber. I suppose they were highly exhilarated,
for they made a great noise of talking and laughing, and my
father began to knock at the chamber door. He called out that
he had M. de Treuil, and that they were cold and hungry.
The Baronne said that she had a fire and they might come in.
She was glad enough, poor lady, to get news of the ball, and
to catch their impressions before they had been dulled by
sleep. So they came in and sat by the fire, and M. de Treuil
looked for some wine and some little cakes where my mother
told him. I was wide awake and heard it all. I heard my
mother protesting and crying out, and the Vicomte laughing,
when he looked into the wrong place; and I am afraid that in
my mother's room there were a great many wrong places.
Before long, in my little stuffy, dark closet, I began to feel
hungry too; whereupon I got out of bed and ventured forth
into the room. I remember the whole picture, as one remem-
bers isolated scenes of childhood: my mother's bed, with its
great curtains half drawn back at the side, and her little eager

face and dark eyes peeping out of the recess; then the two
men at the fire,—my father with his hat on, sitting and looking
drowsily into the flames, and the Vicomte standing before
the hearth, talking, laughing, and gesticulating, with the
candlestick in one hand, and a glass of wine in the other,—
dropping the wax on one side and the wine on the other. He
was dressed from head to foot in white velvet and white silk,
with embroideries of silver, and an immense *jabot*. He was
very pale, and he looked lighter and slighter and wittier and
more elegant than ever. He had a weak voice, and when he
laughed, after one feeble little spasm, it went off into nothing,
and you only knew he was laughing by his nodding his head
and lifting his eyebrows and showing his handsome teeth.
My father was in crimson velvet, with tarnished gold facings.
My mother bade me get back into bed, but my father took me
on his knees and held out my bare feet to the fire. In a little
while, from the influence of the heat, he fell asleep in his
chair, and I sat in my place and watched M. de Treuil as he
stood in the firelight drinking his wine and telling stories to
my mother, until at last I too relapsed into the innocence of
slumber. They were very good friends, the Vicomte and my
mother. He admired the turn of her mind. I remember his
telling me several years later, at the time of her death, when
I was old enough to understand him, that she was a very
brave, keen little woman, and that in her musty solitude of
Bergerac she said a great many more good things than the
world ever heard of.

During the winter which preceded Coquelin's arrival,
M. de Treuil used to show himself at Bergerac in a friendly
manner; but about a month before this event, his visits became
more frequent and assumed a special import and motive. In
a word, my father and his friend between them had conceived
it to be a fine thing that the latter should marry Mlle de
Bergerac. Neither from his own nor from his friend's point of

view was Gaston de Treuil a marrying man or a desirable
parti. He was too fond of pleasure to conciliate a rich wife,
and too poor to support a penniless one. But I fancy that my
father was of the opinion that if the Vicomte came into his
kinsman's property, the best way to insure the preservation
of it, and to attach him to his duties and responsibilities, would
be to unite him to an amiable girl, who might remind him of
the beauty of a domestic life and lend him courage to mend
his ways. As far as the Vicomte was concerned, this was
assuredly a benevolent scheme, but it seems to me that it
made small account of the young girl's own happiness. M. de
Treuil was supposed, in the matter of women, to have known
everything that can be known and to be as *blasé* with regard
to their charms as he was proof against their influence. And,
in fact, his manner of dealing with women, and of discussing
them, indicated a profound disenchantment,—no bravado of
contempt, no affectation of cynicism, but a cold, civil,
absolute lassitude. A simply charming woman, therefore,
would never have served the purpose of my father's theory.
A very sound and liberal instinct led him to direct his thoughts
to his sister. There were, of course, various auxiliary reasons
for such disposal of Mlle de Bergerac's hand. She was now a
woman grown, and she had as yet received no decent proposals. She had no marriage portion of her own, and my
father had no means to endow her. Her beauty, moreover,
could hardly be called a dowry. It was without those vulgar
allurements which, for many a poor girl, replace the glitter
of cash. If within a very few years more she had not succeeded
in establishing herself creditably in the world, nothing would
be left for her but to withdraw from it, and to pledge her
virgin faith to the chilly sanctity of a cloister. I was destined
in the course of time to assume the lordship and the slender
revenues of Bergerac, and it was not to be expected that I
should be burdened on the very threshold of life with the
maintenance of a dowerless maiden aunt. A marriage with

M. de Treuil would be in all senses a creditable match, and, in the event of his becoming his kinsman's legatee, a thoroughly comfortable one.

It was some time before the color of my father's intentions, and the milder hue of the Vicomte's acquiescence, began to show in our common daylight. It is not the custom, as you know, in our excellent France, to admit a lover on probation. He is expected to make up his mind on a view of the young lady's endowments, and to content himself before marriage with the bare cognition of her face. It is not thought decent (and there is certainly reason in it) that he should dally with his draught, and hold it to the light, and let the sun play through it, before carrying it to his lips. It was only on the ground of my father's warm good-will to Gaston de Treuil, and the latter's affectionate respect for the Baron, that the Vicomte was allowed to appear as a lover, before making his proposals in form. M. de Treuil, in fact, proceeded gradually, and made his approaches from a great distance. It was not for several weeks, therefore, that Mlle de Bergerac became aware of them. And now, as this dear young girl steps into my story, where, I ask you, shall I find words to describe the broad loveliness of her person, to hint at the perfect beauty of her mind, to suggest the sweet mystery of her first suspicion of being sought, from afar, in marriage? Not in my fancy, surely; for there I should disinter the flimsy elements and tarnished properties of a superannuated comic opera. My taste, my son, was formed once for all fifty years ago. But if I wish to call up Mlle de Bergerac, I must turn to my earliest memories, and delve in the sweet-smelling virgin soil of my heart. For Mlle de Bergerac is no misty sylphid nor romantic moonlit nymph. She rises before me now, glowing with life, with the sound of her voice just dying in the air,—the more living for the mark of her crimson death-stain.

There was every good reason why her dawning consciousness of M. de Treuil's attentions—although these were little more than projected as yet—should have produced a serious tremor in her heart. It was not that she was aught of a coquette; I honestly believe that there was no latent coquetry in her nature. At all events, whatever she might have become after knowing M. de Treuil, she was no coquette to speak of in her ignorance. Her ignorance of men, in truth, was great. For the Vicomte himself, she had as yet known him only distantly, formally, as a gentleman of rank and fashion; and for others of his quality, she had seen but a small number, and not seen them intimately. These few words suffice to indicate that my aunt led a life of unbroken monotony. Once a year she spent six weeks with certain ladies of the Visitation, in whose convent she had received her education, and of whom she continued to be very fond. Half a dozen times in the twelvemonth she went to a ball, under convoy of some haply ungrudging *châtelaine*. Two or three times a month, she received a visit at Bergerac. The rest of the time she paced, with the grace of an angel and the patience of a woman, the dreary corridors and unclipt garden walks of Bergerac. The discovery, then, that the brilliant Vicomte de Treuil was likely to make a proposal for her hand was an event of no small importance. With precisely what feelings she awaited its coming, I am unable to tell; but I have no hesitation in saying that even at this moment (that is, in less than a month after my tutor's arrival) her feelings were strongly modified by her acquaintance with Pierre Coquelin.

The word "acquaintance" perhaps exaggerates Mlle de Bergerac's relation to this excellent young man. Twice a day she sat facing him at table, and half a dozen times a week she met him on the staircase, in the saloon, or in the park. Coquelin had been accommodated with an apartment in a small untenanted pavilion, within the enclosure of our domain, and except at meals, and when his presence was especially requested at the château, he confined himself to his own precinct. It was there, morning and evening, that I took my lesson. It was impossible, therefore, that an intimacy should have arisen between these two young persons, equally separated as they were by material and conventional barriers. Nevertheless, as the sequel proved, Coquelin must, by his mere presence, have begun very soon to exert a subtle action on Mlle de Bergerac's thoughts. As for the young girl's influence on Coquelin, it is my belief that he fell in love with her the very first moment he beheld her,—that morning when he trudged wearily up our avenue. I need certainly make no apology for the poor fellow's audacity. You tell me that you fell in love at first sight with my aunt's portrait; you will readily excuse the poor youth for having been smitten with the original. It is less logical perhaps, but it is certainly no less natural, that Mlle de Bergerac should have ventured to think of my governor as a decidedly interesting fellow. She saw so few men that one the more or the less made a very great difference. Coquelin's importance, moreover, was increased rather than diminished by the fact that, as I may say, he was a son of the soil. Marked as he was, in aspect and utterance, with the genuine plebeian stamp, he opened a way for the girl's fancy into a vague, unknown world. He stirred her imagination, I conceive, in very much the same way as such a man as Gaston de Treuil would have stirred—actually had stirred, of course—the grosser sensibilities of many a little *bourgeoise*. Mlle de Bergerac was so thoroughly at peace with the consequences of her social position, so little inclined to derogate in act or in thought from the perfect dignity of her birth, that with the best conscience in the world, she entertained, as they came, the feelings provoked by Coquelin's manly virtues and graces. She had been educated in the faith that *noblesse oblige*, and she had seen none but gentlefolks and peasants. I think that she felt a vague, unavowed curiosity to see what sort of a figure you might make when you were under no obligations to nobleness. I think, finally, that unconsciously and in the interest simply of her unsubstantial

dreams (for in those long summer days at Bergerac, without
finery, without visits, music, or books, or anything that a
well-to-do grocer's daughter enjoys at the present day, she
must, unless she was a far greater simpleton that I wish you
to suppose, have spun a thousand airy, idle visions), she contrasted Pierre Coquelin with the Vicomte de Treuil. I protest
that I don't see how Coquelin bore the contrast. I frankly
admit that, in her place, I would have given all my admiration to the Vicomte. At all events, the chief result of any such
comparison must have been to show how, in spite of real
trials and troubles, Coquelin had retained a certain masculine
freshness and elasticity, and how, without any sorrows but
those of his own wanton making, the Vicomte had utterly
rubbed off this primal bloom of manhood. There was that
about Gaston de Treuil that reminded you of an actor by
daylight. His little row of foot-lights had burned itself out.
But this is assuredly a more pedantic view of the case than
any that Mlle de Bergerac was capable of taking. The Vicomte
had but to learn his part and declaim it, and the illusion was
complete.

Mlle de Bergerac may really have been a great simpleton,
and my theory of her feelings—vague and imperfect as it is—
may be put together quite after the fact. But I see you protest; you glance at the picture; you frown. *C'est bon;* give me
your hand. She received the Vicomte's gallantries, then, with
a modest, conscious dignity, and courtesied to exactly the
proper depth when he made her one of his inimitable bows.

One evening—it was, I think, about ten days after Coquelin's arrival—she was sitting reading to my mother, who was
ill in bed. The Vicomte had been dining with us, and after
dinner we had gone into the drawing-room. At the drawing-
room door Coquelin had made his bow to my father, and
carried me off to his own apartment. Mlle de Bergerac and the
two gentlemen had gone into the drawing-room together.
At dusk I had come back to the château, and, going up to

my mother, had found her in company with her sister-in-law. In a few moments my father came in, looking stern and black.

"Sister," he cried, "why did you leave us alone in the drawing-room? Didn't you see I wanted you to stay?"

Mlle de Bergerac laid down her book and looked up at her brother before answering. "I had to come to my sister," she said: "I couldn't leave her alone."

My mother, I'm sorry to say, was not always just to my aunt. She used to lose patience with her sister's want of coquetry, of ambition, of desire to make much of herself. She divined wherein my aunt had offended. "You're very devoted to your sister, suddenly," she said. "There are duties and duties, mademoiselle. I'm very much obliged to you for reading to me. You can put down the book."

"The Vicomte swore very hard when you went out," my father went on.

Mlle de Bergerac laid aside her book. "Dear me!" she said, "if he was going to swear, it's very well I went."

"Are you afraid of the Comte?" said my mother. "You're twenty-two years old. You're not a little girl."

"Is she twenty-two?" cried my father. "I told him she was twenty-one."

"Frankly, brother," said Mlle de Bergerac, "what does he want? Does he want to marry me?"

My father stared a moment. "*Pardieu!*" he cried.

"She looks as if she didn't believe it," said my mother. "Pray, did you ever ask him?"

"No, madam; did you? You are very kind." Mlle de Bergerac was excited; her cheek flushed.

"In the course of time," said my father, gravely, "the Vicomte proposes to demand your hand."

"What is he waiting for?" asked Mlle de Bergerac, simply.

"*Fi donc, mademoiselle!*" cried my mother.

"He is waiting for M. de Sorbières to die," said I, who had got this bit of news from my mother's waiting-woman.

My father stared at me, half angrily; and then,—"He expects to inherit," he said, boldly. "It's a very fine property."

"He would have done better, it seems to me," rejoined Mlle de Bergerac, after a pause, "to wait till he had actually come into possession of it."

"M. de Sorbières," cried my father, "has given him his word a dozen times over. Besides, the Vicomte loves you."

Mlle de Bergerac blushed, with a little smile, and as she did so her eyes fell on mine. I was standing gazing at her as a child gazes at a familiar friend who is presented to him in a new light. She put out her hand and drew me towards her. "The truth comes out of the mouths of children," she said. "Chevalier, does he love me?"

"Stuff!" cried the Baronne; "one doesn't speak to children of such things. A young girl should believe what she's told. I believed my mother when she told me that your brother loved me. He didn't but I believed it, and as far as I know I'm none the worse for it."

For ten days after this I heard nothing more of Mlle de Bergerac's marriage, and I suppose that, childlike, I ceased to think of what I had already heard. One evening, about midsummer, M. de Treuil came over to supper, and announced that he was about to set out in company with poor M. de Sorbières for some mineral springs in the South, by the use of which the latter hoped to prolong his life.

I remember that, while we sat at table, Coquelin was appealed to as an authority upon some topic broached by the Vicomte, by which he found himself at variance with my father. It was the first time, I fancy, that he had been so honored and that his opinions had been deemed worth hearing. The point under discussion must have related to the history of the American War, for Coquelin spoke with the firmness and fulness warranted by personal knowledge. I fancy that he was a little frightened by the sound of his own voice, but he acquitted himself with perfect good grace and success. We all sat attentive; my mother even staring a little, surprised to find in a beggarly pedagogue a perfect *beau diseur*. My father, as became so great a gentleman, knew by a ·certain rough instinct when a man had something amusing to say. He leaned back, with his hands in his pockets, listening and paying the poor fellow the tribute of a half-puzzled frown. The Vicomte, like a man of taste, was charmed. He told stories himself, he was a good judge.

After supper we went out on the terrace. It was a perfect summer night, neither too warm nor too cool. There was no moon, but the stars flung down their languid light, and the earth, with its great dark masses of vegetation and the gently swaying tree-tops, seemed to answer back in a thousand vague perfumes. Somewhere, close at hand, out of an enchanted tree, a nightingale raved and carolled in delirious music. We had the good taste to listen in silence. My mother sat down on a bench against the house, and put out her hand and made my father sit beside her. Mlle de Bergerac strolled to the edge of the terrace, and leaned against the balustrade, whither M. de Treuil soon followed her. She stood motionless, with her head raised, intent upon the music. The Vicomte seated himself upon the parapet, with his face towards her and his arms folded. He may perhaps have been talking, under cover of the nightingale. Coquelin seated himself near the other end of the terrace, and drew me between his knees. At last the nightingale ceased. Coquelin got up, and bade good night to the company, and made his way across the park to his lodge. I went over to my aunt and the Vicomte.

"M. Coquelin is a clever man," said the Vicomte, as he disappeared down the avenue. "He spoke very well this evening."

"He never spoke so much before," said I. "He's very shy."

"I think," said my aunt, "he's a little proud."

"I don't understand," said the Vicomte, "how a man with any pride can put up with the place of a tutor. I had rather dig in the fields."

"The Chevalier is much obliged to you," said my aunt, laughing. "In fact, M. Coquelin has to dig a little, hasn't he, Chevalier?"

"Not at all," said I. "But he keeps some plants in pots."

At this my aunt and the Vicomte began to laugh. "He keeps one precious plant," cried my aunt, tapping my face with her fan.

At this moment my mother called me away. "He makes them laugh," I heard her say to my father, as I went to her.

"She had better laugh about it than cry," said my father.

Before long, Mlle de Bergerac and her companion came back toward the house.

"M. le Vicomte, brother," said my aunt, "invites me to go down and walk in the park. May I accept?"

"By all means," said my father. "You may go with the Vicomte as you would go with me."

"Ah!" said the Vicomte.

"Come then, Chevalier," said my aunt. "In my turn, I invite you."

"My son," said the Baronne, "I forbid you."

"But my brother says," rejoined Mlle de Bergerac, "that I may go with M. de Treuil as I would go with himself. He would not object to my taking my nephew." And she put out her hand.

"One would think," said my mother, "that you were setting out for Siberia."

"For Siberia!" cried the Victomte, laughing; "O no!"

I paused, undecided. But my father gave me a push. "After all," he said, "it's better."

When I overtook my aunt and her lover, the latter, losing no time, appeared to have come quite to the point.

"Your brother tells me, mademoiselle," he had begun, "that he has spoken to you."

The young girl was silent.

"You may be indifferent," pursued the Vicomte, "but I can't believe you're ignorant."

"My brother has spoken to me," said Mlle de Bergerac at last, with an apparent effort,—"my brother has spoken to me of his project."

"I'm very glad he seemed to you to have espoused my cause so warmly that you call it his own. I did my best to convince him that I possess what a person of your merit is entitled to exact of the man who asks her hand. In doing so, I almost convinced myself. The point is now to convince you.'

"I listen."

"You admit, then, that your mind is not made up in advance against me."

"*Mon Dieu!*" cried my aunt, with some emphasis, "a poor girl like me doesn't make up her mind. You frighten me, Vicomte. This is a serious question. I have the misfortune to have no mother. I can only pray God. But prayer helps me not to choose, but only to be resigned."

"Pray often, then, mademoiselle. I'm not an arrogant lover, and since I have known you a little better, I have lost all my vanity. I'm not a good man nor a wise one. I have no doubt you think me very light and foolish, but you can't begin to know how light and foolish I am. Marry me and you'll never know. If you don't marry me, I'm afraid you'll never marry."

"You're very frank, Vicomte. If you think I'm afraid of never marrying, you're mistaken. One can be very happy as

an old maid. I spend six weeks every year with the ladies of
the Visitation. Several of them are excellent women, charming
women. They read, they educate young girls, they visit the
poor—"

The Vicomte broke into a laugh. "They get up at five
o'clock in the morning; they breakfast on boiled cabbage;
they make flannel waistcoats, and very good sweetmeats!
Why do you talk so, mademoiselle? Why do you say that
you would like to lead such a life? One might almost believe
it is coquetry. *Tenez*, I believe it's ignorance,—ignorance of
your own feelings, your own nature, and your own needs."
M. de Treuil paused a moment, and, although I had a very
imperfect notion of the meaning of his words, I remember
being struck with the vehement look of his pale face, which
seemed fairly to glow in the darkness. Plainly, he was in love.
"You are not made for solitude," he went on; "you are not
made to be buried in a dingy old château, in the depths of a
ridiculous province. You are made for the world, for the
court, for pleasure, to be loved, admired, and envied. No, you
don't know yourself, nor does Bergerac know you, nor his
wife! I, at least, appreciate you. I know that you are supremely
beautiful—"

"Vicomte," said Mlle de Bergerac, "you forget—the
child."

"Hang the child! Why did you bring him along? *You* are
no child. You can understand me. You are a woman, full of
intelligence and goodness and beauty. They don't know you
here, they think you a little demoiselle in pinafores. Before
Heaven, mademoiselle, there is that about you,—I see it, I
feel it here at your side, in this rustling darkness—there is
that about you that a man would gladly die for."

Mlle de Bergerac interrupted him with energy. "You
talk extravagantly. I don't understand you; you frighten
me."

"I talk as I feel. I frighten you? So much the better. I wish to stir your heart and get some answer to the passion of my own."

Mlle de Bergerac was silent a moment, as if collecting her thoughts. "If I talk with you on this subject, I must do it with my wits about me," she said at last. "I must know exactly what we each mean."

"It's plain then that I can't hope to inspire you with any degree of affection."

"One doesn't promise to love, Vicomte; I can only answer for the present. My heart is so full of good wishes toward you that it costs me comparatively little to say I don't love you."

"And anything I may say of my own feelings will make no difference to you?"

"You have said you love me. Let it rest there."

"But you look as if you doubted my word."

"You can't see how I look; Vicomte, I believe you."

"Well then, there is one point gained. Let us pass to the others. I'm thirty years old. I have a very good name and a very bad reputation. I honestly believe that, though I've fallen below my birth, I've kept above my fame. I believe that I have no vices of temper; I'm neither brutal, nor jealous, nor miserly. As for my fortune, I'm obliged to admit that it consists chiefly in my expectations. My actual property is about equal to your brother's and you know how your sister-in-law is obliged to live. My expectations are thought particularly good. My great-uncle, M. de Sorbières, possesses, chiefly in landed estates, a fortune of some three millions of livres. I have no important competitors, either in blood or devotion. He is eighty-seven years old and paralytic, and within the past year I have been laying siege to his favor with such constancy that his surrender, like his extinction, is only a question of time. I received yesterday a summons to go with him to the Pyrenees, to drink certain medicinal waters. The least he can do, on my return, is to make me a handsome allowance, which with my own revenues will make—*en attendant* better things—a sufficient income for a reasonable couple."

There was a pause of some moments, during which we slowly walked along in the obstructed starlight, the silence broken only by the train of my aunt's dress brushing against the twigs and pebbles.

"What a pity," she said, at last, "that you are not able to speak of all this good fortune as in the present rather than in the future."

"There it is! Until I came to know you, I had no thoughts of marriage. What did I want of wealth? If five years ago I had foreseen this moment, I should stand here with something better than promises."

"Well, Vicomte," pursued the young girl, with singular composure, "you do me the honor to think very well of me: I hope you will not be vexed to find that prudence is one of my virtues. If I marry, I wish to marry well. It's not only the husband, but the marriage that counts. In accepting you as you stand, I should make neither a sentimental match nor a brilliant one."

"Excellent. I love you, prudence and all, Say, then, that I present myself here three months hence with the titles and tokens of property amounting to a million and a half of livres, will you consider that I am a *parti* sufficiently brilliant to make you forget that you don't love me?"

"I should never forget that."

"Well, nor I either. It makes a sort of sorrowful harmony! If three months hence, I repeat, I offer you a fortune instead of this poor empty hand, will you accept the one for the sake of the other?"

My aunt stopped short in the path. "I hope, Vicomte," she said, with much apparent simplicity, "that you are going to do nothing indelicate."

"God forbid, mademoiselle! It shall be a clean hand and a clean fortune."

"If you ask then a promise, a pledge—"

"You'll not give it. I ask then only for a little hope. Give it in what form you will."

We walked a few steps farther and came out from among the shadows, beneath the open sky. The voice of M. de Treuil, as he uttered these words, was low and deep and tender and full of entreaty. Mlle de Bergerac cannot but have been deeply moved. I think she was somewhat awe-struck at having called up such a force of devotion in a nature deemed cold and inconstant. She put out her hand. "I wish success to any honorable efforts. In any case you will be happier for your wealth. In one case it will get you a wife, and in the other it will console you."

"Console me! I shall hate it, despise it, and throw it into the sea!"

Mlle de Bergerac had no intention, of course, of leaving her companion under an illusion. "Ah, but understand, Vicomte," she said, "I make no promise. My brother claims the right to bestow my hand. If he wishes our marriage now, of course he will wish it three months hence. I have never gainsaid him."

"From now to three months a great deal may happen."

"To you, perhaps, but not to me."

"Are you going to your friends of the Visitation?"

"No, indeed. I have no wish to spend the summer in a cloister. I prefer the green fields."

"Well, then, va for the green fields! They're the next best thing. I recommend you to the Chevalier's protection."

We had made half the circuit of the park and turned into an alley which stretched away towards the house, and about midway in its course separated into two paths, one leading to the main avenue, and the other to the little pavilion inhabited by Coquelin. At the point where the alley was divided stood an enormous oak of great circumference, with a circular bench surrounding its trunk. It occupied, I believe, the central point of the whole domain. As we reached the oak, I looked down along the footpath towards the pavilion, and saw Coquelin's light shining in one of the windows. I immediately proposed that we should pay him a visit. My aunt objected, on the ground that he was doubtless busy and would not thank us for interrupting him. And then, when I insisted, she said it was not proper.

"How not proper?"

"It's not proper for me. A lady doesn't visit young men in their own apartments."

At this the Vicomte cried out. He was partly amused, I think, at my aunt's attaching any compromising power to poor little Coquelin, and partly annoyed at her not considering his own company, in view of his pretensions, a sufficient guaranty.

"I should think," he said, "that with the Chevalier and me you might venture—"

"As you please, then," said my aunt. And I accordingly led the way to my governor's abode.

It was a small edifice of a single floor, standing prettily enough among the trees, and still habitable, although very much in disrepair. It had been built by that same ancestor to whom Bergerac was indebted, in the absence of several of the necessities of life, for many of its elegant superfluities, and had been designed, I suppose, as a scene of pleasure,— such pleasure as he preferred to celebrate elsewhere than beneath the roof of his domicile. Whether it had ever been used I know not; but it certainly had very little of the look of a pleasure-house. Such furniture as it had once possessed had long since been transferred to the needy saloons of the château, and it now looked dark and bare and cold. In front, the shrubbery had been left to grow thick and wild and almost totally to exclude the light from the windows; but behind, outside of the two rooms which he occupied, and which had been provided from the château with the articles necessary for comfort, Coquelin had obtained my father's permission to effect a great clearance in the foliage, and he now enjoyed plenty of sunlight and a charming view of the neighboring country. It was in the larger of these two rooms, arranged as a sort of study, that we found him.

He seemed surprised and somewhat confused by our visit, but he very soon recovered himself sufficiently to do the honours of his little establishment.

"It was an idea of my nephew," said Mlle de Bergerac. "We were walking in the park, and he saw your light. Now that we are here, Chevalier, what would you have us do?"

"M. Coquelin has some very pretty things to show you," said I.

Coquelin turned very red. "Pretty things, Chevalier? Pray, what do you mean? I have some of your nephew's copy-books," he said, turning to my aunt.

"Nay, you have some of your own," I cried. "He has books full of drawings, made by himself."

"Ah, you draw?" said the Vicomte.

"M. le Chevalier does me the honor to think so. My drawings are meant for no critics but children."

"In the way of criticism," said my aunt, gently, "we too are children." Her beautiful eyes, as she uttered these words, must have been quite as gentle as her voice. Coquelin looked at her, thinking very modestly of his little pictures, but loth to refuse the first request she had ever made him.

"Show them, at any rate," said the Vicomte, in a somewhat peremptory tone. In those days, you see, a man occupying Coquelin's place was expected to hold all his faculties and talents at the disposal of his patron, and it was thought an unwarrantable piece of assumption that he should cultivate any of the arts for his own peculiar delectation. In withholding his drawings, therefore, it may have seemed to the Vicomte that Coquelin was unfaithful to the service to which he was held,

—that, namely, of instructing, diverting, and edifying the household of Bergerac. Coquelin went to a little cupboard in the wall, and took out three small albums and a couple of portfolios. Mlle de Bergerac sat down at the table, and Coquelin drew up the lamp and placed his drawings before her. He turned them over, and gave such explanations as seemed necessary. I have only my childish impressions of the character of these sketches, which, in my eyes, of course, seemed prodigiously clever. What the judgment of my companions was worth I know not, but they appeared very well pleased. The Vicomte probably knew a good sketch from a poor one, and he very good-naturedly pronounced my tutor an extremely knowing fellow. Coquelin had drawn anything and everything—peasants and dumb brutes, landscapes and Parisian types and figures, taken indifferently from high and low life. But the best pieces in the collection were a series of illustrations and reminiscences of his adventures with the American army, and of the figures and episodes he had observed in the Colonies. They were for the most part rudely enough executed, owing to his want of time and materials, but they were full of *finesse* and character. M. de Treuil was very much amused at the rude equipments of your ancestors. There were sketches of the enemy too, whom Coquelin apparently had not been afraid to look in the face. While he was turning over these designs for Mlle de Bergerac, the Vicomte took up one of his portfolios, and, after a short inspection, drew from it, with a cry of surprise, a large portrait in pen and ink.

"*Tiens!*" said I; "it's my aunt!"

Coquelin turned pale. Mlle de Bergerac looked at him, and turned the least bit red. As for the Vicomte, he never changed color. There was no eluding the fact that it was a likeness, and Coquelin had to pay the penalty of his skill.

"I didn't know," he said, at random, "that it was in that portfolio. Do you recognize it, mademoiselle?"

"Ah," said the Vicomte, dryly, "M. Coquelin meant to hide it."

"It's too pretty to hide," said my aunt; "and yet it's too pretty to show. It's flattered."

"Why should I have flattered you, mademoiselle?" asked Coquelin. "You were never to see it."

"That's what it is, mademoiselle," said the Vicomte, "to have such dazzling beauty. It penetrates the world. Who knows where you'll find it reflected next?"

However pretty a compliment this may have been to Mlle de Bergerac, it was decidedly a back-handed blow to Coquelin. The young girl perceived that he felt it.

She rose to her feet. "My beauty," she said, with a slight tremor in her voice, "would be a small thing without M. Coquelin's talent. We are much obliged to you. I hope that you'll bring your pictures to the château, so that we may look at the rest."

"Are you going to leave him this?" asked M. de Treuil, holding up the portrait.

"If M. Coquelin will give it to me, I shall be very glad to have it."

"One doesn't keep one's own portrait," said the Vicomte. "It ought to belong to me." In those days, before the invention of our sublime machinery for the reproduction of the human face, a young fellow was very glad to have his mistress's likeness in pen and ink.

But Coquelin had no idea of contributing to the Vicomte's gallery. "Excuse me," he said, gently, but looking the nobleman in the face. "The picture isn't good enough for Mlle de Bergerac, but it's too good for any one else"; and he drew it out of the other's hands, tore it across and applied it to the flame of the lamp.

We went back to the château in silence. The drawing-room was empty; but as we went in, the Vicomte took a lighted candle from a table and raised it to the young girl's face.

"*Parbleu!*" he exclaimed, "the vagabond had looked at you to good purpose!"

Mlle de Bergerac gave a half-confused laugh. "At any rate," she said, "he didn't hold a candle to me as if I were my old smoke-stained grandame, yonder!" and she blew out the light. "I'll call my brother," she said, preparing to retire.

"A moment," said her lover; "I shall not see you for some weeks. I shall start to-morrow with my uncle. I shall think of you by day, and dream of you by night. And meanwhile I shall very much doubt whether you think of me."

Mlle de Bergerac smiled. "Doubt, doubt. It will help you to pass the time. With faith alone it would hang very heavy."

"It seems hard," pursued M. de Treuil, "that I should give you so many pledges, and that you should give me none."

"I give all I ask."

"Then, for Heaven's sake, ask for something!"

"Your kind words are all I want."

"Then give me some kind word yourself."

"What shall I say, Vicomte?"

"Say—say that you'll wait for me."

They were standing in the centre of the great saloon, their figures reflected by the light of a couple of candles in the shining inlaid floor. Mlle de Bergerac walked away a few steps with a look of agitation. Then turning about, "Vicomte," she asked, in a deep, full voice, "do you truly love me?"

"Ah, Gabrielle!" cried the young man.

I take it that no woman can hear her baptismal name uttered for the first time as that of Mlle de Bergerac then came from her suitor's lips without being thrilled with joy and pride.

"Well, M. de Treuil," she said, "I will wait for you."

II

I REMEMBER distinctly the incidents of that summer at
Bergerac; or at least its general character, its tone. It was a
hot, dry season; we lived with doors and windows open.
M. Coquelin suffered very much from the heat, and sometimes, for days together, my lessons were suspended. We put
our books away and rambled out for a long day in the fields.
My tutor was perfectly faithful; he never allowed me to
wander beyond call. I was very fond of fishing, and I used to
sit for hours, like a little old man, with my legs dangling over
the bank of our slender river, patiently awaiting the bite that
so seldom came. Near at hand, in the shade, stretched at his
length on the grass, Coquelin read and re-read one of his
half-dozen Greek and Latin poets. If we had walked far from
home, we used to go and ask for some dinner at the hut of a
neighboring peasant. For a very small coin we got enough
bread and cheese and small fruit to keep us over till supper.
The peasants, stupid and squalid as they were, always
received us civilly enough, though on Coquelin's account
quite as much as on my own. He addressed them with an easy
familiarity, which made them feel, I suppose, that he was, if
not quite one of themselves, at least by birth and sympathies
much nearer to them than to the future Baron de Bergerac.
He gave me in the course of these walks a great deal of good
advice; and without perverting my signorial morals or in-
stilling any notions that were treason to my rank and position,
he kindled in my childish breast a little democratic flame
which has never quite become extinct. He taught me the
beauty of humanity, justice, and tolerance; and whenever he
detected me in a precocious attempt to assert my baronial
rights over the wretched little *manants* who crossed my path,

he gave me morally a very hard drubbing. He had none of the base complaisance and cynical nonchalance of the traditional tutor of our old novels and comedies. Later in life I might have found him too rigorous a moralist; but in those days I liked him all the better for letting me sometimes feel the curb. It gave me a highly agreeable sense of importance and maturity. It was a tribute to half-divined possibilities of naughtiness. In the afternoon, when I was tired of fishing, he would lie with his thumb in his book and his eyes half closed and tell me fairy-tales till the eyes of both of us closed together. Do the instructors of youth nowadays condescend to the fairy-tale pure and simple? Coquelin's stories belonged to the old, old world: no political economy, no physics, no application to anything in life. Do you remember in Doré's illustrations to Perrault's tales, the picture of the enchanted castle of the Sleeping Beauty? Back in the distance, in the bosom of an ancient park and surrounded by thick baronial woods which blacken all the gloomy horizon, on the farther side of a great abysmal hollow of tangled forest verdure, rise the long façade, the moss-grown terraces, the towers, the purple roofs, of a château of the time of Henry IV. Its massive foundations plunge far down into the wild chasm of the woodland, and its cold pinnacles of slate tower upwards, close to the rolling autumn clouds. The afternoon is closing in and a chill October wind is beginning to set the forest a-howling. In the foreground, on an elevation beneath a mighty oak, stand a couple of old woodcutters pointing across into the enchanted distance and answering the questions of the young prince. They are the bent and blackened woodcutters of old France, of La Fontaine's Fables and the *Médecin malgré lui*. What does the castle contain? What secret is locked in its stately walls? What revel is enacted in its long saloons? What strange figures stand aloof from its vacant windows? You ask the question, and the answer is a long revery. I never look at the picture without thinking of those summer afternoons in the woods and of Coquelin's long stories. His fairies were the fairies of the *Grand Siècle*, and his princes and shepherds the godsons of Perrault and Madame d'Aulnay. They lived in such palaces and they hunted in such woods.

Mlle de Bergerac, to all appearance, was not likely to break her promise to M. de Treuil,—for lack of the opportunity, quite as much as of the will. Those bright summer days must have seemed very long to her, and I can't for my life imagine what she did with her time. But she, too, as she had told the Vicomte, was very fond of the green fields; and although she never wandered very far from the house, she spent many an hour in the open air. Neither here nor within doors was she likely to encounter the happy man of whom the Vicomte might be jealous. Mlle de Bergerac had a friend, a single intimate friend, who came sometimes to pass the day with her, and whose visits she occasionally returned. Marie de Chalais, the granddaughter of the Marquis de Chalais, who lived some ten miles away, was in all respects the exact counterpart and foil of my aunt. She was extremely plain, but with that sprightly, highly seasoned ugliness which is often so agreeable to men. Short, spare, swarthy, light, with an immense mouth, a most impertinent little nose, an imperceptible foot, a charming hand, and a delightful voice, she was, in spite of her great name and her fine clothes, the very ideal of the old stage *soubrette*. Frequently, indeed, in her dress and manner, she used to provoke a comparison with this incomparable type. A cap, an apron, and a short petticoat were all sufficient; with these and her bold, dark eyes she could impersonate the very genius of impertinence and intrigue. She was a thoroughly light creature, and later in life, after her marriage, she became famous for her ugliness, her witticisms, and her adventures; but that she had a good heart is shown by her real attachment to my aunt. They were forever at cross-purposes, and yet they were excellent friends. When

my aunt wished to walk, Mlle de Chalais wished to sit still;
when Mlle de Chalais wished to laugh, my aunt wished to
meditate; when my aunt wished to talk piety, Mlle de Chalais
wished to talk scandal. Mlle de Bergerac, however, usually
carried the day and set the tune. There was nothing on earth
that Marie de Chalais so despised as the green fields; and yet
you might have seen her a dozen times that summer wandering over the domain of Bergerac, in a short muslin dress and a
straw hat, with her arm entwined about the waist of her more
stately friend. We used often to meet them, and as we drew
near Mlle de Chalais would always stop and offer to kiss the
Chevalier. By this pretty trick Coquelin was subjected for a
few moments to the influence of her innocent *agaceries;* for
rather than have no man at all to prick with the little darts of
her coquetry, the poor girl would have gone off and made eyes
at the scarecrow in the wheat-field. Coquelin was not at all
abashed by her harmless advances; for although, in addressing my aunt, he was apt to lose his voice or his countenance,
he often showed a very pretty wit in answering Mlle de
Chalais.

On one occasion she spent several days at Bergerac, and
during her stay she proffered an urgent entreaty that my aunt
should go back with her to her grandfather's house, where,
having no parents, she lived with her governess. Mlle de
Bergerac declined, on the ground of having no gowns fit to
visit in; whereupon Mlle de Chalais went to my mother,
begged the gift of an old blue silk dress, and with her own
cunning little hands made it over for my aunt's figure. That
evening Mlle de Bergerac appeared at supper in this renovated
garment,—the first silk gown she had ever worn. Mlle de Chalais
had also dressed her hair, and decked her out with a number of
trinkets and furbelows; and when the two came into the room
together, they reminded me of the beautiful Duchess in Don
Quixote, followed by a little dark-visaged Spanish waiting-
maid. The next morning Coquelin and I rambled off as usual

in search of adventures, and the day after that they were to leave the château. Whether we met with any adventures or not I forget; but we found ourselves at dinner-time at some distance from home, very hungry after a long tramp. We directed our steps to a little roadside hovel, where we had already purchased hospitality, and made our way in unannounced. We were somewhat surprised at the scene that met our eyes.

On a wretched bed at the farther end of the hut lay the master of the household, a young peasant whom we had seen a fortnight before in full health and vigor. At the head of the bed stood his wife, moaning, crying, and wringing her hands. Hanging about her, clinging to her skirts, and adding their piping cries to her own lamentations, were four little children, unwashed, unfed, and half clad. At the foot, facing the dying man, knelt his old mother—a horrible hag, so bent and brown and wrinkled with labor and age that there was nothing womanly left of her but her coarse, rude dress and cap, nothing of maternity but her sobs. Beside the pillow stood the priest, who had apparently just discharged the last offices of the Church. On the other side, on her knees, with the poor fellow's hand in her own, knelt Mlle de Bergerac, like a consoling angel. On a stool near the door, looking on from a distance, sat Mlle de Chalais, holding a little bleating kid in her arms. When she saw us, she started up. "Ah, M. Coquelin!" she cried, "do persuade Mlle de Bergerac to leave this horrible place."

I saw Mlle de Bergerac look at the curé and shake her head, as if to say that it was all over. She rose from her knees and went round to the wife, telling the same tale with her face. The poor, squalid *paysanne* gave a sort of savage, stupid cry, and threw herself and her rags on the young girl's neck. Mlle de Bergerac caressed her, and whispered heaven knows what divinely simple words of comfort. Then, for the first time, she saw Coquelin and me, and beckoned us to approach.

"Chevalier," she said, still holding the woman on her breast, "have you got any money?"

At these words the woman raised her head. I signified that I was penniless.

My aunt frowned impatiently. "M. Coquelin, have you?"

Coquelin drew forth a single small piece, all that he possessed; for it was the end of the month. Mlle de Bergerac took it, and pursued her inquiry.

"Curé, have you any money?"

"Not a sou," said the curé, smiling sweetly.

"Bah!" said Mlle de Bergerac, with a sort of tragic petulance. "What can I do with twelve sous?"

"Give it all the same," said the woman doggedly, putting out her hand.

"They want money," said Mlle de Bergerac, lowering her voice to Coquelin. "They have had this great sorrow, but a *louis d'or* would dull the wound. But we're penniless. O for the sight of a little gold!"

"I have a *louis* at home," said I; and I felt Coquelin lay his hand on my head.

"What was the matter with the husband?" he asked.

"*Mon Dieu!*" said my aunt, glancing round at the bed. "I don't know."

Coquelin looked at her, half amazed, half worshipping.

"Who are they, these people? What are they?" she asked.

"Mademoiselle," said Coquelin, fervently, "you're an angel!"

"I wish I were," said Mlle de Bergerac, simply; and she turned to the old mother.

We walked home together—the curé with Mlle de Chalais and me, and Mlle de Bergerac in front with Coquelin. Asking how the two young girls had found their way to the deathbed we had just left, I learned from Mlle de Chalais that they had set out for a stroll together, and, striking into a footpath across the fields, had gone farther than they supposed, and lost their way. While they were trying to recover it, they came upon the wretched hut where we had found them, and were struck by the sight of two children, standing crying at the door. Mlle de Bergerac had stopped and questioned them to ascertain the cause of their sorrow, which with some difficulty she found to be that their father was dying of a fever. Whereupon, in spite of her companion's lively opposition, she had entered the miserable abode, and taken her place at the wretched couch, in the position in which we had discovered her. All this, doubtless, implied no extraordinary merit on Mlle de Bergerac's part; but it placed her in a gracious pleasing light.

The next morning the young girls went off in the great coach of M. de Chalais, which had been sent for them overnight, my father riding along as an escort. My aunt was absent a week, and I think I may say we keenly missed her. When I say we, I mean Coquelin and I, and when I say Coquelin and I, I mean Coquelin in particular; for it had come to this, that my tutor was roundly in love with my aunt. I didn't know it then, of course; but looking back, I see that he must already have been stirred to his soul's depths. Young as I was, moreover, I believe that I even then suspected his passion, and, loving him as I did, watched it with a vague, childish awe and sympathy. My aunt was to me, of course, a very old story, and I am sure she neither charmed nor dazzled my boyish fancy. I was quite too young to apprehend the meaning or the consequences of Coquelin's feelings; but I knew that he had a secret, and I wished him joy of it. He kept so jealous a guard on it that I would have defied my elders to discover the least reason for accusing him; but with a simple child of ten, thinking himself alone and uninterpreted, he showed himself plainly a lover. He was absent, restless, preoccupied; now steeped in languid revery, now pacing up and down with the exaltation of something akin to hope. Hope itself he could never have felt; for it must have seemed to him that his passion was so audacious as almost to be criminal. Mlle de Bergerac's absence showed him, I imagine, that to know her had been the event of his life; to see her across the table, to hear her voice, her tread, to pass her, to meet her eye, a deep, consoling, healing joy. It revealed to him the force with which she had grasped his heart, and I think he was half frightened at the energy of his passion.

One evening, while Mlle de Bergerac was still away, I sat in his window, committing my lesson for the morrow by the waning light. He was walking up and down among the shadows. "Chevalier," said he, suddenly, "what should you do if I were to leave you?"

My poor little heart stood still. "Leave me?" I cried, aghast; "why should you leave me?"

"Why, you know I didn't come to stay forever."

"But you came to stay till I'm a man grown. Don't you like your place?"

"Perfectly."

"Don't you like my father?"

"Your father is excellent."

"And my mother?"

"Your mother is perfect."

"And me, Coquelin?"

"You, Chevalier, are a little goose."

And then, from a sort of unreasoned instinct that Mlle de Bergerac was somehow connected with his idea of going away, "And my aunt?" I added.

"How, your aunt?"

"Don't you like her?"

Coquelin had stopped in his walk, and stood near me and above me. He looked at me some moments without answering, and then sat down beside me in the window-seat, and laid his hand on my head.

"Chevalier," he said, "I will tell you something."

"Well?" said I, after I had waited some time.

"One of these days you will be a man grown, and I shall have left you long before that. You'll learn a great many things that you don't know now. You'll learn what a strange, vast world it is, and what strange creatures men are—and women; how strong, how weak, how happy, how unhappy. You'll learn how many feelings and passions they have, and what a power of joy and of suffering. You'll be Baron de Bergerac and master of the château and of this little house. You'll sometimes be very proud of your title, and you'll sometimes feel very sad that it's little more than a bare title. But neither your pride nor your grief will come to anything beside this, that one day, in the prime of your youth and strength and good looks, you'll see a woman whom you will love more than all these things—more than your name, your lands, your youth, and strength, and beauty. It happens to all men, especially the good ones, and you'll be a good one. But the woman you love will be far out of your reach. She'll be a princess, perhaps she'll be the Queen. How can a poor little Baron de Bergerac expect her to look at him? You will give up your life for a touch of her hand; but what will she care for your life or your death? You'll curse your love, and and yet you'll bless it, and perhaps—not having your living to get—you'll come up here and shut yourself up with your dreams and regrets. You'll come perhaps into this pavilion, and sit here alone in the twilight. And then, my child, you'll remember this evening; that I foretold it all and gave you my blessing in advance and—kissed you." He bent over, and I felt his burning lips on my forehead.

I understood hardly a word of what he said; but whether it was that I was terrified by his picture of the possible insignificance of a Baron de Bergerac, or that I was vaguely overawed by his deep, solemn tones, I know not; but my eyes very quietly began to emit a flood of tears. The effect of my grief was to induce him to assure me that he had no present intention of leaving me. It was not, of course, till later in life, that, thinking over the situation, I understood his impulse to arrest his hopeless passion for Mlle de Bergerac by immediate departure. He was not brave in time.

At the end of a week she returned one evening as we were at supper. She came in with M. de Chalais, an amiable old man, who had been so kind as to accompany her. She greeted us severally, and nodded to Coquelin. She talked, I remember, with great volubility, relating what she had seen and done in her absence, and laughing with extraordinary freedom. As we left the table, she took my hand, and I put out the other and took Coquelin's.

"Has the Chevalier been a good boy?" she asked.

"Perfect," said Coquelin; "but he has wanted his aunt sadly."

"Not at all," said I, resenting the imputation as derogatory to my independence.

"You have had a pleasant week, mademoiselle?" said Coquelin.

"A charming week. And you?"

"M. Coquelin has been very unhappy," said I. "He thought of going away."

"Ah?" said my aunt.

Coquelin was silent.

"You think of going away?"

"I merely spoke of it, mademoiselle. I must go away some time, you know. The Chevalier looks upon me as something eternal."

"What's eternal?" asked the Chevalier.

"There is nothing eternal, my child," said Mlle de Bergerac. "Nothing lasts more than a moment."

"O," said Coquelin, "I don't agree with you!"

"You don't believe that in this world everything is vain and fleeting and transitory?"

"By no means; I believe in the permanence of many things."

"Of what, for instance?"

"Well, of sentiments and passions."

"Very likely. But not of the hearts that hold them. 'Lovers die, but love survives.' I heard a gentleman say that at Chalais."

"It's better, at least, than if he had put it the other way. But lovers last too. They survive; they outlive the things that would fain destroy them—indifference, denial, and despair."

"But meanwhile the loved object disappears. When it isn't one, it's the other."

"O, I admit that it's a shifting world. But I have a philosophy for that."

"I'm curious to know your philosophy."

"It's a very old one. It's simply to make the most of life while it lasts. I'm very fond of life," said Coquelin, laughing.

"I should say that as yet, from what I know of your history, you have had no great reason to be."

"Nay, it's like a cruel mistress," said Coquelin. "When once you love her, she's absolute. Her hard usage doesn't affect you. And certainly I have nothing to complain of now."

"You're happy here then?"

"Profoundly, mademoiselle, in spite of the Chevalier."

"I should suppose that with your tastes you would prefer something more active, more ardent."

"*Mon Dieu*, my tastes are very simple. And then—happiness, *cela ne se raisonne pas*. You don't find it when you go in quest of it. It's like fortune; it comes to you in your sleep."

"I imagine," said Mlle de Bergerac, "that I was never happy."

"That's a sad story," said Coquelin.

The young girl began to laugh. "And never unhappy."

"Dear me, that's still worse. Never fear, it will come."

"What will come?"

"That which is both bliss and misery at once."

Mlle de Bergerac hesitated a moment. "And what is this strange thing?" she asked.

On his side Coquelin was silent. "When it comes to you," he said, at last, "you'll tell me what you call it."

About a week after this, at breakfast, in pursuance of an urgent request of mine, Coquelin proposed to my father to allow him to take me to visit the ruins of an ancient feudal castle some four leagues distant, which he had observed and explored while he trudged across the country on his way to Bergerac, and which, indeed, although the taste for ruins was at that time by no means so general as since the Revolution (when one may say it was in a measure created), enjoyed a certain notoriety throughout the province. My father good-naturedly consented; and as the distance was too great to be achieved on foot, he placed his two old coach-horses at our service. You know that although I affected, in boyish sort, to have been indifferent to my aunt's absence, I was really very fond of her, and it occurred to me that our excursion would be more solemn and splendid for her taking part in it. So I appealed to my father and asked if Mlle de Bergerac might be allowed to go with us. What the Baron would have decided had he been left to himself I know not; but happily for our cause my mother cried out that, to her mind, it was highly improper that her sister-in-law should travel twenty miles alone with two young men.

"One of your young men is a child," said my father, "and her nephew into the bargain; and the other"—and he laughed, coarsely but not ill-humoredly,—"the other is—Coquelin!"

"Coquelin is not a child nor is mademoiselle either," said my mother.

"All the more reason for their going. Gabrielle, will you go?" My father, I fear, was not remarkable in general for his tenderness or his *prévenance* for the poor girl whom fortune had given him to protect; but from time to time he would wake up to a downright sense of kinship and duty, kindled by the pardonable aggressions of my mother, between whom and her sister-in-law there existed a singular antagonism of temper.

Mlle de Bergerac looked at my father intently and with a little blush. "Yes, brother, I'll go. The Chevalier can take me *en croupe.*'

So we started, Coquelin on one horse, and I on the other, with my aunt mounted behind me. Our sport for the first part of the journey consisted chiefly in my urging my beast into a somewhat ponderous gallop, so as to terrify my aunt, who was not very sure of her seat, and who, at moments, between pleading and laughing, had hard work to preserve her balance. At these times Coquelin would ride close along-side of us, at the same cumbersome pace, declaring himself ready to catch the young girl if she fell. In this way we jolted along, in a cloud of dust, with shouts and laughter.

"Madame the Baronne was wrong," said Coquelin, "in denying that we are children."

"O, this is nothing yet," cried my aunt.

The castle of Fossy lifted its dark and crumbling towers with a decided air of feudal arrogance from the summit of a gentle eminence in the recess of a shallow gorge among the hills. Exactly when it had flourished and when it had decayed I knew not, but in the year of grace of our pilgrimage it was a truly venerable, almost a formidable, ruin. Two great towers were standing,—one of them diminished by half its upper elevation, and the other sadly scathed and shattered, but still exposing its hoary head to the weather, and offering the sullen hospitality of its empty skull to a colony of swallows. I shall never forget that day at Fossy; it was one of those long raptures of childhood which seem to imprint upon the mind an ineffaceable stain of light. The novelty and mystery of the dilapidated fortress,—its antiquity, its intricacy, its sounding vaults and corridors, its inaccessible heights and impenetrable depths, the broad sunny glare of its grass-grown courts and yards, the twilight of its passages and midnight of its dungeons, and along with all this my freedom to rove and scramble, my perpetual curiosity, my lusty absorption of the sun-warmed air, and the contagion of my companions' careless and sensuous mirth,—all these things combined to make our excursion one of the memorable events of my youth. My two companions accepted the situation and drank in the beauty of the day and the richness of the spot with all my own reckless freedom. Coquelin was half mad with the joy of spending a whole unbroken summer's day with the woman whom he secretly loved. He was all motion and humor and resonant laughter; and yet intermingled with his random gayety there lurked a solemn sweetness and reticence, a feverish concentration of thought, which to a woman with a woman's senses must have fairly betrayed his passion. Mlle de Bergerac, without quite putting aside her natural dignity and gravity of mien, lent herself with a charming girlish energy to the undisciplined spirit of the hour.

Our first thoughts, after Coquelin had turned the horses to pasture in one of the grassy courts of the castle, were naturally bestowed upon our little basket of provisions; and our first act was to sit down on a heap of fallen masonry and divide its contents. After that we wandered. We climbed the still practicable staircases, and wedged ourselves into the turrets and strolled through the chambers and halls; we started from their long repose every echo and bat and owl within the innumerable walls.

Finally, after we had rambled a couple of hours. Mlle de Bergerac betrayed signs of fatigue. Coquelin went with her in search of a place of rest, and I was left to my own devices. For an hour I found plenty of diversion, at the end of which I returned to my friends. I had some difficulty in finding them. They had mounted by an imperfect and somewhat perilous ascent to one of the upper platforms of the castle. Mlle de Bergerac was sitting in a listless posture on a block of stone, against the wall, in the shadow of the still surviving tower; opposite, in the light, half leaning, half sitting on the parapet of the terrace, was her companion.

"For the last half-hour, mademoiselle," said Coquelin, as I came up, "you've not spoken a word."

"All the morning," said Mlle de Bergerac, "I've been scrambling and chattering and laughing. Now, by reaction, I'm *triste*."

"I protest, so am I," said Coquelin. "The truth is, this old feudal fortress is a decidedly melancholy spot. It's haunted with the ghost of the past. It smells of tragedies, sorrows, and cruelties." He uttered these words with singular emphasis. "It's a horrible place," he pursued, with a shudder.

Mlle de Bergerac began to laugh. "It's odd that we should only just now have discovered it!"

"No, it's like the history of that abominable past of which it's a relic. At the first glance we see nothing but the great proportions, the show, and the splendor; but when we come to explore, we detect a vast underground world of iniquity and suffering. Only half this castle is above the soil; the rest is dungeons and vaults and *oubliettes*."

"Nevertheless," said the young girl, "I should have liked to live in those old days. Shouldn't you?"

"Verily, no, mademoiselle!" And then after a pause, with a certain irrepressible bitterness: "Life is hard enough now."

Mlle de Bergerac stared but said nothing.

"In those good old days," Coquelin resumed, "I should have been a brutal, senseless peasant, yoked down like an ox, with my forehead in the soil. Or else I should have been a trembling, groaning, fasting monk, moaning my soul away in the ecstacies of faith."

Mlle de Bergerac rose and came to the edge of the platform. "Was no other career open in those days?"

"To such a one as me—no. As I say, mademoiselle, life is hard now, but it was a mere dead weight then. I know it was. I feel in my bones and pulses that awful burden of despair under which my wretched ancestors struggled. *Tenez*, I'm the great man of the race. My father came next; he was one of four brothers, who all thought it a prodigious rise in the world when he became a village tailor. If we had lived five hundred years ago, in the shadow of these great towers, we should never have risen at all. We should have stuck with our feet in the clay. As I'm not a fighting man, I suppose I should have gone into the Church. If I hadn't died from an overdose of inanition, very likely I might have lived to be a cardinal."

Mlle de Bergerac leaned against the parapet, and with a meditative droop of the head looked down the little glen toward the plain and the highway. "For myself," she said, "I can imagine very charming things of life in this castle of Fossy."

"For yourself, very likely."

"Fancy the great moat below filled with water and sheeted with lilies, and the drawbridge lowered, and a company of knights riding into the gates. Within, in one of those vaulted, quaintly timbered rooms, the châtelaine stands ready to receive them, with her women, her chaplain, her physician, and her little page. They come clanking up the staircase, with ringing swords, sweeping the ground with their plumes. They are all brave and splendid and fierce, but one of them far more than the rest. They each bend a knee to the lady—"

"But he bends two," cried Coquelin. "They wander apart into one of those deep embrasures and spin the threads of perfect love. Ah, I could fancy a sweet life, in those days, mademoiselle, if I could only fancy myself a knight!"

"And you can't," said the young girl, gravely, looking at him.

"It's an idle game; it's not worth trying."

"Apparently then, you're a cynic; you have an equally small opinion of the past and the present."

"No; you do me injustice."

"But you say that life is hard."

"I speak not for myself, but for others; for my brothers and sisters and kinsmen in all degrees; for the great mass of *petits gens* of my own class."

"Dear me, M. Coquelin, while you're about it, you can speak for others still; for poor portionless girls, for instance."

"Are they very much to be pitied?"

Mlle de Bergerac was silent. "After all," she resumed, "they oughtn't to complain."

"Not when they have a great name and beauty," said Coquelin.

"O heaven!" said the young girl, impatiently, and turned away. Coquelin stood watching her, his brow contracted, his lips parted. Presently, she came back. "Perhaps you think," she said, "that I care for my name—my great name, as you call it."

"Assuredly, I do."

She stood looking at him, blushing a little and frowning. As he said these words, she gave an impatient toss of the head and turned away again. In her hand she carried an ornamental fan, an antiquated and sadly dilapidated instrument. She suddenly raised it above her head, swung it a moment, and threw it far across the parapet. "There goes the name of Bergerac!" she said; and sweeping round, made the young man a very low courtesy.

There was in the whole action a certain passionate freedom which set poor Coquelin's heart a-throbbing. "To have a good name, mademoiselle," he said, "and to be indifferent to it, is the sign of a noble mind." (In parenthesis, I may say that I think he was quite wrong.)

"It's quite as noble, monsieur," returned my aunt, "to have a small name and not to blush for it."

With these words I fancy they felt as if they had said enough; the conversation was growing rather too pointed.

"I think," said my aunt, "that we had better prepare to

go." And she cast a farewell glance at the broad expanse of country which lay stretched out beneath us, striped with the long afternoon shadows.

Coquelin followed the direction of her eyes. "I wish very much," he said, "that before we go we might be able to make our way up into the summit of the great tower. It would be worth the attempt. The view from here, charming as it is, must be only a fragment of what you see from the topmost platform."

"It's not likely," said my aunt, "that the staircase is still in a state to be used."

"Possibly not; but we can see."

"Nay," insisted my aunt, "I'm afraid to trust the Chevalier. There are great breaches in the sides of the ascent, which are so many open doors to destruction."

I strongly opposed this view of the case; but Coquelin, after scanning the elevation of the tower and such of the fissures as were visible from our standpoint, declared that my aunt was right and that it was my duty to comply. "And you, too, mademoiselle," he said, "had better not try it, unless you pride yourself on your strong head."

"No, indeed, I have a particularly weak one. And you?"

"I confess I'm very curious to see the view. I always want to read to the end of a book, to walk to the turn of a road, and to climb to the top of a building."

"Good," said Mlle de Bergerac. "We'll wait for you."

Although in a straight line from the spot which we occupied, the distance through the air to the rugged sides of the great cylinder of masonry which frowned above us was not more than thirty yards, Coquelin was obliged, in order to strike at the nearest accessible point the winding staircase which clung to its massive ribs, to retrace his steps through the interior of the castle and made a *détour* of some five minutes' duration. In ten minutes more he showed himself at an aperture in the wall, facing our terrace.

"How do you prosper?" cried my aunt, raising her voice.

"I've mounted eighty steps," he shouted; "I've a hundred more." Presently he appeared again at another opening. "The steps have stopped," he cried.

"You've only to stop too," rejoined Mlle de Bergerac. Again he was lost to sight and we supposed he was returning. A quarter of an hour elapsed, and we began to wonder at his not having overtaken us, when we heard a loud call high above our heads. There he stood, on the summit of the edifice, waving his hat. At this point he was so far above us that it was difficult to communicate by sounds, in spite of our curiosity to know how, in the absence of a staircase, he had effected the rest of the ascent. He began to represent, by gestures of pretended rapture, the immensity and beauty of the prospect. Finally Mlle de Bergerac beckoned to him to descend, and pointed to the declining sun, informing him at the same time that we would go down and meet him in the lower part of the castle. We left the terrace accordingly, and, making the best of our way through the intricate passages of the edifice, at last, not without a feeling of relief, found ourselves on the level earth. We waited quite half an hour without seeing anything of our companion. My aunt, I could see, had become anxious, although she endeavored to appear at her ease. As the time elapsed, however, it became so evident that Coquelin had encountered some serious obstacle to his descent, that Mlle de Bergerac proposed we should, in so far as was possible, betake ourselves to his assistance. The point was to approach him within speaking distance.

We entered the body of the castle again, climbed to one of the upper levels, and reached a spot where an extensive destruction of the external wall partially exposed the great tower. As we approached this crumbling breach, Mlle de Bergerac drew back from its brink with a loud cry of horror. It was not long before I discerned the cause of her movement. The side of the tower visible from where we stood presented a vast yawning fissure, which explained the interruption of the staircase, the latter having fallen for want of support. The central column, to which the steps had been fastened, seemed, nevertheless, still to be erect, and to have formed, with the agglomeration of fallen fragments and various occasional projections of masonry, the means by which Coquelin, with extraordinary courage and skill, had reached the topmost platform. The ascent, then, had been possible; the descent, curiously enough, he seemed to have found another matter; and after striving in vain to retrace his footsteps, had been obliged to commit himself to the dangerous experiment of passing from the tower to the external surface of the main fortress. He had accomplished half his journey and now stood directly over against us in a posture which caused my young limbs to stiffen with dismay. The point to which he had directed himself was apparently the breach at which we stood; meanwhile he had paused, clinging in mid-air to heaven knows what narrow ledge or flimsy iron clump in the stone-work, and straining his nerves to an agonized tension in the effort not to fall, while his eyes vaguely wandered in quest of another footing. The wall of the castle was so immensely thick, that wherever he could embrace its entire section, progress was comparatively easy; the more especially as, above our heads, this same wall had been demolished in such a way as to maintain a rapid upward inclination to the point where it communicated with the tower.

I stood staring at Coquelin with my heart in my throat, forgetting (or rather too young to reflect) that the sudden shock of seeing me where I was might prove fatal to his equipose. He perceived me, however, and tried to smile. "Don't be afraid," he cried, "I'll be with you in a moment." My aunt, who had fallen back, returned to the aperture, and gazed at him with pale cheecks and clasped hands. He made a long step forward, successfully, and, as he recovered himself, caught sight of her face and looked at her with fearful intentness.

Then seeing, I suppose, that she was sickened by his insecurity, he disengaged one hand and motioned her back. She retreated, paced in a single moment the length of the enclosure in which we stood, returned and stopped just short of the point at which she would have seen him again. She buried her face in her hands, like one muttering a rapid prayer, and then advanced once more within range of her friend's vision. As she looked at him, clinging in mid-air and planting step after step on the jagged and treacherous edge of the immense perpendicular chasm, she repressed another loud cry only by thrusting her handkerchief into her mouth. He caught her eyes again, gazed into them with piercing keenness, as if to drink in coolness and confidence, and then, as she closed them again in horror, motioned me with his head to lead her away. She returned to the farther end of the apartment and leaned her head against the wall. I remained staring at poor Coquelin, fascinated by the spectacle of his mingled danger and courage. Inch by inch, yard by yard, I saw him lessen the interval which threatened his life. It was a horrible, beautiful sight. Some five minutes elapsed; they seemed like fifty. The last few yards he accomplished with a rush; he reached the window which was the goal of his efforts, swung himself in and let himself down by a prodigious leap to the level on which we stood. Here he stopped, pale, lacerated, and drenched with perspiration. He put out his hand to Mlle de Bergerac who, at the sound of his steps, had turned herself about. On seeing him she made a few steps forward and burst into tears. I took his extended hand. He bent over me and kissed me, and then giving me a push, "Go and kiss your poor aunt," he said. Mlle de Bergerac clasped me to her breast with a most convulsive pressure. From that moment till we reached home, there was very little said. Both my companions had matter for silent reflection—Mlle de Bergerac in the deep significance of that offered hand, and Coquelin in the rich avowal of her tears.

III

A WEEK after this memorable visit to Fossy, in emulation of
my good preceptor, I treated my friends, or myself at least,
to a five minutes' fright. Wandering beside the river one day
when Coquelin had been detained within doors to overlook
some accounts for my father, I amused myself, where the
bank projected slightly over the stream, with kicking the earth
away in fragments, and watching it borne down the current.
The result may be anticipated; I came very near going the
way of those same fragments. I lost my foothold and fell into
the stream, which, however, was so shallow as to offer no
great obstacle to self-preservation. I scrambled ashore, wet
to the bone, and, feeling rather ashamed of my misadventure,
skulked about in the fields for a couple of hours, in my dripping clothes. Finally, there being no sun and my garments
remaining inexorably damp, my teeth began to chatter and
my limbs to ache. I went home and surrendered myself. Here
again the result may be foreseen: the next day I was laid up
with a high fever.

Mlle de Bergerac, as I afterwards learned, immediately
appointed herself my nurse, removed me from my little
sleeping-closet to her own room, and watched me with the
most tender care. My illness lasted some ten days, my con-
valescence a week. When I began to mend, my bed was transferred to an unoccupied room adjoining my aunt's. Here, late
one afternoon, I lay languidly singing to myself and watching
the western sunbeams shimmering on the opposite wall. If
you were ever ill as a child, you will remember such moments.
You look by the hour at your thin, white hands; you listen
to the sounds in the house, the opening of doors and the
tread of feet; you murmur strange odds and ends of talk; and

you watch the fading of the day and the dark flowering of the night. Presently my aunt came in, introducing Coquelin, whom she left by my bedside. He sat with me a long time, talking in the old, kind way, and gradually lulled me to sleep with the gentle murmur of his voice. When I awoke again it was night. The sun was quenched on the opposite wall, but through a window on the same side came a broad ray of moonlight. In the window sat Coquelin, who had apparently not left the room. Near him was Mlle de Bergerac.

Some time elapsed between my becoming conscious of their presence and my distinguishing the sense of the words that were passing between them. When I did so, if I had reached the age when one ponders and interprets what one hears, I should readily have perceived that since those last thrilling moments at Fossy their friendship had taken a very long step, and that the secret of each heart had changed place with its mate. But even now there was little that was careless and joyous in their young love; the first words of Mlle de Bergerac that I distinguished betrayed the sombre tinge of their passion.

"I don't care what happens now," she said. "It will always be something to have lived through these days."

"You're stronger than I, then," said Coquelin. "I haven't the courage to defy the future. I'm afraid to think of it. Ah, why can't we make a future of our own?"

"It would be a greater happiness than we have a right to. Who are you, Pierre Coquelin, that you should claim the right to marry the girl you love, when she's a demoiselle de Bergerac to begin with? And who am I, that I should expect to have deserved a greater blessing than that one look of your eyes, which I shall never, never forget? It is more than enough to watch you and pray for you and worship you in silence."

"What am I? what are you? We are two honest mortals, who have a perfect right to repudiate the blessings of God. If ever a passion deserved its rewards, mademoiselle, it's the absolute love I bear you. It's not a spasm, a miracle, or a delusion; it's the most natural emotion of my nature."

"We don't live in a natural world, Coquelin. If we did, there would be no need of concealing this divine affection. Great heavens! who's natural? Is it my sister-in-law? Is it M. de Treuil? Is it my brother? My brother is sometimes so natural that he's brutal. Is it I myself? There are moments when I'm afraid of my nature."

It was too dark for me to distinguish my companions' faces in the course of this singular dialogue; but it's not hard to imagine how, as my aunt uttered these words, with a burst of sombre *naïveté*, her lover must have turned upon her face the puzzled brightness of his eyes.

"What do you mean?" he asked.

"*Mon Dieu!* think how I have lived! What a senseless, thoughtless, passionless life! What solitude, ignorance, and languor! What trivial duties and petty joys! I have fancied myself happy at times, for it was God's mercy that I didn't know what I lacked. But now that my soul begins to stir and throb and live, it shakes me with its mighty pulsations. I feel as if in the mere wantonness of strength and joy it might drive me to some extravagance. I seem to feel myself making a great rush, with my eyes closed and my heart in my throat. And then the earth sinks away from under my feet, and in my ears is the sound of a dreadful tumult."

"Evidently we have very different ways of feeling. For you our love is action, passion; for me it's rest. For you it's romance; for me it's reality. For me it's a necessity; for you (how shall I say it?) it's a luxury. In point of fact, mademoiselle, how should it be otherwise? When a demoiselle de Bergerac bestows her heart upon an obscure adventurer, a man born in poverty and servitude, it's a matter of charity, of noble generosity."

Mlle de Bergerac received this speech in silence, and for some moments nothing was said. At last she resumed: "After all that has passed between us, Coquelin, it seems to me a matter neither of generosity nor of charity to allude again to that miserable fact of my birth."

"I was only trying to carry out your own idea, and to get at the truth with regard to our situation. If our love is worth a straw, we needn't be afraid of that. Isn't it true—blessedly true, perhaps, for all I know—that you shrink a little from taking me as I am? Except for my character, I'm so little! It's impossible to be less of a *personage*. You can't quite reconcile it to your dignity to love a nobody, so you fling over your weakness a veil of mystery and romance and exaltation. You regard your passion, perhaps, as more of an escapade, an adventure, than it needs to be."

"My 'nobody,'" said Mlle de Bergerac, gently, "is a very wise man, and a great philosopher. I don't understand a word you say."

"Ah, so much the better!" said Coquelin with a little laugh.

"Will you promise me," pursued the young girl, "never again by word or deed to allude to the difference of our birth? If you refuse, I shall consider you an excellent pedagogue, but no lover."

"Will you in return promise me—"

"Promise you what?"

Coquelin was standing before her, looking at her, with folded arms. "Promise me likewise to forget it!"

Mlle de Bergerac stared a moment, and also rose to her feet. "Forget it! Is this generous?" she cried. "Is it delicate? I had pretty well forgot it, I think, on that dreadful day at Fossy!" Her voice trembled and swelled; she burst into tears. Coquelin attempted to remonstrate, but she motioned him aside, and swept out of the room.

It must have been a very genuine passion between these two, you'll observe, to allow this handling without gloves. Only a plant of hardy growth could have endured this chilling blast of discord and disputation. Ultimately, indeed, its effect seemed to have been to fortify and consecrate their love. This was apparent several days later; but I know not what manner of communication they had had in the interval. I was much better, but I was still weak and languid. Mlle de Bergerac brought me my breakfast in bed, and then, having helped me to rise and dress, led me out into the garden, where she had caused a chair to be placed in the shade. While I sat watching the bees and butterflies, and pulling the flowers to pieces, she strolled up and down the alley close at hand, taking slow stitches in a piece of embroidery. We had been so occupied about ten minutes, when Coquelin came towards us from his lodge,—by appointment, evidently, for this was a roundabout way to the house. Mlle de Bergerac met him at the end of the path, where I could not hear what they said, but only see their gestures. As they came along together, she raised both hands to her ears, and shook her head with vehemence, as if to refuse to listen to what he was urging. When they drew near my resting-place, she had interrupted him.

"No, no, no!" she cried, "I will never forget it to my dying day. How should I? How can I look at you without remembering it? It's in your face, your figure, your movements, the tones of your voice. It's you—it's what I love in you! It was that which went through my heart that day at Fossy. It was the look, the tone, with which you called the place horrible; it was your bitter plebeian hate. When you spoke of the misery and baseness of your race, I could have cried out in an anguish of love! When I contradicted you, and pretended that I prized and honored all these tokens of your servitude,— just heaven! you know now what my words were worth!"

Coquelin walked beside her with his hands clasped behind him, and his eyes fixed on the ground with a look of re- pressed sensibility. He passed his poor little convalescent pupil without heeding him. When they came down the path again, the young girl was still talking with the same feverish volubility.

"But most of all, the first day, the first hour, when you came up the avenue to my brother! I had never seen any one like you. I had seen others, but you had something that went to my soul. I devoured you with my eyes,—your dusty clothes, your uncombed hair, your pale face, the way you held yourself not to seem tired. I went down on my knees, then; I haven't been up since."

The poor girl, you see, was completely possessed by her passion, and yet she was in a very strait place. For her life she wouldn't recede; and yet how was she to advance? There must have been an odd sort of simplicity in her way of bestowing her love; or perhaps you'll think it an odd sort of subtlety. It seems plain to me now, as I tell the story, that Coquelin, with his perfect good sense, was right, and that there was, at this moment, a large element of romance in the composition of her feelings. She seemed to feel no desire to realize her passion. Her hand was already bestowed; fate was inexorable. She wished simply to compress a world of bliss into her few remaining hours of freedom.

The day after this interview in the garden I came down to dinner; on the next I sat up to supper, and for some time afterwards, thanks to my aunt's preoccupation of mind. On rising from the table, my father left the château; my mother, who was ailing, returned to her room. Coquelin disappeared, under pretence of going to his own apartments; but, Mlle de Bergerac having taken me into the drawing-room and detained me there some minutes, he shortly rejoined us.

"Great heaven, mademoiselle, this must end!" he cried, as he came into the room. "I can stand it no longer."

"Nor can I," said my aunt. "But I have given my word."

"Take back your word, then! Write him a letter—go to him—send me to him—anything! I can't stay here on the footing of a thief and impostor. I'll do anything," he continued, as she was silent. "I'll go to him in person; I'll go to your brother; I'll go to your sister even. I'll proclaim it to the world. Or, if you don't like that, I'll keep it a mortal secret. I'll leave the château with you without an hour's delay. I'll defy pursuit and discovery. We'll go to America—anywhere you wish, if it's only action. Only spare me the agony of seeing you drift along into that man's arms."

Mlle de Bergerac made no reply for some moments. At last, "I will never marry M. de Treuil," she said.

To this declaration Coquelin made no response; but after a pause, "Well, well, well?" he cried.

"Ah, you're pitiless!" said the young girl.

"No, mademoiselle, from the bottom of my heart I pity you."

"Well, then, think of all you ask! Think of the inexpiable criminality of my love. Think of me standing here—here before my mother's portrait—murmuring out my shame, scorched by my sister's scorn, buffeted by my brother's curses! Gracious heaven, Coquelin, suppose after all I were a bad, hard girl!"

"I'll suppose nothing; this is no time for hair-splitting." And then, after a pause, as if with a violent effort, in a voice hoarse and yet soft: "Gabrielle, passion is blind. Reason alone is worth a straw. I'll not counsel you in passion, let us wait till reason comes to us." He put out his hand; she gave him her own; he pressed it to his lips and departed.

On the following day, as I still professed myself too weak to resume my books, Coquelin left the château alone, after breakfast, for a long walk. He was going, I suppose, into the woods and meadows in quest of Reason. She was hard to find, apparently, for he failed to return to dinner. He reappeared, however, at supper, but now my father was absent. My mother, as she left the table, expressed the wish that Mlle de Bergerac should attend her to her own room. Coquelin, meanwhile, went with me into the great saloon, and for half an hour talked to me gravely and kindly about my studies, and questioned me on what we had learned before my illness. At the end of this time Mlle de Bergerac returned.

"I got this letter to-day from M. de Treuil," she said, and offered him a missive which had apparently been handed to her since dinner.

"I don't care to read it," he said.

She tore it across and held the pieces to the flame of the candle. "He is to be here to-morrow," she added finally.

"Well?" asked Coquelin gravely.

"You know my answer."

"Your answer to him, perfectly. But what is your answer to me?"

She looked at him in silence. They stood for a minute, their eyes locked together. And then, in the same posture,— her arms loose at her sides, her head slightly thrown back,— "To you," she said, "my answer is—farewell."

The word was little more than whispered; but, although he heard it, he neither started nor spoke. He stood unmoved, all his soul trembling under his brows and filling the space between his mistress and himself with a sort of sacred stillness. Then, gradually, his head sank on his breast, and his eyes dropped on the ground.

"It's reason," the young girl began. "Reason has come to me. She tells me that if I marry in my brother's despite, and in opposition to all the traditions that have been kept sacred in my family, I shall neither find happiness nor give it. I must choose the simplest course. The other is a gulf; I can't leap it. It's harder than you think. Something in the air forbids it,—something in the very look of these old walls, within which I was born and I've lived. I shall never marry; I shall go into religion. I tried to fling away my name; it was sowing dragons' teeth. I don't ask you to forgive me. It's small enough comfort that you should have the right to think of me as a poor, weak heart. Keep repeating that: it will console you.

I shall not have the compensation of doubting the perfection of what I love."

Coquelin turned away in silence. Mlle de Bergerac sprang after him. "In Heaven's name," she cried, "say something! Rave, storm, swear, but don't let me think I've broken your heart."

"My heart's sound," said Coquelin, almost with a smile. "I regret nothing that has happened. Oh, how I love you!"

The young girl buried her face in her hands.

"This end," he went on, "is doubtless the only possible one. It's thinking very lightly of life to expect any other. After all, what call had I to interrupt your life,—to burden you with a trouble, a choice, a decision? As much as anything that I have ever known in you I admire your beautiful delicacy of conscience."

"Ah," said the young girl, with a moan, "don't kill me with fine names!"

And then came the farewell. "I feel," said poor Coquelin, "that I can't see you again. We must not meet. I will leave Bergerac immediately,—to-night,—under pretext of having been summoned home by my mother's illness. In a few days I will write to your brother that circumstances forbid me to return."

My own part in this painful interview I shall not describe at length. When it began to dawn upon my mind that my friend was actually going to disappear, I was seized with a convulsion of rage and grief. "Ah," cried Mlle de Bergerac bitterly, "that was all that was wanting!" What means were taken to restore me to composure, what promises were made me, what pious deception was practised, I forget; but, when at last I came to my senses, Coquelin had made his exit.

My aunt took me by the hand and prepared to lead me up to bed, fearing naturally that my ruffled aspect and swollen visage would arouse suspicion. At this moment I heard the clatter of hoofs in the court, mingled with the sound of voices. From the window, I saw M. de Treuil and my father alighting from horseback. Mlle de Bergerac, apparently, made the same observation; she dropped my hand and sank down in a chair. She was not left long in suspense. Perceiving a light in the saloon, the two gentlemen immediately made their way to this apartment. They came in together, arm in arm, the Vicomte dressed in mourning. Just within the threshold they stopped; my father disengaged his arm, took his companion by the hand and led him to Mlle de Bergerac. She rose to her feet as you may imagine a sitting statue to rise. The Vicomte bent his knee.

"At last, mademoiselle," said he,—"sooner than I had hoped,—my long probation is finished."

The young girl spoke, but no one would have recognized her voice. "I fear, M. le Vicomte," she said, "that it has only begun."

The Vicomte broke into a harsh, nervous laugh.

"Fol de rol, mademoiselle," cried my father, "your pleasantry is in very bad taste."

But the Vicomte had recovered himself. "Mademoiselle is quite right," he declared; "she means that I must now begin to deserve my happiness." This little speech showed a very brave fancy. It was in flagrant discord with the expression of the poor girl's figure, as she stood twisting her hands together and rolling her eyes,—an image of sombre desperation.

My father felt there was a storm in the air. "M. le Vicomte is in mourning for M. de Sorbières," he said. "M. le Vicomte is his sole legatee. He comes to exact the fulfilment of your promise."

"I made no promise," said Mlle de Bergerac.

"Excuse me, mademoiselle; you gave your word that you'd wait for me."

"Good heaven!" cried the young girl; "haven't I waited for you!"

"*Ma toute belle*," said the Baron, trying to keep his angry voice within the compass of an undertone, and reducing it in the effort to a very ugly whisper, "if I had supposed you were going to make us a scene, *nom de Dieu!* I would have taken my precautions beforehand! You know what you're to expect. Vicomte, keep her to her word. I'll give you half an hour. Come, Chevalier." And he took me by the hand.

We had crossed the threshold and reached the hall, when I heard the Vicomte give a long moan, half plaintive, half indignant. My father turned, and answered with a fierce, inarticulate cry, which I can best describe as a roar. He straightway retraced his steps, I, of course, following. Exactly what, in the brief interval, had passed between our companions I am unable to say; but it was plain that Mlle de Bergerac, by some cruelly unerring word or act, had discharged the bolt of her refusal. Her gallant lover had sunk into a chair, burying his face in his hands, and stamping his feet on the floor in a frenzy of disappointment. She stood regarding him in a sort of helpless, distant pity. My father had been going to break out into a storm of imprecations; but he suppressed them, and folded his arms.

"And now, mademoiselle," he said, "will you be so good as to inform me of your intentions?"

Beneath my father's gaze the softness passed out of my aunt's face and gave place to an angry defiance, which he must have recognized as cousin-german, at least, to the passion in his own breast. "My intentions had been," she said, "to let M. le Vicomte know that I couldn't marry him, with as little offence as possible. But you seem determined, my brother to thrust in a world of offence somewhere."

You must not blame Mlle de Bergerac for the sting of her retort. She foresaw a hard fight; she had only sprung to her arms.

My father looked at the wretched Vicomte, as he sat sobbing and stamping like a child. His bosom was wrung with pity for his friend. "Look at that dear Gaston, that charming man, and blush for your audacity."

"I know a great deal more about my audacity than you, brother. I might tell you things that would surprise you."

"Gabrielle, you are mad!" the Baron broke out.

"Perhaps I am," said the young girl. And then, turning to M. de Treuil, in a tone of exquisite reproach, "M. le Vicomte, you suffer less well than I had hoped."

My father could endure no more. He seized his sister by her two wrists, so that beneath the pressure her eyes filled with tears. "Heartless fool!" he cried, "do you know what I can do to you?"

"I can imagine, from this specimen," said the poor creature.

The Baron was beside himself with passion. "Down, down on your knees," he went on, "and beg our pardon all round for your senseless, shameless, perversity!" As he spoke, he increased the pressure of his grasp to that degree that, after a vain struggle to free herself, she uttered a scream of pain. The Vicomte sprang to his feet. "In heaven's name, Gabrielle," he cried,—and it was the only real *naïveté* that he had ever uttered,—"isn't it all a horrible jest?"

Mlle de Bergerac shook her head. "It seems hard, Vicomte," she said, "that I should be answerable for your happiness."

"You hold it there it your hand. Think of what I suffer. To have lived for weeks in the hope of this hour, and to find it what you would fain make it! To have dreamed of rapturous bliss, and to wake to find it hideous misery! Think of it once again!"

"She shall have a chance to think of it," the Baron declared; "she shall think of it quite at her ease. Go to your room, mademoiselle, and remain there till further notice."

Gabrielle prepared to go, but, as she moved away, "I used to fear you, brother," she said with homely scorn, "but I don't fear you now. Judge whether it's because I love you more!"

"Gabrielle," the Vicomte cried out, "I haven't given you up."

"Your feelings are your own, M. le Vicomte. I would have given more than I can say rather than have caused you to suffer. Your asking my hand has been the great honor of my life; my withholding it has been the great trial." And she walked out of the room with the step of unacted tragedy. My father, with an oath, despatched me to bed in her train. Heavy-headed with the recent spectacle of so much half-apprehended emotion, I speedily fell asleep.

I was aroused by the sound of voices, and the grasp of a heavy hand on my shoulder. My father stood before me, holding a candle, with M. de Treuil beside him. "Chevalier," he said, "open your eyes like a man, and come to your senses."

Thus exhorted, I sat up and stared. The Baron sat down on the edge of the bed. "This evening," he began, "before the Vicomte and I came in, were you alone with your aunt?"— My dear friend, you see the scene from here. I answered with the cruel directness of my years. Even if I had had the wit to dissemble, I should have lacked the courage. Of course I had no story to tell. I had drawn no inferences; I didn't say that my tutor was my aunt's lover. I simply said that he had been with us after supper, and that he wanted my aunt to go away with him. Such was my part in the play. I see the whole picture again,—my father brandishing the candlestick, and devouring my words with his great flaming eyes; and the Vicomte behind, portentously silent, with his black clothes and his pale face.

They had not been three minutes out of the room when the door leading to my aunt's chamber opened and Mlle de Bergerac appeared. She had heard sounds in my apartment, and suspected the visit of the gentlemen and its motive. She immediately won from me the recital of what I had been forced to avow. "Poor Chevalier," she cried, for all commentary. And then, after a pause, "What made them suspect that M. Coquelin had been with us?"

"They saw him, or some one, leave the château as they came in."

"And where have they gone now?"

"To supper. My father said to M. de Treuil that first of all they must sup."

Mlle de Bergerac stood a moment in meditation. Then suddenly, "Get up, Chevalier," she said, "I want you to go with me."

"Where are you going?"

"To M. Coquelin's."

I needed no second admonition. I hustled on my clothes; Mlle de Bergerac left the room and immediately returned, clad in a light mantle. We made our way undiscovered to one of the private entrances of the château, hurried across the park and found a light in the window of Coquelin's lodge. It was about half past nine. Mlle de Bergerac gave a loud knock at the door, and we entered her lover's apartment.

Coquelin was seated at his table writing. He sprang to his feet with a cry of amazement. Mlle de Bergerac stood panting, with one hand pressed to her heart, while rapidly moving the other as if to enjoin calmness.

"They are come back," she began,—"M. de Treuil and my brother!"

"I thought he was to come to-morrow. Was it a deception?"

"Ah, no! not from him,—an accident. Pierre Coquelin, I've had such a scene! But it's not your fault."

"What made the scene?"

"My refusal, of course."

"You turned off the Vicomte?"

"Holy Virgin! You ask me?"

"Unhappy girl!" cried Coquelin.

"No, I was a happy girl to have had a chance to act as my heart bade me. I had faltered enough. But it was hard!"

"It's all hard."

"The hardest is to come," said my aunt. She put out her hand; he sprang to her and seized it, and she pressed his own with vehemence. "They have discovered our secret,—don't ask how. It was Heaven's will. From this moment, of course—"

"From this moment, of course," cried Coquelin, "I stay where I am!"

With an impetuous movement she raised his hand to her lips and kissed it. "You stay where you are. We have nothing to conceal, but we have nothing to avow. We have no confessions to make. Before God we have done our duty. You may expect them, I fancy, to-night; perhaps, too, they will honor me with a visit. They are supping between two battles. They will attack us with fury, I know; but let them dash themselves against our silence as against a wall of stone. I have taken my stand. My love, my errors, my longings, are my own affair. My reputation is a sealed book. Woe to him who would force it open!"

The poor girl had said once, you know, that she was afraid of her nature. Assuredly it had now sprung erect in its strength; it came hurrying into action on the wings of her indignation. "Remember, Coquelin," she went on, "you are still and always my friend. You are the guardian of my weakness, the support of my strength."

"Say it all, Gabrielle!" he cried. "I'm for ever and ever your lover!"

Suddenly, above the music of his voice, there came a great rattling knock at the door. Coquelin sprang forward; it opened in his face and disclosed my father and M. de Treuil. I have no words in my dictionary, no images in my rhetoric, to represent the sudden horror that leaped into my father's face as his eye fell upon his sister. He staggered back a step and then stood glaring, until his feelings found utterance in a single word: "*Coureuse!*" I have never been able to look upon the word as trivial since that moment.

The Vicomte came striding past him into the room, like a bolt of lightning from a rumbling cloud, quivering with baffled desire, and looking taller by the head for his passion. "And it was for this, mademoiselle," he cried, "and for *that!*" and he flung out a scornful hand toward Coquelin. "For a beggarly, boorish, ignorant pedagogue!"

Coquelin folded his arms. "Address me directly, M. le Vicomte," he said, "don't fling mud at me over mademoiselle's head."

"You? Who are you?" hissed the nobleman. "A man doesn't address you; he sends his lackeys to flog you!"

"Well, M. le Vicomte, you're complete," said Coquelin, eyeing him from head to foot.

"Complete?" and M. de Treuil broke into an almost hysterical laugh. "I only lack having married your mistress!"

"Ah!" cried Mlle de Bergerac.

"O, you poor, insensate fool!" said Coquelin.

"Heaven help me," the young man went on, "I'm ready to marry her still."

While these words were rapidly exchanged, my father stood choking with the confusion of amazement and rage. He was stupefied at his sister's audacity—at the dauntless spirit which ventured to flaunt its shameful passion in the very face of honor and authority. Yet that simple interjection which I have quoted from my aunt's lips stirred a secret tremor in his heart; it was like the striking of some magic silver bell, portending monstrous things. His passion faltered, and, as his eyes glanced upon my innocent head (which, it must be confessed, was sadly out of place in that pernicious scene), alighted on this smaller wrong. "The next time you go on your adventures, mademoiselle," he cried, "I'd thank you not to pollute my son by dragging him at your skirts."

"I'm not sorry to have my family present," said the young girl, who had had time to collect her thoughts. "I should be glad even if my sister were here. I wish simply to bid you farewell."

Coquelin, at these words, made a step towards her. She passed her hand through his arm. "Things have taken place —and chiefly within the last moment—which change the face of the future. You've done the business, brother," and she fixed her glittering eyes on the Baron; "you've driven me back on myself. I spared you, but you never spared me. I cared for my name; you loaded it with dishonor. I chose between happiness and duty,—duty as you would have laid it down; I preferred duty. But now that happiness has become one with simple safety from violence and insult, I go back to happiness. I give you back your name; though I have kept it more jealously than you. I have another ready for me. O Messieurs!" she cried, with a burst of rapturous exaltation, "for what you have done to me I thank you."

My father began to groan and tremble. He had clasped my hand in his own, which was clammy with perspiration. "For the love of God, Gabrielle," he implored, "or the fear of the Devil, speak so that a sickened, maddened Christian can understand you! For what purpose did you come here to-night?"

"*Mon Dieu*, it's a long story. You made short work with it. I might in justice do as much. I came here, brother, to guard my reputation, and not to lose it."

All this while my father had neither looked at Coquelin nor spoken to him, either because he thought him not worth his words, or because he had kept some transcendent insult in reserve. Here my governor broke in. "It seems to me time, M. le Baron, that I should inquire the purpose of your own visit."

My father stared a moment. "I came, M. Coquelin, to take you by the shoulders and eject you through that door, with the further impulsion, if necessary, of a vigorous kick."

"Good! And M. le Vicomte?"

"M. le Vicomte came to see it done."

"Perfect! A little more and you had come too late. I was

on the point of leaving Bergerac. I can put the story into three words. I have been so happy as to secure the affections of Mlle de Bergerac. She asked herself, devoutly, what course of action was possible under the circumstances. She decided that the only course was that we should immediately separate. I had no hesitation in bringing my residence with M. le Chevalier to a sudden close. I was to have quitted the château early to-morrow morning, leaving mademoiselle at absolute liberty. With her refusal of M. de Treuil I have nothing to do. Her action in this matter seems to have been strangely precipitated, and my own departure anticipated in consequence. It was at her adjuration that I was preparing to depart. She came here this evening to command me to stay. In our relations there was nothing that the world had a right to lay a finger upon. From the moment that they were suspected it was of the first importance to the security and sanctity of Mlle de Bergerac's position that there should be no appearance on my part of elusion or flight. The relations I speak of had ceased to exist; there was, therefore, every reason why for the present I should retain my place. Mlle de Bergerac had been here some three minutes, and had just made known her wishes, when you arrived with the honorable intentions which you avow, and under that illusion the perfect stupidity of which is its least reproach. In my own turn, Messieurs, I thank you!"

"Gabrielle," said my father, as Coquelin ceased speaking, "the long and short of it appears to be that after all you needn't marry this man. Am I to understand that you intend to?"

"Brother, I mean to marry M. Coquelin."

My father stood looking from the young girl to her lover. The Vicomte walked to the window, as if he were in want of air. The night was cool and the window closed. He tried the sash, but for some reason it resisted. Whereupon he raised his sword-hilt and with a violent blow shivered a pane into fragments. The Baron went on: "On what do you propose to live?"

"It's for me to propose," said Coquelin. "My wife shall not suffer."

"Whither do you mean to go?"

"Since you're so good as to ask,—to Paris."

My father had got back his fire. "Well, then," he cried, "my bitterest unforgiveness go with you, and turn your unholy pride to abject woe! My sister may marry a base-born vagrant if she wants, but I shall not give her away. I hope you'll enjoy the mud in which you've planted yourself. I hope your marriage will be blessed in the good old fashion, and that you'll regard philosophically the sight of a half-dozen starving children. I hope you'll enjoy the company of chandlers and cobblers and scribblers!" The Baron could go no further. "Ah, my sister!" he half exclaimed. His voice broke; he gave a great convulsive sob, and fell into a chair.

"Coquelin," said my aunt, "take me back to the château."

As she walked to the door, her hand in the young man's arm, the Vicomte turned short about from the window, and stood with his drawn sword, grimacing horribly.

"Not if I can help it!" he cried through his teeth, and with a sweep of his weapon he made a savage thrust at the young girl's breast. Coquelin, with equal speed, sprang before her, threw out his arm, and took the blow just below the elbow.

"Thank you, M. le Vicomte," he said, "for the chance of calling you a coward! There was something I wanted."

Mlle de Bergerac spent the night at the château, but by early dawn she had disappeared. Whither Coquelin betook himself with his gratitude and his wound, I know not. He lay, I suppose, at some neighboring farmer's. My father and the Vicomte kept for an hour a silent, sullen vigil in my preceptor's vacant apartment,—for an hour and perhaps longer, for at the end of this time I fell asleep, and when I came to my senses, the next morning, I was in my own bed.

M. de Bergerac had finished his tale.

"But the marriage," I asked, after a pause,—"was it happy?"

"Reasonably so, I fancy. There is no doubt that Coquelin was an excellent fellow. They had three children, and lost them all. They managed to live. He painted portraits and did literary work."

"And his wife?"

"Her history, I take it, is that of all good wives: she loved her husband. When the Revolution came, they went into politics; but here, in spite of his base birth, Coquelin acted with that superior temperance which I always associate with his memory. He was no *sans-culotte*. They both went to the scaffold among the Girondists."

TRAVELLING COMPANIONS

I

THE most strictly impressive picture in Italy is incontestably the Last Supper of Leonardo at Milan. A part of its immense solemnity is doubtless due to its being one of the first of the great Italian masterworks that you encounter in coming down from the North. Another secondary source of interest resides in the very completeness of its decay. The mind finds a rare delight in filling each of its vacant spaces, effacing its rank defilement, and repairing, as far as possible, its sad disorder. Of the essential power and beauty of the work there can be no better evidence than this fact that, having lost so much, it has yet retained so much. An unquenchable elegance lingers in those vague outlines and incurable scars; enough remains to place you in sympathy with the unfathomable wisdom of the painter. The fresco covers a wall, the reader will remember, at the end of the former refectory of a monastery now suppressed, the precinct of which is occupied by a regiment of cavalry. Horses stamp, soldiers rattle their oaths, in the cloisters which once echoed to the sober tread of monastic sandals and the pious greetings of meek-voiced friars.

It was the middle of August, and summer sat brooding fiercely over the streets of Milan. The great brick-wrought dome of the church of St Mary of the Graces rose black with the heat against the brazen sky. As my *fiacre* drew up in front of the church, I found another vehicle in possession of the little square of shade which carpeted the glaring pavement before the adjoining convent. I left the two drivers to share this advantage as they could, and made haste to enter the cooler presence of the Cenacolo. Here I found the occupants of the *fiacre* without, a young lady and an elderly man. Here also, besides the official who takes your tributary franc, sat a long-haired copyist, wooing back the silent secrets of the great fresco into the cheerfullest commonplaces of yellow and blue. The gentleman was earnestly watching this ingenious operation; the young lady sat with her eyes fixed on the picture, from which she failed to move them when I took my place on a line with her. I too, however, speedily became as unconscious of her presence as she of mine, and lost myself in the study of the work before us. A single glance had assured me that she was an American.

Since that day, I have seen all the great art treasures of Italy: I have seen Tintoretto at Venice, Michael Angelo at Florence and Rome, Correggio at Parma; but I have looked at no other picture with an emotion equal to that which rose within me as this great creation of Leonardo slowly began to dawn upon my intelligence from the tragical twilight of its ruin. A work so nobly conceived can never utterly die, so long as the half-dozen main lines of its design remain. Neglect and malice are less cunning than the genius of the great painter. It has stored away with masterly skill such a wealth of beauty as only perfect love and sympathy can fully detect. So, under my eyes, the restless ghost of the dead fresco returned to its mortal abode. From the beautiful central image of Christ I perceived its radiation right and left along the sadly broken line of the disciples. One by one, out of the depths of their grim dismemberment, the figures trembled into meaning and life, and the vast, serious beauty of the work stood revealed. What is the ruling force of this magnificent design? Is it art? is it science? is it sentiment? is it knowledge? I am sure I can't say; but in moments of doubt and depression I find it of excellent use to recall the great picture with all possible distinctness. Of all the works of man's hands it is the least superficial.

The young lady's companion finished his survey of the

copyist's work and came and stood behind his chair. The reader will remember that a door has been rudely cut in the wall, a part of it entering the fresco.

"He hasn't got in that door," said the old gentleman, speaking apparently of the copyist.

The young lady was silent. "Well, my dear," he continued. "What do you think of it?"

The young girl gave a sigh. "I see it," she said.

"You see it, eh? Well, I suppose there is nothing more to be done."

The young lady rose slowly, drawing on her glove. As her eyes were still on the fresco, I was able to observe her. Beyond doubt she was American. Her age I fancied to be twenty-two. She was of middle stature, with a charming slender figure. Her hair was brown, her complexion fresh and clear. She wore a white piqué dress and a black lace shawl, and on her thick dark braids a hat with a purple feather. She was largely characterized by that physical delicacy and that personal elegance (each of them sometimes excessive) which seldom fail to betray my young countrywomen in Europe. The gentleman, who was obviously her father, bore the national stamp as plainly as she. A shrewd, firm, generous face, which told of many dealings with many men, of stocks and shares and current prices,—a face, moreover, in which there lingered the mellow afterglow of a sense of excellent claret. He was bald and grizzled, this perfect American, and he wore a short-bristled white moustache between the two hard wrinkles forming the sides of a triangle of which his mouth was the base and the ridge of his nose, where his eyeglass sat, the apex. In deference perhaps to this exotic growth, he was better dressed than is common with the typical American citizen, in a blue necktie, a white waistcoat, and a pair of gray trousers. As his daughter still lingered, he looked at me with an eye of sagacious conjecture.

"Ah, that beautiful, beautiful, beautiful Christ," said the

young lady, in a tone which betrayed her words in spite of its softness. "O father, what a picture!"

"Hum!" said her father, "I don't see it."

"I must get a photograph," the young girl rejoined. She turned away and walked to the farther end of the hall, where the custodian presides at a table of photographs and prints. Meanwhile her father had perceived my Murray.

"English, sir?" he demanded.

"No, I'm an American, like yourself, I fancy."

"Glad to make your acquaintance, sir. From New York?"

"From New York. I have been absent from home, however, for a number of years."

"Residing in this part of the world?"

"No. I have been living in Germany. I have only just come into Italy."

"Ah, so have we. The young lady is my daughter. She is crazy about Italy. We were very nicely fixed at Interlaken, when suddenly she read in some confounded book or other that Italy should be seen in summer. So she dragged me over the mountains into this fiery furnace. I'm actually melting away. I have lost five pounds in three days."

I replied that the heat was indeed intense, but that I agreed with his daughter that Italy should be seen in summer. What could be pleasanter than the temperature of that vast cool hall?"

"Ah, yes," said my friend; "I suppose we shall have plenty of this kind of thing. It makes no odds to me, so long as my poor girl has a good time."

"She seems," I remarked, "to be having a pretty good time with the photographs." In fact, she was comparing photographs with a great deal of apparent energy, while the salesman lauded his wares in the Italian manner. We strolled over to the table. The young girl was seemingly in treaty for a large photograph of the head of Christ, in which the blurred and fragmentary character of the original was largely intensified, though much of its exquisite pathetic beauty was also preserved. "They'll not think much of that at home," said the old gentleman.

"So much the worse for them," said his daughter, with an accent of delicate pity. With the photograph in her hand, she walked back to the fresco. Her father engaged in an English dialogue with the custodian. In the course of five minutes, wishing likewise to compare the copy and the original, I returned to the great picture. As I drew near it the young lady turned away. Her eyes then for the first time met my own. They were deep and dark and luminous,—I fancied streaming with tears. I watched her as she returned to the table. Her walk seemed to me peculiarly graceful; light, and rapid, and yet full of decision and dignity. A thrill of delight passed through my heart as I guessed at her moistened lids.

"Sweet fellow-countrywoman," I cried in silence, "you have the divine gift of feeling." And I returned to the fresco with a deepened sense of its virtue. When I turned around, my companions had left the room.

In spite of the great heat, I was prepared thoroughly to "do" Milan. In fact, I rather enjoyed the heat; it seemed to my Northern senses to deepen the Italian, the Southern, the local character of things. On that blazing afternoon, I have not forgotten, I went to the church of St Ambrose, to the Ambrosian Library, to a dozen minor churches. Every step distilled a richer drop into the wholesome cup of pleasure. From my earliest manhood, beneath a German sky, I had dreamed of this Italian pilgrimage, and, after much waiting and working and planning, I had at last undertaken it in a spirit of fervent devotion. There had been moments in Germany when I fancied myself a clever man; but it now seemed to me that for the first time I really *felt* my intellect. Imagination, panting and exhausted, withdrew from the game; and Observation stepped into her place, trembling and glowing with open-eyed desire.

I had already been twice to the Cathedral, and had wandered through the clustering inner darkness of the high arcades which support those light-defying pinnacles and spires. Towards the close of the afternoon I found myself strolling once more over the great column-planted, altar-studded pavement, with the view of ascending to the roof. On presenting myself at the little door in the right transept, through which you gain admission to the upper regions, I perceived my late fellow-visitors of the fresco preparing apparently for an upward movement, but not without some reluctance on the paternal side. The poor gentleman had been accommodated with a chair, on which he sat fanning himself with his hat and looking painfully apoplectic. The sacristan meanwhile held open the door with an air of invitation. But my corpulent friend, with his thumb in his Murray, balked at the ascent. Recognizing me, his face expressed a sudden sense of vague relief.

"Have you been up, sir?" he inquired, groaningly.

I answered that I was about to ascend; and recalling then the fact, which I possessed rather as information than experience, that young American ladies may not improperly detach themselves on occasion from the parental side, I ventured to declare that, if my friend was unwilling to encounter the fatigue of mounting to the roof in person, I should be most happy, as a fellow-countryman, qualified already perhaps to claim a traveller's acquaintance, to accompany and assist his daughter.

"You're very good, sir," said the poor man; "I confess that I'm about played out. I'd far rather sit here and watch these pretty Italian ladies saying their prayers. Charlotte, what do you say?"

"Of course if you're tired I should be sorry to have you make the effort," said Charlotte. "But I believe the great thing is to see the view from the roof. I'm much obliged to the gentleman."

It was arranged accordingly that we should ascend together. "Good luck to you," cried my friend, "and mind you take good care of her."

Those who have rambled among the marble immensities of the summit of Milan Cathedral will hardly expect me to describe them. It is only when they have been seen as a complete concentric whole that they can be properly appreciated. It was not as a whole that I saw them; a week in Italy had assured me that I have not the architectural *coup d'œil*. In looking back on the scene into which we emerged from the stifling spiral of the ascent, I have chiefly a confused sense of an immense skyward elevation and a fierce blinding efflorescence of fantastic forms of marble. There, reared for the action of the sun, you find a vast marble world. The solid whiteness lies in mighty slabs along the iridescent slopes of nave and transept, like the lonely snow-fields of the higher Alps. It leaps and climbs and shoots and attacks the unsheltered blue with a keen and joyous incision. It meets the pitiless sun with a more than equal glow; the day falters, declines, expires, but the marble shines forever, unmelted and unintermittent. You will know what I mean if you have looked upward from the Piazza at midnight. With confounding frequency too, on some uttermost point of a pinnacle, its plastic force explodes into satisfied rest in some perfect flower of a figure. A myriad carven statues, known only to the circling air, are poised and niched beyond reach of human vision, the loss of which to mortal eyes is, I suppose, the gain of the Church and the Lord. Among all the jewelled shrines and overwrought tabernacles of Italy, I have seen no such magnificent waste of labor, no such glorious synthesis of cunning secrets. As you wander, sweating and blinking, over the changing levels of the edifice, your eye catches at a hundred points the little profile of a little saint, looking out into the dizzy air, a pair of folded hands praying to the bright immediate heavens, a sandalled monkish foot planted on the edge of the white abyss. And then, besides this mighty world of the great Cathedral itself, you possess the view of all green Lombardy,—vast, lazy Lombardy, resting from its Alpine upheavals.

My companion carried a little white umbrella, with a violet lining. Thus protected from the sun, she climbed and gazed with abundant courage and spirit. Her movements, her glance, her voice, were full of intelligent pleasure. Now that I could observe her closely, I saw that, though perhaps without regular beauty, she was yet, for youth, summer, and Italy, more than pretty enough. Owing to my residence in Germany, among Germans, in a small university town, Americans had come to have for me, in a large degree, the interest of novelty and remoteness. Of the charm of American women, in especial, I had formed a very high estimate, and I was more than ready to be led captive by the far-famed graces of their frankness and freedom. I already felt that in the young girl beside me there was a different quality of womanhood from any that I had recently known; a keenness, a maturity, a conscience, which deeply stirred my curiosity. It was positive, not negative maidenhood.

"You're an American," I said, as we stepped to look at the distance.

"Yes; and you?" In her voice alone the charm faltered. It was high, thin, and nervous.

"Oh, happily, I'm also one."

"I shouldn't have thought so. I should have taken you for a German."

"By education I am a German. I knew you were an American the moment I looked at you."

"I suppose so. It seems that American women are easily recognized. But don't talk about America." She paused and swept her dark eye over the whole immensity of prospect. "This is Italy," she cried, "Italy, Italy!"

"Italy indeed. What do you think of the Leonardo?"

"I fancy there can be only one feeling about it. It must be the saddest and finest of all pictures. But I know nothing of art. I have seen nothing yet but that lovely Raphael in the Brera."

"You have a vast deal before you. You're going southward, I suppose."

"Yes, we are going directly to Venice. There I shall see Titian."

"Titian and Paul Veronese."

"Yes, I can hardly believe it. Have you ever been in a gondola?"

"No; this is my first visit to Italy."

"Ah, this is all new, then, to you as well."

"Divinely new," said I, with fervor.

She glanced at me, with a smile,—a ray of friendly pleasure in my pleasure. "And you are not disappointed!"

"Not a jot. I'm too good a German."

"I'm too good an American. I live at Araminta, New Jersey!"

We thoroughly "did" the high places of the church, concluding with an ascent into the little gallery of the central spire. The view from this spot is beyond all words, especially the view toward the long mountain line which shuts out the North. The sun was sinking: clear and serene upon their blue foundations, the snow-peaks sat clustered and scattered, and shrouded in silence and light. To the south the long shadows fused and multiplied, and the bosky Lombard flats melted away into perfect Italy. This prospect offers a great emotion to the Northern traveller. A vague, delicious impulse of conquest stirs in his heart. From his dizzy vantage-point, as he looks down at her, beautiful, historic, exposed, he embraces the whole land in the far-reaching range of his desire. "That is Monte Rosa," I said; "that is the Simplon pass; there is the triple glitter of those lovely lakes."

"Poor Monte Rosa," said my companion.

"I'm sure I never thought of Monte Rosa as an object of pity."

"You don't know what she represents. She represents the genius of the North. There she stands, frozen and fixed, resting her head upon that mountain wall, looking over at this lovely southern world and yearning towards it forever in vain."

"It is very well she can't come over. She would melt."

"Very true. She is beautiful, too, in her own way. I mean to fancy that I am her chosen envoy, and that I have come up here to receive her blessing."

I made an attempt to point out a few localities. "Yonder lies Venice, out of sight. In the interval are a dozen divine little towns. I hope to visit them all. I shall ramble all day in their streets and churches, their little museums, and their great palaces. In the evening I shall sit at the door of a café in the little piazza, scanning some lovely civic edifice in the moonlight, and saying, 'Ah! this is Italy!'"

"You gentlemen are certainly very happy. I'm afraid we must go straight to Venice."

"Your father insists upon it?"

"He wishes it. Poor father! in early life he formed the habit of being in a hurry, and he can't break it even now, when, being out of business, he has nothing on earth to do."

"But in America I thought daughters insisted as well as fathers."

The young girl looked at me, half serious, half smiling. "Have you a mother?" she asked; and then, blushing the least bit at her directness and without waiting for an answer, "This is not America," she said. "I should like to think I might become for a while a creature of Italy."

Somehow I felt a certain contagion in her momentary flash of frankness. "I strongly suspect," I said, "that you are American to the depths of your soul, and that you'll never be anything else; I hope not."

In this hope of mine there was perhaps a little impertinence;

but my companion looked at me with a gentle smile, which seemed to hint that she forgave it. "You, on the other hand," she said, "are a perfect German, I fancy; and you'll never be anything else."

"I am sure I wish with all my heart," I answered, "to be a good American. I'm open to conversion. Try me."

"Thank you; I haven't the ardor; I'll make you over to my father. We mustn't forget, by the way, that he is waiting for us."

We did forget it, however, a while longer. We came down from the tower and made our way to the balustrade which edges the front of the edifice, and looked down on the city and the piazza below. Milan had, to my sense, a peculiar charm of temperate gayety,—the softness of the South without its laxity; and I felt as if I could gladly spend a month there. The common life of the streets was beginning to stir and murmur again, with the subsiding heat and the approaching night. There came up into our faces a delicious emanation as from the sweetness of Transalpine life. At the little balconies of the windows, beneath the sloping awnings, with their feet among the crowded flower-pots and their plump bare arms on the iron rails, lazy, dowdy Italian beauties would appear, still drowsy with the broken *siesta*. Beautiful, slim young officers had begun to dot the pavement, glorious with their clanking swords, their brown moustaches, and their legs of azure. In gentle harmony with these, various ladies of Milan were issuing forth to enjoy the cool; elegant, romantic, provoking, in short black dresses and lace mantillas depending from their *chignons*, with a little cloud of powder artfully enhancing the darkness of their hair and eyes. How it all wasn't Germany! how it couldn't have been Araminta, New Jersey! "It's the South, the South," I kept repeating,—"the South in nature, in man, in manners." It was a brighter world. "It's the South," I said to my companion. "Don't you feel it in all your nerves?"

"O, it's very pleasant," she said.

"We must forget all our cares and duties and sorrows. We must go in for the beautiful. Think of this great trap for the sunbeams, in this city of yellows and russets and crimsons, of liquid vowels and glancing smiles being, like one of our Northern cathedrals, a temple to Morality and Conscience. It doesn't belong to heaven, but to earth,—to love and light and pleasure."

My friend was silent a moment. "I'm glad I'm not a Catholic," she said at last. "Come, we must go down."

We found the interior of the Cathedral delightfully cool and shadowy. The young lady's father was not at our place of ingress, and we began to walk through the church in search of him. We met a number of Milanese ladies, who charmed us with their sombre elegance and the Spanish romance of their veils. With these pale penitents and postulants my companion had a lingering sisterly sympathy.

"Don't you wish you were a Catholic now?" I asked. "It would be so pleasant to wear one of those lovely mantillas."

"The mantillas are certainly becoming," she said. "But who knows what horrible old-world sorrows and fears and remorses they cover? Look at this person." We were standing near the great altar. As she spoke, a woman rose from her knees, and as she drew the folds of her lace mantle across her bosom, fixed her large dark eyes on us with a peculiar significant intensity. She was of less than middle age, with a pale, haggard face, a certain tarnished elegance of dress, and a remarkable nobleness of gesture and carriage. She came towards us, with an odd mixture, in her whole expression, of decency and defiance. "Are you English?" she said in Italian. "You are very pretty. Is he a brother or a lover?"

"He is neither," said I, affecting a tone of rebuke.

"Neither? only a friend! You are very happy to have a friend, Signorina. Ah, you are pretty! You were watching me at my prayers just now; you thought me very curious, apparently. I don't care. You may see me here any day. But I devoutly hope you may never have to pray such bitter, bitter prayers as mine. A thousand excuses." And she went her way.

"What in the world does she mean?" said my companion.

"Monte Rosa," said I, "was the genius of the North. This poor woman is the genius of the Picturesque. She shows us the essential misery that lies behind it. It's not an unwholesome lesson to receive at the outset. Look at her sweeping down the aisle. What a poise of the head! The picturesque is handsome, all the same."

"I do wonder what is her trouble," murmured the young girl. "She has swept away an illusion in the folds of those black garments."

"Well," said I, "here is a solid fact to replace it." My eyes had just lighted upon the object of our search. He sat in a chair, half tilted back against a pillar. His chin rested on his shirt-bosom, and his hands were folded together over his waistcoat, where it most protruded. Shirt and waistcoat rose and fell with visible, audible regularity. I wandered apart and left his daughter to deal with him. When she had fairly aroused him, he thanked me heartily for my care of the young lady, and expressed the wish that we might meet again. "We start to-morrow for Venice," he said. "I want awfully to get a whiff of the sea-breeze and to see if there is anything to be got out of a gondola."

As I expected also to be in Venice before many days, I had little doubt of our meeting. In consideration of this circumstance, my friend proposed that we should exchange cards; which we accordingly did, then and there, before the high altar, above the gorgeous chapel which enshrines the relics of St Charles Borromeus. It was thus that I learned his name to be Mr Mark Evans.

"Take a few notes for us!" said Miss Evans, as I shook her hand in farewell.

I spent the evening, after dinner, strolling among the crowded streets of the city, tasting of Milanese humanity. At the door of a café I perceived Mr Evans seated at a little round table. He seemed to have discovered the merits of absinthe. I wondered where he had left his daughter. She was in her room, I fancied, writing her journal.

The fortnight which followed my departure from Milan was in all respects memorable and delightful. With an interest that hourly deepened as I read, I turned the early pages of the enchanting romance of Italy. I carried out in detail the programme which I had sketched for Miss Evans. Those few brief days, as I look back on them, seem to me the sweetest, fullest, calmest of my life. All personal passions, all restless egotism, all worldly hopes, regrets, and fears were stilled and absorbed in the steady perception of the material present. It exhaled the pure essence of romance. What words can reproduce the picture which these Northern Italian towns project upon a sympathetic retina? They are shabby, deserted, dreary, decayed, unclean. In those August days the southern sun poured into them with a fierceness which might have seemed fatal to any lurking shadow of picturesque mystery. But taking them as cruel time had made them and left them, I found in them an immeasurable instruction and charm. My perception seemed for the first time to live a sturdy creative life of its own. How it fed upon the mouldy crumbs of the festal past! I have always thought the observant faculty a windy impostor, so long as it refuses to pocket pride and doff its bravery and crawl on all-fours, if need be, into the un-illumined corners and crannies of life. In these dead cities of Verona, Mantua, Padua, how life had revelled and postured in its strength! How sentiment and passion had blossomed and flowered! How much of history had been performed! What a wealth of mortality had ripened and decayed! I have never elsewhere got so deep an impression of the social secrets of mankind. In England, even, in those verdure-stifled haunts

of domestic peace which muffle the sounding chords of
British civilization, one had a fainter sense of the possible
movement and fruition of individual character. Beyond a
certain point you fancy it merged in the general medium of
duty, business, and politics. In Italy, in spite of your knowledge of the strenuous public conscience which once inflamed
these compact little states, the unapplied, spontaneous moral
life of society seems to have been more active and more
subtle. I walked about with a volume of Stendhal in my
pocket; at every step I gathered some lingering testimony to
the exquisite vanity of ambition.

But the great emotion, after all, was to feel myself among
scenes in which art had ranged so freely. It had often enough
been bad, but it had never ceased to be art. An invincible
instinct of beauty had presided at life,—an instinct often
ludicrously crude and primitive. Wherever I turned I found
a vital principle of grace,—from the smile of a chambermaid
to the curve of an arch. My memory reverts with an especial
tenderness to certain hours in the dusky, faded saloons of
those vacant, ruinous palaces which boast of "collections."
The pictures are frequently poor, but the visitor's impression
is generally rich. The brick-tiled floors are bare; the doors
lack paint; the great windows, curtains; the chairs and tables
have lost their gilding and their damask drapery; but the ghost
of a graceful aristocracy treads at your side and does the
melancholy honors of the abode with a dignity that brooks
no sarcasm. You feel that art and piety here have been blind,
generous instincts. You are reminded in persuasive accents
of the old personal regimen in human affairs. Certain pictures are veiled and curtained *virginibus puerisque*. Through
these tarnished halls lean and patient abbés led their youthful
virginal pupils. Have you read Stendhal's *Chartreuse de
Parme*? There was such a gallery in the palace of the Duchess
of San Severino. After a long day of strolling, lounging, and
staring, I found a singularly perfect pleasure in sitting at the

door of a café in the warm starlight, eating an ice and making an occasional experiment in the way of talk with my neighbors. I recall with peculiar fondness and delight three sweet sessions in the delicious Piazza dei Signori at Verona. The Piazza is small, compact, private almost, accessible only to pedestrians, paved with great slabs which have known none but a gentle human tread. On one side of it rises in elaborate elegance and grace, above its light arched *loggia*, the image-bordered mass of the ancient palace of the Council; facing these stand two sterner, heavier, buildings, dedicated to municipal offices and to the lodgement of soldiers. Step through the archway which leads out of the Piazza and you will find a vast quadrangle with a staircase climbing sunward, along the wall, a row of gendarmes sitting in the shade, a group of soldiers cleaning their muskets, a dozen persons of either sex leaning downward from the open windows. At one end of the little square rose into the pale darkness the high slender shaft of a brick campanile; in the centre glittered steadily a colossal white statue of Dante. Behind this statue was the Caffè Dante, where on three successive days I sat till midnight, feeling the scene, learning its sovereign "distinction." But of Verona I shall not pretend to speak. As I drew near Venice I began to feel a soft impatience, an expectant tremor of the heart. The day before reaching it I spent at Vicenza. I wandered all day through the streets, of course, looking at Palladio's palaces and enjoying them in defiance of reason and Ruskin. They seemed to me essentially rich and palatial. In the evening I resorted, as usual, to the city's generous heart, the decayed ex-glorious Piazza. This spot at Vicenza affords you a really soul-stirring premonition of Venice. There is no Byzantine Basilica and no Ducal Palace; but there is an immense impressive hall of council, and a soaring campanile, and there are two discrowned columns telling of defeated Venetian dominion. Here I seated myself before a café door, in a group of gossiping votaries of the

Southern night. The tables being mostly occupied, I had some difficulty in finding one. In a short time I perceived a young man walking through the crowd, seeking where he might bestow himself. Passing near me, he stopped and asked me with irresistible grace if he might share my table. I cordially assented; he sat down and ordered a glass of sugar and water. He was of about my own age, apparently, and full of the opulent beauty of the greater number of young Italians. His dress was simple even to shabbiness; he might have been a young prince in disguise, a Haroun-al-Raschid. With small delay we engaged in conversation. My companion was boyish, modest, and gracious; he nevertheless discoursed freely on the things of Vicenza. He was so good as to regret that we had not met earlier in the day; it would have given him such pleasure to accompany me on my tour of the city. He was passionately fond of art: he was in fact an artist. Was I fond of pictures? Was I inclined to purchase? I answered that I had no desire to purchase modern pictures, that in fact I had small means to purchase any. He informed me that he had a beautiful ancient work which, to his great regret, he found himself compelled to sell; a most divine little Correggio. Would I do him the favor to look at it? I had small belief in the value of this unrenowned masterpiece; but I felt a kindness for the young painter. I consented to have him call for me the next morning and take me to his house, where for two hundred years, he assured me, the work had been jealously preserved.

He came punctually, beautiful, smiling, shabby, as before. After a ten minutes' walk we stopped before a gaudy half-palazzo which rejoiced in a vague Palladian air. In the basement, looking on the court, lived my friend; with his mother, he informed me, and his sister. He ushered me in, through a dark antechamber, into which, through a gaping kitchen door, there gushed a sudden aroma of onions. I found myself in a high, half-darkened saloon. One of the windows was

open into the court, from which the light entered verdantly
through a row of flowering plants. In an arm-chair near the
window sat a young girl in a dressing-gown, empty-handed,
pale, with wonderful eyes, apparently an invalid. At her side
stood a large elderly woman in a rusty black silk gown, with
an agreeable face, flushed a little, apparently with the expectation of seeing me. The young man introduced them as his
mother and his sister. On a table near the window, propped
upright in such a way as to catch the light, was a small picture
in a heavy frame. I proceeded to examine it. It represented in
simple composition a Madonna and Child; the mother facing
you, pressing the infant to her bosom, faintly smiling, and
looking out of the picture with a solemn sweetness. It was
pretty, it was good; but it was not Correggio. There was
indeed a certain suggestion of his exquisite touch; but it was
a likeness merely, and not the precious reality. One fact,
however, struck swiftly home to my consciousness: the face
of the Madonna bore a singular resemblance to that of Miss
Evans. The lines, the character, the expression, were the
same; the faint half-thoughtful smile was hers, the feminine
frankness and gentle confidence of the brow, from which the
dark hair waved back with the same even abundance. All this,
in the Madonna's face, was meant for heaven; and on Miss
Evans's in a fair degree, probably, for earth. But the mutual
likeness was, nevertheless, perfect, and it quickened my
interest in the picture to a point which the intrinsic merit of
the work would doubtless have failed to justify; although I
confess that I was now not slow to discover a great deal of
agreeable painting in it.

"But I doubt of its being a Correggio," said I.

"A Correggio, I give you my word of honor, sir!" cried
my young man.

"*Ecco!* my son's word of honor," cried his mother.

"I don't deny," I said, "that it is a very pretty work. It is
perhaps Parmigianino."

"O no, sir," the elder insisted, "a true Correggio! We have had it two hundred years! Try another light; you will see. A true Correggio! Isn't it so, my daughter?"

The young man put his arm in mine, played his fingers airily over the picture, and whispered of a dozen beauties.

"O, I grant you," said I, "it's a very pretty picture." As I looked at it I felt the dark eyes of the young girl in the armchair fixed upon me with almost unpleasant intensity. I met her gaze for a moment: I found in it a strange union of defiant pride and sad despondent urgency.

"What do you ask for the picture?" I said.

There was a silence.

"Speak, *madre mia*," said the young man.

"*La senta!*" and the lady played with her broken fan. "We should like you to name a price."

"O, if I named a price, it would not be as for a Correggio. I can't afford to buy Correggios. If this were a real Correggio, you would be rich. You should go to a duke, a prince, not to me."

"We should be rich! Do you hear, my children? We are very poor, sir. You have only to look at us. Look at my poor daughter. She was once beautiful, fresh, gay. A year ago she fell ill: a long story, sir, and a sad one. We have had doctors; they have ordered five thousand things. My daughter gets no better. There it is, sir. We are very poor."

The young girl's look confirmed her mother's story. That she had been beautiful I could easily believe; that she was ill was equally apparent. She was still remarkable indeed for a touching, hungry, unsatisfied grace. She remained silent and motionless, with her eyes fastened upon my face. I again examined the pretended Correggio. It was wonderfully like Miss Evans. The young American rose up in my mind with irresistible vividness and grace. How she seemed to glow with strength, freedom, and joy, beside this sombre, fading, Southern sister! It was a happy thought that, under the benediction of her image, I might cause a ray of healing sunshine to fall at this poor girl's feet.

"Have you ever tried to sell the picture before?"

"Never!" said the old lady, proudly. "My husband had it from his father. If we have made up our minds to part with it now,—most blessed little Madonna!—it is because we have had an intimation from heaven."

"From heaven?"

"From heaven, Signore. My daughter had a dream. She dreamed that a young stranger came to Vicenza, and that he wandered about the streets saying, 'Where, ah where, is my blessed Lady?' Some told him in one church, and some told him in another. He went into all the churches and lifted all the curtains, giving great fees to the sacristans! But he always came out shaking his head and repeating his question, 'Where is my blessed Lady? I have come from over the sea, I have come to Italy to find her!'" The woman delivered herself of this recital with a noble florid unction and a vast redundancy, to my Northern ear, of delightful liquid sounds. As she paused momentarily, her daughter spoke for the first time.

"And then I fancied," said the young girl, "that I heard his voice pausing under my window at night. 'His blessed Lady is here,' I said, 'we must not let him lose her.' So I called my brother and bade him go forth in search of you. I dreamed that he brought you back. We made an altar with candles and lace and flowers, and on it we placed the little picture. The stranger had light hair, light eyes, a flowing beard like you. He kneeled down before the little Madonna and worshipped her. We left him at his devotions and went away. When we came back the candles on the altar were out: the Madonna was gone, too; but in its place there burned a bright pure light. It was a purse of gold!"

"What a very pretty story!" said I. "How many pieces were there in the purse?"

The young man burst into a laugh. "Twenty thousand!" he said.

I made my offer for the picture. It was esteemed generous apparently; I was cordially thanked. As it was inconvenient, however, to take possession of the work at that moment, I agreed to pay down but half the sum, reserving the other half to the time of delivery. When I prepared to take my departure the young girl rose from her chair and enabled me to measure at once her weakness and her beauty. "Will you come back for the picture yourself?" she asked.

"Possibly. I should like to see you again. You must get better."

"O, I shall never get better."

"I can't believe that. I shall perhaps have a dream to tell you!"

"I shall soon be in heaven. I shall send you one."

"Listen to her!" cried the mother. "But she is already an angel."

With a farewell glance at my pictured Madonna I departed. My visit to this little Vicenza household had filled me with a painful, indefinable sadness. So beautiful they all were, so civil, so charming, and yet so mendacious and miserable! As I hurried along in the train toward the briny cincture of Venice, my heart was heavy with the image of that sombre, dying Italian maiden. Her face haunted me. What fatal wrong had she suffered? What hidden sorrow had blasted the fresh-ness of her youth? As I began to smell the nearing Adriatic, my fancy bounded forward to claim asylum in the calmer presence of my bright American friend. I have no space to tell the story of my arrival in Venice and my first impressions. Mr Evans had not mentioned his hotel. He was not at the Hotel de l'Europe, whither I myself repaired. If he was still in Venice, however, I foresaw that we should not fail to meet. The day succeeding my arrival I spent in a restless fever of curiosity and delight, now lost in the sensuous ease of my

gondola, now lingering in charmed devotion before a canvas
of Tintoretto or Paul Veronese. I exhausted three gondoliers
and saw all Venice in a passionate fury and haste. I wished to
probe its fulness and learn at once the best—or the worst.
Late in the afternoon I disembarked at the Piazzetta and took
my way haltingly and gazingly to the many-domed Basilica,
—that shell of silver with a lining of marble. It was that
enchanting Venetian hour when the ocean-touching sun sits
melting to death, and the whole still air seems to glow with
the soft effusion of his golden substance. Within the church,
the deep brown shadow-masses, the heavy thick-tinted air,
the gorgeous composite darkness, reigned in richer, quainter,
more fantastic gloom than my feeble pen can reproduce the
likeness of. From those rude concavities of dome and semi-
dome, where the multitudinous facets of pictorial mosaic
shimmer and twinkle in their own dull brightness; from the
vast antiquity of innumerable marbles, incrusting the walls
in roughly mated slabs, cracked and polished and triple-
tinted with eternal service; from the wavy carpet of compacted
stone, where a thousand once-bright fragments glimmer
through the long attrition of idle feet and devoted knees;
from sombre gold and mellow alabaster, from porphyry and
malachite, from long dead crystal and the sparkle of undying
lamps,—there proceeds a dense rich atmosphere of splendor
and sanctity which transports the half-stupefied traveller to
the age of a simpler and more awful faith. I wandered for
half an hour beneath those reverted cups of scintillating darkness, stumbling on the great stony swells of the pavement as
I gazed upward at the long mosaic saints who curve giganti-
cally with the curves of dome and ceiling. I had left Europe;
I was in the East. An overwhelming sense of the sadness of
man's spiritual history took possession of my heart. The
clustering picturesque shadows about me seemed to represent
the darkness of a past from which he had slowly and painfully struggled. The great mosaic images, hideous, grotesque,

inhuman, glimmered like the cruel spectres of early super-
stitions and terrors. There came over me, too, a poignant
conviction of the ludicrous folly of the idle spirit of travel.
How with Murray and an opera-glass it strolls and stares
where omniscient angels stand diffident and sad! How blunted
and stupid are its senses! How trivial and superficial its
imaginings! To this builded sepulchre of trembling hope and
dread, this monument of mighty passions, I had wandered in
search of pictorial effects. O vulgarity! Of course I remained,
nevertheless, still curious of effects. Suddenly I perceived a
very agreeable one. Kneeling on a low *prie-dieu*, with her
hands clasped, a lady was gazing upward at the great mosaic
Christ in the dome of the choir. She wore a black lace shawl
and a purple hat. She was Miss Evans. Her attitude slightly
puzzled me. Was she really at her devotions, or was she only
playing at prayer? I walked to a distance, so that she might
have time to move before I addressed her. Five minutes afterwards, however, she was in the same position. I walked
slowly towards her, and as I approached her attracted her
attention. She immediately recognized me and smiled and
bowed, without moving from her place.

"I saw you five minutes ago," I said, "but I was afraid of
interrupting your prayers."

"O, they were only half-prayers," she said.

"Half-prayers are pretty well for one who only the other
day was thanking Heaven that she was not a Catholic."

"Half-prayers are no prayers. I'm not a Catholic, yet."

Her father, she told me, had brought her to the church, but
had returned on foot to the hotel for his pocket-book. They
were to dine at one of the restaurants in the Piazza. Mr Evans
was vastly contented with Venice, and spent his days and
nights in gondolas. Awaiting his return, we wandered over
the church. Yes, incontestably, Miss Evans resembled my
little Vicenza picture. She looked a little pale with the heat
and the constant nervous tension of sight-seeing; but she

pleased me now as effectually as she had pleased me before. There was an even deeper sweetness in the freedom and breadth of her utterance and carriage. I felt more even than before that she was an example of woman active, not of woman passive. We strolled through the great Basilica in serious, charmed silence. Miss Evans told me that she had been there much: she seemed to know it well. We went into the dark Baptistery and sat down on a bench against the wall, trying to discriminate in the vaulted dimness the harsh mediæval reliefs behind the altar and the mosaic Crucifixion above it.

"Well," said I, "what has Venice done for you?"

"Many things. Tired me a little, saddened me, charmed me."

"How have you spent your time?"

"As people spend it. After breakfast we get into our gondola and remain in it pretty well till bedtime. I believe I know every canal, every canaletto, in Venice. You must have learned already how sweet it is to lean back under the awning, to feel beneath you that steady, liquid lapse, to look out at all this bright, sad elegance of ruin. I have been reading two or three of George Sand's novels. Do you know *La Dernière Aldini?* I fancy a romance in every palace."

"The reality of Venice seems to me to exceed all romance. It's romance enough simply to be here."

"Yes; but how brief and transient a romance!"

"Well," said I, "we shall certainly cease to be here, but we shall never cease to have been here. You are not to leave directly, I hope."

"In the course of ten days or a fortnight, we go to Florence."

"And then to Rome?"

"To Rome and Naples, and then by sea, probably, to Genoa, and thence to Nice and Paris. We must be at home by the new year. And you?"

"I hope to spend the winter in Italy."

"Are you never coming home again?"

"By no means. I shall probably return in the spring. But I wish you, too, were going to remain."

"You are very good. My father pronounces it impossible. I have only to make the most of it while I'm here."

"Are you going back to Araminta?"

Miss Evans was silent a moment. "O, don't ask!" she said.

"What kind of a place is Araminta?" I asked, maliciously.

Again she was silent. "That is John the Baptist on the cover of the basin," she said, at last, rising to her feet, with a light laugh.

On emerging from the Baptistery we found Mr Evans, who greeted me cordially and insisted on my coming to dine with them. I think most fondly of our little dinner. We went to the Caffè Quadri and occupied a table beside an open window, looking out into the Piazza, which was beginning to fill with evening loungers and listeners to the great band of music in the centre. Miss Evans took off her hat and sat facing me in friendly silence. Her father sustained the larger burden of conversation. He seemed to feel its weight, however, as the dinner proceeded and when he had attacked his second bottle of wine. Miss Evans then questioned me about my journey from Milan. I told her the whole story, and felt that I infused into it a great deal of color and heat. She sat charming me forward with her steady, listening smile. For the first time in my life I felt the magic of sympathy. After dinner we went down into the Piazza and established ourselves at one of Florian's tables. Night had become perfect; the music was magnificent. At a neighboring table was a group of young Venetian gentlemen, splendid in dress, after the manner of their kind, and glorious with the wondrous physical glory of the Italian race.

"They only need velvet and satin and plumes," I said, "to be subjects for Titian and Paul Veronese."

They sat rolling their dark eyes and kissing their white hands at passing friends, with smiles that were like the moon-flashes on the Adriatic.

"They are beautiful exceedingly," said Miss Evans; "the most beautiful creatures in the world, except——"

"Except, you mean, this other gentleman."

She assented. The person of whom I had spoken was a young man who was just preparing to seat himself at a vacant table. A lady and gentleman, elderly persons, had passed near him and recognized him, and he had uncovered himself and now stood smiling and talking. They were all genuine Anglo-Saxons. The young man was rather short of stature, but firm and compact. His hair was light and crisp, his eye a clear blue, face and neck violently tanned by exposure to the sun. He wore a pair of small blonde whiskers.

"Do you call him beautiful?" demanded Mr Evans. "He reminds me of myself when I was his age. Indeed, he looks like you, sir."

"He's not beautiful," said Miss Evans, "but he is hand-some."

The young man's face was full of decision and spirit; his whole figure had been moulded by action, tempered by effort. He looked simple and keen, upright, downright.

"Is he English?" asked Miss Evans, "or American?"

"He is both," I said, "or either. He is made of that precious clay that is common to the whole English-speaking race."

"He's American."

"Very possibly," said I; and indeed we never learned. I repeat the incident because I think it has a certain value in my recital. Before we separated I expressed the hope that we might meet again on the morrow.

"It's very kind of you to propose it," said Miss Evans; "but you'll thank us for refusing. Take my advice, as for an old Venetian, and spend the coming three days alone. How can you enjoy Tintoretto and Bellini, when you are racking your brains for small talk for me?"

"With you, Miss Evans, I shouldn't talk small. But you shape my programme with a liberal hand. At the end of three days, pray, where will you be?"

They would still be in Venice, Mr Evans declared. It was a capital hotel, and then those jolly gondolas! I was unable to impeach the wisdom of the young girl's proposition. To be so wise, it seemed to me, was to be extremely charming.

For three days, accordingly, I wandered about alone. I often thought of Miss Evans and I often fancied I should enjoy certain great pictures none the less for that deep associated contemplation and those fine emanations of assent and dissent which I should have known in her society. I wandered far; I penetrated deep, it seemed to me, into the heart of Venetian power. I shook myself free of the sad and sordid present, and embarked on that silent contemplative sea whose irresistible tides expire at the base of the mighty canvases in the Scuola di San Rocco. But on my return to the hither shore, I always found my sweet young countrywoman waiting to receive me. If Miss Evans had been an immense coquette, she could not have proceeded more cunningly than by this injunction of a three days' absence. During this period, in my imagination, she increased tenfold in value. I don't mean to say that there were not hours together when I quite forgot her, and when I had no heart but for Venice and the lessons of Venice, for the sea and sky and the great painters and builders. But when my mind had executed one of these great passages of appreciation, it turned with a sudden sense of solitude and lassitude to those gentle hopes, those fragrant hints of intimacy, which clustered about the person of my friend. She remained modestly uneclipsed by the women of Titian. She was as deeply a woman as they, and yet so much more of a person; as fit as the broadest and blondest to be loved for herself, yet full of serene superiority as an active friend. To the old, old sentiment what an exquisite modern turn she might give! I so far overruled her advice as that, with her father, we made a trio every evening, after the day's labors, at one of Florian's tables. Mr Evans drank absinthe and discoursed upon the glories of our common country, of which he declared it was high time I should make the acquaintance. He was not the least of a bore: I relished him vastly. He was in many ways an excellent representative American. Without taste, without culture or polish, he nevertheless produced an impression of substance in character, keenness in perception, and intensity in will, which effectually redeemed him from vulgarity. It often seemed to me, in fact, that his good-humored tolerance and easy morality, his rank self-confidence, his nervous decision and vivacity, his fearlessness of either gods or men, combined in proportions of which the union might have been very fairly termed aristocratic. His voice, I admit, was of the nose, nasal; but possibly, in the matter of utterance, one eccentricity is as good as another. At all events, with his clear, cold gray eye, with that just faintly impudent, more than level poise of his ample chin, with those two hard lines which flanked the bristling wings of his gray moustache, with his general expression of unchallenged security and practical aptitude and incurious scorn of tradition, he impressed the sensitive beholder as a man of incontestable force. He was entertaining, too, partly by wit and partly by position. He was weak only in his love of absinthe. After his first glass he left his chair and strolled about the piazza, looking for possible friends and superbly unconscious of possible enemies. His daughter sat back in her chair, her arms folded, her ungloved hands sustaining them, her prettiness half defined, her voice enhanced and subdued by the gas-tempered starlight. We had infinite talk. Without question, she had an admirable feminine taste; she was worthy to know Venice. I remember telling her so in a sudden explosion of homage. "You are really worthy to know Venice, Miss Evans. We must learn to know it together. Who knows what hidden treasures we may help each other to find?"

II

AT the end of my three days' probation, I spent a week constantly with my friends. Our mornings were, of course, devoted to churches and galleries, and in the late afternoon we passed and repassed along the Grand Canal or betook ourselves to the Lido. By this time Miss Evans and I had become thoroughly intimate; we had learned to know Venice together, and the knowledge had helped us to know each other. In my own mind, Charlotte Evans and Venice had played the game most effectively into each other's hands. If my fancy had been called upon to paint her portrait, my fancy would have sketched her with a background of sunset-flushed palace wall, with a faint reflected light from the green lagoon playing up into her face. And if I had wished to sketch a Venetian scene, I should have painted it from an open window, with a woman leaning against the casement,—as I had often seen her lean from a window in her hotel. At the end of a week we went one afternoon to the Lido, timing our departure so as to allow us to return at sunset. We went over in silence, Mr Evans sitting with reverted head, blowing his cigar-smoke against the dazzling sky, which told so fiercely of sea and summer; his daughter motionless and thickly veiled; I facing them, feeling the broken swerve of our gondola, and watching Venice grow level and rosy beyond the liquid interval. Near the landing-place on the hither side of the Lido is a small *trattoria* for the refreshment of visitors. An arbor outside the door, a horizontal vine checkering still further a dirty tablecloth, a pungent odour of *frittata*, an admiring circle of gondoliers and beggars, are the chief attractions of this suburban house of entertainment,—attractions sufficient, however, to have arrested the inquisitive steps of an elderly American gentleman, in whom Mr Evans speedily recognized a friend of early years, a comrade in affairs. A hearty greeting ensued. This worthy man had ordered dinner: he besought Mr Evans at least to sit down and partake of a bottle of wine. My friend vacillated between his duties as a father and the prospect of a rich old-boyish revival of the delectable interests of home; but his daughter graciously came to his assistance. "Sit down with Mr Munson, talk till you are tired, and then walk over to the beach and find us. We shall not wander beyond call."

She and I accordingly started slowly for a stroll along the barren strand which averts its shining side from Venice and takes the tides of the Adriatic. The Lido has for me a peculiar melancholy charm, and I have often wondered that I should have felt the presence of beauty in a spot so destitute of any exceptional elements of beauty. For beyond the fact that it knows the changing moods and hues of the Adriatic, this narrow strip of sand-stifled verdure has no very rare distinction. In my own country I know many a sandy beach, and many a stunted copse, and many a tremulous ocean line of little less purity and breadth of composition, with far less magical interest. The secret of the Lido is simply your sense of adjacent Venice. It is the salt-sown garden of the city of the sea. Hither came short-paced Venetians for a meagre taste of *terra firma*, or for a wider glimpse of their parent ocean. Along a narrow line in the middle of the island are market-gardens and breeze-twisted orchards, and a hint of hedges and lanes and inland greenery. At one end is a series of low fortifications duly embanked and moated and sentinelled. Still beyond these, half over-drifted with sand and over-clambered with rank grasses and coarse thick shrubbery, are certain quaintly lettered funereal slabs, tombs of former Jews of Venice. Toward these we slowly wandered and sat down in the grass.

Between the sand-heaps, which shut out the beach, we saw
in a dozen places the blue agitation of the sea. Over all the
scene there brooded the deep bright sadness of early autumn.
I lay at my companion's feet and wondered whether I was in
love. It seemed to me that I had never been so happy in my
life. They say, I know, that to be in love is not pure happiness;
that in the mood of the unconfessed, unaccepted lover there
is an element of poignant doubt and pain. Should I at once
confess myself and taste of the perfection of bliss? It seemed
to me that I cared very little for the meaning of her reply. I
only wanted to talk of love; I wanted in some manner to
enjoy in that atmosphere of romance the woman who was
so blessedly fair and wise. It seemed to me that all the agitation of fancy, the excited sense of beauty, the fervor and joy
and sadness begotten by my Italian wanderings, had suddenly
resolved themselves into a potent demand for expression.
Miss Evans was sitting on one of the Hebrew tombs, her chin
on her hand, her elbow on her knee, watching the broken
horizon. I was stretched on the grass on my side, leaning on
my elbow and on my hand, with my eyes on her face. She
bent her own eyes and encountered mine; we neither of us
spoke or moved, but exchanged a long steady regard; after
which her eyes returned to the distance. What was her feeling
toward me? Had she any sense of my emotion or of any
answering trouble in her own wonderful heart? Suppose she
should deny me: should I suffer, would I persist? At any rate,
I should have struck a blow for love. Suppose she were to
accept me; would my joy be any greater than in the mere
translation of my heartbeats? Did I in truth long merely for
a bliss which should be of that hour and that hour alone? I
was conscious of an immense respect for the woman beside
me. I was unconscious of the least desire even to touch the
hem of her garment as it lay on the grass, touching my own.
After all, it was but ten days that I had known her. How little
I really knew of her! how little else than her beauty and her

wit! How little she knew of me, of my vast outlying, unsentimental, spiritual self! We knew hardly more of each other than had appeared in this narrow circle of our common impressions of Venice. And yet if into such a circle Love had forced his way, let him take his way! Let him widen the circle! Transcendent Venice! I rose to my feet with a violent movement, and walked ten steps away. I came back and flung myself again on the grass.

"The other day at Vicenza," I said, "I bought a picture."

"Ah? an 'original'?"

"No, a copy."

"From whom?"

"From you!"

She blushed. "What do you mean?"

"It was a little pretended Correggio; a Madonna and Child."

"Is it good?"

"No, it's rather poor."

"Why, then, did you buy it?"

"Because the Madonna looked singularly like you."

"I'm sorry, Mr Brooke, you hadn't a better reason. I hope the picture was cheap."

"It was quite reason enough. I admire you more than any woman in the world."

She looked at me a moment, blushing again. "You don't know me."

"I have a suspicion of you. It's ground enough for admiration."

"O, don't talk about admiration. I'm tired of it all beforehand."

"Well, then," said I, "I'm in love."

"Not with me, I hope."

"With you, of course. With whom else?"

"Has it only just now occurred to you?"

"It has just occurred to me to say it."

Her blush had deepened a little; but a genuine smile came to its relief. "Poor Mr Brooke!" she said.

"Poor Mr Brooke indeed, if you take it in that way."

"You must forgive me if I doubt of your love."

"Why should you doubt?"

"Love, I fancy, doesn't come in just this way."

"It comes as it can. This is surely a very good way."

"I know it's a very pretty way, Mr Brooke; Venice behind us, the Adriatic before us, these old Hebrew tombs! Its very prettiness makes me distrust it."

"Do you believe only in the love that is born in darkness and pain? Poor love! it has trouble enough, first and last. Allow it a little ease."

"Listen," said Miss Evans, after a pause. "It's not with me you're in love, but with that painted picture. All this Italian beauty and delight has thrown you into a romantic state of mind. You wish to make it perfect. I happened to be at hand, so you say, 'Go to, I'll fall in love.' And you fancy me, for the purpose, a dozen fine things that I'm not."

"I fancy you beautiful and good. I'm sorry to find you so dogmatic."

"You mustn't abuse me, or we shall be getting serious."

"Well," said I, "you can't prevent me from adoring you."

"I should be very sorry to. So long as you 'adore' me, we're safe! I can tell you better things than that I'm in love with you."

I looked at her impatiently. "For instance?"

She held out her hand. "I like you immensely. As for love, I'm in love with Venice."

"Well, I like Venice immensely, but I'm in love with you."

"In that way I am willing to leave it. Pray don't speak of it again to-day. But my poor father is probably wandering up to his knees in the sand."

I had been happy before, but I think I was still happier for the words I had spoken. I had cast them abroad at all events; my heart was richer by a sense of their possible fruition. We walked far along the beach. Mr Evans was still with his friend.

"What is beyond that horizon?" said my companion.

"Greece, among other things."

"Greece! only think of it! Shall you never go there?"

I stopped short. "If you will believe what I say, Miss Evans, we may both go there." But for all answer she repeated her request that I should forbear. Before long, retracing our steps, we met Mr Evans, who had parted with his friend, the latter having returned to Venice. He had arranged to start the next morning for Milan. We went back over the lagoon in the glow of the sunset, in a golden silence which suffered us to hear the far-off ripple in the wake of other gondolas, a golden clearness so perfect that the rosy flush on the marble palaces seemed as light and pure as the life-blood on the forehead of a sleeping child. There is no Venice like the Venice of that magical hour. For that brief period her ancient glory returns. The sky arches over her like a vast imperial canopy crowded with its clustering mysteries of light. Her whole aspect is one of unspotted splendor. No other city takes the crimson evanescence of day with such magnificent effect. The lagoon is sheeted with a carpet of fire. All torpid, pallid hues of marble are transmuted to a golden glow. The dead Venetian tone brightens and quickens into life and lustre, and the spectator's enchanted vision seems to rest on an embodied dream of the great painter who wrought his immortal reveries into the ceilings of the Ducal Palace.

It was not till the second day after this that I again saw Miss Evans. I went to the little church of San Cassiano, to see a famous Tintoretto, to which I had already made several vain attempts to obtain access. At the door in the little bustling *campo* which adjoins the church I found her standing expectant. A little boy, she told me, had gone for the sacristan and his key. Her father, she proceeded to explain, had suddenly been summoned to Milan by a telegram from Mr Munson, the friend whom he had met at the Lido, who had suddenly been taken ill.

"And so you're going about alone? Do you think that's altogether proper? Why didn't you send for me?" I stood lost in wonder and admiration at the exquisite dignity of her self-support. I had heard of American girls doing such things; but I had yet to see them done.

"Do you think it less proper for me to go about alone than to send for you? Venice has seen so many worse improprieties that she'll forgive me mine."

The little boy arrived with the sacristan and his key, and we were ushered into the presence of Tintoretto's Crucifixion. This great picture is one of the greatest of the Venetian school. Tintoretto, the travelled reader will remember, has painted two masterpieces on this tremendous theme. The larger and more complex work is at the Scuola di San Rocco; the one of which I speak is small, simple, and sublime. It occupies the left side of the narrow choir of the shabby little church which we had entered, and is remarkable as being, with two or three exceptions, the best preserved work of its incomparable author. Never, in the whole range of art, I imagine, has so powerful an effect been produced by means so simple and select; never has the intelligent choice of means to an effect been pursued with such a refinement of perception. The picture offers to our sight the very central essence of the great tragedy which it depicts. There is no swooning Madonna, no consoling Magdalen, no mockery of contrast, no cruelty of an assembled host. We behold the silent summit of Calvary. To the right are the three crosses, that of the Saviour foremost. A ladder pitched against it supports a turbaned executioner, who bends downward to receive the sponge offered him by a comrade. Above the crest of the hill the helmets and spears of a line of soldiery complete the grimness of the scene. The reality of the picture is beyond all words: it is hard to say which is more impressive, the naked horror of the fact represented, or the sensible power of the artist. You breathe a silent prayer of thanks that you, for your part, are without the terrible clairvoyance of genius. We sat and looked at the picture in silence. The sacristan loitered about; but finally, weary of waiting, he retired to the *campo* without. I observed my companion; pale, motionless, oppressed, she evidently felt with poignant sympathy the commanding force of the work. At last I spoke to her; receiving no answer, I repeated my question. She rose to her feet and turned her face upon me, illumined with a vivid ecstasy of pity. Then passing me rapidly, she descended into the aisle of the church, dropped into a chair, and, burying her face in her hands, burst into an agony of sobs. Having allowed time for her feeling to expend itself, I went to her and recommended her not to let the day close on this painful emotion. "Come with me to the Ducal Palace," I said; "let us look at the Rape of Europa." But before departing we went back to our Tintoretto, and gave it another solemn half-hour. Miss Evans repeated aloud a dozen verses from St Mark's Gospel.

"What is it here," I asked, "that has moved you most, the painter or the subject?"

"I suppose it's the subject. And you?"

"I'm afraid it's the painter."

We went to the Ducal Palace, and immediately made our way to that transcendent shrine of light and grace, the room which contains the masterpiece of Paul Veronese, and the Bacchus and Ariadne of his solemn comrade. I steeped myself with unprotesting joy in the gorgeous glow and salubrity of that radiant scene, wherein, against her bosky screen of immortal verdure, the rosy-footed, pearl-circled, nymph-flattered victim of a divine delusion rustles her lustrous satin against the ambrosial hide of bovine Jove. "It makes one think more agreeably of life," I said to my friend, "that such visions have blessed the eyes of men of mortal mould. What has been may be again. We may yet dream as brightly, and some few of us translate our dreams as freely."

"This, I think, is the brighter dream of the two," she answered, indicating the Bacchus and Ariadne. Miss Evans, on the whole, was perhaps right. In Tintoretto's picture there is no shimmer of drapery, no splendor of flowers and gems; nothing but the broad, bright glory of deep-toned sea and sky, and the shining purity and symmetry of deified human flesh. "What do you think," asked my companion, "of the painter of that tragedy at San Cassiano being also the painter of this dazzling idyl; of the great painter of darkness being also the great painter of light?"

"He was also a colorist! Let us thank the great man, and be colorists too. To understand this Bacchus and Ariadne we ought to spend a long day on the lagoon, beyond sight of Venice. Will you come to-morrow to Torcello?" The proposition seemed to me audacious; I was conscious of blushing a little as I made it. Miss Evans looked at me and pondered. She then replied with great calmness that she preferred to wait for her father, the excursion being one that he would probably enjoy. "Will you come, then,—somewhere?" I asked.

Again she pondered. Suddenly her face brightened. "I should very much like to go to Padua. It would bore my poor father to go. I fancy he would thank you for taking me. I should be almost willing," she said with a smile, "to go alone."

It was easily arranged that on the morrow we should go for the day to Padua. Miss Evans was certainly an American to perfection. Nothing remained for me, as the good American which I aspired to be, but implicitly to respect her confidence. To Padua, by an early train, we accordingly went. The day stands out in my memory delightfully curious and rich. Padua is a wonderful little city. Miss Evans was an excellent walker, and, thanks to the broad arcades which cover the footways in the streets, we rambled for hours in perpetual shade. We spent an hour at the famous church of St Anthony, which boasts one of the richest and holiest shrines in all church-burdened Italy. The whole edifice is nobly and darkly ornate and picturesque, but the chapel of its patron saint—a wondrous combination of chiselled gold and silver and alabaster and perpetual flame—splendidly outshines and outshadows the rest. In all Italy, I think, the idea of palpable, material sanctity is nowhere more potently enforced.

"O the Church, the Church!" murmured Miss Evans, as we stood contemplating.

"What a real pity," I said, "that we are not Catholics; that that dazzling monument is not something more to us than a mere splendid show! What a different thing this visiting of churches would be for us, if we occasionally felt the prompting to fall on our knees. I begin to grow ashamed of this perpetual attitude of bald curiosity. What a pleasant thing it must be, in such a church as this, for two good friends to say their prayers together!"

"*Ecco!*" said Miss Evans. Two persons had approached the glittering shrine,—a young woman of the middle class and a man of her own rank, some ten years older, dressed with a good deal of cheap elegance. The woman dropped on her knees; her companion fell back a few steps, and stood gazing idly at the chapel. "Poor girl!" said my friend, "she believes; he doubts."

"He doesn't look like a doubter. He's a vulgar fellow. They're a betrothed pair, I imagine. She is very pretty." She had turned round and flung at her companion a liquid glance of entreaty. He appeared not to observe it; but in a few moments he slowly approached her, and bent a single knee at her side. When presently they rose to their feet, she passed her arm into his with a beautiful, unsuppressed lovingness. As they passed us, looking at us from the clear darkness of their Italian brows, I keenly envied them. "They are better off than we," I said. "Be they husband and wife, or lovers, or simply friends, we I think, are rather vulgar beside them."

"My dear Mr Brooke," said Miss Evans, "go by all means and say your prayers." And she walked away to the other side of the church. Whether I obeyed her injunction or not, I feel under no obligation to report. I rejoined her at the beautiful frescoed chapel in the opposite transept. She was sitting listlessly turning over the leaves of her Murray. "I suppose," she said, after a few moments, "that nothing is more vulgar than to make a noise about having been called vulgar. But really, Mr Brooke, don't call me so again. I have been of late so fondly fancying I am not vulgar."

"My dear Miss Evans, you are—"

"Come, nothing vulgar!"

"You're divine!"

"*A la bonne heure!* Divinities needn't pray. They are prayed to."

I have no space and little power to enumerate and describe the various curiosities of Padua. I think we saw them all. We left the best, however, for the last, and repaired in the late afternoon, after dining fraternally at a restaurant, to the Chapel of Giotto. This little empty church, standing unshaded and forlorn in the homely market-garden which was once a Roman arena, offers one of the deepest lessons of Italian travel. Its four walls are covered, almost from base to ceiling, with that wonderful series of dramatic paintings which usher in the golden prime of Italian art. I had been so ill-informed as to fancy that to talk about Giotto was to make more or less of a fool of one's self, and that he was the especial property of the mere sentimentalists of criticism. But you no sooner cross the threshold of that little ruinous temple—a mere empty shell, but coated as with the priceless substance of fine pearls and vocal with a murmured eloquence as from the infinite of art—than you perceive with whom you have to deal: a complete painter of the very strongest sort. In one respect, assuredly, Giotto has never been surpassed—in the art of presenting a story. The amount of dramatic expression compressed into those quaint little scenic squares would equip a thousand later masters. How, beside him, they seem to fumble and grope and trifle! And he, beside them, how direct he seems, how essential, how masculine! What a solid simplicity, what an immediate purity and grace! The exhibition suggested to my friend and me more wise reflections than we had the skill to utter. "Happy, happy art," we said, as we seemed to see it beneath Giotto's hand tremble and thrill and sparkle, almost, with a presentiment of its immense career, "for the next two hundred years what a glorious felicity will be yours!" The chapel door stood open into the sunny corn-field, and the lazy litter of verdure enclosed by the crumbling oval of Roman masonry. A loutish boy who had come with the key lounged on a bench, awaiting tribute, and gazing at us as we gazed. The ample light flooded the inner precinct, and lay hot upon the coarse, pale surface of the painted wall. There seemed an irresistible pathos in such a combination of shabbiness and beauty. I thought of this subsequently at the beautiful Museum at Bologna, where mediocrity is so richly enshrined. Nothing that we had yet seen together had filled us with so deep a sense of enjoyment. We stared, we laughed, we wept almost, we raved with a decent delight. We went over the little compartments one by one: we lingered and returned and compared; we studied; we melted together in unanimous homage. At last the light began to fade and the little saintly figures to grow quaint and terrible in the gathering dusk. The loutish boy had transferred himself significantly to the door-post: we lingered for a farewell glance.

"Mr Brooke," said my companion, "we ought to learn from all this to be *real;* real even as Giotto is real; to discriminate between genuine and factitious sentiment; between the substantial and the trivial; between the essential and the superfluous; sentiment and sentimentality."

"You speak," said I, "with appalling wisdom and truth. You strike a chill to my heart of hearts."

She spoke unsmiling, with a slightly contracted brow and an apparent sense of effort. She blushed as I gazed at her.

"Well," she said, "I'm extremely glad to have been here. Good, wise Giotto! I should have liked to know you,—Nay, let me pay the boy." I saw the piece she put into his hand; he was stupefied by its magnitude.

"We shall not have done Padua," I said, as we left the garden, "unless we have been to the Caffè Pedrocchi. Come to the Caffè Pedrocchi. We have more than an hour before our train,—time to eat an ice." So we drove to the Caffè Pedrocchi, the most respectable *café* in the world; a *café* monumental, scholastic, classical.

We sat down at one of the tables on the cheerful external platform, which is washed by the gentle tide of Paduan life. When we had finished our ices, Miss Evans graciously allowed me a cigar. How it came about I hardly remember, but, prompted by some happy accident of talk, and gently encouraged perhaps by my smoke-wreathed quietude, she lapsed, with an exquisite feminine reserve, into a delicate auto-biographical strain. For a moment she became egotistical; but with a modesty, a dignity, a lightness of touch which filled my eyes with admiring tears. She spoke of her home, her family, and the few events of her life. She had lost her mother in her early years; her two sisters had married young; she and her father were equally united by affection and habit. Upon one theme she touched, in regard to which I should be at loss to say whether her treatment told more, by its frank-ness, of our friendship, or, by its reticence, of her modesty. She spoke of having been engaged, and of having lost her betrothed in the Civil War. She made no story of it; but I felt from her words that she had tasted of sorrow. Having finished my cigar, I was proceeding to light another. She drew out her watch. Our train was to leave at eight o'clock. It was now a quarter past. There was no later evening train.

The reader will understand that I tell the simple truth when I say that our situation was most disagreeable and that we were deeply annoyed. "Of course," said I, "you are utterly disgusted."

She was silent. "I am extremely sorry," she said, at last, just vanquishing a slight tremor in her voice.

"Murray says the hotel is good," I suggested.

She made no answer. Then, rising to her feet, "Let us go immediately," she said. We drove to the principal inn and bespoke our rooms. Our want of luggage provoked, of course, a certain amount of visible surprise. This, however, I fancy, was speedily merged in a more flattering emotion, when my companion, having communed with the chambermaid, sent her forth with a list of purchases.

We separated early. "I hope," said I, as I bade her goodnight, "that you will be fairly comfortable."

She had recovered her equanimity. "I have no doubt of it."

"Good night."

"Good night." Thank God, I silently added, for the dignity of American women. Knowing to what suffering a similar accident would have subjected a young girl of the orthodox European training, I felt devoutly grateful that among my own people a woman and her reputation are more indissolubly one. And yet I was unable to detach myself from my Old-World associations effectually enough not to wonder whether, after all, Miss Evans's calmness might not be the simple calmness of despair. The miserable words rose to my lips, "Is she Compromised?" If she were, of course, as far as I was concerned, there was but one possible sequel to our situation.

We met the next morning at breakfast. She assured me that she had slept, but I doubted it. I myself had not closed my eyes,—not from the excitement of vanity. Owing partly, I suppose, to a natural reaction against our continous talk on the foregoing day, our return to Venice was attended with a good deal of silence. I wondered whether it was a mere fancy that Miss Evans was pensive, appealing, sombre. As we entered the gondola to go from the railway station to the Hotel Danieli, she asked me to request the gondoliers to pass along the Canalezzo rather than through the short cuts of the smaller canals. "I feel as if I were coming home," she said, as we floated beneath the lovely façade of the Ca' Doro. Suddenly she laid her hand on my arm. "It seems to me," she said, "that I should like to stop for Mrs L—," and she mentioned the wife of the American Consul. "I have promised to show her some jewelry. This is a particularly good time. I shall ask her to come home with me." We stopped accordingly at the American Consulate. Here we found, on inquiry, to my great regret, that the Consul and his wife had gone for a week to the Lake of Como. For a moment my companion meditated. Then, "To the hotel," she said with decision. Our arrival attracted apparently little notice. I went with Miss Evans to the door of her father's sitting-room, where we met a servant, who informed us with inscrutable gravity that Monsieur had returned the evening before, but that he had gone out after breakfast and had not reappeared.

"Poor father," she said. "It was very stupid of me not to have left a note for him." I urged that our absence for the night was not to have been foreseen, and that Mr Evans had in all likelihood very plausibly explained it. I withdrew with a handshake and permission to return in the evening.

I went to my hotel and slept, a long, sound, dreamless sleep. In the afternoon I called my gondola, and went over to the Lido. I crossed to the outer shore and sought the spot where a few days before I had lain at the feet of Charlotte Evans. I stretched myself on the grass and fancied her present. To say that I *thought* would be to say at once more and less than the literal truth. I was in a tremulous glow of feeling. I listened to the muffled rupture of the tide, vaguely conscious of my beating heart. Was I or was I not in love? I was able to settle nothing. I wandered musingly further and further from the point. Every now and then, with a deeper pulsation of the heart, I would return to it, but only to start afresh and follow some wire-drawn thread of fancy to a nebulous goal of doubt. That she was a most lovely woman seemed to me of all truths the truest, but it was a hard-featured fact of the senses rather than a radiant mystery of faith. I felt that I was not possessed by a passion; perhaps I was incapable of passion. At last, weary of self-bewilderment, I left the spot and wandered beside the sea. It seemed to speak more musingly than ever of the rapture of motion and freedom. Beyond the horizon was Greece, beyond and below was the wondrous Southern world which blooms about the margin of the Mid-land Sea. To marry, somehow, meant to abjure all this, and in the prime of youth and manhood to sink into obscurity and care. For a moment there stirred in my heart a feeling of anger and pain. Perhaps, after all, I *was* in love!

I went straight across the lagoon to the Hotel Danieli, and as I approached it I became singularly calm and collected. From below I saw Miss Evans alone on her balcony, watching the sunset. She received me with perfect friendly composure. Her father had again gone out, but she had told him of my coming, and he was soon to return. He had not been pain-fully alarmed at her absence, having learned through a chambermaid, to whom she had happened to mention her intention, that she had gone for the day to Padua.

"And what have you been doing all day?" I asked.

"Writing letters,—long, tiresome, descriptive letters. I have also found a volume of Hawthorne, and have been reading 'Rappacini's Daughter.' You know the scene is laid in Padua." And what had I been doing?

Whether I was in a passion of love or not, I was enough in

love to be very illogical. I was disappointed, Heaven knows why! that she should have been able to spend her time in this wholesome fashion. "I have been at the Lido, at the Hebrew tombs, where we sat the other day, thinking of what you told me there."

"What I told you?"

"That you liked me immensely."

She smiled; but now that she smiled, I fancied I saw in the movement of her face an undercurrent of pain. Had the peace of her heart been troubled? "You needn't have gone so far away to think of it."

"It's very possible," I said, "that I shall have to think of it, in days to come, farther away still."

"Other places, Mr Brooke, will bring other thoughts."

"Possibly. This place has brought that one." At what prompting it was that I continued I hardly know; I *would* tell her that I loved her. "I value it beyond all other thoughts."

"I do like you, Mr Brooke. Let it rest there."

"It may rest there for you. It can't for me. It begins there! Don't refuse to understand me."

She was silent. Then, bending her eyes on me, "Perhaps," she said, "I understand you too well."

"O, in Heaven's name, don't play at coldness and scepticism!"

She dropped her eyes gravely on a bracelet which she had locked and unlocked on her wrist. "I think," she said, without raising them, "you had better leave Venice." I was about to reply, but the door opened and Mr Evans came in. From his hard, grizzled brow he looked at us in turn; then, greeting me with an extended hand, he spoke to his daughter.

"I have forgotten my cigar-case. Be so good as to fetch it from my dressing-table."

For a moment Miss Evans hesitated and cast upon him a faint protesting glance. Then she lightly left the room. He stood holding my hand, with a very sensible firmness, with his eyes on mine. Then, laying his other hand heavily on my shoulder, "Mr Brooke," he said, "I believe you are an honest man."

"I hope so," I answered.

He paused, and I felt his steady gray eyes. "How the devil," he said, "came you to be left at Padua?"

"The explanation is a very simple one. Your daughter must have told you."

"I have thought best to talk very little to my daughter about it."

"Do you regard it, Mr Evans," I asked, "as a very serious calamity?"

"I regard it as an infernally disagreeable thing. It seems that the whole hotel is talking about it. There is a little beast of an Italian downstairs—"

"Your daughter, I think, was not seriously discomposed."

"My daughter is a d—d proud woman!—'

"I can assure you that my esteem for her is quite equal to your own."

"What does that mean, Mr Brooke?" I was about to answer but Miss Evans reappeared. Her father, as he took his cigar-case from her, looked at her intently, as if he were on the point of speaking, but the words remained on his lips, and, declaring that he would be back in half an hour, he left the room.

His departure was followed by a long silence.

"Miss Evans," I said, at last, "will you be my wife?"

She looked at me with a certain firm resignation. "Do you *feel* that, Mr Brooke? Do you know what you ask?"

"Most assuredly."

"Will you rest content with my answer?"

"It depends on what your answer is."

She was silent.

"I should like to know what my father said to you in my absence."

"You had better learn from himself."

"I think I know. Poor father!"

"But you give me no answer," I rejoined, after a pause.

She frowned a little. "Mr Brooke," she said, "you disappoint me."

"Well, I'm sorry. Don't revenge yourself by disappointing me."

"I fancied that I had answered your proposal; that I had, at least, anticipated it, the other day at the Lido."

"O, that was very good for the other day; but do give me something different now."

"I doubt of your being more in earnest to-day than then."

"It seems to suit you wonderfully well to doubt!"

"I thank you for the honor of your proposal: but I can't be your wife, Mr Brooke."

"That's the answer with which you ask me to remain satisfied!"

"Let me repeat what I said just now. You had better leave Venice, otherwise we must leave it."

"Ah, that's easy to say!"

"You mustn't think me unkind or cynical. You have done your duty."

"My duty—what duty?"

"Come," she said, with a beautiful blush and the least attempt at a smile, "you imagine that I have suffered an injury by my being left with you at Padua. I don't believe in such injuries."

"No more do I."

"Then there is even less wisdom than before in your proposal. But I strongly suspect that if we had not missed the train at Padua, you would not have made it. There is an idea of reparation in it—O Sir!" And she shook her head with a deepening smile.

"If I had flattered myself that it lay in my power to do you an injury," I replied, "I should now be rarely disenchanted. As little almost as to do you a benefit!"

"You have loaded me with benefits. I thank you from the bottom of my heart. I may be very unreasonable, but if I have doubted of my having to decline your offer three days ago, I should have quite ceased to doubt this evening."

"You are an excessively proud woman. I can tell you that."

"Possibly. But I'm not as proud as you think. I believe in my common sense."

"I wish that for five minutes you had a grain of imagination!"

"If only for the same five minutes you were without it. You have too much, Mr Brooke. You imagine you love me."

"Poor fool that I am!"

"You imagine that I'm charming. I assure you I'm not in the least. Here in Venice I have not been myself at all. You should see me at home."

"Upon my word, Miss Evans, you remind me of a German philosopher. I have not the least objection to seeing you at home."

"Don't fancy that I think lightly of your offer. But we have been living, Mr Brooke, in poetry. Marriage is stern prose. Do let me bid you farewell!"

I took up my hat. "I shall go from here to Rome and Naples," I said. "I must leave Florence for the last. I shall write you from Rome and of course see you there."

"I hope not. I had rather not meet you again in Italy. It perverts our dear good old American truth!"

"Do you really propose to bid me a final farewell?"

She hesitated a moment. "When do you return home?"

"Some time in the spring."

"Very well. If a year hence, in America, you are still of your present mind, I shall not decline to see you. I feel very safe! If you are not of your present mind, of course I shall be still more happy. Farewell." She put out her hand; I took it.

"Beautiful, wonderful woman!" I murmured.

"That's rank poetry! Farewell!"

I raised her hand to my lips and released it in silence. At this point Mr Evans reappeared, considering apparently that his half-hour was up. "Are you going?" he asked.

"Yes. I start to-morrow for Rome."

"The deuce! Daughter, when are we to go?"

She moved her hand over her forehead, and a sort of nervous tremor seemed to pass through her limbs. "Oh, you must take me home?" she said. "I'm terribly home-sick!" She flung her arms round his neck and buried her head on his shoulder. Mr Evans with a movement of his head dismissed me.

At the top of the staircase, however, he overtook me. "You made your offer!" And he passed his arm into mine.

"Yes!"

"And she refused you?" I nodded. He looked at me, squeezing my arm. "By Jove, sir, if she had accepted—"

"Well!" said I, stopping.

"Why, it wouldn't in the least have suited me! Not that I don't esteem you. The whole house shall see it." With his arm in mine we passed downstairs, through the hall, to the landing-place, where he called his own gondola and requested me to use it. He bade me farewell with a kindly hand-shake, and the assurance that I was too "nice a fellow not to keep as a friend."

I think, on the whole, that my uppermost feeling was a sense of freedom and relief. It seemed to me on my journey to Florence that I had started afresh, and was regarding things with less of nervous rapture than before, but more of sober insight. Of Miss Evans I forbade myself to think. In my deepest heart I admitted the truth, the partial truth at least, of her assertion of the unreality of my love. The reality I believed would come. The way to hasten its approach was, meanwhile, to study, to watch, to observe,—doubtless even to enjoy. I certainly enjoyed Florence and the three days I spent there. But I shall not attempt to deal with Florence in a parenthesis. I subsequently saw that divine little city under circumstances which peculiarly colored and shaped it. In Rome, to begin with, I spent a week and went down to Naples, dragging the heavy Roman chain which she rivets about your limbs forever. In Naples I discovered the real South—the Southern South,—in art, in nature, in man, and the least bit in woman. A German lady, an old kind friend, had given me a letter to a Neapolitan lady whom she assured me she held in high esteem. The Signora B—— was at Sorrento, where I presented my letter. It seemed to me that "esteem" was not exactly the word; but the Signora B—— was charming. She assured me on my first visit that she was a "true Neapolitan," and I think, on the whole, she was right. She told me that I was a true German, but in this she was altogether wrong. I spent four days in her house; on one of them we went to Capri, where the Signora had an infant—her only one—at nurse. We saw the Blue Grotto, the Tiberian ruins, the tarantella and the infant, and returned late in the evening by moonlight. The Signora sang on the water in a magnificent contralto. As I looked upward at Northern Italy, it seemed, in contrast, a cold, dark hyperborean clime, a land of order, conscience, and virtue. How my heart went out to that brave, rich, compact little Verona! How there Nature seemed to have mixed her colors with potent oil, instead of as here with crystalline water, drawn though it was from the Neapolitan Bay! But in Naples, too, I pursued my plan of vigilance and study. I spent long mornings at the Museum and learned to know Pompeii; I wrote once to Miss Evans, about the statues in the Museum, without a word of wooing, but received no answer. It seemed to me that I returned to Rome a wiser man. It was the middle of October when I reached it. Unless Mr Evans had altered his programme, he would at this moment be passing down to Naples.

A fortnight elapsed without my hearing of him, during

which I was in the full fever of initiation into Roman wonders. I had been introduced to an old German archæologist, with whom I spent a series of memorable days in the exploration of ruins and the study of the classical topography. I thought, I lived, I ate and drank, in Latin, and German Latin at that. But I remember with especial delight certain long lonely rides on the Campagna. The weather was perfect. Nature seemed only to slumber, ready to wake far on the hither side of wintry death. From time to time, after a passionate gallop, I would pull up my horse on the slope of some pregnant mound and embrace with the ecstasy of quickened senses the tragical beauty of the scene; strain my ear to the soft low silence, pity the dark dishonored plain, watch the heavens come rolling down in tides of light, and breaking in waves of fire against the massive stillness of temples and tombs. The aspect of all this sunny solitude and haunted vacancy used to fill me with a mingled sense of exaltation and dread. There were moments when my fancy swept that vast funereal desert with passionate curiosity and desire, moments when it felt only its potent sweetness and its high historic charm. But there were other times when the air seemed so heavy with the exhalation of unburied death, so bright with sheeted ghosts, that I turned short about and galloped back to the city. One afternoon after I had indulged in one of these super-sensitive flights on the Campagna, I betook myself to St Peter's. It was shortly before the opening of the recent Council, and the city was filled with foreign ecclesiastics, the increase being of course especially noticeable in the churches. At St Peter's they were present in vast numbers; great armies encamped in prayer on the marble plains of its pavement: an inexhaustible physiognomical study. Scattered among them were squads of little tonsured neophytes, clad in scarlet, marching and counter-marching, and ducking and flapping, like poor little raw recruits for the heavenly host. I had never before, I think, received an equal impression of the greatness of this church of churches, or, standing beneath the dome, beheld such a vision of erected altitude,—of the builded sublime. I lingered awhile near the brazen image of St Peter, observing the steady procession of his devotees. Near me stood a lady in mourning, watching with a weary droop of the head the grotesque deposition of kisses. A peasant-woman advanced with the file of the faithful and lifted up her little girl to the well-worn toe. With a sudden movement of impatience the lady turned away, so that I saw her face to face. She was strikingly pale, but as her eyes met mine the blood rushed into her cheeks. This lonely mourner was Miss Evans. I advanced to her with an outstretched hand. Before she spoke I had guessed at the truth.

"You're in sorrow and trouble!"

She nodded, with a look of simple gravity.

"Why in the world haven't you written to me?"

"There was no use. I seem to have sufficed to myself."

"Indeed, you have not sufficed to yourself. You are pale and worn; you look wretchedly." She stood silent, looking about her with an air of vague unrest. "I have as yet heard nothing," I said. "Can you speak of it?"

"O Mr Brooke!" she said with a simple sadness that went to my heart. I drew her hand through my arm and led her to the extremity of the left transept of the church. We sat down together, and she told me of her father's death. It had happened ten days before, in consequence of a severe apoplectic stroke. He had been ill but a single day, and had remained unconscious from first to last. The American physician had been extremely kind, and had relieved her of all care and responsibility. His wife had strongly urged her to come and stay in their house, until she should have determined what to do; but she had preferred to remain at her hotel. She had immediately furnished herself with an attendant in the person of a French maid, who had come with her to the church and was now at confession. At first she had wished greatly to

leave Rome, but now that the first shock of grief had passed
away she found it suited her mood to linger on from day to
day. "On the whole," she said, with a sober smile, "I have
got through it all rather easily than otherwise. The common
cares and necessities of life operate strongly to interrupt and
dissipate one's grief. I shall feel my loss more when I get
home again." Looking at her while she talked, I found a
pitiful difference between her words and her aspect. Her pale
face, her wilful smile, her spiritless gestures, spoke most
forcibly of loneliness and weakness. Over this gentle weakness and dependence I secretly rejoiced; I felt in my heart an
immense uprising of pity,—of the pity that goes hand in
hand with love. At its bidding I hastily, vaguely sketched a
magnificent scheme of devotion and protection.

"When I think of what you have been through," I said,
"my heart stands still for very tenderness. Have you made
any plans?" She shook her head with such a perfection of
helplessness that I broke into a sort of rage of compassion:
"One of the last things your father said to me was that you
are a very proud woman."

She colored faintly. "I may have been! But there is not
among the most abject peasants who stand kissing St Peter's
foot a creature more bowed in humility than I."

"How did you expect to make that weary journey home?"

She was silent a moment and her eyes filled with tears.
"O don't cross-question me, Mr Brooke!" she softly cried;
"I expected nothing. I was waiting for my stronger self."

"Perhaps your stronger self has come." She rose to her
feet as if she had not heard me, and went forward to meet
her maid. This was a decent, capable-looking person, with a
great deal of apparent deference of manner. As I rejoined them,
Miss Evans prepared to bid me farewell. "You haven't yet
asked me to come and see you," I said.

"Come, but not too soon?"

"What do you call too soon? This evening?"

"Come to-morrow." She refused to allow me to go with her to her carriage. I followed her, however, at a short interval, and went as usual to my restaurant to dine. I remember that my dinner cost ten francs,—it usually cost me five. Afterwards, as usual, I adjourned to the Caffè Greco, where I met my German archæologist. He discoursed with even more than his wonted sagacity and eloquence; but at the end of half an hour he rapped his fist on the table and asked me what the deuce was the matter; he would wager I hadn't heard a word of what he said.

I went forth the next morning into the Roman streets, doubting heavily of my being able to exist until evening without seeing Miss Evans. I felt, however, that it was due to her to make the effort. To help myself through the morning, I went into the Borghese Gallery. The great treasure of this collection is a certain masterpiece of Titian. I entered the room in which it hangs by the door facing the picture. The room was empty, save that before the great Titian, beside the easel of an absent copyist, stood a young woman in mourning. This time, in spite of her averted head, I immediately knew her and noiselessly approached her. The picture is one of the finest of its admirable author,—rich and simple and brilliant with the true Venetian fire. It unites the charm of an air of latent symbolism with a steadfast splendor and solid perfection of design. Beside a low sculptured well sit two young and beautiful women: one richly clad, and full of mild dignity and repose; the other with unbound hair, naked, ungirdled by a great reverted mantle of Venetian purple, and radiant with the frankest physical sweetness and grace. Between them a little winged cherub bends forward and thrusts his chubby arm into the well. The picture glows with the inscrutable chemistry of the prince of colorists.

"Does it remind you of Venice?" I said, breaking a long silence, during which she had not noticed me.

She turned and her face seemed bright with reflected color.

We spoke awhile of common things; she had come alone. "What an emotion, for one who has loved Venice," she said, "to meet a Titian in other lands."

"They call it," I answered—and as I spoke my heart was in my throat,—"a representation of Sacred and Profane Love. The name perhaps roughly expresses its meaning. The serious, stately woman is the likeness, one may say, of love as an experience,—the gracious, impudent goddess of love as a sentiment; this of the passion that fancies, the other of the passion that knows." And as I spoke I passed my arm, in its strength, around her waist. She let her head sink on my shoulders and looked up into my eyes.

"One may stand for the love I denied," she said; "and the other—"

"The other," I murmured, "for the love which, with this kiss, you accept." I drew her arm into mine, and before the envious eyes that watched us from gilded casements we passed through the gallery and left the palace. We went that afternoon to the Pamfili-Doria Villa. Saying just now that my stay in Florence was peculiarly colored by circumstances, I meant that I was there with my wife.

A PASSIONATE PILGRIM

I

INTENDING to sail for America in the early part of June, I determined to spend the interval of six weeks in England, of which I had dreamed much but as yet knew nothing. I had formed in Italy and France a resolute preference for old inns, deeming that what they sometimes cost the ungratified body they repay the delighted mind. On my arrival in London, therefore, I lodged at a certain antique hostelry far to the east of Temple Bar, deep in what I used to denominate the Johnsonian city. Here, on the first evening of my stay, I descended to the little coffee-room and bespoke my dinner of the genius of decorum, in the person of the solitary waiter. No sooner had I crossed the threshold of this apartment than I felt I had mown the first swath in my golden-ripe crop of British "impressions." The coffee-room of the Red-Lion, like so many other places and things I was destined to see in England, seemed to have been waiting for long years, with just that sturdy sufferance of time written on its visage, for me to come and gaze, ravished but unamazed.

The latent preparedness of the American mind for even the most delectable features of English life is a fact which I never fairly probed to its depths. The roots of it are so deeply buried in the virgin soil of our primary culture, that, without some great upheaval of experience, it would be hard to say exactly when and where and how it begins. It makes an American's enjoyment of England an emotion more fatal and sacred than his enjoyment, say, of Italy or Spain. I had seen the coffee-room of the Red-Lion years ago, at home,—at Saragossa, Illinois,—in books, in visions, in dreams, in

Dickens, in Smollett, and Boswell. It was small, and sub-divided into six small compartments by a series of perpendicular screens of mahogany, something higher than a man's stature, furnished on either side with a narrow uncushioned ledge, denominated in ancient Britain a seat. In each of the little dining-boxes thus immutably constituted was a small table, which in crowded seasons was expected to accommodate the several agents of a fourfold British hungriness. But crowded seasons had passed away from the Red-Lion forever. It was crowded only with memories and ghosts and atmosphere. Round the room there marched, breast-high, a magnificent panelling of mahogany, so dark with time and so polished with unremitted friction, that by gazing awhile into its lucid blackness I fancied I could discern the lingering images of a party of gentlemen in periwigs and short-clothes, just arrived from York by the coach. On the dark yellow walls, coated by the fumes of English coal, of English mutton, of Scotch whiskey, were a dozen melancholy prints, sallow-toned with age,—the Derby favorite of the year 1807, the Bank of England, her Majesty the Queen. On the floor was a Turkey carpet—as old as the mahogany, almost, as the Bank of England, as the Queen,—into which the waiter in his lonely revolutions had trodden so many massive soot-flakes and drops of overflowing beer, that the glowing looms of Smyrna would certainly not have recognized it. To say that I ordered my dinner of this superior being would be altogether to misrepresent the process, owing to which, having dreamed of lamb and spinach, and a charlotte-russe, I sat down in penitence to a mutton-chop and a rice pudding. Bracing my feet against the cross-beam of my little oaken table, I opposed to the mahogany partition behind me that vigorous dorsal resistance which expresses the old-English idea of repose. The sturdy screen refused even to creak; but my poor Yankee joints made up the deficiency. While I was waiting for my chop there came into the room a person whom I took to be

my sole fellow-lodger. He seemed, like myself, to have submitted to proposals for dinner; the table on the other side of
my partition had been prepared to receive him. He walked
up to the fire, exposed his back to it, consulted his watch, and
looked apparently out of the window, but really at me. He
was a man of something less than middle age and more than
middle stature, though indeed you would have called him
neither young nor tall. He was chiefly remarkable for his
exaggerated leanness. His hair, very thin on the summit of
his head, was dark, short, and fine. His eye was of a pale,
turbid gray, unsuited, perhaps, to his dark hair and brow, but
not altogether out of harmony with his colorless, bilious
complexion. His nose was aquiline and delicate; beneath it
hung a thin, comely, dark mustache. His mouth and chin
were meagre and uncertain of outline; not vulgar, perhaps, but
weak. A cold, fatal, gentlemanly weakness, indeed, seemed
expressed in his attentuated person. His eye was restless and
deprecating; his whole physiognomy, his manner of shifting
his weight from foot to foot, the spiritless droop of his head,
told of exhausted purpose, of a will relaxed. His dress was
neat and careful, with an air of half-mourning. I made up my
mind on three points: he was unmarried, he was ill, he was
not an Englishman. The waiter approached him, and they
murmured momentarily in barely audible tones. I heard the
words "claret," "sherry," with a tentative inflection, and
finally "beer," with a gentle affirmative. Perhaps he was a
Russian in reduced circumstances; he reminded me of a certain
type of Russian which I had met on the Continent. While I
was weighing this hypothesis,—for you see I was interested,—
there appeared a short, brisk man with reddish-brown hair,
a vulgar nose, a sharp blue eye, and a red beard, confined to
his lower jaw and chin. My impecunious Russian was still
standing on the rug, with his mild gaze bent on vacancy; the
other marched up to him, and with his umbrella gave him
a playful poke in the concave frontage of his melancholy

waistcoat. "A penny-ha'penny for your thoughts!" said the new-comer.

His companion uttered an exclamation, stared, then laid his two hands on the other's shoulders. The latter looked round at me keenly, compassing me in a momentary glance. I read in its own high light that this was an American eye-beam; and with such confidence that I hardly needed to see its owner, as he prepared, with his friend, to seat himself at the table adjoining my own, take from his overcoat-pocket three New York papers and lay them beside his plate. As my neighbors proceeded to dine, I became conscious that, through no indiscretion of my own, a large portion of their conversation made its way over the top of our dividing partition and mingled its savor with that of my simple re-past. Occasionally their tone was lowered, as with the inten-tion of secrecy; but I heard a phrase here and a phrase there distinctly enough to grow very curious as to the burden of the whole, and, in fact, to succeed at last in guessing it. The two voices were pitched in an unforgotten key, and equally native to our Cisatlantic air; they seemed to fall upon the muffled medium of surrounding parlance as the rattle of pease on the face of a drum. They were American, however, with a difference; and I had no hesitation in assigning the lighter and softer of the two to the pale, thin gentleman, whom I decidedly preferred to his comrade. The latter began to question him about his voyage.

"Horrible, horrible! I was deadly sick from the hour we left New York."

"Well, you do look considerably reduced," his friend affirmed.

"Reduced! I've been on the verge of the grave. I haven't slept six hours in three weeks." This was said with great gravity. "Well, I have made the voyage for the last time."

"The deuce you have! You mean to stay here forever?"

"Here, or somewhere! It's likely to be a short forever."

There was a pause; after which: "You're the same cheerful old boy, Searle. Going to die to-morrow, eh!"

"I almost wish I were."

"You're not in love with England, then? I've heard people say at home that you dressed and talked and acted like an Englishman. But I know Englishmen, and I know you. You're not one of them, Searle, not you. You'll go under here, sir; you'll go under as sure as my name is Simmons."

Following this, I heard a sudden clatter, as of the dropping of a knife and fork. "Well, you're a delicate sort of creature, Simmons! I have been wandering about all day in this accursed city, ready to cry with home-sickness and heart-sickness and every possible sort of sickness, and thinking, in the absence of anything better, of meeting you here this evening, and of your uttering some syllable of cheer and comfort, and giving me some feeble ray of hope. Go under? Am I not under now? I can't sink lower, except to sink into my grave!"

Mr Simmons seems to have staggered a moment under this outbreak of passion. But the next, "Don't cry, Searle," I heard him say. "Remember the waiter. I've grown Englishman enough for that. For heaven's sake, don't let us have any feelings. Feelings will do nothing for you here. It's best to come to the point. Tell me in three words what you expect of me."

I heard another movement, as if poor Searle had collapsed in his chair. "Upon my word, Simmons, you are inconceivable. You got my letter?"

"Yes, I got your letter. I was never sorrier to get anything in my life."

At this declaration Mr Searle rattled out an oath, which it was well perhaps that I but partially heard. "John Simmons," he cried, "what devil possesses you? Are you going to betray me here in a foreign land, to turn out a false friend, a heartless rogue?"

"Go on, sir," said sturdy Simmons. "Pour it all out. I'll wait till you have done.—Your beer is very bad," to the waiter. "I'll have some more."

"For God's sake, explain yourself!" cried Searle.

There was a pause, at the end of which I heard Mr Simmons set down his empty tankard with emphasis. "You poor morbid man," he resumed, "I don't want to say anything to make you feel sore. I pity you. But you must allow me to say that you have acted like a blasted fool!"

Mr Searle seemed to have made an effort to compose himself. "Be so good as to tell me what was the meaning of your letter."

"I was a fool, myself, to have written that letter. It came of my infernal meddlesome benevolence. I had much better have let you alone. To tell you the plain truth, I never was so horrified in my life as when I found that on the strength of that letter you had come out here to seek your fortune."

"What did you expect me to do?"

"I expected you to wait patiently till I had made further inquiries and had written to you again."

"You have made further inquiries now?"

"Inquiries! I have made assaults."

"And you find I have no claim?"

"No claim to call a claim. It looked at first as if you had a very pretty one. I confess the idea took hold of me—"

"Thanks to your preposterous benevolence!"

Mr Simmons seemed for a moment to experience a difficulty in swallowing. "Your beer is undrinkable," he said to the waiter. "I'll have some brandy.—Come, Searle," he resumed, "don't challenge me to the arts of debate, or I'll settle right down on you. Benevolence, as I say, was part of it. The reflection that if I put the thing through it would be a very pretty feather in my cap and a very pretty penny in my purse was part of it. And the satisfaction of seeing a poor nobody of a Yankee walk right into an old English estate was a good deal of it. Upon my word, Searle, when I think of it, I wish with all my heart that, erratic genius as you are, you had a claim, for the very beauty of it! I should hardly care what you did with the confounded property when you got it. I could leave you alone to turn it into Yankee notions,—into ducks and drakes, as they call it here. I should like to see you stamping over it and kicking up its sacred dust in their very faces!"

"You don't know me, Simmons!" said Searle, for all response to this untender benediction.

"I should be very glad to think I didn't, Searle. I have been to no small amount of trouble for you. I have consulted by main force three first-rate men. They smile at the idea. I should like you to see the smile negative of one of these London big-wigs. If your title were written in letters of fire, it wouldn't stand being sniffed at in that fashion. I sounded in person the solicitor of your distinguished kinsman. He seemed to have been in a manner forewarned and forearmed. It seems your brother George, some twenty years ago, put forth a feeler. So you are not to have the glory of even frightening them."

"I never frightened any one," said Searle, "I shouldn't begin at this time of day. I should approach the subject like a gentleman."

"Well, if you want very much to do something like a gentleman, you've got a capital chance. Take your disappointment like a gentleman."

I had finished my dinner, and I had become keenly interested in poor Mr Searle's mysterious claim; so interested that it was vexatious to hear his emotions reflected in his voice without noting them in his face. I left my place, went over to the fire, took up the evening paper, and established a post of observation behind it.

Lawyer Simmons was in the act of choosing a soft chop from the dish,—an act accompanied by a great deal of prying and poking with his own personal fork. My disillusioned compatriot had pushed away his plate; he sat with his elbows on the table, gloomily nursing his head with his hands. His companion stared at him a moment, I fancied half tenderly; I am not sure whether it was pity or whether it was beer and brandy. "I say, Searle,"—and for my benefit, I think, taking me for an impressible native, he attuned his voice to something of a pompous pitch—"in this country it is the inestimable privilege of a loyal citizen, under whatsoever stress of pleasure or of pain, to make a point of eating his dinner."

Searle disgustedly gave his plate another push. "Anything may happen, now!" he said. "I don't care a straw."

"You ought to care. Have another chop, and you *will* care. Have some brandy. Take my advice!"

Searle from between his two hands looked at him. "I have had enough of your advice!" he said.

"A little more," said Simmons, mildly; "I shan't trouble you again. What do you mean to do!"

"Nothing."

"O, come!"

"Nothing, nothing, nothing!"

"Nothing but starve. How about your money?"

"Why do you ask? You don't care."

"My dear fellow, if you want to make me offer you twenty pounds, you set most clumsily about it. You said just now I don't know you. Possibly! There is, perhaps, no such enormous difference between knowing you and not knowing you. At any rate, you don't know me. I expect you to go home."

"I won't go home! I have crossed the ocean for the last time."

"What is the matter? Are you afraid?"

"Yes, I'm afraid! 'I thank thee, Jew, for teaching me that word!'"

"You're more afraid to go than to stay?"

"I sha'n't stay. I shall die."

"O, are you sure of that?"

"One can always be sure of that."

Mr Simmons started and stared: his mild cynic had turned grim stoic. "Upon my soul," he said, "one would think that Death had named the day!"

"We have named it, between us."

This was too much even for Mr Simmon's easy morality. "I say, Searle," he cried, "I'm not more of a stickler than the next man, but if you are going to blaspheme, I shall wash my hands of you. If you'll consent to return home with me by the steamer of the 23rd, I'll pay your passage down. More than that, I'll pay your wine bill."

Searle meditated. "I believe I never willed anything in my life," he said; "but I feel sure that I have willed this, that I stay here till I take my leave for a newer world than that poor old New World of ours. It's an odd feeling—I rather like it! What should I do at home?"

"You said just now you were homesick."

"So I was—for a morning. But haven't I been all my life long sick for Europe? And now that I've got it, am I to cast it off again? I'm much obliged to you for your offer. I have enough for the present. I have about my person some forty pounds' worth of British gold and the same amount, say, of Yankee vitality. They'll last me out together! After they are gone, I shall lay my head in some English churchyard, beside some ivied tower, beneath an English yew."

I had thus far distinctly followed the dialogue; but at this point the landlord came in, and, begging my pardon, would suggest that No. 12, a most superior apartment, having now been vacated, it would give him pleasure, etc. The fate of No. 12 having been decreed, I transferred my attention back to my friends. They had risen to their feet; Simmons had put on his overcoat; he stood polishing his rusty black hat with his napkin. "Do you mean to go down to the place?" he asked.

"Possibly. I have dreamed of it so much I should like to see it."

"Shall you call on Mr Searle?"

"Heaven forbid!"

"Something has just occurred to me," Simmons pursued, with an unhandsome grin, as if Mephistopheles were playing at malice. "There's a Miss Searle, the old man's sister."

"Well?" said the other, frowning.

"Well, sir! suppose, instead of dying, you should marry!"

Mr Searle frowned in silence. Simmons gave him a tap on the stomach. "Line those ribs a bit first!" The poor gentleman blushed crimson and his eyes filled with tears. "You *are* a coarse brute," he said. The scene was pathetic. I was prevented from seeing the conclusion of it by the reappearance of the landlord, on behalf of No. 12. He insisted on my coming to inspect the premises. Half an hour afterwards I was rattling along in a Hansom toward Covent Garden, where I heard Madame Bosio in the Barber of Seville. On my return from the opera I went into the coffee-room, vaguely fancying I might catch another glimpse of Mr Searle. I was not disappointed. I found him sitting before the fire, with his head fallen on his breast, sunk in the merciful stupor of tardy sleep. I looked at him for some moments. His face, pale and refined in the dim lamplight, impressed me with an air of helpless, ineffective delicacy. They say fortune comes while we sleep. Standing there I felt benignant enough to be poor Mr Searle's fortune. As I walked away, I perceived amid the shadows of one of the little dining stalls which I have described the lonely ever-dressed waiter, dozing attendance on my friend, and shifting aside for a while the burden of waiterhood. I lingered a moment beside the old inn-yard, in which, upon a time, the coaches and postchaises found space to turn and disgorge. Above the upward vista of the enclosing galleries, from which lounging lodgers and crumpled chambermaids and all the picturesque domesticity of an antique tavern must have watched the great entrances and exits of the posting and coaching drama, I descried the distant lurid twinkle of the London constellations. At the foot of the stairs, enshrined in the glittering niche of her well-appointed bar, the landlady sat napping like some solemn idol amid votive brass and plate.

The next morning, not finding the innocent object of my benevolent curiosity in the coffee-room, I learned from the waiter that he had ordered breakfast in bed. Into this asylum I was not yet prepared to pursue him. I spent the morning running about London, chiefly on business, but snatching by the way many a vivid impression of its huge metropolitan interest. Beneath the sullen black and gray of that hoary civic world the hungry American mind detects the magic colors of association. As the afternoon approached, however, my impatient heart began to babble of green fields; it was of English meadows I had chiefly dreamed. Thinking over the suburban lions, I fixed upon Hampton Court. The day was the more propitious that it yielded just that dim, subaqueous light which sleeps so fondly upon the English landscape.

At the end of an hour I found myself wandering through the multitudinous rooms of the great palace. They follow each other in infinite succession, with no great variety of interest or aspect, but with a sort of regal monotony, and a fine specific flavor. They are most exactly of their various times. You pass from green painted and panelled bedchambers and closets, anterooms, drawing-rooms, council-rooms, through king's suite, queen's suite, and prince's suite, until you feel as if you were strolling through the appointed hours and stages of some decorous monarchical day. On one side are the old monumental upholsteries, the vast cold tarnished beds and canopies, with the circumference of disapparelled royalty attested by a gilded balustrade, and the great carved and yawning chimney-places, where dukes-in-waiting may have warmed their weary heels; on the other side, in deep recesses, the immense windows, the framed and draped embrasures where the sovereign whispered and favorites smiled, looking out on the terraced gardens and the misty glades of Bushey Park. The dark walls are gravely decorated by innumerable dark portraits of persons attached to Court and State, more especially with various members of the Dutch-looking *entourage* of William of Orange, the restorer of the palace; with good store, too, of the lily-bosomed models of Lely and Kneller. The whole tone of this long-drawn interior is immensely sombre, prosaic, and sad. The tints of all things have sunk to a cold and melancholy brown, and the great palatial void seems to hold no stouter tenantry than a sort of pungent odorous chill. I seemed to be the only visitor. I held ungrudged communion with the formal genius of the spot. Poor mortalized kings! ineffective lure of royalty! This, or something like it, was the murmured burden of my musings. They were interrupted suddenly by my coming upon a person standing in devout contemplation before a simpering countess of Sir Peter Lely's creation. On hearing my footstep this person turned his head, and I recognized my fellow-lodger at the Red-Lion. I was apparently recognized as well; I detected an air of overture in his glance. In a few moments, seeing I had a catalogue, he asked the name of the portrait. On my ascertaining it, he inquired, timidly, how I liked the lady.

"Well," said I, not quite timidly enough, perhaps, "I confess she seems to me rather a light piece of work."

He remained silent, and a little abashed, I think. As we strolled away he stole a sidelong glance of farewell at his leering shepherdess. To speak with him face to face was to feel keenly that he was weak and interesting. We talked of our inn, of London, of the palace; he uttered his mind freely, but he seemed to struggle with a weight of depression. It was a simple mind enough, with no great culture, I fancied, but with a certain appealing native grace. I foresaw that I should find him a true American full of that perplexing interfusion of refinement and crudity which marks the American mind. His perceptions, I divined, were delicate; his opinions, possibly, gross. On my telling him that I too was an American, he stopped short and seemed overcome with emotion: then silently passing his arm into my own, he suffered me to lead him through the rest of the palace and down into the gardens. A vast gravelled platform stretches itself before the basement of the palace, taking the afternoon sun. A portion of the edifice is reserved as a series of private apartments, occupied by state pensioners, reduced gentlewomen in receipt of the Queen's bounty, and other deserving persons. Many of these apartments have their little private gardens; and here and there, between their verdure-coated walls, you catch a glimpse of these dim horticultural closets. My companion and I took many a turn up and down this spacious level, looking down on the antique geometry of the lower garden and on the stoutly woven tapestry of vine and blossom which muffles the foundations of the huge red pile. I thought of the various images of old-world gentility, which, early and late, must have strolled upon that ancient terrace and felt the great protecting quietude of the solemn palace. We looked through an antique grating into one of the little private gardens, and saw an old lady with a black mantilla on her head, a decanter of water in one hand and a crutch in the other, come forth, followed by three little dogs and a cat, to sprinkle a plant. She had an opinion, I fancied, on the virtue of Queen Caroline. There are few sensations so exquisite in life as to stand with a companion in a foreign land and inhale to the depths of your consciousness the alien savor of the air and the tonic picturesqueness of things. This common relish of local color makes comrades of strangers. My companion seemed oppressed with vague amazement. He stared and lingered and scanned the scene with a gentle scowl. His enjoyment appeared to give him pain. I proposed, at last, that we should dine in the neighborhood and take a late train to town. We made our way out of the gardens into the adjoining village, where we found an excellent inn. Mr Searle sat down to table with small apparent interest in the repast, but gradually warming to his work, he declared at the end of half an hour that for the first time in a month he felt an appetite.

"You're an invalid?" I said.

"Yes," he answered. "A hopeless one!"

The little village of Hampton Court stands clustered about the broad entrance of Bushey Park. After we had dined we lounged along into the hazy vista of the great avenue of horse-chestnuts. There is a rare emotion, familiar to every intelligent traveller, in which the mind, with a great passionate throb, achieves a magical synthesis of its impressions. You feel England; you feel Italy. The reflection for the moment has an extraordinary poignancy. I had known it from time to time in Italy, and had opened my soul to it as to the spirit of the Lord. Since my arrival in England I had been waiting for it to come. A bottle of excellent Burgundy at dinner had perhaps unlocked to it the gates of sense; it came now with a conquering tread. Just the scene around me was the England of my visions. Over against us, amid the deep-hued bloom of its ordered gardens, the dark red palace, with its formal copings and its vacant windows, seemed to tell of a proud and splendid past; the little village nestling between park and palace, around a patch of turfy common, with its tavern of gentility, its ivy-towered church, its parsonage, retained to my modernized fancy the lurking semblance of a feudal hamlet. It was in this dark composite light that I had read all English prose; it was this mild moist air that had blown from the verses of English poets; beneath these broad acres of rain-deepened greenness a thousand honored dead lay buried.

"Well," I said to my friend, "I think there is no mistake about this being England. We may like it or not, it's positive! No more dense and stubborn fact ever settled down on an expectant tourist. It brings my heart into my throat."

Searle was silent. I looked at him; he was looking up at the sky, as if he were watching some visible descent of the elements. "On me too," he said, "it's settling down!" Then with a forced smile: "Heaven give me strength to bear it!"

"O mighty world," I cried, "to hold at once so rare an Italy and so brave an England!"

"To say nothing of America," added Searle.

"O," I answered, "America has a world to herself!"

"You have the advantage over me," my companion resumed, after a pause, "in coming to all this with an educated eye. You already know the old. I have never known it but by report. I have always fancied I should like it. In a small way at home, you know, I have tried to stick to the old. I must be a conservative by nature. People at home—a few people—used to call me a snob."

"I don't believe you were a snob," I cried. "You look too amiable."

He smiled sadly. "There it is," he said. "It's the old story! I'm amiable! I know what that means! I was too great a fool to be even a snob! If I had been I should probably have come abroad earlier in life—before—before—" He paused, and his head dropped sadly on his breast.

The bottle of Burgundy had loosened his tongue. I felt that my learning his story was merely a question of time. Something told me that I had gained his confidence and he would unfold himself. "Before you lost your health," I said.

"Before I lost my health," he answered. "And my property, —the little I had. And my ambition. And my self-esteem."

"Come!" I said. "You shall get them all back. This tonic English climate will wind you up in a month. And with the return of health, all the rest will return."

He sat musing, with his eyes fixed on the distant palace. "They are too far gone,—self-esteem, especially! I should like to be an old genteel pensioner, lodged over there in the palace, and spending my days in maundering about these classic haunts. I should go every morning, at the hour when it gets the sun, into that long gallery where all those pretty women of Lely's are hung,—I know you despise them!—and stroll up and down and pay them compliments. Poor, precious forsaken creatures! So flattered and courted in their day, so neglected now! Offering up their shoulders and ringlets and smiles to that inexorable solitude!"

I patted my friend on the shoulder. "You shall be yourself again yet," I said.

Just at this moment there came cantering down the shallow glade of the avenue a young girl on a fine black horse,—one of those lovely budding gentlewomen, perfectly mounted and equipped, who form to American eyes the sweetest incident of English scenery. She had distanced her servant, and, as she came abreast of us, turned slightly in her saddle and looked back at him. In the movement she dropped her whip. Drawing in her horse, she cast upon the ground a glance of maidenly alarm. "This is something better than a Lely," I said. Searle hastened forward, picked up the whip, and removing his hat with an air of great devotion, presented it to the young girl. Fluttered and blushing, she reached forward, took it with softly murmured gratitude, and the next moment was bounding over the elastic turf. Searle stood watching her; the servant, as he passed us, touched his hat. When Searle turned toward me again, I saw that his face was glowing with a violent blush. "I doubt of your having come abroad too late!" I said, laughing.

A short distance from where we had stopped was an old stone bench. We went and sat down on it and watched the light mist turning to sullen gold in the rays of the evening sun. "We ought to be thinking of the train back to London, I suppose," I said at last.

"O, hang the train!" said Searle.

"Willingly! There could be no better spot than this to feel the magic of an English twilight." So we lingered, and the twilight lingered around us,—a light and not a darkness. As we sat, there came trudging along the road an individual whom, from afar, I recognized as a member of the genus "tramp." I had read of the British tramp, but I had never yet encountered him, and I brought my historic consciousness to bear upon the present specimen. As he approached us he slackened pace and finally halted, touching his cap. He was a man of middle age, clad in a greasy bonnet, with greasy ear-locks depending from its sides. Round his neck was a grimy red scarf, tucked into his waistcoat; his coat and trousers had a remote affinity with those of a reduced hostler. In one hand he had a stick; on his arm he bore a tattered basket, with a handful of withered green stuff in the bottom. His face was pale, haggard, and degraded beyond description,—a singular mixture of brutality and finesse. He had a history. From what height had he fallen, from what depth had he risen? Never was a form of rascally beggarhood more complete. There was a merciless fixedness of outline about him which filled me with a kind of awe. I felt as if I were in the presence of a personage,—an artist in vagrancy.

"For God's sake, gentlemen," he said, in that raucous tone of weather-beaten poverty suggestive of chronic sore-throat exacerbated by perpetual gin,—"for God's sake, gentlemen, have pity on a poor fern-collector!"—turning up his stale dandelions. "Food hasn't passed my lips, gentlemen, in the last three days."

We gaped responsive, in the precious pity of guileless Yankeeism. "I wonder," thought I, "if half a crown would be enough?" And our fasting botanist went limping away through the park with a mystery of satirical gratitude super-added to his general mystery.

"I feel as if I had seen my *doppel-ganger*," said Searle. "He reminds me of myself. What am I but a tramp?"

Upon this hint I spoke. "What are you, my friend?" I asked. "Who are you?"

A sudden blush rose to his pale face, so that I feared I had offended him. He poked a moment at the sod with the point of his umbrella, before answering. "Who am I?" he said at last. "My name is Clement Searle. I was born in New York. I have lived in New York. What am I? That's easily told. Nothing! I assure you, nothing."

"A very good fellow, apparently," I protested.

"A very good fellow! Ah, there it is! You've said more than you mean. It's by having been a very good fellow all my days that I've come to this. I have drifted through life. I'm a failure, sir,—a failure as hopeless and helpless as any that ever swallowed up the slender investments of the widow and the orphan. I don't pay five cents on the dollar. Of what I was to begin with no memory remains. I have been ebbing away, from the start, in a steady current which, at forty, has left this arid sand-bank behind. To begin with, certainly, I was not a fountain of wisdom. All the more reason for a definite channel,—for will and purpose and direction. I walked by chance and sympathy and sentiment. Take a turn through New York and you'll find my tattered sympathies and sentiments dangling on every bush and fluttering in every breeze; the men to whom I lent money, the women to whom I made love, the friends I trusted, the dreams I cherished, the poisonous fumes of pleasure, amid which nothing was sweet or precious but the manhood they stifled! It was my fault that I believed in pleasure here below. I believe in it still, but as I believe in God and not in man! I believed in eating your cake and having it. I respected Pleasure, and she made a fool of me. Other men, treating her like the arrant strumpet she is, enjoyed her for the hour, but kept their good manners for plain-faced Business, with the larger dowry, to whom they are now lawfully married. My taste was to be delicate; well, perhaps I was so! I had a little money; it went the way of my little wit. Here in my pocket I have forty pounds of it left. The only thing I have to show for my money and my wit is a little volume of verses, printed at my own expense, in which fifteen years ago I made bold to sing the charms of love and idleness. Six months since I got hold of the volume; it reads like the poetry of fifty years ago. The form is incredible. I hadn't seen Hampton Court then. When I was thirty I married. It was a sad mistake, but a generous one. The young girl was poor and obscure, but beautiful and proud. I fancied she would make an incomparable woman. It was a sad mistake! She died at the end of three years, leaving no children. Since then I have idled long. I have had bad habits. To this impalpable thread of existence the current of my life has shrunk. To-morrow I shall be high and dry. Was I meant to come to this? Upon my soul I wasn't! If I say what I feel, you'll fancy my vanity quite equal to my folly, and set me down as one of those dreary theorizers after the fact, who draw any moral from their misfortunes but the damning moral that vice is vice and that's an end of it. Take it for what it's worth. I have always fancied that I was meant for a gentler world. Before heaven, sir,—whoever you are,—I'm in practice so absurdly tender-hearted that I can afford to say it,—I came into the world an aristocrat. I was born with a soul for the picturesque. It condemns me, I confess; but in a measure, too, it absolves me. I found it nowhere. I found a world all hard lines and harsh lights, without shade, without composition, as they say of pictures, without the lovely mystery of color. To furnish color, I melted down the very substance of my own soul. I went about with my brush, touching up and toning down; a very pretty chiaroscuro you'll find in my track! Sitting here, in this old park, in this old land, I feel—I feel that I hover on the misty verge of what might have been! I should have been born here and not there; here my vulgar idleness would have been—don't laugh now!—would have been elegant leisure. How it was that I never came abroad is more than I can say. It might have cut the knot; but the knot was too tight. I was always unwell or in debt or entangled.

Besides, I had a horror of the sea—with reason, heaven knows! A year ago I was reminded of the existence of an old claim to a portion of an English estate, cherished off and on by various members of my family for the past eighty years. It's undeniably slender and desperately hard to define. I am by no means sure that to this hour I have mastered it. You look as if you had a clear head. Some other time, if you'll consent, we'll puzzle it out, such as it is, together. Poverty was staring me in the face; I sat down and got my claim by heart, as I used to get nine times nine as a boy. I dreamed about it for six months, half expecting to wake up some fine morning to hear through a latticed casement the cawing of an English rookery. A couple of months since there came out here on business of his own a sort of half-friend of mine, a sharp New York lawyer, an extremely common fellow, but a man with an eye for the weak point and the strong point. It was with him yesterday that you saw me dining. He undertook, as he expressed it, to 'nose round' and see if anything could be made of this pretended right. The matter had never seriously been taken up. A month later I got a letter from Simmons, assuring me that things looked mighty well, that he should be vastly amazed if I hadn't a case. I took fire in a humid sort of way; I acted, for the first time in my life; I sailed for England. I have been here three days: it seems three months. After keeping me waiting for thirty-six hours, last evening my precious Simmons makes his appearance, and informs me, with his mouth full of mutton, that I was a blasted fool to have taken him at his word; that he had been precipitate; that I had been precipitate; that my claim was moonshine; and that I must do penance and take a ticket for another fortnight of seasickness in his agreeable society. My friend, my friend! Shall I say I was disappointed? I'm already resigned. I doubted the practicability of my claim. I felt in my deeper consciousness that it was the crowning illusion of a life of illusions. Well, it was a pretty one. Poor Simmons!

I forgive him with all my heart. But for him I shouldn't be sitting in this place, in this air, with these thoughts. This is a world I could have loved. There's a great fitness in its having been kept for the last. After this nothing would have been tolerable. I shall now have a month of it, I hope, and I shall not have a chance to be disenchanted. There's one thing!—and here, pausing, he laid his hand on mine; I rose and stood before him,—"I wish it were possible you should be with me to the end."

"I promise you," I said, "to leave you only at your own request. But it must be on condition of your omitting from your conversation this intolerable flavor of mortality. The end! Perhaps it's the beginning."

He shook his head. "You don't know me. It's a long story. I'm incurably ill."

"I know you a little. I have a strong suspicion that your illness is in great measure a matter of mind and spirits. All that you've told me is but another way of saying that you have lived hitherto in yourself. The tenement's haunted! Live abroad! Take an interest!"

He looked at me for a moment with his sad weak eyes. Then with a faint smile: "Don't cut down a man you find hanging. He has had a reason for it. I'm bankrupt."

"O, health is money!" I said. "Get well, and the rest will take care of itself. I'm interested in your claim."

"Don't ask me to expound it now! It's a sad muddle. Let it alone. I know nothing of business. If I myself were to take the matter in hand, I should break short off the poor little silken thread of my expectancy. In a better world than this I think I should be listened to. But in this hard world there's small bestowal of ideal justice. There is no doubt, I fancy, that, a hundred years ago, we suffered a palpable wrong. But we made no appeal at the time, and the dust of a century now lies heaped upon our silence. Let is rest!"

"What is the estimated value of your interest?"

"We were instructed from the first to accept a compromise. Compared with the whole property, our utmost right is extremely small. Simmons talked of eighty-five thousand dollars. Why eighty-five I'm sure I don't know. Don't beguile me into figures."

"Allow me one more question. Who is actually in possession?"

"A certain Mr Richard Searle. I know nothing about him."

"He is in some way related to you?"

"Our great-grandfathers were half-brothers. What does that make?"

"Twentieth cousins, say. And where does your twentieth cousin live?"

"At Lockley Park, Herefordshire."

I pondered awhile. "I'm interested in you. Mr Searle," I said. "In your story, in your title, such as it is, and in this Lockley Park, Herefordshire. Suppose we go down and see it."

He rose to his feet with a certain alertness. "I shall make a sound man of him, yet," I said to myself.

"I shouldn't have the heart," he said, "to accomplish the melancholy pilgrimage alone. But with you I'll go anywhere."

On our return to London we determined to spend three days there together, and then to go into the country. We felt to excellent purpose the sombre charm of London, the mighty mother-city of our mighty race, the great distributing heart of our traditional life. Certain London characteristics—monuments, relics, hints of history, local moods and memories—are more deeply suggestive to an American soul than anything else in Europe. With an equal attentive piety my friend and I glanced at these things. Their influence on Searle was deep and singular. His observation I soon perceived to be extremely acute. His almost passionate relish for the old, the artificial, and social, wellnigh extinct from its long inanition, began now to tremble and thrill with a tardy vitality. I watched in silent wonderment this strange metaphysical renascence.

Between the fair boundaries of the counties of Hereford and Worcester rise in a long undulation the sloping pastures of the Malvern Hills. Consulting a big red book on the castles and manors of England, we found Lockley Park to be seated near the base of this grassy range,—though in which county I forget. In the pages of this genial volume, Lockley Park and its appurtenances made a very handsome figure. We took up our abode at a certain little wayside inn, at which in the days of leisure the coach must have stopped for lunch, and burnished pewters of rustic ale been tenderly exalted to "outsides" athirst with breezy progression. Here we stopped, for sheer admiration of its steep thatched roof, its latticed windows, and its homely porch. We allowed a couple of days to elapse in vague, undirected strolls and sweet sentimental observance of the land, before we prepared to execute the especial purpose of our journey. This admirable region is a compendium of the general physiognomy of England. The noble friendliness of the scenery, its subtle old-friendliness, the magical familiarity of multitudinous details, appealed to us at every step and at every glance. Deep in our souls a natural affection answered. The whole land, in the full, warm rains of the last of April, had burst into sudden perfect spring. The dark walls of the hedgerows had turned into blooming screens; the sodden verdure of lawn and meadow was streaked with a ranker freshness. We went forth without loss of time for a long walk on the hills. Reaching their summits, you find half England unrolled at your feet. A dozen broad counties, within the vast range of your vision, commingle their green exhalations. Closely beneath us lay the dark, rich flats of hedgy Worcestershire and the copse-checkered slopes of rolling Hereford, white with the blossom of apples. At widely opposite points of the large expanse two great cathedral towers rise sharply, taking the light, from the settled shadow of their circling towns,—the light, the ineffable English light! "Out of England," cried Searle, "it's but a garish world!"

The whole vast sweep of our surrounding prospect lay answering in a myriad fleeting shades the cloudy process of the tremendous sky. The English heaven is a fit antithesis to the complex English earth. We possess in America the infinite beauty of the blue; England possesses the splendor of combined and animated clouds. Over against us, from our station on the hills, we saw them piled and dissolved, compacted and shifted, blotting the azure with sullen rain spots, stretching, breeze-fretted, into dappled fields of gray, bursting into a storm of light or melting into a drizzle of silver. We made our way along the rounded summits of these well-grazed heights,—mild, breezy inland downs,—and descended through long-drawn slopes of fields, green to cottage doors, to where a rural village beckoned us from its seat among the meadows. Close beside it, I admit, the railway shoots fiercely from its tunnel in the hills; and yet there broods upon this charming hamlet an old-time quietude and privacy, which seems to make it a violation of confidence to tell its name so far away. We struck through a narrow lane, a green lane, dim with its height of hedges; it led us to a superb old farmhouse, now jostled by the multiplied lanes and roads which have curtailed its ancient appanage. It stands in stubborn picturesqueness, at the receipt of sad-eyed contemplation and the sufferance of "sketches." I doubt whether out of Nuremberg —or Pompeii!—you may find so forcible an image of the domiciliary genius of the past. It is cruelly complete; its bended beams and joists, beneath the burden of its gables, seem to ache and groan with memories and regrets. The short, low windows, where lead and glass combine in equal proportions to hint to the wondering stranger of the mediæval gloom within, still prefer their darksome office to the grace of modern day. Such an old house fills an American with an indefinable feeling of respect. So propped and patched and tinkered with clumsy tenderness, clustered so richly about its central English sturdiness, its oaken vertebrations, so human-ized with ages of use and touches of beneficent affection, it seemed to offer to our grateful eyes a small, rude synthesis of the great English social order. Passing out upon the high-road, we came to the common browsing-patch, the "village green" of the tales of our youth. Nothing was wanting; the shaggy, mouse-coloured donkey, nosing the turf with his mild and huge proboscis, the geese, the old woman—*the* old woman, in person, with her red cloak and her black bonnet, frilled about the face and double-frilled beside her decent, placid cheeks,—the towering ploughman with his white smock-frock, puckered on chest and back, his short corduroys, his mighty calves, his big, red, rural face. We greeted these things as children greet the loved pictures in a story-book, lost and mourned and found again. It was marvellous how well we knew them. Beside the road we saw a ploughboy straddle, whistling, on a stile. Gainsborough might have painted him. Beyond the stile, across the level velvet of a meadow, a footpath lay, like a thread of darker woof. We followed it from field to field and from stile to stile. It was the way to church. At the church we finally arrived, lost in its rook-haunted churchyard, hidden from the work-day world by the broad stillness of pastures,—a gray, gray tower, a huge black yew, a cluster of village graves, with crooked head-stones, in grassy, low relief. The whole scene was deeply ecclesiastical. My companion was overcome.

"You must bury me here," he cried. "It's the first church I have seen in my life. How it makes a Sunday where it stands!"

The next day we saw a church of statelier proportions. We walked over to Worcester, through such a mist of local color, that I felt like one of Smollett's pedestrian heroes, faring tavernward for a night of adventures. As we neared the provincial city we saw the steepled mass of the cathedral, long and high, rise far into the cloud-freckled blue. And as we came nearer still, we stopped on the bridge and viewed the solid minster reflected in the yellow Severn. And going farther yet we entered the town,—where surely Miss Austen's heroines, in chariots and curricles, must often have come a shopping for swan's-down boas and high lace mittens;— we lounged about the gentle close and gazed insatiably at that most soul-soothing sight, the waning, wasting afternoon light, the visible ether which feels the voices of the chimes, far aloft on the broad perpendicular field of the cathedral tower; saw it linger and nestle and abide, as it loves to do on all bold architectural spaces, converting them graciously into registers and witnesses of nature; tasted, too, as deeply of the peculiar stillness of this clerical precinct; saw a rosy English lad come forth and lock the door of the old foundation school, which marries its hoary basement to the soaring Gothic of the church, and carry his big responsible key into one of the quiet canonical houses; and then stood musing together on the effect on one's mind of having in one's boyhood haunted such cathedral shades as a King's scholar, and yet kept ruddy with much cricket in misty meadows by the Severn. On the third morning we betook ourselves to Lockley Park, having learned that the greater part of it was open to visitors, and that, indeed, on application, the house was occasionally shown.

Within its broad enclosure many a declining spur of the great hills melted into parklike slopes and dells. A long avenue wound and circled from the outermost gate through an un- trimmed woodland, whence you glanced at further slopes and glades and copses and bosky recesses,—at everything except the limits of the place. It was as free and wild and untended as the villa of an Italian prince; and I have never seen the stern English fact of property put on such an air of innocence. The weather had just become perfect; it was one of the dozen exquisite days of the English year,—days stamped with a refinement of purity unknown in more liberal climes. It was as if the mellow brightness, as tender as that of the primroses which starred the dark waysides like petals wind-scattered over beds of moss, had been meted out to us by the cubic foot,—tempered, refined, recorded! From this external region we passed into the heart of the park, through a second lodge-gate, with weather-worn gilding on its twisted bars, to the smooth slopes where the great trees stood singly and the tame deer browsed along the bed of a woodland stream. Hence, before us, we perceived the dark Elizabethan manor among its blooming parterres and terraces.

"Here you can wander all day," I said to Searle, "like a proscribed and exiled prince, hovering about the dominion of the usurper."

"To think," he answered, "of people having enjoyed this all these years! I know what I am,—what might I have been? What does all this make of you?"

"That it makes you happy," I said, "I should hesitate to believe. But it's hard to suppose that such a place has not some beneficent action of its own."

"What a perfect scene and background it forms!" Searle went on. "What legends, what histories it knows! My heart is breaking with unutterable visions. There's Tennyson's Talking Oak. What summer days one could spend here! How I could lounge my bit of life away on this shady stretch of turf! Haven't I some maiden-cousin in yon moated grange who would give me kind leave?" And then turning almost fiercely upon me: "Why did you bring me here? Why did you drag me into this torment of vain regrets?"

At this moment there passed near us a servant who had emerged from the gardens of the great house. I hailed him and inquired whether we should be likely to gain admittance. He answered that Mr Searle was away from home, and that he thought it probable the housekeeper would consent to do the honors of the mansion. I passed my arm into Searle's. "Come," I said. "Drain the cup, bitter-sweet though it be. We shall go in." We passed another lodge-gate and entered the gardens. The house was an admirable specimen of complete Elizabethan, a multitudinous cluster of gables and porches, oriels and turrets, screens of ivy and pinnacles of slate. Two broad terraces commanded the great wooded horizon of the adjacent domain. Our summons was answered by the butler in person, solemn and *tout de noir habillé*. He repeated the statement that Mr Searle was away from home, and that he would present our petition to the housekeeper. We would be so good, however, as to give him our cards. This request, following so directly on the assertion that Mr Searle was absent, seemed to my companion not distinctly pertinent. "Surely not for the housekeeper," he said.

The butler gave a deferential cough. "Miss Searle is at home."

"Yours alone will suffice," said Searle. I took out a card and pencil, and wrote beneath my name, *New York*. Standing with the pencil in my hand I felt a sudden impulse. Without in the least weighing proprieties or results, I yielded to it. I added above my name, *Mr Clement Searle*. What would come of it?

Before many minutes the housekeeper attended us—a fresh rosy little old woman in a dowdy clean cap and a scanty calico gown; an exquisite specimen of refined and venerable servility. She had the accent of the country, but the manners of the house. Under her guidance we passed through a dozen apartments, duly stocked with old pictures, old tapestry, old carvings, old armor, with all the constituent properties of an English manor. The pictures were especially valuable. The two Vandykes, the trio of rosy Rubenses, the sole and sombre Rembrandt, glowed with conscious authenticity. A Claude, a Murillo, a Greuze, and a Gainsborough hung gracious in their chosen places. Searle strolled about silent, pale and, grave, with bloodshot eyes and lips compressed. He uttered no comment and asked no question. Missing him, at last, from my side, I retraced my steps and found him in a room we had just left, on a tarnished silken divan, with his face buried in his hands. Before him, ranged on an antique buffet, was a magnificent collection of old Italian majolica; huge platters radiant with their steady colors, jugs and vases nobly bellied and embossed. There came to me, as I looked, a sudden vision of the young English gentleman, who, eighty years ago, had travelled by slow stages to Italy and been waited on at his inn by persuasive toymen. "What is it, Searle?" I asked. "Are you unwell?"

He uncovered his haggard face and showed a burning blush. Then smiling in hot irony: "A memory of the past! I was thinking of a china vase that used to stand on the parlor mantel-shelf while I was a boy, with the portrait of General Jackson painted on one side and a bunch of flowers on the other. How long do you suppose that majolica has been in the family?"

"A long time probably. It was brought hither in the last century, into old, old England, out of old, old Italy, by some old young buck of this excellent house with a taste for *chinoiseries*. Here it has stood for a hundred years, keeping its clear, firm hues in this aristocratic twilight."

Searle sprang to his feet. "I say," he cried, "in heaven's name take me away! I can't stand this. Before I know it I shall do something I shall be ashamed of. I shall steal one of their d—d majolicas. I shall proclaim my identity and assert my rights! I shall go blubbering to Miss Searle and ask her in pity's name to keep me here for a month!"

If poor Searle could ever have been said to look "dangerous," he looked so now. I began to regret my officious presentation of his name, and prepared without delay to lead him out of the house. We overtook the housekeeper in the last room of the suite, a small, unused boudoir, over the chimney-piece of which hung a noble portrait of a young man in a powdered wig and a brocaded waistcoat. I was immediately struck with his resemblance to my companion.

"This is Mr Clement Searle, Mr Searle's great-uncle, by Sir Joshua Reynolds," quoth the housekeeper. "He died young, poor gentleman. He perished at sea, going to America.'

"He's the young buck," I said, "who brought the majolica out of Italy."

"Indeed, sir, I believe he did," said the housekeeper, staring.

"He's the image of you, Searle," I murmured.

"He's wonderfully like the gentleman, saving his presence," said the housekeeper.

My friend stood gazing. "Clement Searle—at sea—going to America—" he muttered. Then harshly, to the housekeeper, "Why the deuce did he go to America?"

"Why, indeed, sir? You may well ask. I believe he had kinsfolk there. It was for them to come to him."

Searle broke into a laugh. "It was for them to have come to him! Well, well," he said, fixing his eyes on the little old woman, "they have come to him at last!"

She blushed like a wrinkled rose-leaf. "Indeed, sir," she said, "I verily believe that you are one of *us!*"

"My name is the name of that lovely youth," Searle went on. "Kinsman, I salute you! Attend!" And he grasped me by the arm. "I have an idea! He perished at sea. His spirit came ashore and wandered forlorn till it got lodgment again in my poor body. In my poor body it has lived, homesick, these forty years, shaking its rickety cage, urging me, stupid, to carry it back to the scenes of its youth. And I never knew what was the matter with me! Let me exhale my spirit here!"

The housekeeper essayed a timorous smile. The scene was embarrassing. My confusion was not allayed when I suddenly perceived in the doorway the figure of a lady. "Miss Searle?" whispered the housekeeper. My first impression of Miss

Searle was that she was neither young nor beautiful. She stood with a timid air on the threshold, pale, trying to smile, and twirling my card in her fingers. I immediately bowed. Searle, I think, gazed marvelling.

"If I am not mistaken," said the lady, "one of you gentlemen is Mr Clement Searle."

"My friend is Mr Clement Searle," I replied. "Allow me to add that I alone am responsible for your having received his name."

"I should have been sorry not to receive it," said Miss Searle, beginning to blush. "Your being from America has led me to—to interrupt you."

"The interruption, madam, has been on our part. And with just that excuse,—that we are from America."

Miss Searle, while I spoke, had fixed her eyes on my friend, as he stood silent beneath Sir Joshua's portrait. The housekeeper, amazed and mystified, took a liberty. "Heaven preserve us, Miss! It's your great-uncle's picture come to life."

"I'm not mistaken, then," said Miss Searle. "We are distantly related." She had the aspect of an extremely modest woman. She was evidently embarrassed at having to proceed unassisted in her overture. Searle eyed her with gentle wonder from head to foot. I fancied I read his thoughts. This, then, was Miss Searle, his maiden-cousin, prospective heiress of these manorial acres and treasures. She was a person of about thirty-three years of age, taller than most women, with health and strength in the rounded amplitude of her shape. She had a small blue eye, a massive chignon of yellow hair, and a mouth at once broad and comely. She was dressed in a lustreless black satin gown, with a short train. Around her neck she wore a blue silk handkerchief, and over this handkerchief, in many convolutions, a string of amber beads. Her appearance was singular; she was large, yet not imposing; girlish, yet mature. Her glance and accent, in addressing us, were simple, too simple. Searle, I think, had been fancying some proud cold beauty of five-and-twenty; he was relieved at finding the lady timid and plain. His person was suddenly illumined with an old disused gallantry.

"We are distant cousins, I believe. I am happy to claim a relationship which you are so good as to remember. I had not in the least counted on your doing so."

"Perhaps I have done wrong," and Miss Searle blushed anew and smiled. "But I have always known of there being people of our blood in America, and I have often wondered and asked about them; without learning much, however. To-day, when this card was brought me and I knew of a Clement Searle wandering about the house like a stranger, I felt as if I ought to do something. I hardly knew what! My brother is in London. I have done what I think he would have done. Welcome, as a cousin." And with a gesture at once frank and shy, she put out her hand.

"I'm welcome indeed," said Searle, taking it, "if he would have done it half as graciously."

"You've seen the show," Miss Searle went on. "Perhaps now you'll have some lunch." We followed her into a small breakfast-room, where a deep bay-window opened on the mossy flags of the great terrace. Here, for some moments, she remained silent and shy, in the manner of a person resting from a great effort. Searle, too, was formal and reticent, so that I had to busy myself with providing small-talk. It was of course easy to descant on the beauties of park and mansion. Meanwhile I observed our hostess. She had small beauty and scanty grace; her dress was out of taste and out of season; yet she pleased me well. There was about her a sturdy sweetness, a homely flavor of the sequestered *châtelaine* of feudal days. To be so simple amid this massive luxury, so mellow and yet so fresh, so modest and yet so placid, told of just the spacious leisure in which I had fancied human life to be steeped in many a park-circled home. Miss Searle was to the Belle au

Bois Dormant what a fact is to a fairy-tale, an interpretation to a myth. We, on our side, were to our hostess objects of no light scrutiny. The best possible English breeding still marvels visibly at the native American. Miss Searle's wonderment was guileless enough to have been more overt and yet inoffensive; there was no taint of offence indeed in her utterance of the unvarying amenity that she had met an American family on the Lake of Como whom she would have almost taken to be English.

"If I lived here," I said, "I think I should hardly need to go away, even to the Lake of Como."

"You might perhaps get tired of it. And then the Lake of Como! If I could only go abroad again!"

"You have been but once?"

"Only once. Three years ago my brother took me to Switzerland. We thought it extremely beautiful. Except for this journey, I have always lived here. Here I was born. It's a dear old place, indeed, and I know it well. Sometimes I fancy I'm a little tired." And on my asking her how she spent her time and what society she saw, "It's extremely quiet," she went on, proceeding by short steps and simple statements, in the manner of a person summoned for the first time to define her situation and enumerate the elements of her life. "We see very few people. I don't think there are many nice people hereabouts. At least we don't know them. Our own family is very small. My brother cares for little else but riding and books. He had a great sorrow ten years ago. He lost his wife and his only son, a dear little boy, who would have succeeded him in the estates. Do you know that I'm likely to have them now! Poor me! Since his loss my brother has preferred to be quite alone. I'm sorry he's away. But you must wait till he comes back. I expect him in a day or two." She talked more and more, with a rambling, earnest vapidity, about her circumstances, her solitude, her bad eyes, so that she couldn't read, her flowers, her ferns, her dogs, and the curate, recently inducted by her brother and warranted sound orthodox, who had lately begun to light his altar candles; pausing every now and then to blush in self-surprise, and yet moving steadily from point to point in the deepening excitement of temptation and occasion. Of all the old things I had seen in England, this mind of Miss Searle's seemed to me the oldest, the quaintest, the most ripely verdant; so fenced and protected by convention and precedent and usage; so passive and mild and docile. I felt as if I were talking with a potential heroine of Miss Burney. As she talked, she rested her dull, kind eyes upon her kinsman with a sort of fascinated stare. At last, "Did you mean to go away," she demanded, "without asking for us?"

"I had thought it over, Miss Searle, and had determined not to trouble you. You have shown me how unfriendly I should have been."

"But you knew of the place being ours and of our relationship?"

"Just so. It was because of these things that I came down here—because of them, almost, that I came to England. I have always liked to think of them."

"You merely wished to look, then? We don't pretend to be much to look at."

"You don't know what you are, Miss Searle," said my friend, gravely.

"You like the old place, then?"

Searle looked at her in silence. "If I could only tell you," he said at last.

"Do tell me! You must come and stay with us."

Searle began to laugh. "Take care, take care," he cried. "I should surprise you. At least I should bore you. I should never leave you."

"O, you'd get homesick for America!"

At this Searle laughed the more. "By the way," he cried to me, "tell Miss Searle about America!" And he stepped through the window out upon the terrace. followed by two beautiful dogs, a pointer and a young stag-hound, who from the moment we came in had established the fondest relation with him. Miss Searle looked at him as he went, with a certain tender wonder in her eye. I read in her glance, methought, that she was interested. I suddenly recalled the last words I had heard spoken by my friend's adviser in London: "Instead of dying you'd better marry." If Miss Searle could be gently manipulated. O for a certain divine tact! Something assured me that her heart was virgin soil; that sentiment had never bloomed there. If I could but sow the seed! There lurked within her the perfect image of one of the patient wives of old.

"He has lost his heart to England," I said. "He ought to have been born here."

"And yet," said Miss Searle, "he's not in the least an Englishman."

"How do you know that?"

"I hardly know how. I never talked with a foreigner before; but he looks and talks as I have fancied foreigners."

"Yes, he's foreign enough!"

"Is he married?"

"He's a widower,—without children."

"Has he property?"

"Very little."

"But enough to travel?"

I meditated. "He has not expected to travel far," I said at last. "You know he's in poor health."

"Poor gentleman! So I fancied."

"He's better, though, than he thinks. He came here because he wanted to see your place before he dies."

"Poor fellow!" And I fancied I perceived in her eye the lustre of a rising tear. "And he was going off without my seeing him?"

"He's a modest man, you see."

"He's very much of a gentleman."

"Assuredly!"

At this moment we heard on the terrace a loud, harsh cry. "It's the great peacock!" said Miss Searle, stepping to the window and passing out. I followed her. Below us on the terrace, leaning on the parapet, stood our friend, with his arm round the neck of the pointer. Before him, on the grand walk, strutted a splendid peacock, with ruffled neck and expanded tail. The other dog had apparently indulged in a momentary attempt to abash the gorgeous fowl; but at Searle's voice he had bounded back to the terrace and leaped upon the parapet, where he now stood licking his new friend's face. The scene had a beautiful old-time air; the peacock flaunting in the foreground, like the very genius of antique gardenry; the broad terrace, which flattered an innate taste of mine for all deserted promenades to which people may have adjourned from formal dinners, to drink coffee in old Sèvres, and where the stiff brocade of women's dresses may have rustled autumnal leaves; and far around us, with one leafy circle melting into another, the timbered acres of the park. "The very beasts have made him welcome," I said, as we rejoined our companion.

"The peacock has done for you, Mr Searle," said his cousin, "what he does only for very great people. A year ago there came here a duchess to see my brother. I don't think that since then he has spread his tail as wide for anyone else by a dozen feathers."

"It's not alone the peacock," said Searle. "Just now there came slipping across my path a little green lizard, the first I ever saw, the lizard of literature! And if you have a ghost, broad daylight though it be, I expect to see him here. Do you know the annals of your house, Miss Searle?"

"O dear no! You must ask my brother for all those things."

"You ought to have a book full of legends and traditions.

You ought to have loves and murders and mysteries by the roomful. I count upon it."

"O Mr Searle! We have always been a very well-behaved family. Nothing out of the way has ever happened, I think."

"Nothing out of the way? O horrors! We have done better than that in America. Why, I myself!"—and he gazed at her a moment with a gleam of malice, and then broke into a laugh. "Suppose I should turn out a better Searle than you? Better than you, nursed here in romance and picturesqueness. Come, don't disappoint me. You have some history among you all, you have some poetry. I have been famished all my days for these things. Do you understand? Ah, you can't understand! Tell me something! When I think of what must have happened here! when I think of the lovers who must have strolled on this terrace and wandered through those glades! of all the figures and passions and purposes that must have haunted these walls! of the births and deaths, the joys and sufferings, the young hopes and the old regrets, the intense experience—" And here he faltered a moment, with the increase of his vehemence. The gleam in his eye, which I have called a gleam of malice, had settled into a deep unnatural light. I began to fear he had become over-excited. But he went on with redoubled passion. "To see it all evoked before me," he cried, "if the Devil alone could do it, I'd make a bargain with the Devil! O Miss Searle, I'm a most unhappy man!"

"O dear, O dear!" said Miss Searle.

"Look at that window, that blessed oriel!" And he pointed to a small, protruding casement above us, relieved against the purple brick-work, framed in chiselled stone, and curtained with ivy.

"It's my room," said Miss Searle.

"Of course it's a woman's room. Think of the forgotten loveliness which has peeped from that window; think of the old-time women's lives which have known chiefly that out-look on this bosky world. O gentle cousins! And you, Miss Searle, you're one of them yet." And he marched to-wards her and took her great white hand. She surrendered it, blushing to her eyes, and pressing her other hand to her breast. "You're a woman of the past. You're nobly simple. It has been a romance to see you. It doesn't matter what I say to you. You didn't know me yesterday, you'll not know me to-morrow. Let me to-day do a mad, sweet thing. Let me fancy you the soul of all the dead women who have trod these terrace-flags, which lie here like sepulchral tablets in the pavement of a church. Let me say I worship you!" And he raised her hand to his lips. She gently withdrew it, and for a moment averted her face. Meeting her eyes the next moment, I saw that they were filled with tears. The Belle au Bois Dormant was awake.

There followed an embarrassed pause. An issue was suddenly presented by the appearance of the butler bearing a letter. "A telegram, Miss," he said.

"Dear me!" cried Miss Searle, "I can't open a telegram. Cousin, help me."

Searle took the missive, opened it, and read aloud: "*I shall be home to dinner. Keep the American.*"

II

"KEEP the American!" Miss Searle, in compliance with the injunction conveyed in her brother's telegram (with something certainly of telegraphic curtness), lost no time in expressing the pleasure it would give her to have my companion remain. "Really you must," she said; and forthwith repaired to the housekeeper, to give orders for the preparation of a room.

"How in the world," asked Searle, "did he know of my being here?"

"He learned, probably," I expounded, "from his solicitor of the visit of your friend Simmons. Simmons and the solicitor must have had another interview since your arrival in England. Simmons, for reasons of his own, has communicated to the solicitor your journey to this neighborhood, and Mr Searle, learning this, has immediately taken for granted that you have formally presented yourself to his sister. He's hospitably inclined, and he wishes her to do the proper thing by you. More, perhaps! I have my little theory that he is the very Phœnix of usurpers, that his nobler sense has been captivated by the exposition of the men of law, and that he means gracefully to surrender you your fractional interest in the estate."

"I give it up!" said my friend, musing. "Come what come will!"

"You of course," said Miss Searle, reappearing and turning to me, "are included in my brother's invitation. I have bespoken your lodging as well. Your luggage shall immediately be sent for."

It was arranged that I in person should be driven over to our little inn, and that I should return with our effects in time to meet Mr Searle at dinner. On my arrival, several hours later, I was immediately conducted to my room. The servant pointed out to me that it communicated by a door and a private passage with that of my companion. I made my way along this passage,—a low, narrow corridor, with a long latticed casement, through which there streamed, upon a series of grotesquely sculptured oaken closets and cupboards, the lurid animating glow of the western sun,—knocked at his door, and, getting no answer, opened it. In an arm-chair by the open window sat my friend, sleeping, with arms and legs relaxed and head placidly reverted. It was a great relief to find him resting from his rhapsodies, and I watched him for some moments before waking him. There was a faint glow of color in his cheek and a light parting of his lips, as in a smile; something nearer to mental soundness than I had yet seen in him. It was almost happiness, it was almost health. I laid my hand on his arm and gently shook it. He opened his eyes, gazed at me a moment, vaguely recognized me, then closed them again. "Let me dream, let me dream!" he said.

"What are you dreaming about?"

A moment passed before his answer came. "About a tall woman in a quaint black dress, with yellow hair, and a sweet, sweet smile, and a soft, low, delicious voice! I'm in love with her."

"It's better to see her," I said, "than to dream about her. Get up and dress, and we shall go down to dinner and meet her."

"Dinner—dinner—" And he gradually opened his eyes again. "Yes, upon my word, I shall dine!"

"You're a well man!" I said, as he rose to his feet. "You'll live to bury Mr Simmons." He had spent the hours of my absence, he told me, with Miss Searle. They had strolled together over the park and through the gardens and greenhouses. "You must already be intimate!" I said, smiling.

"She is intimate with me," he answered. "Heaven knows what rigmarole I've treated her to!" They had parted an hour ago, since when, he believed, her brother had arrived.

The slow-fading twilight still abode in the great drawing-room as we entered it. The housekeeper had told us that this apartment was rarely used, there being a smaller and more convenient one for the same needs. It seemed now, however, to be occupied in my comrade's honor. At the farther end of it, rising to the roof, like a ducal tomb in a cathedral, was a great chimney-piece of chiselled white marble, yellowed by time, in which a light fire was crackling. Before the fire stood a small short man with his hands behind him; near him stood

Miss Searle, so transformed by her dress that at first I scarcely
knew her. There was in our entrance and reception something
profoundly chilling and solemn. We moved in silence up the
long room. Mr Searle advanced slowly a dozen steps to meet
us. His sister stood motionless. I was conscious of her masking
her visage with a large white tinselled fan, and of her eyes,
grave and expanded, watching us intently over the top of it.
The master of Lockley Park grasped in silence the proffered
hand of his kinsman, and eyed him from head to foot, sup-
pressing, I think, a start of surprise at his resemblance to Sir
Joshua's portrait. "This is a happy day!" he said. And then
turning to me with a bow, "My cousin's friend is my friend."
Miss Searle lowered her fan.

The first thing that struck me in Mr Searle's appearance
was his short and meagre stature, which was less by half a
head than that of his sister. The second was the preternatural
redness of his hair and beard. They intermingled over his
ears and surrounded his head like a huge lurid nimbus. His
face was pale and attenuated, like the face of a scholar, a
dilettante, a man who lives in a library, bending over books
and prints and medals. At a distance it had an oddly innocent
and youthful look; but on a nearer view it revealed a number
of finely etched and scratched wrinkles, of a singularly aged
and cunning effect. It was the complexion of a man of sixty.
His nose was arched and delicate, identical almost with the
nose of my friend. In harmony with the effect of his hair was
that of his eyes, which were large and deep-set, with a sort of
vulpine keenness and redness, but full of temper and spirit.
Imagine this physiognomy—grave and solemn in aspect,
grotesquely solemn, almost, in spite of the bushy brightness
in which it was encased—set in motion by a smile which
seemed to whisper terribly, "I am *the* smile, the sole and
official, the grin to command," and you will have an imperfect
notion of the remarkable presence of our host; something
better worth seeing and knowing, I fancied as I covertly

scrutinized him, than anything our excursion had yet introduced us to. Of how thoroughly I had entered into sympathy with my companion and how effectually I had associated my sensibilities with his, I had small suspicion until, within the short five minutes which preceded the announcement of dinner, I distinctly perceived him place himself, morally speaking, on the defensive. To neither of us was Mr Searle as the Italians would say, sympathetic. I might have fancied from her attitude that Miss Searle apprehended our thoughts. A signal change had been wrought in her since the morning; during the hour, indeed (as I read in the light of the wondering glance he cast at her), that had elapsed since her parting with her cousin. She had not yet recovered from some great agitation. Her face was pale and her eyes red with weeping. These tragic betrayals gave an unexpected dignity to her aspect, which was further enhanced by the rare picturesqueness of her dress.

Whether it was taste or whether it was accident, I know not; but Miss Searle, as she stood there, half in the cool twilight, half in the arrested glow of the fire as it spent itself in the vastness of its marble cave, was a figure for a cunning painter. She was dressed in the faded splendor of a beautiful tissue of combined and blended silk and crape of a tender sea-green color, festooned and garnished and puffed into a massive *bouillonnement;* a piece of millinery which, though it must have witnessed a number of stately dinners, preserved still an air of admirable elegance. Over her white shoulders she wore an ancient web of the most precious and venerable lace, and about her rounded throat a necklace of heavy pearls. I went with her in to dinner, and Mr Searle, following with my friend, took his arm (as the latter afterwards told me) and pretended sportively to conduct him. As dinner proceeded, the feeling grew within me that a drama had begun to be played in which the three persons before me were actors, each of a most exacting part. The part of my friend, however, seemed the most heavily charged, and I was filled with a strong desire that he should acquit himself with honor. I seemed to see him summon his shadowy faculties to obey his shadowy will. The poor fellow sat playing solemnly at self-esteem. With Miss Searle, credulous, passive, and pitying, he had finally flung aside all vanity and propriety, and shown her the bottom of his fantastic heart. But with our host there might be no talking of nonsense nor taking of liberties; there and then, if ever, sat a double-distilled conservative, breathing the fumes of hereditary privilege and security. For an hour, then, I saw my poor friend turn faithfully about to speak graciously of barren things. He was to prove himself a sound American, so that his relish of this elder world might seem purely disinterested. What his kinsman had expected to find him, I know not; but, with all his finely adjusted urbanity, he was unable to repress a shade of annoyance at finding him likely to speak graciously at all. Mr Searle was not the man to show his hand, but I think his best card had been a certain implicit confidence that this exotic parasite would hardly have good manners. Our host, with great decency, led the conversation to America, talking of it rather as if it were some fabled planet, alien to the British orbit, lately proclaimed indeed to have the proportion of atmospheric gases required to support animal life, but not, save under cover of a liberal afterthought, to be admitted into one's regular conception of things. I, for my part, felt nothing but regret that the spheric smoothness of his universe should be strained to cracking by the intrusion of our square shoulders.

"I knew in a general way," said Mr Searle, "of my having relations in America; but you know one hardly realizes those things. I could hardly more have imagined people of our blood there, than I could have imagined being there myself. There was a man I knew at college, a very odd fellow, a nice fellow too; he and I were rather cronies; I think he afterwards went to America; to the Argentine Republic, I believe. Do you know the Argentine Republic? What an extraordinary name, by the way! And then, you know, there was that great-uncle of mine whom Sir Joshua painted. He went to America, but he never got there. He was lost at sea. You look enough like him to have one fancy he *did* get there, and that he has lived along till now. If you are he, you've not done a wise thing to show yourself here. He left a bad name behind him. There's a ghost who comes sobbing about the house every now and then, the ghost of one against whom he wrought a great evil!"

"O brother!" cried Miss Searle, in simple horror.

"Of course you know nothing of such things," said Mr Searle. "You're too sound a sleeper to hear the sobbing of ghosts."

"I'm sure I should like immensely to hear the sobbing of a ghost!" said my friend, with the light of his previous eagerness playing up into his eyes. "Why does it sob? Unfold the wondrous tale."

Mr Searle eyed his audience for a moment gaugingly; and then, as the French say, *se recueillit*, as if he were measuring his own imaginative force.

He wished to do justice to his theme. With the five finger-nails of his left hand nervously playing against the tinkling crystal of his wineglass, and his bright eye telling of a gleeful sense that, small and grotesque as he sat there, he was for the moment profoundly impressive, he distilled into our un-tutored minds the sombre legend of his house. "Mr Clement Searle, from all I gather, was a young man of great talents but a weak disposition. His mother was left a widow early in life, with two sons, of whom he was the older and the more promising. She educated him with the utmost fondness and care. Of course, when he came to manhood she wished him to marry well. His means were quite sufficient to enable him to overlook the want of means in his wife; and Mrs Searle selected a young lady who possessed, as she conceived, every good gift save a fortune,—a fine, proud, handsome girl, the daughter of an old friend,—an old lover, I fancy, of her own. Clement, however, as it appeared, had either chosen otherwise or was as yet unprepared to choose. The young lady discharged upon him in vain the battery of her attractions; in vain his mother urged her cause. Clement remained cold, insensible, inflexible. Mrs Searle possessed a native force of which in its feminine branch the family seems to have lost trick. A proud, passionate, imperious woman, she had had great cares and a number of lawsuits; they had given her a great will. She suspected that her son's affections were lodged elsewhere, and lodged amiss. Irritated by his stubborn defiance of her wishes, she persisted in her urgency. The more she watched him the more she believed that he loved in secret. If he loved in secret, of course he loved beneath him. He went about sombre, sullen, and preoccupied. At last, with the fatal indiscretion of an angry woman, she threatened to bring the young lady of her choice—who, by the way, seems to have been no shrinking blossom—to stay in the house. A stormy scene was the result. He threatened that if she did so, he would leave the country and sail for America. She probably disbelieved him; she knew him to be weak, but she overrated his weakness. At all events, the fair rejected arrived and Clement departed. On a dark December day he took ship at Southampton. The two women, desperate with rage and sorrow, sat alone in this great house, mingling their tears and imprecations. A fortnight later, on Christmas eve, in the midst of a great snow-storm, long famous in the country, there came to them a mighty quickening of their bitterness. A young woman, soaked and chilled by the storm, gained entrance to the house and made her way into the presence of the mistress and her guest. She poured out her tale. She was a poor curate's daughter of Hereford. Clement Searle had loved her; loved her all too well. She had been turned out in wrath from her father's house; his mother, at least, might pity her; if not for herself, then for the child she was soon to bring forth. The poor girl had been a second time too trustful. The women, in scorn, in horror, with blows, possibly, turned her forth again into the storm. In the storm she wandered, and in the deep snow she died. Her lover, as you know, perished in that hard winter weather at sea; the news came to his mother late, but soon enough. We are haunted by the curate's daughter!"

There was a pause of some moments. "Ah, well we may be!" said Miss Searle, with a great pity.

Searle blazed up into enthusiasm. "Of course you know," —and suddenly he began to blush violently,—"I should be sorry to claim any identity with my faithless namesake, poor fellow. But I shall be hugely tickled if this poor ghost should be deceived by my resemblance and mistake me for her cruel lover. She's welcome to the comfort of it. What one can do in the case I shall be glad to do. But can a ghost haunt a ghost? I *am* a ghost!"

Mr Searle stared a moment, and then smiling superbly: "I could almost believe you are!" he said.

"Oh brother—cousin!" cried Miss Searle, with the gentlest, yet most appealing dignity, "how can you talk so horribly?"

This horrible talk, however, evidently possessed a potent magic for my friend; and his imagination, chilled for a while by the frigid contact of his kinsman, began to glow again with its earlier fire. From this moment he ceased to steer his cockle-shell, to care what he said or how he said it, so long as he expressed his passionate satisfaction in the scene about him. As he talked I ceased even mentally to protest. I have wondered since that I should not have resented the exhibition of so rank and florid an egotism. But a great frankness for the time makes its own law, and a great passion its own channel. There was, moreover, an immense sweetness in the manner of my friend's speech. Free alike from either adulation or envy, the very soul of it was a divine apprehension, an imaginative mastery, free as the flight of Ariel, of the poetry of his companions' situation and of the contrasted prosiness of their attitude.

"How does the look of age come?" he demanded, at dessert. "Does it come of itself, unobserved, unrecorded, unmeasured? Or do you woo it and set baits and traps for it, and watch it like the dawning brownness of a meerschaum pipe, and nail it down when it appears, just where it peeps out, and light a votive taper beneath it and give thanks to it daily? Or do you forbid it and fight it and resist it, and yet feel it settling and deepening about you, as irresistible as fate?"

"What the deuce is the man talking about?" said the smile of our host.

"I found a gray hair this morning," said Miss Searle.

"Good heavens! I hope you respected it," cried Searle.

"I looked at it for a long time in my little glass," said his cousin, simply.

"Miss Searle, for many years to come, can afford to be amused at gray hairs," I said.

"Ten years hence I shall be forty-three," she answered.

"That's my age," said Searle. "If I had only come here ten years ago! I should have had more time to enjoy the feast, but I should have had less of an appetite. I needed to get famished for it."

"Why did you wait for the starving point?" asked Mr Searle. "To think of these ten years that we might have been enjoying you!" And at the thought of these wasted ten years Mr Searle broke into a violent nervous laugh.

"I always had a notion,—a stupid, vulgar notion, if there ever was one,—that to come abroad properly one ought to have a pot of money. My pot was too nearly empty. At last I came with my empty pot!"

Mr Searle coughed with an air of hesitation. "You're a— you're in limited circumstances?"

My friend apparently was vastly tickled to have his bleak

situation called by so soft a name. "Limited circumstances!"
he cried with a long, light laugh; "I'm in no circumsatnces
at all!"

"Upon my word!" murmured Mr Searle, with an air of
being divided between his sense of the indecency and his sense
of the rarity of a gentleman taking just that tone about his
affairs. "Well—well—well!" he added, in a voice which
might have meant everything or nothing; and proceeded,
with a twinkle in his eye, to finish a glass of wine. His spark-
ling eye, as he drank, encountered mine over the top of his
glass, and, for a moment, we exchanged a long deep glance,—
a glance so keen as to leave a slight embarrassment on the
face of each. "And you," said Mr Searle, by way of carrying
it off, "how about your circumstances?"

"O, his," said my friend, "his are unlimited! He could
buy up Lockley Park!" He had drunk, I think, a rather
greater number of glasses of port—I admit that the port was
infinitely drinkable—than was to have been desired in the
interest of perfect self-control. He was rapidly drifting beyond
any tacit dissuasion of mine. A certain feverish harshness in
his glance and voice warned me that to attempt to direct him
would simply irritate him. As we rose from the table he caught
my troubled look. Passing his arm for a moment into mine,
"This is the great night!" he whispered. "The night of
fatality, the night of destiny!"

Mr Searle had caused the whole lower region of the house
to be thrown open and a multitude of lights to be placed in
convenient and effective positions. Such a marshalled wealth
of ancient candlesticks and flambeaux I had never beheld.
Niched against the dark panellings, casting great luminous
circles upon the pendent stiffness of sombre tapestries, enhancing and completing with admirable effect the vastness
and mystery of the ancient house, they seemed to people the
great rooms, as our little group passed slowly from one to
another, with a dim, expectant presence. We had a delightful

hour of it. Mr Searle at once assumed the part of cicerone, and
—I had not hitherto done him justice—Mr Searle became
agreeable. While I lingered behind with Miss Searle, he walked
in advance with his kinsman. It was as if he had said, "Well,
if you want the old place, you shall have it—metaphysically!"
To speak vulgarly, he rubbed it in. Carrying a great silver
candlestick in his left hand, he raised it and lowered it and
cast the light hither and thither, upon pictures and hangings
and bits of carving and a hundred lurking architectural
treasures. Mr Searle knew his house. He hinted at innumerable
traditions and memories, and evoked with a very pretty wit
the figures of its earlier occupants. He told a dozen anecdotes
with an almost reverential gravity and neatness. His companion attended, with a sort of brooding intelligence. Miss
Searle and I, meanwhile, were not wholly silent.

"I suppose that by this time," I said, "you and your
cousin are almost old friends."

She trifled a moment with her fan, and then raising her
homely candid gaze: "Old friends, and at the same time
strangely new! My cousin,—my cousin,"—and her voice
lingered on the word,—"it seems so strange to call him my
cousin, after thinking these many years that I had no cousin!
He's a most singular man."

"It's not so much he as his circumstances that are singular,"
I ventured to say.

"I'm so sorry for his circumstances. I wish I could help
him in some way. He interests me so much." And here Miss
Searle gave a rich, mellow sigh. "I wish I had known him a
long time ago. He told me that he is but the shadow of what
he was."

I wondered whether Searle had been consciously playing
upon the fancy of this gentle creature. If he had, I believed
he had gained his point. But in fact, his position had become
to my sense so charged with opposing forces, that I hardly
ventured wholly to rejoice. "His better self just now," I

said, "seems again to be taking shape. It will have been a good deed on your part, Miss Searle, if you help to restore him to soundness and serenity."

"Ah, what can I do?"

"Be a friend to him. Let him like you, let him love you! You see in him now, doubtless, much to pity and to wonder at. But let him simply enjoy awhile the grateful sense of your nearness and dearness. He will be a better and stronger man for it, and then you can love him, you can respect him without restriction."

Miss Searle listened with a puzzled tenderness of gaze. "It's a hard part for poor me to play!"

Her almost infantine gentleness left me no choice but to be absolutely frank. "Did you ever play any part at all?" I asked.

Her eyes met mine, wonderingly; she blushed, as with a sudden sense of my meaning. "Never! I think I have hardly lived."

"You've begun now, perhaps. You have begun to care for something outside the narrow circle of habit and duty. (Excuse me if I am rather too outspoken: you know I'm a foreigner.) It's a great moment: I wish you joy!"

"I could almost fancy you are laughing at me. I feel more trouble than joy."

"Why do you feel trouble?"

She paused, with her eyes fixed on our two companions. "My cousin's arrival," she said at last, "is a great disturbance."

"You mean that you did wrong in recognizing him? In that case the fault is mine. He had no intention of giving you the opportunity."

"I did wrong, after a fashion! But I can't find it in my heart to regret it. I never shall regret it! I did what I thought proper. Heaven forgive me!"

"Heaven bless you, Miss Searle! Is any harm to come of it? I did the evil; let me bear the brunt!"

She shook her head gravely. "You don't know my brother!"

"The sooner I do know him, then, the better!" And hereupon I felt a dull irritation which had been gathering force for more than an hour explode into sudden wrath. "What on earth *is* your brother?" I demanded. She turned away. "Are you afraid of him?" I asked.

She gave me a tearful sidelong glance. "He's looking at me!" she murmured.

I looked at him. He was standing with his back to us, holding a large Venetian hand-mirror, framed in rococo silver, which he had taken from a shelf of antiquities, in just such a position that he caught the reflection of his sister's person. Shall I confess it? Something in this performance so tickled my sense of the picturesque, that it was with a sort of blunted anger that I muttered, "The sneak!" Yet I felt passion enough to urge me forward. It seemed to me that by implication I, too, was being covertly watched. I should not be watched for nothing! "Miss Searle," I said, insisting upon her attention, "promise me something."

She turned upon me with a start and the glance of one appealing from some great pain. "O, don't ask me!" she cried. It was as if she were standing on the verge of some sudden lapse of familiar ground and had been summoned to make a leap. I felt that retreat was impossible, and that it was the greater kindness to beckon her forward.

"Promise me," I repeated.

Still with her eyes she protested. "O, dreadful day!" she cried, at last.

"Promise me to let him speak to you, if he should ask you, any wish you may suspect on your brother's part notwithstanding."

She colored deeply. "You mean," she said,—"you mean that he—has something particular to say."

"Something most particular!"

"Poor cousin!"

I gave her a deeply questioning look. "Well, poor cousin! But promise me."

"I promise," she said, and moved away across the long room and out of the door.

"You're in time to hear the most delightful story!" said my friend, as I rejoined the two gentlemen. They were standing before an old sombre portrait of a lady in the dress of Queen Anne's time, with her ill-painted flesh-tints showing livid in the candlelight against her dark drapery and background. "This is Mistress Margaret Searle,—a sort of Beatrix Esmond,—who did as she pleased. She married a paltry Frenchman, a penniless fiddler, in the teeth of her whole family. Fair Margaret, my compliments! Upon my soul, she looks like Miss Searle! Pray go on. What came of it all?"

Mr Searle looked at his kinsman for a moment with an air of distaste for his boisterous homage, and of pity for his crude imagination. Then resuming, with a very effective dryness of tone: "I found a year ago, in a box of very old papers, a letter from Mistress Margaret to Cynthia Searle, her elder sister. It was dated from Paris and dreadfully ill-spelled. It contained a most passionate appeal for—a—for pecuniary assistance. She had just been confined, she was starving, and neglected by her husband; she cursed the day she left England. It was a most dismal effusion. I never heard that she found means to return."

"So much for marrying a Frenchman!" I said, sententiously.

Mr Searle was silent for some moments. "This was the first," he said finally, "and the last of the family who has been so d—d un-English!"

"Does Miss Searle know her history?" asked my friend, staring at the rounded whiteness of the lady's heavy cheek.

"Miss Searle knows nothing!" said our host, with zeal.

This utterance seemed to kindle in my friend a generous opposing zeal. "She shall know at least the tale of Mistress Margaret," he cried, and walked rapidly away in search of her.

Mr Searle and I pursued our march through the lighted rooms. "You've found a cousin," I said, "with a vengeance."

"Ah, a vengeance?" said my host, stiffly.

"I mean that he takes as keen an interest in your annals and possessions as yourself."

"O, exactly so!" and Mr Searle burst into resounding laughter. "He tells me," he resumed, in a moment, "that he is an invalid. I should never have fancied it."

"Within the past few hours," I said, "he's a changed man. Your place and your kindness have refreshed him immensely."

Mr Searle uttered the little shapeless ejaculation with which many an Englishman is apt to announce the concussion of any especial courtesy of speech. He bent his eyes on the floor frowningly, and then, to my surprise, he suddenly stopped and looked at me with a penetrating eye. "I'm an honest man!" he said. I was quite prepared to assent; but he went on, with a sort of fury of frankness, as if it was the first time in his life that he had been prompted to expound himself, as if the process was mightily unpleasant to him and he was hurrying through it as a task. "An honest man, mind you! I know nothing about Mr Clement Searle! I never expected to see him. He has been to me a—a—" And here Mr Searle paused to select a word which should vividly enough express what, for good or for ill, his kinsman had been to him. "He has been to me an *amazement!* I have no doubt he is a most amiable man! You'll not deny, however, that he's a very odd style of person. I'm sorry he's ill! I'm sorry he's poor! He's my fiftieth cousin! Well and good! I'm an honest man. He shall not have it to say that he was not received at my house."

"He, too, thank heaven! is an honest man!" I said, smiling.

"Why the deuce, then," cried Mr Searle, turning almost fiercely upon me, "has he established this underhand claim to my property?"

This startling utterance flashed backward a gleam of light upon the demeanor of our host and the suppressed agitation of his sister. In an instant the jealous soul of the unhappy gentleman revealed itself. For a moment I was so amazed and scandalized at the directness of his attack that I lacked words to respond. As soon as he had spoken, Mr Searle appeared to feel that he had struck too hard a blow. "Excuse me, sir," he hurried on, "if I speak of this matter with heat. But I have seldom suffered so grievous a shock as on learning, as I learned this morning from my solicitor, the monstrous proceedings of Mr Clement Searle. Great heaven, sir, for what does the man take me? He pretends to the Lord knows what fantastic passion for my place. Let him respect it, then. Let him, with his tawdry parade of imagination, imagine a tithe of what I feel. I love my estate; it's my passion, my life, myself! Am I to make a great hole in it for a beggarly foreigner, a man without means, without proof, a stranger, an adventurer, a Bohemian? I thought America boasted that she had land for all men! Upon my soul, sir, I have never been so shocked in my life."

I paused for some moments before speaking, to allow his passion fully to expend itself and to flicker up again if it chose; for on my own part it seemed well that I should answer him once for all. "Your really absurd apprehensions, Mr Searle," I said at last,—"your terrors, I may call them,—have fairly overmastered your common-sense. You are attacking a man of straw, a creature of base illusion; though I'm sadly afraid you have wounded a man of spirit and of conscience. Either my friend has no valid claim on your estate, in which case your agitation is superfluous; or he *has* a valid claim—"

Mr Searle seized my arm and glared at me, as I may say; his pale face paler still with the horror of my suggestion, his great keen eyes flashing, and his flamboyant hair erect and quivering.

"A valid claim!" he whispered. "Let him try it!"

We had emerged into the great hall of the mansion and stood facing the main doorway. The door stood open into the porch, through whose stone archway I saw the garden glittering in the blue light of a full moon. As Mr Searle uttered the words I have just repeated, I beheld my companion come slowly up into the porch from without, bareheaded, bright in the outer moonlight, dark then in the shadow of the archway, and bright again in the lamplight on the threshold of the hall. As he crossed the threshold the butler made his appearance at the head of the staircase on our left, faltered visibly a moment on seeing Mr Searle; but then, perceiving my friend, he gravely descended. He bore in his hand a small plated salver. On the salver, gleaming in the light of the suspended lamp, lay a folded note. Clement Searle came forward, staring a little and startled, I think, by some fine sense of a near explosion. The butler applied the match. He advanced toward my friend, extending salver and note. Mr Searle made a movement as if to spring forward, but controlled himself. "Tottenham!" he shouted, in strident voice.

"Yes, sir!" said Tottenham, halting.

"Stand where you are. For whom is that note?"

"For Mr Clement Searle," said the butler, staring straight before him as if to discredit a suspicion of his having read the direction.

"Who gave it to you?"

"Mrs Horridge, sir." (The housekeeper.)

"Who gave it Mrs Horridge?"

There was on Tottenham's part just an infinitesimal pause before replying.

"My dear sir," broke in Searle, completely sobered by the sense of violated courtesy, "isn't that rather my business?"

"What happens in my house is my business; and mighty strange things seem to be happening." Mr Searle had become exasperated to that point that, a rare thing for an Englishman, he compromised himself before a servant.

"Bring me the note!" he cried. The butler obeyed.

"Really, this is too much!" cried my companion, affronted and helpless.

I was disgusted. Before Mr Searle had time to take the note, I possessed myself of it. "If you have no regard for your sister," I said, "let a stranger, at least, act for her." And I tore the disputed thing into a dozen pieces.

"In the name of decency," cried Searle, "what does this horrid business mean?"

Mr Searle was about to break out upon him; but at this moment his sister appeared on the staircase, summoned evidently by our high-pitched and angry voices. She had exchanged her dinner-dress for a dark dressing-gown, removed her ornaments, and begun to disarrange her hair, a heavy truss of which escaped from the comb. She hurried downward, with a pale, questioning face. Feeling distinctly that, for ourselves, immediate departure was in the air, and divining Mr Tottenham to be a butler of remarkable intuitions and extreme celerity, I seized the opportunity to request him, *sotto voce*, to send a carriage to the door without delay. "And put up our things," I added.

Our host rushed at his sister and seized the white wrist which escaped from the loose sleeve of her dress. "What was in that note?" he demanded.

Miss Searle looked first at its scattered fragments and then at her cousin. "Did you read it?" she asked.

"No, but I thank you for it!" said Searle.

Her eyes for an instant communed brightly with his own; then she transferred them to her brother's face, where the light went out of them and left a dull, sad patience. An inexorable patience he seemed to find it; he flushed crimson with rage and the sense of his unhandsomeness, and flung her away. "You're a child!" he cried. "Go to bed."

In poor Searle's face as well the gathered serenity was twisted into a sickened frown, and the reflected brightness of his happy day turned to blank confusion. "Have I been dealing these three hours with a madman?" he asked plaintively.

"A madman, yes, if you will! A man mad with the love of his home and the sense of its stability. I have held my tongue till now, but you have been too much for me. Who are you, what are you? From what paradise of fools do you come, that you fancy I shall cut off a piece of my land, my home, my heart, to toss to you? Forsooth, I shall share my land with you? Prove your infernal claim! There isn't *that* in it!" And he kicked one of the bits of paper on the floor.

Searle received this broadside gaping. Then turning away, he went and seated himself on a bench against the wall and rubbed his forehead amazedly. I looked at my watch, and listened for the wheels of our carriage.

Mr Searle went on. "Wasn't it enough that you should have practised against my property? Need you have come into my very house to practise against my sister?"

Searle put his two hands to his face. "Oh, oh, oh!" he softly roared.

Miss Searle crossed rapidly and dropped on her knees at his side.

"Go to bed, you fool!" shrieked her brother.

"Dear cousin," said Miss Searle, "it's cruel that you are to have to think of us so!"

"O, I shall think of you!" he said. And he laid a hand on her head.

"I believe you have done nothing wrong!" she murmured.

"I've done what I could," her brother pursued. "But it's arrant folly to pretend to friendship when this abomination lies between us. You were welcome to my meat and my wine, but I wonder you could swallow them. The sight spoiled my appetite!" cried the furious little man, with a laugh. "Proceed with your case! My people in London are instructed and prepared."

"I have a fancy," I said to Searle, "that your case has vastly improved since you gave it up."

"Oho! you don't feign ignorance, then?" and he shook his flaming *chevelure* at me. "It is very kind of you to give it up!" And he laughed resoundingly. "Perhaps you will also give up my sister!"

Searle sat in his chair in a species of collapse, staring at his adversary. "O miserable man!" he moaned at last. "I fancied we had become such friends!"

"Boh! you imbecile!" cried our host.

Searle seemed not to hear him. "Am I seriously expected," he pursued, slowly and painfully—"am I seriously expected —to—to sit here and defend myself—to prove I have done nothing wrong? Think what you please." And he rose, with an effort, to his feet. "I know what *you* think!" he added, to Miss Searle.

The carriage wheels resounded on the gravel, and at the same moment the footman descended with our two portmanteaus. Mr Tottenham followed him with our hats and coats.

"Good God!" cried Mr Searle; "you are not going away!" This ejaculation, under the circumstances, had a grand comicality which prompted me to violent laughter. "Bless my soul!" he added; "of course you are going."

"It's perhaps well," said Miss Searle, with a great effort, inexpressibly touching in one for whom great efforts were visibly new and strange, "that I should tell you what my poor little note contained."

"That matter of your note, madam," said her brother, "you and I will settle together!"

"Let me imagine its contents," said Searle.

"Ah! they have been too much imagined!" she answered simply. "It was only a word of warning. I knew something painful was coming."

Searle took his hat. "The pains and the pleasures of this day," he said to his kinsman, "I shall equally never forget. Knowing you," and he offered his hand to Miss Searle, "has been the pleasure of pleasures. I hoped something more was to come of it."

"A deal too much has come of it!" cried our host, irrepressibly.

Searle looked at him mildly, almost benignantly, from head to foot; and then closing his eyes with an air of sudden physical distress: "I'm afraid so! I can't stand more of this." I gave him my arm, and crossed the threshold. As we passed out I heard Miss Searle burst into a torrent of sobs.

"We shall hear from each other yet, I take it!" cried her brother, harassing our retreat.

Searle stopped and turned round on him sharply, almost fiercely. "O ridiculous man!" he cried.

"Do you mean to say you shall not prosecute?" screamed the other. "I shall force you to prosecute! I shall drag you into court, and you shall be beaten—beaten—beaten!" And this soft vocable continued to ring in our ears as we drove away.

We drove, of course, to the little wayside inn whence we had departed in the morning so unencumbered, in all broad England, with either enemies or friends. My companion, as the carriage rolled along, seemed utterly overwhelmed and exhausted. "What a dream!" he murmured stupidly. "What an awakening! What a long, long day! What a hideous scene! Poor me! Poor woman!" When we had resumed possession of our two little neighboring rooms, I asked him if Miss Searle's note had been the result of anything that had passed between them on his going to rejoin her. "I found her on the terrace," he said, "walking a restless walk in the moonlight. I was greatly excited; I hardly knew what I said. I asked her, I think, if she knew the story of Margaret Searle. She seemed frightened and troubled, and she used just the words her brother had used, 'I know nothing.' For the moment, somehow, I felt as a man drunk. I stood before her and told her, with great emphasis, how sweet Margaret Searle had married a beggarly foreigner, in obedience to her heart and in defiance of her family. As I talked the sheeted moonlight seemed to close about us, and we stood in a dream, in a solitude, in a romance. She grew younger, fairer, more gracious. I trembled with a divine loquacity. Before I knew it I had gone too far. I was taking her hand and calling her 'Margaret!' She had said that it was impossible; that she could do nothing; that she was a fool, a child, a slave. Then, with a sudden huge conviction, I spoke of my claim against the estate. 'It exists, then?' she said. 'It exists,' I answered, 'but I have foregone it. Be generous! Pay it from your heart!' For an instant her face was radiant. 'If I marry you,' she cried, 'it will repair the trouble.' 'In our marriage,' I affirmed, 'the trouble will melt away like a rain-drop in the ocean.' 'Our marriage!' she repeated, wonderingly; and the deep, deep ring of her voice seemed to shatter the crystal walls of our illusion. 'I must think, I must think!' she said; and she hurried away with her face in her hands. I walked up and down the terrace for some moments, and then came in and met you. This is the only witchcraft I have used!"

The poor fellow was at once so excited and so exhausted by the day's events, that I fancied he would get little sleep. Conscious, on my own part, of a stubborn wakefulness, I but partly undressed, set my fire a blazing, and sat down to do some writing. I heard the great clock in the little parlor below strike twelve, one, half past one. Just as the vibration of this last stroke was dying on the air the door of communication into Searle's room was flung open, and my companion stood on the threshold, pale as a corpse, in his nightshirt, standing like a phantom against the darkness behind him. "Look at me!" he said, in a low voice, "touch me, embrace me, revere me! You see a man who has seen a ghost!"

"Great heaven, what do you mean?"

"Write it down!" he went on. "There, take your pen. Put it into dreadful words. Make it of all ghost-stories the ghostliest, the truest! How do I look? Am I human? Am I pale? Am I red? Am I speaking English? A ghost, sir! Do you understand?"

I confess, there came upon me, by contact, a great supernatural shock. I shall always feel that I, too, have seen a ghost. My first movement—I can't smile at it even now—was to spring to the door, close it with a great blow, and then turn the key upon the gaping blackness from which Searle had emerged. I seized his two hands; they were wet with perspiration. I pushed my chair to the fire and forced him to sit down in it. I kneeled down before him and held his hands as firmly as possible. They trembled and quivered; his eyes were fixed, save that the pupil dilated and contracted with extraordinary force. I asked no questions, but waited with my heart in my throat. At last he spoke. "I'm not frightened, but I'm—O, EXCITED! This is life! This is living! My nerves—my heart—my brain! They are throbbing with the wildness of a myriad lives! Do you feel it? Do you tingle? Are you hot? Are you cold? Hold me tight—tight—tight! I shall tremble away into waves—waves—waves, and know the universe and approach my Maker!" He paused a moment and then went on: "A woman—as clear as that candle.—No, far clearer! In a blue dress, with a black mantle on her head, and a little black muff. Young, dreadfully pretty, pale and ill, with the sadness of all the women who ever loved and suffered pleading and accusing in her dead dark eyes. God knows I never did any such thing! But she took me for my elder, for the other Clement. She came to me here as she would have come to me there. She wrung her hands and spoke to me. 'Marry me!' she moaned; 'marry me and right me!' I sat up in bed just as I sit here, looked at her, heard her,—heard her voice melt away, watched her figure fade away. Heaven and earth! Here I am!''

I made no attempt either to explain my friend's vision or to discredit it. It is enough that I felt for the hour the irresistible contagion of his own agitation. On the whole, I think my own vision was the more interesting of the two. He beheld but the transient, irresponsible spectre: I beheld the human subject, hot from the spectral presence. Nevertheless, I soon recovered my wits sufficiently to feel the necessity of guarding my friend's health against the evil results of excitement and exposure. It was tacitly established that, for the night, he was not to return to his room; and I soon made him fairly comfortable in his place by the fire. Wishing especially to obviate a chill, I removed my bedding and wrapped him about with multitudinous blankets and counterpanes. I had no nerves either for writing or sleep; so I put out my lights, renewed the fire, and sat down on the opposite side of the hearth. I found a kind of solemn entertainment in watching my friend. Silent, swathed and muffled to his chin, he sat rigid and erect with the dignity of his great adventure. For the most part his eyes were closed; though from time to time he would open them with a vast steady expansion and gaze unblinking into the firelight, as if he again beheld, without terror, the image of that blighted maid. With his cadaverous, emaciated face, his tragic wrinkles, intensified by the upward glow from the hearth, his drooping black mustache, his transcendent gravity, and a certain high fantastical air in the flickering alternations of his brow, he looked like the vision-haunted knight of La Mancha, nursed by the Duke and Duchess. The night passed wholly without speech. Towards its close I slept for half an hour. When I awoke the awakened birds had begun to twitter. Searle sat unperturbed, staring at me. We exchanged a long look; I felt with a pang that his glittering eyes had tasted their last of natural sleep. "How is it? are you comfortable?" I asked.

He gazed for some time without replying. Then he spoke with a strange, innocent grandiloquence, and with pauses between his words, as if an inner voice were slowly prompting him. "You asked me, when you first knew me, what I was. 'Nothing,' I said,—'nothing.' Nothing I have always deemed myself. But I have wronged myself. I'm a personage! I'm rare among men! I'm a haunted man!"

Sleep had passed out of his eyes: I felt with a deeper pang that perfect sanity had passed out of his voice. From this moment I prepared myself for the worst. There was in my friend, however, such an essential gentleness and conservative patience, that to persons surrounding him the worst was likely to come without hurry or violence. He had so confirmed a habit of good manners that, at the core of reason, the process of disorder might have been long at work without finding an issue. As morning began fully to dawn upon us, I brought our grotesque vigil to an end. Searle appeared so weak that I gave him my hands to help him to rise from his chair; he retained them for some moments after rising to his feet, from an apparent inability to keep his balance. "Well," he said, "I've seen one ghost, but I doubt of my living to see another. I shall soon be myself as brave a ghost as the best of them. I shall haunt Mr Searle! It can only mean one thing,—my near, dear death."

On my proposing breakfast, "This shall be my breakfast!" he said; and he drew from his travelling-sack a phial of morphine. He took a strong dose and went to bed. At noon I found him on foot again, dressed, shaved, and apparently refreshed. "Poor fellow!" he said, "you have got more than you bargained for,—a ghost-encumbered comrade. But it won't be for long." It immediately became a question, of course, whither we should now direct our steps.

"As I have so little time," said Searle, "I should like to

see the best, the best alone." I answered that, either for time
or eternity, I had imagined Oxford to be the best thing in
England; and for Oxford in the course of an hour we accordingly departed.

Of Oxford I feel small vocation to speak in detail. It must
long remain for an American one of the supreme gratifications
of travel. The impression it produces, the emotions it stirs,
in an American mind, are too large and various to be com-
passed by words. It seems to embody with undreamed
completeness a kind of dim and sacred ideal of the Western
intellect,—a scholastic city, an appointed home of contemplation. No other spot in Europe, I imagine, extorts from our
barbarous hearts so passionate an admiration. A finer pen
than mine must enumerate the splendid devices by which it
performs this great office; I can bear testimony only to the
dominant tone of its effect. Passing through the various
streets in which the obverse longitude of the hoary college
walls seems to maintain an antique stillness, you feel this to
be the most dignified of towns. Over all, through all, the
great corporate fact of the University prevails and penetrates,
like some steady bass in a symphony of lighter chords, like
the mediæval and mystical presence of the Empire in the
linked dispersion of lesser states. The plain Gothic of the
long street-fronts of the colleges—blessed seraglios of
culture and leisure—irritate the fancy like the blank harem-
walls of Eastern towns. Within their arching portals, however,
you preceive more sacred and sunless courts, and the dark
verdure grateful and restful to bookish eyes. The gray-green
quadrangles stand forever open with a noble and trustful
hospitality. The seat of the humanities is stronger in the
admonitory shadow of her great name than in a marshalled
host of wardens and beadles. Directly after our arrival my
friend and I strolled eagerly forth in the luminous early dusk.
We reached the bridge which passes beneath the walls of
Magdalen and saw the eight-spired tower, embossed with its

slender shaftings, rise in temperate beauty,—the perfect prose of Gothic,—wooing the eyes to the sky, as it was slowly drained of day. We entered the little monkish doorway and stood in that dim, fantastic outer court, made narrow by the dominant presence of the great tower, in which the heart beats faster, and the swallows niche more lovingly in the tangled ivy, I fancied, than elsewhere in Oxford. We passed thence into the great cloister, and studied the little sculptured monsters along the entablature of the arcade. I was pleased to see that Searle became extremely interested; but I very soon began to fear that the influence of the place would prove too potent for his unbalanced imagination. I may say that from this time forward, with my unhappy friend, I found it hard to distinguish between the play of fancy and the labor of thought, and to fix the balance between perception and illusion. He had already taken a fancy to confound his identity with that of the earlier Clement Searle; he now began to speak almost wholly as from the imagined consciousness of his old-time kinsman.

"This was my college, you know," he said, "the noblest in all Oxford. How often I have paced this gentle cloister, side by side with a friend of the hour! My friends are all dead, but many a young fellow as we meet him, dark or fair, tall or short, reminds me of them. Even Oxford, they say, feels about its massive base the murmurs of the tide of time; there are things eliminated, things insinuated! Mine was ancient Oxford,—the fine old haunt of rank abuses, of precedent and privilege. What cared I, who was a perfect gentleman, with my pockets full of money? I had an allowance of two thousand a year."

It became evident to me, on the following day, that his strength had begun to ebb, and that he was unequal to the labor of regular sight-seeing. He read my apprehension in my eyes, and took pains to assure me that I was right. "I am going down hill. Thank heaven it's an easy slope, coated

with English turf and with an English churchyard at the foot."
The almost hysterical emotion produced by our adventure
at Lockley Park had given place to a broad, calm satisfaction,
in which the scene around us was reflected as in the depths of
a lucid lake. We took an afternoon walk through Christ-
Church Meadow, and at the river-bank procured a boat,
which I pulled up the stream to Iffley and to the slanting
woods of Nuneham,—the sweetest, flattest, reediest streamside landscape that the heart need demand. Here, of course,
we encountered in hundreds the mighty lads of England, clad
in white flannel and blue, immense, fair-haired, magnificent
in their youth, lounging down the current in their idle punts,
in friendly couples or in solitude possibly portentous of
scholastic honors; or pulling in straining crews and hoarsely
exhorted from the near bank. When, in conjunction with all
this magnificent sport, you think of the verdant quietude and
the silvery sanctities of the college gardens, you cannot but
consider that the youth of England have their porridge well
salted. As my companion found himself less and less able to
walk, we repaired on three successive days to these scholastic
domains, and spent long hours sitting in their greenest places.
They seemed to us the fairest things in England and the ripest
and sweetest fruits of the English system. Locked in their
antique verdure, guarded (as in the case of New College) by
gentle battlements of silver-gray, outshouldering the matted
leafage of centenary vines, filled with perfumes and privacy
and memories, with students lounging bookishly on the turf
(as if tenderly to spare it the pressure of their boot-heels),
and with the great conservative presence of the college front
appealing gravely from the restless outer world, they seem
places to lie down on the grass in forever, in the happy faith
that life is all a vast old English garden, and time an endless
English afternoon. This charmed seclusion was especially
grateful to my friend, and his sense of it reached its climax,
I remember, on the last afternoon of our three, as we sat

dreaming in the spacious garden of St John's. The long college façade here, perhaps, broods over the lawn with a more
effective air of property than elsewhere. Searle fell into un-
ceasing talk and exhaled his swarming impressions with a
tender felicity, compounded of the oddest mixture of wisdom
and folly. Every student who passed us was the subject of an
extemporized romance, and every feature of the place the
theme of a lyric rhapsody.

"Isn't it all," he demanded, "a delightful lie? Mightn't
one fancy this the very central point of the world's heart,
where all the echoes of the world's life arrive only to falter
and die? Listen! The air is thick with arrested voices. It is
well there should be such places, shaped in the interest of
factitious needs; framed to minister to the book-begotten
longing for a medium in which one may dream unwaked,
and believe unconfuted; to foster the sweet illusion that all is
well in this weary world, all perfect and rounded, mellow and
complete in this sphere of the pitiful unachieved and the
dreadful uncommenced. The world's made! Work's over!
Now for leisure! England's safe! Now for Theocritus and
Horace, for lawn and sky! What a sense it all gives one of the
composite life of England, and how essential a factor of the
educated, British consciousness one omits in not thinking of
Oxford! Thank heaven they had the wit to send me here in
the other time. I'm not much with it, perhaps; but what should
I have been without it? The misty spires and towers of Oxford
seen far off on the level have been all these years one of the
constant things of memory. Seriously, what does Oxford do
for these people? Are they wiser, gentler, richer, deeper? At
moments when its massive influence surges into my mind
like a tidal wave, I take it as a sort of affront to my dignity.
My soul reverts to the naked background of our own education, the dead white wall before which we played our parts.
I assent it to all with a sort of desperate calmness; I bow to it
with a dogged pride. We are nursed at the opposite pole.

Naked come we into a naked world. There is a certain grandeur in the absence of a *mise en scène*, a certain heroic strain
in those young imaginations of the West, which find nothing
made to their hands, which have to concoct their own
mysteries, and raise high into our morning air, with a ringing
hammer and nails, the castles in which they dwell. *Noblesse
oblige:* Oxford obliges. What a horrible thing not to respond
to such obligations. If you pay the pious debt to the last
farthing of interest, you may go through life with her blessing; but if you let it stand unhonored, you are a worse
barbarian than we! But for better or worse, in a myriad
private hearts, think how she must be loved! How the youthful sentiment of mankind seems visibly to brood upon her!
Think of the young lives now taking color in her corridors
and cloisters. Think of the centuries' tale of dead lads,—dead
alike with the close of the young days to which these haunts
were a present world and the ending of the larger lives which
a sterner mother-scene has gathered into her massive history!
What are those two young fellows kicking their heels over
on the grass there? One of them has the Saturday Review;
the other—upon my soul—the other has Artemus Ward!
Where do they live, how do they live, to what end do they
live? Miserable boys! How can they read Artemus Ward
under those windows of Elizabeth? What do you think
loveliest in all Oxford? The poetry of certain windows. Do
you see that one yonder, the second of those lesser bays, with
the broken mullion and open casement? That used to be the
window of my *fidus Achates*, a hundred years ago. Remind
me to tell you the story of that broken mullion. Don't tell
me it's not a common thing to have one's *fidus Achates* at
another college. Pray, was I pledged to common things? He
was a charming fellow. By the way, he was a good deal like
you. Of course his cocked hat, his long hair in a black ribbon,
his cinnamon velvet suit, and his flowered waistcoat made a
difference! We gentlemen used to wear swords."

There was something surprising and impressive in my friend's gushing magniloquence. The poor disheartened loafer had turned rhapsodist and seer. I was particularly struck with his having laid aside the diffidence and shy self-consciousness which had marked him during the first days of our acquaintance. He was becoming more and more a disembodied observer and critic; the shell of sense, growing daily thinner and more transparent, transmitted the tremor of his quickened spirit. He revealed an unexpected faculty for becoming acquainted with the lounging gownsmen whom we met in our vague peregrinations. If I left him for ten minutes, I was sure to find him, on my return, in earnest conversation with some affable wandering scholar. Several young men with whom he had thus established relations invited him to their rooms and entertained him, as I gathered, with boisterous hospitality. For myself, I chose not to be present on these occasions; I shrunk partly from being held in any degree responsible for his vagaries, and partly from witnessing that painful aggravation of them which I feared might be induced by champagne and youthful society. He reported these adventures with less eloquence than I had fancied he might use; but, on the whole, I suspect that a certain method in his madness, a certain firmness in his most melting *bonhomie*, had insured him perfect respect. Two things, however, became evident,—that he drank more champagne than was good for him, and that the boyish grossness of his entertainers tended rather, on reflection, to disturb in his mind the pure image of Oxford. At the same time it completed his knowledge of the place. Making the acquaintance of several tutors and fellows, he dined in Hall in half a dozen colleges, and alluded afterwards to these banquets with a sort of religious unction. One evening, at the close of one of these entertainments, he came back to the hotel in a cab, accompanied by a friendly student, and a physician, looking deadly pale. He had swooned away on leaving table, and had remained so stubbornly unconscious as to excite great alarm among his companions. The following twenty-four hours, of course, he spent in bed; but on the third day he declared himself strong enough to go out. On reaching the street his strength again forsook him, and I insisted upon his returning to his room. He besought me with tears in his eyes not to shut him up. "It's my last chance," he said. "I want to go back for an hour to that garden of St John's. Let me look and feel; to-morrow I die." It seemed to me possible that with a Bath-chair the expedition might be acccomplished. The hotel, it appeared, possessed such a convenience : it was immediately produced. It became necessary hereupon that we should have a person to propel the chair. As there was no one available on the spot, I prepared to perform the office; but just as Searle had got seated and wrapped (he had come to suffer acutely from cold), an elderly man emerged from a lurking-place near the door, and, with a formal salute, offered to wait upon the gentleman. We assented, and he proceeded solemnly to trundle the chair before him. I recognized him as an individual whom I had seen lounging shyly about the hotel doors, at intervals during our stay, with a depressed air of wanting employment and a hopeless doubt of finding any. He had once, indeed, in a half-hearted way, proposed himself as an amateur cicerone for a tour through the colleges; and I now, as I looked at him, remembered with a pang that I had declined his services with untender curtness. Since then, his shyness, apparently, had grown less or his misery greater; for it was with a strange, grim avidity that he now attached himself to our service. He was a pitiful image of shabby gentility and the dinginess of "reduced circumstances." He imparted an original force to to the term "seedy." He was, I suppose, some fifty years of age; but his pale, haggard, unwholesome visage, his plaintive, drooping carriage, and the irremediable decay of his apparel, seemed to add to the burden of his days and experience. His eyes were bloodshot and weak-looking, his handsome nose had turned to purple, and his sandy beard, largely streaked with gray, bristled with a month's desperate indifference to the razor. In all this rusty forlornness there lurked a visible assurance of our friend's having known better days. Obviously, he was the victim of some fatal depreciation in the market value of pure gentility. There had been something terribly pathetic in the way he fiercely merged the attempt to touch the greasy rim of his antiquated hat into a rounded and sweeping bow, as from jaunty equal to equal. Exchanging a few words with him as we went along, I was struck with the refinement of his tone.

"Take me by some long roundabout way," said Searle, "so that I may see as many college walls as possible."

"You can wander without losing your way?" I asked of our attendant.

"I ought to be able to, sir," he said, after a moment, with pregnant gravity. And as we were passing Wadham College, "That's my college, sir," he added.

At these words, Searle commanded him to stop and come and stand in front of him. "You say that is *your* college?" he demanded.

"Wadham might deny me, sir; but Heaven forbid I should deny Wadham. If you'll allow me to take you into the quad, I'll show you my windows, thirty years ago!"

Searle sat staring, with his huge, pale eyes, which now had come to usurp the greatest place in his wasted visage, filled with wonder and pity. "If you'll be so kind," he said, with immense politeness. But just as this degenerate son of Wadham was about to propel him across the threshold of the court, he turned about, disengaged his hands, with his own hand, from the back of the chair, drew him alongside of him and turned to me. "While we are here, my dear fellow," he said, "be so good as to perform this service. You understand?" I smiled sufferance at our companion, and we resumed our way. The latter showed us his window of thirty years ago, where now a rosy youth in a scarlet smoking-fez was puffing a cigarette in the open lattice. Thence we proceeded into the little garden, the smallest, I believe, and certainly the sweetest of all the bosky resorts in Oxford. I pushed the chair along to a bench on the lawn, wheeled it about toward the façade of the college, and sat down on the grass. Our attendant shifted himself mournfully from one foot to the other. Searle eyed him open-mouthed. At length he broke out: "God bless my soul, sir, you don't suppose that I expect you to stand! There's an empty bench."

"Thank you," said our friend, bending his joints to sit.

"You English," said Searle, "are really fabulous! I don't know whether I most admire you or despise you! Now tell me: who are you? what are you? what brought you to this?"

The poor fellow blushed up to his eyes, took off his hat, and wiped his forehead with a ragged handkerchief. "My name is Rawson, sir. Beyond that, it's a long story."

"I ask out of sympathy," said Searle. "I have a fellow-feeling! You're a poor devil; I'm a poor devil too."

"I'm the poorer devil of the two," said the stranger, with a little emphatic nod of the head.

"Possibly. I suppose an English poor devil is the poorest of all poor devils. And then, you have fallen from a height. From Wadham College as a gentleman commoner (is that what they call you?) to Wadham College as a Bath-chair man! Good heavens, man, the fall's enough to kill you!"

"I didn't take it all at once, sir. I dropped a bit one time and a bit another."

"That's me, that's me!" cried Searle, clapping his hands.

"And now," said our friend, "I believe I can't drop further."

"My dear fellow," and Searle clasped his hand and shook it, "there's a perfect similarity in our lot."

Mr Rawson lifted his eyebrows. "Save for the difference of sitting in a Bath-chair and walking behind it!"

"O, I'm at my last gasp, Mr Rawson."

"I'm at my last penny, sir."

"Literally, Mr Rawson?"

Mr Rawson shook his head, with a world of vague bitterness. "I have almost come to the point," he said, "of drinking my beer and buttoning my coat figuratively; but I don't talk in figures."

Fearing that the conversation had taken a turn which might seem to cast a rather fantastic light upon Mr Rawson's troubles, I took the liberty of asking him with great gravity how he made a living.

"I don't make a living," he answered, with tearful eyes, "I can't make a living. I have a wife and three children, starving, sir. You wouldn't believe what I have come to. I sent my wife to her mother's, who can ill afford to keep her, and came to Oxford a week ago, thinking I might pick up a few half-crowns by showing people about the colleges. But it's no use. I haven't the assurance. I don't look decent. They want a nice little old man with black gloves, and a clean shirt, and a silver-headed stick. What do I look as if I knew about Oxford, sir?"

"Dear me," cried Searle, "why didn't you speak to us before?"

"I wanted to; half a dozen times I have been on the point of it. I knew you were Americans."

"And Americans are rich!" cried Searle, laughing. "My dear Mr Rawson, American as I am, I'm living on charity.'

"And I'm not, sir! There it is. I'm dying for the want of charity. You say you're a pauper; it takes an American pauper to go bowling about in a Bath-chair. American's an easy country."

"Ah, me!" groaned Searle. "Have I come to Wadham gardens to hear the praise of America?"

"Wadham gardens are very well!" said Mr Rawson; "but one may sit here hungry and shabby, so long as one isn't too shabby, as well as elsewhere. You'll not persuade me that it's not an easier thing to keep afloat yonder than here. I wish I were there, that's all!" added Mr Rawson, with a sort of feebleminded energy. Then brooding for a moment on his wrongs: "Have you a brother? or you, sir? It matters little to you. But it has mattered to me with a vengeance! Shabby as I sit here, I have a brother with his five thousand a year. Being a couple of years my senior, he gorges while I starve. There's England for you! A very pretty place for *him!*"

"Poor England!" said Searle, softly.

"Has your brother never helped you?" I asked.

"A twenty-pound note now and then! I don't say that there have not been times when I have sorely tried his generosity. I have not been what I should. I married dreadfully amiss. But the devil of it is that he started fair and I started foul; with the tastes, the desires, the needs, the sensibilities of a gentleman,—and nothing else! I can't afford to live in England."

"This poor gentleman," said I, "fancied a couple of months ago that he couldn't afford to live in America."

"I'd change chances with him!" And Mr Rawson gave a passionate slap to his knee.

Searle reclined in his chair with his eyes closed and his face twitching with violent emotion. Suddenly he opened his eyes with a look of awful gravity. "My friend," he said, "you're a failure! Be judged! Don't talk about chances. Don't talk about fair starts and foul starts. I'm at that point myself that I have a right to speak. It lies neither in one's chance nor one's start to make one a success; nor in anything one's brother can do or can undo. It lies in one's own will! You and I, sir, have had none; that's very plain! We have been weak, sir; as weak as water. Here we are, sitting staring in each other's faces and reading our weakness in each other's eyes. We are of no account!"

Mr Rawson received this address with a countenance in which heartfelt conviction was oddly mingled with a vague suspicion that a proper self-respect required him to resent its unflattering candor. In the course of a minute a proper self-respect yielded to the warm, comfortable sense of his being understood, even to his light dishonor. "Go on, sir, go on," he said. "It's wholesome truth." And he wiped his eyes with his dingy handkerchief.

"Dear me!" cried Searle. "I've made you cry. Well! we speak as from man to man. I should be glad to think that you had felt for a moment the side-light of that great undarkening of the spirit which precedes—which precedes the grand illumination of death."

Mr Rawson sat silent for a moment, with his eyes fixed on the ground and his well-cut nose more deeply tinged by the force of emotion. Then at last, looking up: "You're a very good-natured man, sir; and you'll not persuade me that you don't come of a good-natured race. Say what you please about a chance; when a man's fifty,—degraded, penniless, a husband and father,—a chance to get on his legs again is not to be despised. Something tells me that my chance is in your country,—that great home of chances. I can starve here, of course; but I don't want to starve. Hang it, sir, I want to live. I see thirty years of life before me yet. If only, by God's help, I could spend them there! It's a fixed idea of mine. I've had it for the last ten years. It's not that I'm a radical. I've no ideas! Old England's good enough for me, but I'm not good enough for old England. I'm a shabby man that wants to get out of a room full of staring gentlefolks. I'm forever put to the blush. It's a perfect agony of spirit. Everything reminds me of my younger and better self. O, for a cooling, cleansing plunge into the unknowing and the unknown! I lie awake thinking of it."

Searle closed his eyes and shivered with a long-drawn tremor which I hardly knew whether to take for an expression of physical or of mental pain. In a moment I perceived it was neither. "O my country, my country, my country!" he murmured in a broken voice; and then sat for some time abstracted and depressed. I intimated to our companion that it was time we should bring our *séance* to a close, and he, without hesitating, possessed himself of the little handrail of the Bath-chair and pushed it before him. We had got half-way home before Searle spoke or moved. Suddenly in the High Street, as we were passing in front of a chop-house, from whose open doors there proceeded a potent suggestion of juicy joints and suet puddings, he motioned us to halt. "This is my last five pounds," he said, drawing a note from his pocket-book. "Do me the favor, Mr Rawson, to accept it. Go in there and order a colossal dinner. Order a bottle of Burgundy and drink it to my immortal health!" Mr Rawson stiffended himself up and received the gift with momentarily irresponsive fingers. But Mr Rawson had the nerves of a gentleman. I saw the titillation of his pointed finger-tips as they closed upon the crisp paper; I noted the fine tremor in his empurpled nostril as it became more deeply conscious of the succulent flavor of the spot. He crushed the crackling note in his palm with a convulsive pressure.

"It shall be Chambertin!" he said, jerking a spasmodic bow. The next moment the door swung behind him.

Searle relapsed into his feeble stupor, and on reaching the hotel I helped him to get to bed. For the rest of the day he lay in a half-somnolent state, without motion or speech. The doctor, whom I had constantly in attendance, declared that his end was near. He expressed great surprise that he should have lasted so long; he must have been living for a month on a cruelly extorted strength. Toward evening, as I sat by his bedside in the deepening dusk, he aroused himself with a purpose which I had vaguely felt gathering beneath his quietude. "My cousin, my cousin," he said, confusedly. "Is she here?" It was the first time he had spoken of Miss Searle

since our exit from her brother's house. "I was to have
married her," he went on. "What a dream! That day was like
a string of verses—rhymed hours. But the last verse is bad
measure. What's the rhyme to 'love'? *Above!* Was she a
simple person, a sweet person? Or have I dreamed it? She
had the healing gift; her touch would have cured my madness.
I want you to do something. Write three lines, three words:
'Good-bye; remember me; be happy.'" And then, after a long
pause: "It's strange a man in my condition should have a
wish. Need a man eat his breakfast before his hanging? What
a creature is man! what a farce is life! Here I lie, worn down
to a mere throbbing fever-point; I breathe and nothing more,
and yet I *desire!* My desire lives. If I could see her! Help me
out with it and let me die."

Half an hour later, at a venture, I despatched a note to Miss
Searle: "*Your cousin is rapidly dying. He asks to see you.*" I
was conscious of a certain unkindness in doing so. It would
bring a great trouble, and no power to face the trouble. But
out of her distress I fondly hoped a sufficient energy might
be born. On the following day my friend's exhaustion had
become so total that I began to fear that his intelligence was
altogether gone. But towards evening he rallied awhile, and
talked in a maundering way about many things, confounding
in a ghastly jumble the memories of the past weeks and those
of bygone years. "By the way," he said suddenly, "I have
made no will. I haven't much to bequeath. Yet I've something." He had been playing listlessly with a large signet-ring
on his left hand, which he now tried to draw off. "I leave you
this," working it round and round vainly. "if you can get
it off. What mighty knuckles! There must be such knuckles
in the mummies of the Pharaohs. Well, when I'm gone! Nay,
I leave you something more precious than gold,—the sense
of a great kindness. But I have a little gold left. Bring me
those trinkets." I placed on the bed before him several articles
of jewelry, relics of early elegance: his watch and chain, of

great value, a locket and seal, some shirt-buttons and scarf-pins. He trifled with them feebly for some moments, murmuring various names and dates associated with them. At last, looking up with a sudden energy, "What's become of Mr Rawson?"

"You want to see him?"

"How much are these things worth?" he asked, without heeding me. "How much would they bring?" And he held them up in his weak hands. "They have a great weight. Two hundred pounds? I am richer than I thought! Rawson—Rawson—you want to get out of this awful England."

I stepped to the door and requested the servant, whom I kept in constant attendance in the adjoining sitting-room, to send and ascertain if Mr Rawson was on the premises. He returned in a few moments, introducing our shabby friend. Mr Rawson was pale, even to his nose, and, with his suppressed agitation, had an air of great distinction. I led him up to the bed. In Searle's eyes, as they fell on him, there shone for a moment the light of a high fraternal greeting.

"Great God!" said Mr Rawson, fervently.

"My friend," said Searle, "there is to be one American the less. Let there be one the more. At the worst, you'll be as good a one as I. Foolish me! Take these trinkets; let them help you on your way. They are gifts and memories, but this is a better use. Heaven speed you! May America be kind to you. Be kind, at the last, to your own country!"

"Really, this is too much; I can't," our friend protested in a tremulous voice. "Do get well, and I'll stop here!"

"Nay; I'm booked for my journey, you for yours. I hope you don't suffer at sea."

Mr Rawson exhaled a groan of helpless gratitude, appealing piteously from so awful a good fortune. "It's like the angel of the Lord," he said, "who bids people in the Bible to rise and flee!"

Searle had sunk back upon his pillow, exhausted: I led

Mr Rawson back into the sitting-room, where in three words I proposed to him a rough valuation of our friend's trinkets. He assented with perfect good breeding; they passed into my possession and a second bank-note into his.

From the collapse into which this beneficent interview had plunged him, Searle gave few signs of being likely to emerge. He breathed, as he had said, and nothing more. The twilight deepened: I lit the night-lamp. The doctor sat silent and official at the foot of the bed; I resumed my constant place near the head. Suddenly Searle opened his eyes widely. "She'll not come," he murmured. "Amen! she's an English sister." Five minutes passed. He started forward. "She has come, she is here!" he whispered. His words conveyed to my mind so absolute an assurance, that I lightly rose and passed into the sitting-room. At the same moment, through the opposite door, the servant introduced a lady. A lady, I say; for an instant she was simply such; tall, pale, dressed in deep mourning. The next moment I had uttered her name—"Miss Searle!" She looked ten years older.

She met me, with both hands extended, and an immense question in her face. "He has just spoken your name," I said. And then, with a fuller consciousness of the change in her dress and countenance: "What has happened?"

"O death, death!" said Miss Searle. "You and I are left."

There came to me with her words a sort of sickening shock, the sense of poetic justice having been grimly shuffled away. "Your brother?" I demanded.

She laid her hand on my arm, and I felt its pressure deepen as she spoke. "He was thrown from his horse in the park. He died on the spot. Six days have passed.—Six months!"

She took my arm. A moment later we had entered the room and approached the bedside. The doctor withdrew. Searle opened his eyes and looked at her from head to foot. Suddenly he seemed to perceive her mourning. "Already!" he cried, audibly; with a smile, as I believe, of pleasure.

She dropped on her knees and took his hand. "Not for you, cousin," she whispered. "For my poor brother."

He started in all his deathly longitude as with a galvanic shock. "Dead! *he* dead! Life itself!" And then, after a moment, with a slight rising inflection: "You are free?"

"Free, cousin. Sadly free. And now—*now*—with what use for freedom?"

He looked steadily a moment into her eyes, dark in the heavy shadow of her musty mourning veil. "For me," he said, "wear colors!"

In a moment more death had come, the doctor had silently attested it, and Miss Searle had burst into sobs.

We buried him in the little churchyard in which he had expressed the wish to lie; beneath one of the mightiest of English yews and the little tower than which none in all England has a softer and hoarier gray. A year has passed. Miss Searle, I believe, has begun to wear colours.

AT ISELLA

My story begins properly, I suppose, with my journey, and my journey began properly at Lucerne. It had been on the point of beginning a number of times before. About the middle of August I actually started. I had been putting it off from day to day in deference to the opinion of several discreet friends, who solemnly assured me that a man of my make would never outweather the rage of an Italian August. But ever since deciding to winter in Italy, instead of subsiding unimaginatively upon Paris, I had had a standing quarrel with Switzerland. What was Switzerland after all? Little else but brute Nature surely, of which at home we have enough and to spare. What we seek in Europe is Nature refined and transmuted to art. In Switzerland, what a pale historic coloring; what a penury of relics and monuments! I pined for a cathedral or a gallery. Instead of dutifully conning my Swiss Baedeker, I had fretfully deflavored my Murray's North Italy. Lucerne indeed is a charming little city, and I had learned to know it well. I had watched the tumbling Reuss, blue from the melting pinnacles which know the blue of heaven, come rushing and swirling beneath those quaintly-timbered bridges, vaulted with mystical paintings in the manner of Holbein, and through the severed mass of the white, compact town. I had frequented the great, bald, half-handsome, half-hideous church of the Jesuits, and listened in the twilight to the seraphic choir which breathes through its mighty organ-tubes. I had taken the most reckless pleasure in the fact that this was Catholic Switzerland. I had strolled and

restrolled across the narrow market-place at Altorf, and kept
my countenance in the presence of that ludicrous plaster-cast
of the *genius loci* and his cross-bow. I had peregrinated further
to the little hamlet of Bürglen, and peeped into the frescoed
chapel which commemorates the hero's natal scene. I had also
investigated that sordid lake-side sanctuary, with its threshold
lapped by the waves and its walls defiled by cockneys, which
consecrates the spot at which the great mountaineer, leaping
from among his custodians in Gesler's boat, spurned the
stout skiff with his invincible heel. I had contemplated from
the deck of the steamer the images of the immortal trio,
authors of the oath of liberation, which adorn the pier at
Brunnen. I had sojourned at that compact little State of
Gersau, sandwiched between the lake and the great wall of
the Righi, and securely niched somewhere in history as the
smallest and most perpetual of republics. The traveller's
impatience hereabouts is quickened by his nearness to one
of the greatest of the Alpine highways. Here he may catch a
balmy side-wind, stirred from the ranks of southward-
trooping pilgrims. The Saint Gothard route begins at Lucerne,
where you take your place in the diligence and register your
luggage. I used to fancy that a great wave of Southern life
rolled down this mighty channel to expire visibly in the blue
lake, and ripple to its green shores. I used to imagine great
gusts of warm wind hovering about the coach office at Fluelen
scented with oleander and myrtle. I used to buy at Fluelen,
to the great peril of my digestion, certain villainous peaches
and plums, offered by little girls at the steamboat landing,
and of which it was currently whispered that they had ripened
on those further Italian slopes.

One fine morning I marked my luggage *Milan!* with a great
imaginative flourish which may have had something to do
with my subsequent difficulty in recovering it in the Lombard
capital, banished it for a fortnight from sight and mind, and
embarked on the steamboat at Lucerne with the interval's

equipment in a knapsack. It is noteworthy how readily, on leaving Switzerland, I made my peace with it. What a pleasure-giving land it is, in truth! Besides the massive glory of its mountains, how it heaps up the measure of delight with the unbargained grace of town and tower, of remembered name and deed! As we passed away from Lucerne, my eyes lingered with a fresher fondness than before upon an admirable bit of the civic picturesque—a great line of mellow-stuccoed dwellings, with verdurous water-steps and grated basements, rising squarely from the rushing cobalt of the Reuss. It was a palpable foretaste of Venice. I am not ashamed to say how soon I began to look out for premonitions of Italy. It was better to begin too soon than too late; so, to miss nothing, I began to note "sensations" at Altorf, the historic heart of Helvetia. I remember here certain formal burgher mansions, standing back from the dusty highroad beyond spacious, well-swept courts, into which the wayfarer glances through immense gates of antique wrought iron. I had a notion that deserted Italian palazzos took the lingering sunbeams at somewhat such an angle, with just that coarse glare. I wondered of course who lived in them, and how they lived, and what was society in Altorf; longing plaintively, in the manner of roaming Americans, for a few stray crumbs from the native social board; with my fancy vainly beating its wings against the great blank wall, behind which, in travel-haunted Europe, all gentle private interests nestle away from intrusion. Here, as everywhere, I was struck with the mere surface-relation of the Western tourist to the soil he treads. He filters and trickles through the dense social body in every possible direction, and issues forth at last the same virginal water drop. "Go your way," these antique houses seemed to say, from their quiet courts and gardens; "the road is yours and welcome, but the land is ours. You may pass and stare and wonder, but you may never know us." The Western tourist consoles himself, of course, by the reflection that the gentry

of Altorf and other ancient burghs gain more from the
imagination possibly than they might bestow upon it.

I confess that so long as I remained in the land, as I did for
the rest of the afternoon—a pure afternoon of late summer,
charged with mellow shadows from the teeming verdure of
the narrow lowland, beyond which to-morrow and Italy
seemed merged in a vague bright identity—I felt that I was
not fairly under way. The land terminates at Amstaeg, where
I lay that night. Early the next morning I attacked the mighty
slopes. Just beyond Amstaeg, if I am not mistaken, a narrow
granite bridge spans the last mountain-plunge of the Reuss;
and just here the great white road begins the long toil of its
ascent. To my sense, these mighty Alpine highways have a
grand poetry of their own. I lack, doubtless, that stout
stomach for pure loneliness which leads your genuine mountaineer to pronounce them a desecration of the mountain
stillness. As if the mountain stillness were not inviolable!
Gleaming here and there against the dark sides of the gorges,
unrolling their measured bands further and higher, doubling
and stretching and spanning, but always climbing, they break
it only to the anxious eye. The Saint Gothard road is immensely long drawn, and, if the truth be told, somewhat
monotonous. As you follow it to its uppermost reaches, the
landscape takes on a darker local color. Far below the wayside, the yellow Reuss tumbles and leaps and foams over a
perfect torture-bed of broken rock. The higher slopes lie
naked and raw, or coated with slabs of gray. The valley lifts
and narrows and darkens into the scenic mountain pass of
the fancy. I was haunted as I walked by an old steel plate in a
French book that I used to look at as a child, lying on my
stomach on the parlor floor. Under it was written "Saint
Gothard." I remembered distinctly the cold, gray mood which
this picture used to generate; the same tone of feeling is
produced by the actual scene. Coming at last to the Devil's
Bridge, I recognized the source of the steel plate of my

infancy. You have no impulse here to linger fondly. You hurry away after a moment's halt, with an impression fierce and chaotic as the place itself. A great torrent of wind, sweeping from a sudden outlet and snatching uproar and spray from the mad torrent of water leaping in liquid thunderbolts beneath; a giddy, deafened, deluged stare, with my two hands to my hat, and a rapid shuddering retreat—these are my chief impressions of the Devil's Bridge. If, on leaving Amstaeg in the morning, I had been asked whither I was bending my steps, "To Italy!" I would have answered, with a grand absence of detail. The radiance of this broad fact had quenched the possible side-lights of reflection. As I approached the summit of the pass, it became a profoundly solemn thought that I might, by pushing on with energy, lay my weary limbs on an Italian bed. There was something so delightful in the mere protracted, suspended sense of approach, that it seemed a pity to bring it to so abrupt a close. And then suppose, metaphysical soul of mine, that Italy should not, in vulgar parlance, altogether come up to time? Why not prolong awhile the possible bliss of ignorance—of illusion? Something short of the summit of the Saint Gothard pass, the great road of the Furca diverges to the right, passes the Rhône Glacier, enters the Rhône Valley, and conducts you to Brieg and the foot of the Simplon. Reaching in due course this divergence of the Furca road, I tarried awhile beneath the mountain sky, debating whether or not delay would add to pleasure. I opened my Baedeker and read that within a couple of hours' walk from my halting-place was the *Albergo di San Gothardo, vaste et sombre auberge Italienne.* To think of being at that distance from a vast, sombre Italian inn! On the other hand, there were some very pretty things said of the Simplon. I tossed up a napoleon; the head fell uppermost. I trudged away to the right. The road to the Furca lies across one of those high desolate plateaux which represent the hard prose of mountain scenery. Naked and stern it lay before me, rock

and grass, without a shrub, without a tree, without a grace—
like the dry bed of some gigantic river of prehistoric times.

The stunted hamlet of Realp, beside the road dwarfed by
the huge scale of things, seemed little more than a cluster of
naked, sub-blackened boulders. It contained an inn, however,
and the inn contained the usual Alpine larder of cold veal
and cheese, and, as I remember, a very affable maid-servant,
who spoke excellent lowland French, and confessed in the
course of an after-dinner conversation that the winters in
Realp were *un peu tristes*. This conversation took place as I
sat resting outside the door in the later afternoon, watching
the bright, hard light of the scene grow gray and cold beneath
a clear sky, and wondering to find humanity lodged in such
an exaltation of desolation.

The road of the Furca, as I discovered the next morning,
is a road and little else. Its massive bareness, however, gives
it an incontestable grandeur. The broad, serpentine terrace
uncoils its slanting *cordons* with a multiplicity of curves and
angles and patient reaches of circumvention, which give it
the air of some wanton revelry of engineering genius. Finally,
after a brief level of repose, it plunges down to the Rhône
Glacier. I had the good fortune to see this great spectacle on
the finest day of the year. Its perfect beauty is best revealed
beneath the scorching glare of an untempered sun. The sky
was without a cloud—the air incredibly lucid. The glacier
dropped its billowy sheet—a soundless tumult of whiteness,
a torrent of rolling marble—straight from the blue of heaven
to the glassy margin of the road. It seems to gather into its
bosom the whole diffused light of the world, so that round
about it all objects lose their color. The rocks and hills
stand sullen and neutral; the lustre of the sky is turned to
blackness. At the little hotel near the glacier I waited for the
coach to Brieg, and started thitherward in the early afternoon,
sole occupant of the *coupé*.

Let me not, however, forget to commemorate the French

priest whom we took in at one of the squalid villages of the
dreary Haut-Valais, through which on that bright afternoon
we rattled so superbly. It was a Sunday, and throughout
this long dark chain of wayside hamlets the peasants were
straddling stolidly about the little central *place* in the hideous
festal accoutrements of the rustic Swiss. He came forth from
the tavern, gently cleaving the staring crowd, accompanied
by two brother ecclesiastics. These were portly, elderly men;
he was young and pale and priestly in the last degree. They
had a little scene of adieux at the coach door. They whispered
gently, gently holding each other's hands and looking lovingly
into each other's eyes, and then the two elders saluted their
comrade on each cheek, and, as we departed, blew after him
just the least little sacramental kiss. It was all, dramatically
speaking, delightfully low in tone. Before we reached Brieg
the young priest had gained a friend to console him for those
he had lost. He proved to be a most amiable person; full of
homely frankness and appealing innocence of mundane
things; and invested withal with a most pathetic air of sitting
there as a mere passive object of transmission—a simple
priestly particle in the great ecclesiastical body, transposed
by the logic of an inscrutable *thither!* and *thus!* On learning
that I was an American, treated me so implicitly as a travelled
man of the world, that he almost persuaded me for the time
I was one. He was on pins and needles with his sense of the
possible hazards of travel. He asked questions the most
innocently *saugrenues*. He was convinced on general grounds
that our driver was drunk, and that he would surely overturn
us into the Rhône. He seemed possessed at the same time
with a sort of school-boy relish for the profane humor of
things. Whenever the coach made a lurch toward the river-
bank or swung too broadly round a turn, he would grasp my
arm and whisper that our hour had come; and then, before
our pace was quite readjusted, he would fall to nursing his
elbows and snickering gently to himself. It seemed altogether

a larger possibility than any he had been prepared for that on his complaining of the cold I should offer him the use of my overcoat. Of this and of other personal belongings he ventured to inquire the price, and indeed seemed oppressed with the sudden expensiveness of the world. But now that he was fairly launched he was moving in earnest. He was to reach Brieg, if possible, in time for the night diligence over the Simplon, which was to deposit him at the Hospice on the summit.

By a very early hour the next morning I had climbed apace with the sun. Brieg was far below me in the valley. I had, measured an endless number of the giant elbows of the road, and from the bosky flank of the mountain I looked down at nestling gulfs of greenness, cool with shade; at surging billows of forest crested with the early brightness; at slopes in light and cliffs in shadow; at all the heaving mountain zone which belongs to the verdant nearness of earth; and then straight across to the sacred pinnacles which take their tone from heaven.

If weather could bless an enterprise, mine was blessed beyond words. It seemed to me that Nature had taken an interest in my little project and was determined to do the thing handsomely. As I mounted higher, the light flung its dazzling presence on all things. The air stood still to take it; the green glittered within the green, the blue burned beyond it; the dew on the forests gathered to dry into massive crystals, and beyond the brilliant void of space the clear snow-fields stood out like planes of marble inserted in a field of lapis-lazuli. The Swiss side of the Simplon has the beauty of a boundless luxury of green; the view remains gentle even in its immensity. The ascent is gradual and slow, and only when you reach the summit do you get a sense of proper mountain grimness. On this favoring day of mine the snowy horrors of the opposite Aletsch Glacier seemed fairly to twinkle with serenity. It seemed to me when I reached the Hospice that I had been winding for hours along the inner hollow of some

mighty cup of verdure toward a rim of chiselled silver
crowned with topaz. At the Hospice I made bold to ask leave
to rest. It stands on the bare topmost plateau of the pass, bare
itself as the spot it consecrates, and stern as the courage of
the pious brothers who administer its charities. It broods
upon the scene with the true, bold, convent look, with rugged
yellow walls and grated windows, striving to close in human
weakness from blast and avalanche, as in valleys and cities
to close it in from temptation and pollution. A few St Bernard
dogs were dozing outside in the chilly sunshine. I climbed
the great stone steps which lift the threshold above the snow-
land, and tinkled the bell of appeal. Here for a couple of
hours I was made welcome to the cold, hard fare of the convent. There was to my mind a solemn and pleasant fitness in
my thus entering church-burdened Italy through the portal
of the church, for from the convent door to the plain of
Lombardy it was all to be downhill work. I seemed to feel
on my head the hands of especial benediction, and to hear in
my ears the premonition of countless future hours to be passed
in the light of altar-candles. The inner face of the Hospice is
well-nigh as cold and bare as the face it turns defiant to the
Alpine snows. Huge stone corridors and ungarnished rooms,
in which poor unacclimatized friars must sit aching and
itching with chilblains in high midsummer; everywhere that
peculiar perfume of churchiness—the *odeur de sacristie* and
essence of incense—which impart throughout the world an
especial pungency to Catholicism. Having the good fortune,
as it happened, to be invited to dine with the Prior, I found
myself in fine priestly company. A dozen of us sat about the
board in the greasy, brick-paved refectory, lined with sombre
cupboards of ponderous crockery, all in stole and cassock
but myself. Several of the brothers were *in transitu* from below.
Among them I had the pleasure of greeting my companion
in the *coupé* to Brieg, slightly sobered perhaps by his relapse
into the clerical ranks, but still timidly gracious and joyous.

The Prior himself, however, especially interested me, so every inch was he a prior—a priest dominant and militant. He was still young, and familiar, I should say, with the passions of youth; tall and powerful in frame, stout-necked and small-headed, with a brave beak of a nose and closely placed, fine, but sinister eyes. The simple, childish cut of his black cassock, with its little linen band across his great pectoral expanse as he sat at meat, seemed to denote a fantastical, ironical humility. Was it a mere fancy of a romantic Yankee tourist that he was more evil than gentle? Heaven grant, I mused as I glanced at him, that his fierce and massive manhood be guided by the Lord's example. What was such a man as that doing up there on a lonely mountain top, watching the snow clouds from closed windows and doling out restorative cognac to frost-bitten wagoners? He ought to be down in the hard, dense world, fighting and sinning for his mother Church. But he was one who could bide his time. Unless I'm scribbling nonsense, it will come. In deference probably to the esoteric character of a portion of the company, our conversation at dinner was not rigidly clerical. In fact, when my attention wandered back to its theme, I found the good brothers were talking of Alexandre Dumas with a delightful air of protest and hearsay, and a spice of priestly malice. The great romancer, I believe, had among his many fictions somewhere promulgated an inordinate fiction touching the manners and customs of the Hospice. The game being started, each of them said his say and cast his pebble, weighted always with an "*on dit*," and I was amazed to find they were so well qualified to reprobate the author of "Monte Cristo." When we had dined my young Frenchman came and took me by the arm and led me in great triumph over the whole convent, delighted to have something to show me—me who had come from America and had lent him my overcoat. When at last I had under his auspices made my farewell obeisance to the Prior, and started on my down-ward course, he bore me company along the road. But before we lost sight of the Hospice he gave me his fraternal blessing. "*Allons!*" he was pleased to say, "the next time I shall know an American;" and he gathered up his gentle petticoat, and, as I looked behind, I saw his black stockings frolicking back over the stones by a short cut to the monastery.

I should like to be able to tell the veracious tale of that divine afternoon. I should like to be able to trace the soft stages by which those rugged heights melt over into a Southern difference. Now at last in good earnest I began to watch for the *symptoms* of Italy. Now that the long slope began to tend downward unbroken, it was not absurd to fancy a few adventurous tendrils of Southern growth might have crept and clambered upward. At a short distance beyond the Hospice stands the little village of Simplon, where I believe the coach stops for dinner; the uttermost outpost, I deemed it, of the lower world, perched there like an empty shell, with its murmur not yet quenched, tossed upward and stranded by some climbing Southern wave. The little inn at the Italian end of the street, painted in a bright Italian medley of pink and blue, must have been decorated by a hand which had learned its cunning in the land of the fresco. The Italian slope of the Simplon road commands a range of scenery wholly different from the Swiss. The latter winds like a thread through the blue immensity; the former bores its way beneath crag and cliff, through gorge and mountain crevice. But though its channel narrows and darkens, Italy nears and nears none the less. You suspect it first in—what shall I say?—the growing warmth of the air, a fancied elegance of leaf and twig; a little while yet, and they will curl and wanton to your heart's content. The famous Gorge of Gando, at this stage of the road, renews the sombre horrors of the Via Mala. The hills close together above your head, and the daylight filters down their corrugated sides from three inches of blue. The mad torrent of the Dauria, roaring through the straitened vale, fills it forever with a sounding din, as—to compare poetry to prose—a railway train a tunnel. Emerging from the Gorge of Gando, you fairly breathe Italian air. The gusts of a mild climate come wandering along the road to meet you. Lo! suddenly, by the still wayside, I came upon a sensation: a little house painted a hot salmon color, with a withered pine-twig over the door in token of entertainment, and above this inscribed in square chirography—literally in Italics— *Osteria!* I stopped devotedly to quaff a glass of sour wine to Italy gained. The place seemed wrapped in a desolation of stillness, save that as I stood and thumped the doorpost, the piping cry of a baby rose from the loft above and tickled the mountain echoes. Anon came clattering down the stairs a nursing mother of peasants; she gave me her only wine, out of her own bottle, out of her only glass. While she stood to wait on me, the terrible cry of her infant became so painful that I bade her go and fetch him before he strangled; and in a moment she reappeared, holding him in her arms, pacified and utterly naked. Standing there with the little unswaddled child on her breast, and smiling happily from her glowing brow, she made a picture which, in coming weeks, I saw imitated more or less vividly over many an altar and in many a palace. Onward still, through its long-drawn evolutions, the valley keeps darkly together, as if to hold its own to the last against the glittering breadth of level Lombardy. In truth, I had gained my desire. If Italy meant stifling heat, this was the essence of Italy. The afternoon was waning, and the early shadows of the valley deepening into a dead summer night. But the hotter the better, and the more Italian! At last, at a turn in the road, glimpsed the first houses of a shallow village, pressed against the mountain wall. It was Italy—the Dogana Isella! so I quickened my jaded steps. I met a young officer strolling along the road in sky-blue trousers, with a moustache *à la* Victor Emanuel, puffing a cigarette, and yawning with the sensuous *ennui* of Isella—the first of that swarming company of warriors whose cerulean presence, in

many a rich street-scene, in later hours touched up so brightly
the foreground of the picture. A few steps more brought me
to the Dogana, and to my first glimpse of those massive and
shadowy arcades so delightfully native to the South. Here it
was my privilege to hear for the first time the music of an
Italian throat vibrate upon Italian air. "Nothing to declare—
niente?" asked the dark-eyed functionary, emerging from the
arcade. "*Niente*" seemed to me delicious; I would have told a
fib for the sake of repeating the word. Just beyond stood the
inn, which seemed to me somehow not as the inns of Switzerland. Perched something aloft against the hillside, a vague light
tendency to break out into balconies and terraces and trellises
seemed to enhance its simple façade. Its open windows had
an air of being familiar with Southern nights; with balmy
dialogues, possibly, passing between languid ladies leaning
on the iron rails, and lounging gentlemen, star-gazing from
the road beneath at their mistresses' eyes. Heaven grant it
should not be fastidiously neat, scrubbed and furbished and
frotté like those prosy taverns on the Swiss lakes! Heaven
was generous. I was ushered into a room whereof the ceiling
was frescoed with flowers and gems and cherubs, but whose
brick-tiled floor would have been vastly amended by the
touch of a wet cloth and broom. After repairing my toilet
within the limits of my resources, I proceeded to order supper.
The host, I remember, I decreed to have been the *chef de
cuisine* of some princely house of Lombardy. He wore a
grizzled moustache and a red velvet cap, with little gold ear-
rings. I could see him, under proper inspiration, whip a towel
round his waist, turn back his sleeves, and elaborate a masterly
pasticcio. "I shall take the liberty," he said, "of causing
monsieur to be served at the same time with a lady."

"With a lady—an English lady?" I asked.

"An Italian lady. She arrived an hour ago." And mine
host paused a moment and honored me with a genial smile.
"She is alone—she is young—she is pretty."

Stolid child of the North that I was, surely my smile of response was no match for his! But, nevertheless, in my heart I felt that fortune was kind. I went forth to stroll down the road while my repast was being served, and while daylight still lingered, to reach forward as far as possible into the beckoning land beyond. Opposite the inn the mountain stream, still untamed, murmured and tumbled between the stout parapet which edged the road and the wall of rock which enclosed the gorge. I felt indefinably curious, expectant, impatient. Here was Italy at last; but what next? Was I to eat my supper and go contentedly to bed? Was there nothing I could see, or do, or feel? I had been deeply moved, but I was primed for a deeper emotion still. Would it come? Along the road toward Domo d'Ossola the evening shadows deepened and settled, and filled the future with mystery. The future would take care of itself; but ah, for an intenser present! I stopped and gazed wistfully along the broad dim highway. At this moment I perceived beyond me, leaning against the parapet, the figure of a woman, alone and in meditation. Her two elbows rested on the stone coping, her two hands were laid against her ears to deaden the din of the stream, and her face, between them, was bent over upon the waters. She seemed young and comely. She was bare-headed; a black organdy shawl was gathered round her shoulders; her dress, of a light black material, was covered with a multitude of little puffs and flounces, trimmed and adorned with crimson silk. There was an air of intense meditation in her attitude; I passed near her without her perceiving me. I observed her black-brown tresses, braided by a cunning hand, but slightly disarranged by travel, and the crumpled disorder of her half-fantastic dress. She was a lady and an Italian; she was alone, young and pretty; was she possibly my destined companion? A few yards beyond the spot at which she stood, I retraced my steps; she had now turned round. As I approached her she looked at me from a pair of expressive dark eyes. Just a hint of suspicion and defiance I fancied that at this moment they expressed. "Who are you, what are you, roaming so close to me?" they seemed to murmur. We were alone in this narrow pass, I a new comer, she a daughter of the land; moreover, her glance had almost audibly challenged me; instinctively, therefore, and with all the deference I was master of, I bowed. She continued to gaze for an instant; then suddenly she perceived, I think, that I was utterly a foreigner and presumably a gentleman, and hereupon, briefly but graciously, she returned my salute. I went my way and reached the hotel. As I passed in, I saw the fair stranger come slowly along the road as if also to enter the inn. In the little dining-room I found mine host of the velvet cap bestowing the finishing touches upon a small table set *en tête-à-tête* for two. I had heard, I had read, of the gracious loquacity of the Italian race and their sweet familiarities of discourse. Here was a chance to test the quality of the matter. The landlord, having posed two fantastically folded napkins directly *vis-à-vis*, glanced at me with a twinkle in his eye which seemed to bespeak recognition of this cunning arrangement.

"*A propos*," I said, "this lady with whom I am to dine? Does she wear a black dress with red flounces?"

"Precisely, Signore. You have already had a glimpse of her? A pretty woman, isn't it so?"

"Extremely pretty. Who is the lady?"

"Ah!" And the landlord turned back his head and thrust out his chin, with just the least play of his shoulders. "That's the question! A lady of that age, with that face and those red flounces, who travels alone—not even a maid—you may well ask who she is! She arrived here an hour ago in a carriage from Domo d'Ossola, where, her vetturino told me, she had arrived only just before by the common coach from Arona. But though she travels by the common vehicle, she is not a common person; one may see that with half an eye. She comes in great haste, but ignorant of the ways and means. She wishes to go by the diligence to Brieg. She ought to have waited at Domo, where she could have found a good seat. She didn't even take the precaution of engaging one at the office there. When the diligence stops here, she will have to fare as she can. She is pretty enough indeed to fare very well —or very ill; isn't it so, Signore?" demanded the worthy Bonifazio, as I believe he was named. "Ah, but behold her strolling along the road, bare-headed, in those red flounces! What is one to say? After dusk, with the dozen officers in garrison here watching the frontier! Watching the ladies who come and go, *per Dio!* Many of them, saving your presence, Signore, are your own compatriots. You'll not deny that some of them are a little free—a little bold. What will you have? Out of their own country! What else were the use of travel? But this one; eh! she's not out of her own country yet. Italians are Italians, Signore, up to the frontier— eh! eh!" And the Signor Bonifazio indulged in a laugh the most *goguenard.* "Nevertheless, I have not kept an inn these twenty years without learning to know the sheep from the goats. This is an honorable lady, Signore; it is for that reason that I have offered to you to sup with her. The other sort! one can always sup with them!"

It seemed to me that my host's fluent commentary was no meagre foretaste of Italian frankness. I approached the window. The fair object of our conversation stood at the foot of the stone staircase which ascended to the inn door, with the toe of her shoe resting upon the first step. She was looking fixedly and pensively up the road toward Switzerland. Her hand clasped the knob of the iron balustrade and her slight fingers played an impatient measure. She had begun to interest me. Her dark eyes, intent upon the distant turn of the road, seemed to expand with a vague expectancy. Whom was she looking for? Of what romance of Italy was she the heroine? The *maître d'hôtel* appeared at the head of the steps, and with a flourish of his napkin announced that the Signora

was served. She started a little and then lightly shrugged her
shoulders. At the same moment I caught her eye as I stood
gazing from the window. With a just visible deepening of her
color, she slowly ascended the steps. I was suddenly seized
with a sense of being dingy, travel-stained, unpresentable to a
woman so charming. I hastily retreated to my room, and,
surveying myself in my dressing-glass, objurgated fortune
that I lacked the wherewithal to amend my attire. But I
could at least change my cravat. I had no sooner replaced my
black neck-tie by a blue one than it occurred to me that the
Signora would observe the difference; but what then? It
would hardly offend her. With a timid hope that it might
faintly gratify her as my only feasible tribute to the honor of
her presence, I returned to the dining-room. She was seated
and had languidly addressed herself to the contents of her
soup-plate. The worthy Bonifazio had adorned our little table
with four lighted candles and a centre-piece of Alpine flowers.
As I installed myself opposite my companion, after having
greeted her and received a murmured response, it seemed to
me that I was sitting down to one of those factitious repasts
which are served upon the French stage, when the table has
been moved close to the footlights, and the ravishing young
widow and the romantic young artist begin to manipulate
the very *nodus* of the comedy. Was the Signora a widow?
Our attendant, with his crimson cap, his well-salted discourse,
his light-handed gestures, and his smile from behind the
scenes, might have passed for a classic *valet de théâtre*. I had
the appetite of a man who had been walking since sunrise, but
I found ample occasion, while I plied my knife and fork, to
inspect the Signora. She merely pretended to eat; and to
appeal, perhaps, from the over-flattering intentness of my
vision, she opened an idle conversation with Bonifazio. I
listened admiringly, while the glancing shuttle of Italian
speech passed rapidly from lip to lip. It was evident, frequently, that she remained quite heedless of what he said,

losing herself forever in a kind of fretful intensity of thought. The repast was long and multifarious, and as he time and again removed her plate with its contents untouched, mine host would catch my eye and roll up his own with an air of mock commiseration, turning back his thumb at the same moment toward the region of his heart. "*Un coup de tête*," he took occasion to murmur as he reached over me to put down a dish. But the more I looked at the fair unknown, the more I came to suspect that the source of her unrest lay deeper than in the petulance of wounded vanity. Her face wore to my eye the dignity of a deep resolution—a resolution taken in tears and ecstasy. She was some twenty-eight years of age, I imagined; though at moments a painful gravity resting upon her brow gave her the air of a woman who in youth has anticipated old age. How beautiful she was by natural gift I am unable to say; for at this especial hour of her destiny, her face was too serious to be fair and too interesting to be plain. She was pale, worn, and weary-looking; but in the midst of her weariness there flickered a fierce impatience of delay and forced repose. She was a gentle creature, turned brave and adventurous by the stress of fate. It burned bright in her soft, grave eyes, this longing for the larger freedom of the tarrying morrow. A dozen chance gestures indicated the torment of her spirit—the constant rapping of her knife against the table, her bread crumbed to pieces but uneaten, the frequent change from posture to posture of her full and flexible figure, shifting through that broad range of attitude—the very gamut of gracefulness—familiar to Italian women.

The repast advanced without my finding a voice to address her. Her secret puzzled me, whatever it was, but I confess that I was afraid of it. A *coup de tête!* Heaven only knew how direful a *coup!* My mind was flooded by the memory of the rich capacity of the historic womanhood of Italy. I thought of Lucrezia Borgia, of Bianca Capello, of the heroines of

Stendhal. My fair friend seemed invested with an atmosphere of candid passion, which placed her quite apart from the ladies of my own land. The gallant soul of the Signor Bonifazio, however, had little sufferance for this pedantic view of things. Shocked by my apparent indifference to the privilege of my rare position, he thrust me by the shoulders into the conversation. The Signora eyed me for a moment not ungraciously, and then, "Do you understand Italian?" she asked.

I had come to Italy with an ear quite unattuned, of course, to the spoken tongue; but the mellow cadence of the Signora's voice rang in upon my senses like music. "I understand *you*," I said.

She looked at me gravely, with the air of a woman used to receive compliments without any great flutter of vanity. "Are you English?" she abruptly asked.

"English is my tongue."

"Have you come from Switzerland?"

"He has walked from Brieg!" proclaimed our host.

"Ah, you happy men, who can walk—who can run—who needn't wait for coaches and conductors!" The Signora uttered these words with a smile of acute though transient irony. They were followed by a silence. Bonifazio, seeing the ice was broken, retired with a flourish of his napkin and a contraction of his eyelids as much in the nature of a wink as his respect for me, for the Signora, and for himself allowed. What was the motive of the Signora's impatience? I had a presentiment that I should learn. The Italians are confidential; of this I had already received sufficient assurance; and my companion, with her lucid eye and her fine pliable lips, was a bright example of the eloquent genius of her race. She sat idly pressing with her fork the crimson substance out of a plateful of figs, without raising them to her lips.

"You are going over into Switzerland," I said, "and you are in haste."

She eyed me a minute suspiciously. "Yes, I'm in haste!"

"I, who have just begun to feel the charm of Italy," I rejoined, "can hardly understand being in haste to leave it."

"The charm of Italy!" cried the Signora, with a slightly cynical laugh. "Foreigners have a great deal to say about it."

"But you, a good Italian, certainly know what we mean."

She shrugged her shoulders—an operation she performed more gracefully than any woman I ever saw, unless it be Mlle Madeleine Brohan of the Théâtre Français. "For me it has no charm! I have been unhappy here. Happiness for me is *there!*" And with a superb nod of her head she indicated the Transalpine world. Then, as if she had spoken a thought too freely, she rose suddenly from her chair and walked away to the window. She stepped out on the narrow balcony, looked intently for an instant up and down the road and at the band of sky above it, and then turned back into the room. I sat in my place, divided between my sense of the supreme sweetness of figs and my wonder at my companion's mystery. "It's a fine night!" she said. And with a little jerk of impatience she flung herself into an arm-chair near the table. She leaned back, with her skirt making a great wave around her and her arms folded. I went on eating figs. There was a long silence. "You've eaten at least a dozen figs. You'll be ill!" said the Signora at last.

This was friendly in its frankness. "Ah, if you only knew how I enjoy them!" I cried, laughing. "They are the first I ever tasted. And this the first Asti wine. We don't have either in the North. If figs and Asti wine are for anything in your happiness, Signora," I added, "you had better not cross the Alps. See, the figs are all gone. Do you think it would hurt me to have any more?"

"Truly," cried the Signora, "I don't know what you English are made of!"

"You think us very coarse, and given up altogether to eating and drinking?" She gave another shrug tempered by a smile. "To begin with, I am not an Englishman. And in the second place, you'd not call me coarse if you knew—if you only knew what I feel this evening. Eh! such thick-coming fancies!"

"What are your fancies?" she demanded, with a certain curiosity gleaming in her dark eye.

"I *must* finish this Asti!" This I proceeded to do. I am very glad I did, moreover, as I borrowed from its mild and luscious force something of the courage with which I came to express myself. "I don't know how it is that I'm talking Italian as such a rate. Somehow the words come to me. I know it only from books. I have never talked it."

"You speak as well," the Signora graciously affirmed, "as if you had lived six months in the country."

"Half an hour in your society," said I, "is as profitable as six months elsewhere."

"Bravo!" she responded. "An Italian himself couldn't say it better."

Sitting before me in the vague candlelight, beautiful, pale, dark-browed, sad, the Signora seemed to me an incorporate image of her native land. I had come to pay it my devotions. Why not perform them at her feet? "I have come on a pilgrimage," I said. "To understand what I mean, you must have lived, as I have lived, in a land beyond the seas, barren of romance and grace. This Italy of yours, on whose threshold I stand, is the home of history, of beauty, of the arts—of all that makes life splendid and sweet. Italy, for us dull strangers, is a magic word. We cross ourselves when we pronounce it. We are brought up to think that when we have earned leisure and rest—at some bright hour, when fortune smiles—we may go forth and cross oceans and mountains and see on Italian soil the primal substance—the Platonic 'idea'—of our consoling dreams and our richest fancies. I have been brought

up in these thoughts. The happy hour has come to me—
Heaven be praised!—while I am still young and strong and
sensitive. Here I sit for the first time in the enchanted air in
which love and faith and art and knowledge are warranted to
become deeper passions than in my own chilly clime. I begin
to behold the promise of my dreams. It's Italy. How can I
tell you what that means to one of us? Only see already how
fluent and tender of speech I've become. The air has a perfume; everything that enters my soul, at every sense, is a
suggestion, a promise, a performance. But the best thing of all
is that I have met *you, bella donna!* If I were to tell you how
you seem to me, you would think me either insincere or
impertinent. *Ecco!*"

She listened to me without changing her attitude or without removing her fathomless eyes from my own. Their blue-
black depths, indeed, seemed to me the two wells of poetic
unity, from which I drew my somewhat transcendental
allocution. She was puzzled, I think, and a little amused, but
not offended. Anything from an Inglese! But it was doubtless
grateful to feel these rolling waves of sentiment break softly
at her feet, chained as she was, like Andromeda, to the rock
of a lonely passion. With an admirable absence of *minauderie*,
"How is it that I seem to you, Signore?" she asked.

I left my place and came round and stood in front of her.
"Ever since I could use my wits," I said, "I have done little
else than fancy dramas and romances and love-tales, and
lodge them in Italy. You seem to me as the heroine of all my
stories."

There was perhaps a slight movement of coquetry in her
reply: "Your stories must have been very dull, Signore," and
she gave a sad smile.

"Nay, in future," I said, "my heroines shall be more like
you than ever. Where do you come from?" I seated myself
in the chair she had quitted. "But it's none of my business."
I added. "From anywhere. In Milan or Venice, in Bologna

or Florence, Rome or Naples, every grave old palazzo I pass,
I shall fancy your home. I'm going the whole length of Italy.
My soul, what things I shall see!"

"You please me, Signore. I say to you what I wouldn't
say to another. I came from Florence. Shall you surely go
there?"

"I have reasons," I said, "for going there more than elsewhere. In Florence"—and I hesitated, with a momentary
horror at my perfect unreserve—"in Florence I am to meet
my—my *promessa sposa.*"

The Signora's face was instantly irradiated by a generous
smile. "Ah!" she said, as if now for the first time she really
understood me.

"As I say, she has been spending the summer at the Baths
of Lucca. She comes to Florence with her mother in the
middle of September."

"Do you love her?"

"Passionately."

"Is she pretty?"

"Extremely. But not like you. Very fair, with blue eyes."

"How long since you have seen her?"

"A year."

"And when are you to be married?"

"In November, probably, in Rome."

She covered me for a moment with a glance of the largest
sympathy. "Ah, what happiness!" she cried abruptly.

"After our marriage," I said, "we shall go down to Naples.
Do you know Naples?"

Instead of answering, she simply gazed at me, and her
beautiful eyes seemed to grow larger and more liquid. Suddenly, while I sat in the benignant shadow of her vision, I
saw the tears rise to her lids. Her face was convulsed and she
burst into sobs. I remember that in my amazement and regret
I suddenly lost my Italian. "Dearest lady," I cried in my
mother tongue, "forgive me that I have troubled you. Share

with me at least the sorrow that I have aroused." In an instant, however, she had brushed away her tears and her face had recovered its pale composure. She tried even to smile.

"What will you think of me?" she asked. "What do you think of me already?"

"I think you are an extremely interesting woman. You are in trouble. If there is anything I can do for you, pray say the word."

She gave me her hand. I was on the point of raising it to my lips. "No—*à l'Anglaise*," she said, and she lightly shook my own. "I like you—you're an honest man—you don't try to make love to me. I should like to write a note to your *promessa sposa* to tell her she may trust you. You can't help me. I have committed myself to God and the Holy Virgin. They will help me. Besides, it's only a little longer. Eh, it's a long story, Signore! What is said in your country of a woman who travels alone at night without even a servant?"

"Nothing is said. It's very common."

"Ah! women must be very happy there, or very unhappy! Is it never supposed of a woman that she has a lover? That is worst of all."

"Fewer things are 'supposed' of women there than here. They live more in the broad daylight of life. They make their own law."

"They must be very good then—or very bad. So that a man of fancy like you, with a taste for romance, has to come to poor Italy, where he can suppose at leisure! But we are not all romance, I assure you. With me, I promise you, it's no light-minded *coup de tête*." And the Signora enforced her candid assurance with an almost imperious nod. "I know what I'm doing. Eh! I'm an old woman. I've waited and waited. But now my hour has come! Ah, the heavenly freedom of it! Ah, the peace—the joy! Just God, I thank thee!" And sitting back in her chair, she folded her hands on her bosom and closed her eyes in a kind of ecstasy. Opening them

suddenly, she perceived, I suppose, my somewhat intent and
dilated countenance. Breaking then into a loud, excited
laugh, "How you stare at me!" she cried. "You think I've
at least poisoned my husband. No, he's safe and sound and
strong! On the contrary, I've forgiven him. I forgive him
with all my heart, with all my soul; there! I call upon you to
witness it. I bear him no rancor. I wish never to think of him
again; only let me never see him—never hear of him! Let him
never come near me: I shall never trouble him! Hark!" She
had interrupted herself and pressed her hand with a startled
air upon my arm. I listened, and in a moment my ear caught
the sound of rolling wheels on the hard highroad. With a
great effort at self-composure, apparently, she laid her fingers
on her lips. "If it should be he—if it should be he!" she
murmured. "Heaven preserve me! Do go to the window
and see."

I complied, and perceived a two-horse vehicle advancing
rapidly from the Italian quarter. "It's a carriage of some sort
from Italy," I said. "But what—whom do you fear?"

She rose to her feet. "That my husband should overtake
me," and she gave a half-frantic glance round the room, like
a hunted stag at bay. "If it should be he, protect me! Do
something, say something—anything! Say I'm not fit to go
back to him. He wants me because he thinks me good. Say
I'm not good—to your knowledge. Oh, Signore—Holy
Virgin!" Recovering herself, she sank into a chair, and sat
stiff and superb, listening to the deepening sound of the
wheels. The vehicle approached, reached the inn, passed it,
and went on to the Dogana.

"You're safe," I said, "It's not a posting-chaise, but a
common wagon with merchandise."

With a hushed sigh of relief she passed her hand over her
brow, and then looking at me: "I have lived these three days
in constant terror. I believe in my soul he has come in pursuit
of me; my hope is in my having gained time through his being

absent when I started. My nerves are broken. I have neither slept nor eaten, nor till now have I spoken. But I *must* speak! I'm frank; it's good to take a friend when you find one."

I confess that to have been thus freely admitted by the fair fugitive into the whirling circle of her destiny was one of the keenest emotions of my life. "I know neither the motive of your flight nor the goal of your journey," I answered; "but if I may help you and speed you, I will joyfully turn back from the threshold of Italy and give you whatever furtherance my company may yield. To go with you," I added, smiling, "will be to remain in Italy, I assure you."

She acknowledged my offer with a glance more potent than words. "I'm going to a friend," she said, after a silence. "To accept your offer would be to make friendship cheap. He is lying ill at Geneva; otherwise I shouldn't be *thus!* But my head is on fire. This room is close; it smells of supper. Do me the favor to accompany me into the air."

She gathered her shawl about her shoulders, I offered her my arm, and we passed into the entry toward the door. In the doorway stood mine host, with his napkin under his arm. He drew himself up as we approached, and, as if to deprecate a possible imputation of scandal, honored us with a bow of the most ceremonious homage. We descended the steps and strolled along the road toward the Swiss frontier. A vague remnant of daylight seemed to linger imprisoned in the narrow gorge. We passed the Dogana and left the village behind us. My thoughts reverted as we went, to the aching blank of my fancy as I entered Isella an hour before. It seemed to palpitate now with a month's experience. Beyond the village a narrow bridge spans the stream and leads to a path which climbs the opposite hillside. We diverged from the road and lingered on the bridge while the sounding torrent gushed beneath us, flashing in the light of the few stars which sparkled in our narrow strip of sky, like diamonds tacked upon a band of velvet. I remained silent, thinking a passive silence

the most graceful tribute to the Signora's generous intentions. "I will tell you all!" she said at last. "Do you think
me pretty? But you needn't answer. The less you think so,
the more you'll say it. I *was* pretty! I don't pretend to be so
now. I have suffered too much. I have a miserable fear that
when *he* sees me, after these three years, he'll notice the loss
of my beauty. But, *poverino!* he is perhaps too ill to notice
anything. He is young—a year younger than I—twenty-
seven. He is a painter; he has a most beautiful talent. He
loved me four years ago, before my marriage. He was a friend
of my poor brother, who was fatally wounded at the battle
of Mentana, where he fought with Garibaldi. My brother,
Giuseppino, was brought home with his wound; he died in a
week. Ernesto came to make a drawing of his face before we
lost it forever. It was not the first time I had seen him, but it
was the first time we understood each other. I was sitting by
poor Giuseppino's bedside, crying—crying! He, too, cried
while he drew and made great blisters on the paper. I know
where to look for them still. They loved each other devotedly.
I, too, had loved my brother! for my mother was dead, and
my father was not a mother—not even a father! Judge for
yourself! We placed together the love which each of us had
borne for Giuseppino, and it made a great love for each other.
It was a misfortune; but how could we help it? He had
nothing but his talent, which as yet was immature. I had
nothing at all but the poor little glory of my father's being a
Marchese, without a *soldo*, and my prettiness! But you see what
has become of that! My father was furious to have given his
only son to that scoundrel of a Garibaldi, for he is of that way
of thinking. You should have heard the scene he made me
when poor Ernesto is despair asked leave to marry me. My
husband, whom I had never seen or at least never noticed,
was at that time in treaty for my hand. By his origin he was
little better than a peasant, but he had made a fortune in trade,
and he was very well pleased to marry a *marchesina*. It's not

every man who is willing to take a penniless girl; it was the first chance and perhaps the best. So I was given over blindfold, bound hand and foot, to that brute. Eh! what I hadn't brought in cash I had to pay down in patience. If I were to tell you what I've suffered these three years, it would bring tears to your eyes—Inglese as you are. But they are things which can't be told. He is a peasant, with the soul of a peasant—the taste, the manners, the vices of a peasant. It was my great crime that I was proud. I had much to be proud of. If I had only been a woman of his own sort! to pay him in his own coin! Ernesto, of course, had been altogether suppressed. He proposed to me to escape with him before my marriage, and I confess to you that I would have done if it I could. I tried in vain; I was too well watched. I implored him then to go away till better days; and he at last consented to go to Paris and pursue his studies. A week after my marriage he came to bid me farewell. My husband had taken me to Naples, to make me believe I was not wretched. Ernesto followed me, and I contrived to see him. It lasted three minutes by the clock: I have not seen him since. In three years I have had five letters from him; they are here in my dress. I am sure of his love; I don't need to have him write, to tell me. I have answered him twice. These letters—seven in all, in three years!—are all my husband has to reproach me with. He is furious at not having more. He knows of course that I love another; he knows that to bear such things a woman must borrow strength somewhere. I have had faith, but it has not been all faith! My husband has none; nothing is sacred to him, not the Blessed Virgin herself. If you were to hear the things he says about the Holy Father! I have waited and waited. I confess it, I have hoped at times that my husband would die. But he has the health of a peasant. He used to strike me—to starve me—to lock me up without light or fire. I appealed to my father, but, I'm sorry to say it, my father is a coward! Heaven forgive me! I'm saying dreadful things here! But, ah, Signore, let me breathe at last! I've waited and waited, as I say, for this hour! Heaven knows I have been good. Though I stand here now, I have not trifled with my duties. It's not coquetry! I determined to endure as long as I could, and then to break—to break forever! A month ago strength and courage left me; or rather, they came to me! I wrote to Ernesto that I would come to him. He answered that he would come down to meet me—if possible at Milan. Just afterwards he wrote me in a little scrawl in pencil that he had been taken ill in Geneva, and that if I could I must come alone, before he got worse. Here I am then, alone, pursued, frantic with ignorance and dread. Heaven only keep him till I come. I shall do the rest! Exactly how I left home, I can't tell you. It has been like a dream! My husband—God be praised!—was obliged to make a short absence on business, of which I took advantage. My great trouble was getting a little money. I never have any. I sold a few trinkets for a few francs—hardly enough! The people saw I was too frightened to make a stand, so that they cheated me. But if I can only come to the end! I'm certain that my husband has pursued me. Once I get to Switzerland, we can hide. Meanwhile I'm in a fever. I've lost my head. I began very well, but all this delay has so vexed and confused me. I hadn't even the wit to secure a place in the coach at Domo d'Ossola. But I shall go, if I have to sit on the roof—to crouch upon the doorstep. If I had only a little more money, so that I needn't wait for coaches. To overtake me my husband, for once in his life, won't count his *lire!*"

I listened with a kind of awe to this torrent of passionate confidence. I had got more even that I had bargained for. The current of her utterance seemed to gather volume as it came, and she poured out her tragic story with a sort of rapturous freedom. She had unburdened at last her heavy heart. As she spoke, the hot breath of her eloquence seemed to pass far beyond my single attentive sense, and mingle joyously with the free air of the night. Her tale, in a measure, might be untrue or imperfect; but her passion, her haste, her sincerity, were imperiously real. I felt, as I had never felt it, the truth of the poet's claim for his touch of nature. I became conscious of a hurrying share in my companion's dread. I seemed to hear in the trembling torrent the sound of rapid wheels. I expected every moment to see the glare of lights along the road, before the inn, then a strong arm locked about her waist, and, in the ray of a lantern from the carriage window to catch the mute agony of her solemn eyes. My heart beat fast; I was part and parcel of a romance! Come! the *dénouement* shouldn't fail by any prosy fault of mine.

"How I've talked!" cried the Signora, after a brief pause. "And how you stare at me! Eh! don't be afraid. I've said all, and it has done me good. You'll laugh with your *promessa sposa* about that crazy creature who was flying from her husband. The idea of people not being happy in marriage, you'll say to her!"

"I thank you with all my heart," I said, "for having trusted me as you have. But I'm almost sorry you have taken the time. You oughtn't to be lingering here while your husband is making the dust fly."

"That's easy to say, Signore; but I can't walk to Brieg, like you. A carriage costs a hundred and fifty francs. I have only just enough to pay my place in the coach."

I drew out my portemonnaie and emptied it in my hand; it contained a hundred and seventy francs. "*Ecco!*" I said, holding them out to her.

She glanced at them an instant, and then, with a movement which effectually rounded and completed my impression of her simple and passionate sincerity, seized with both her hands my own hand as it held them. "Ah, the Blessed Virgin be praised!" she cried. "Ah, you're an angel from heaven! Quick, quick! A carriage, a carriage!"

She thrust the money into her pocket, and, without waiting

for an answer, hurried back to the road, and moved swiftly toward the inn. I overtook her as she reached the doorstep, where our host was enjoying a pipe in the cool. "A carriage!" she cried. "I must be off. Quick, without delay! I have the money; you shall be well paid. Don't tell me you haven't one. There must be one here. Find one, prepare it, lose not a moment. Do you think I can lie tossing here all night? I shall put together my things, and give you ten minutes! You, sir, see that they hurry!" And she rapidly entered the house.

Bonifazio stared, somewhat aghast at the suddenness and the energy of her requisition. Fearing that he might not be equal to the occasion, I determined to take him by his gallantry. "Come, my friend," I said, "don't stand scratching your head, but *act*. I know you admire the Signora. You don't want to see so charming a woman in trouble. You don't wish to have a scandal in your inn. It is of the first importance that she should leave in ten minutes. Stir up your hostler."

A wise grin illumined his face. "Ah," said he, "it's as bad as that. I had my notions. I'll do what I can." He exerted himself to such good purpose that in the incredibly short period of twenty minutes a small closed carriage was drawn by a couple of stout horses to the door. Going in to summon the fair fugitive, I found her in the dining-room, where, fretting with impatience, and hooded and shawled, she had suffered a rather bungling chambermaid to attempt the insertion of a couple of necessary pins. She swept past me on her exit as if she had equally forgotten my face and her obligations, and entered the carriage with passionate adjurations of haste. I followed her and watched her take her place; but she seemed not even to see me. My hour was over. I had added an impulse to her straining purpose; its hurrying current had left me alone on the brink. I could not resist the influence of a poignant regret at having dropped from her consciousness. Learning from a peasant who was lounging near at hand that an easy footpath wound along the side of the mountain and struck the highroad at the end of half an hour's walk, I immediately discovered and followed it. I saw beneath me in the dimness as I went the white highroad, with the carriage slowly beginning its ascent. Descending at last from the slope, I met the vehicle well on its way up the mountain, and motioned to the driver to stop. The poor Signora, haunted with the fear of interruption, thrust her pale face from the window. Seeing me, she stared an instant almost vacantly, and then passing her hand over her face broke into a glorious smile. Flinging open the carriage door from within, she held out her two hands in farewell.

"Give me your blessing," she cried, "and take mine! I had almost forgotten you. Love is selfish, Signore. But I should have remembered you later and cried with gratitude. My Ernesto will write to you. Give me your card—write me your address, there in the carriage lamp. No? As you please, then. Think of me kindly. And the young girl you marry—use her well—love her if only a little—it will be enough. We ask but a little, but we need that. Addio!" and she raised her two hands to her lips, seemed for an instant to exhale her whole soul upon her finger tips, and flung into the air a magnificent Italian kiss.

I returned along the winding footpath more slowly, a wiser, possibly a sadder man than a couple of hours before. I had entered Italy, I had tasted of sentiment, I had assisted at a drama. It was a good beginning. I found Bonifazio finishing his pipe before the inn. "Well, well, Signore," he cried, "what does it all mean?"

"Aren't you enough of an Italian to guess?" I asked.

"Eh, eh, it's better to be an Inglese and to be told," cried Bonifazio with a twinkle.

"You must sleep to-night with an ear open," I said. "A personage will arrive post-haste from Domo. Stop him if you can."

Bonifazio scratched his head. "If a late supper or an early

breakfast will stop him!" he murmured. I looked deep into his little round eye, expecting to read there the recipe for the infusion of a sleeping potion into *café au lait*.

My room that night was close and hot, and my bed none of the best. I tossed about in a broken sleep. I dreamed that I was lying ill in a poor tavern at Naples, waiting, waiting with an aching heart, for the arrival from the Baths of Lucca of a certain young lady, who had been forced by her mother, Mrs B. of Philadelphia, into a cruel marriage with a wealthy Tuscan *contadino*. At last I seemed to hear a great noise without and a step on the stairs; through the opened door rushed in my *promessa sposa*. Her blue eyes were bright with tears, and she wore a flounced black dress trimmed with crimson silk. The next moment she was kneeling at my bedside crying, "Ernesto, Ernesto!" At this point I awoke into the early morning. The noise of horses and wheels and voices came up from outside. I sprang from my bed and stepped to my open window. The huge, high-piled, yellow diligence from Domo d'Ossola had halted before the inn. The door of the *coupé* was open; from the aperture half emerged the Personage. "A peasant," she had called him, but he was well *dicrotti*, though he *had* counted his *lire* and taken the diligence. He struck me as of an odd type for an Italian: dark sandy hair, a little sandy mustache, waxed at the ends, and sandy whiskers *à l'Anglaise*. He had a broad face, a large nose, and a small keen eye, without any visible brows. He wore a yellow silk handkerchief tied as a nightcap about his head, and in spite of the heat he was very much muffled. On the steps stood Bonifazio, cap in hand, smiling and obsequious.

"Is there a lady here?" demanded the gentleman from the *coupé*. "A lady alone—good-looking—with little luggage?"

"No lady, Signore," said Bonifazio. "Alas! I have an empty house. If *eccellenza* would like to descend——"

"Have you had a lady—yesterday, last night? Don't lie."

"We had three, *eccellenza*, a week ago—three Scotch ladies going to Baveno. Nay, three days since we had a *prima donna* on her way to Milan."

"Damn your Scotch *prima donna!*" said the other. "Have you had my wife?"

"The wife of *eccellenza?* Save the ladies I mention, we have had neither wife nor maid. Would *eccellenza* like a cup of coffee?"

"*Sangue di Dio!*" was *eccellenza's* sole response. The *coupé* door closed with a slam, the conductor mounted, the six horses started, and the great mountain coach rolled away.

MASTER EUSTACE

I

HAVING handed me my cup of tea, she proceeded to make her own—an operation she performed with an old-maidish precision I delighted to observe.

The story is not my own (she then began), but that of persons with whom for a time I was intimately connected. I have led a very quiet life; that is my only romance—and it's the romance of others. When I was a young woman of twenty-two my poor mother died, after a long, weary illness, and I found myself obliged to seek a new home. Making a home requires time and money. I had neither to spare, so I advertised for a "situation," rating my accomplishments modestly, and asking rather for kind treatment than high wages. Mrs Garnyer immediately answered my advertisement. She offered me a fair salary and a peaceful asylum. I was to teach her little boy the rudiments of my slender stock of science and to make myself generally useful. Something in her tone and manner assured me that in accepting this latter condition, I was pledging myself to no very onerous servitude, and I never found reason to repent of my bargain. I had always valued my freedom before all things, and it seemed to me that in trading it away even partially I was surrendering a priceless treasure; but Mrs Garnyer made bondage very easy. I liked her from the first, and I doubt if she ever fully appreciated my fidelity and affection. She knew she could trust me, and she always spoke of me as "a good creature"; but she never measured the trouble I saved her, or the little burdens I lifted from her pretty, feeble shoulders. Both in her position and her person there was something singularly appealing. She was in those days—indeed she always remained—a very attractive woman; but she had grace even more than beauty. She was young, and looked even younger than her years; slight, fluttering, with frequent gestures and not many words, and fairer, whiter, purer, in complexion than any woman I have seen. She reminded me of a sketch from which the "shading" has been omitted. She had her shadows indeed, as well as her lights; but they were all turned inward. She might have been made up of the airy substance of lights and shadows. Nature in putting her together had left out the harder, heavier parts, the selfishness, the ambition, the power to insist and to calculate. Experience, however, had given her a burden to carry; she was evidently sorrow-laden. She shifted the cruel weight from shoulder to shoulder, she ached and sighed under it, and in the depths of her sweet natural smile you saw it pressing the tears from her very soul. Mrs Garnyer's distresses, I confess, were in my eyes an added charm. I was desperately fond of a bit of romance, and as I was plainly never to have one of my own, I made the most of my neighbour's. This secret sadness would have covered more sins than I ever had to forgive her. At first, naturally, I connected it with the death of her husband; but, as time went on, I found reason to believe that there had been little love between the pair. She had been married against her will; Mr Garnyer was fifteen years her senior, and, as she frankly mentioned, coarsely and cruelly dissipated. Their married life had lasted but three years, and had come to an end to her great and manifest relief. Had he done her while it lasted some irreparable wrong? I suspected so; she was like a garden-rose with half its petals plucked. He had left her with diminished means, though her property (mostly her own) was still ample for her needs. These, with those of her son, were extremely simple. To certain little luxuries she was obstinately attached; but her manner of life was so monotonous and frugal that she must have spent but a fraction of her income. It was

her single son—the heir of her hopes, the apple of her eye—
that she entrusted to my care. He was five years old, and she
had taught him his letters—a great feat she seemed to think;
she was as proud of it as if she had invented the alphabet for
the occasion. She had called him Eustace, for she meant that
he should have the best of everything—the prettiest clothes,
the prettiest playthings and the prettiest name. He was himself as pretty as his name, though not at all in the manner of
his mother. He was slight like her, but far more nervous and
decided, and he had neither her features nor her colouring.
Least of all had he her expression. Mrs Garnyer's attitude
was one of tender, pensive sufferance modified by hopes—a
certain half-mystical hope which seemed akin to religion, but
which was not all religion, for the heaven she dreamed of was
situated here below. The boy from his early childhood presented himself as a little man who would take a line of his
own. He was not one who would ever wait for things, good
or evil; he would snatch boldly at the one sort and snap his
fingers at the other. He had a pale, dark skin, not altogether
healthy in tone; a mass of fine brown hair, which seemed
given him just to emphasise by its dancing sweep the petulant
little nods and shakes of his head; and a deep, wilful, malicious
eye. His eye told me from the first that I should have no easy
work with him, and with every possible relaxation of the
nursery-code my place never became in the least a sinecure.
His wits were so quick, however, and his imagination so
lively, that I gradually managed to fill out his mother's
meagre little programme of study. This had been drawn up
with a sparing hand; her only fear was of his being over-
worked. The poor lady had but a dim conception of what a
man of the world is expected to know. She thought, I believe,
that with his handsome face, his handsome property, and his
doting mother, he would need to know little more than how
to sign that pretty name of Eustace to replies to invitations to
dinner. I wonder now that with her constant interference I

contrived to set the child intellectually on his legs. Later, when he had a tutor, I received a compliment for my perseverance.

The truth is, I became fond of him; his very imperfections fascinated me. He would soon enough have to take his chance of the world's tolerance, and society would cease to consist for him of a couple of coaxing women. I told Mrs Garnyer that there was never an easier child to spoil, and that those fondling hands of hers would sow a crop of formidable problems for future years. But Mrs Garnyer was utterly incapable of taking a rational view of matters, or of sacrificing to-day to to-morrow; and her folly was the more incurable as it was founded on a strange, perverse little principle—a crude, passionate theory—that love, love, pure love, is the sum and substance of maternal duty, and that the love which reasons and requires and refuses is cruel and wicked. "I know you think I am a silly goose," she said, "and not fit to have a child at all. But you are wrong—I promise you you are wrong. I am very reasonable, I am very patient; I have a great deal to bear—more than you know—and I bear it very well. But one can't be always on the stretch—always hard and wise and good. In some things one must break down and be one's poor natural, lonely self. Eustace can't turn out wrong; it's impossible; it would be too cruel. You must not say it nor hint it. I shall do with him what my heart bids me; he is all I have; he consoles me."

My notions perhaps were a little old-fashioned; but surely it will never altogether go out of fashion to teach a child that he is not to have the moon by crying for it. Now Eustace had a particular fancy for the moon, for everything bright, inaccessible and absurd. His will was as sharp as a steel spring, and it was vain to attempt to bend it or break it. He had an indefeasible conviction that he was number one among men; and if he had been born in the purple, as they say, of some far-off Eastern court, or found himself the final morbid little offshoot of a long line of despots, he couldn't have had a greater idea of his prerogative. The poor child had no sense of justice—he had the extra virtues, but not the regular ones. He could condescend, he could forgive, he could allow things, if his leave had been asked, but he couldn't endure the hint of a conflicting right. He could love, love passionately; but he was so jealous and exacting that his love cost you very much more than it was worth. If he liked me and confided in me, I had worked hard for it—I had to "live up" to it. He thought it a very great honour that he should care to harness me up as his horse, to throw me his ball by the hour, to make me joggle with him on the see-saw (sitting close to the middle) till my poor bones ached. Nevertheless, in this frank, childish arrogance there was an almost irresistible charm and, I was absurdly flattered at his liking me. Poor me! at twenty-three I was his first "conquest"—the first in a long list, as I believe it came to be. If he required a great margin, he used it with a peculiar grace of his own, and he admitted the corresponding obligation of being clever and brilliant. As a child even, he had a kind of personal distinction. His talents were excellent, and teaching him, whatever it may have been, was at least not dull work. It was indeed less to things really needful than to the luxuries of learning that he took most kindly. He had an excellent ear for music, and though he never practised properly he turned off an air with wonderful expression. In this he resembled his mother, who was a natural musician. She, however, was always at the piano, and whenever I think of her in those early years I see her sitting before it musingly, half sadly, with her pretty head on one side, her fair braids thrust behind her ears—ears from which a couple of small but admirable diamonds were never absent—and her white hands wandering over the notes, seeking vaguely for a melody they seemed hardly to dare to remember. Eustace had an unsatiable appetite for stories, though he was one of the coolest and most merciless of critics. I can imagine him now at my knee, with his big eyes fastened on my lips, demanding more wonders and more, till my short-winded invention had to cry for breath. Do my best, I could never startle him; my giants were never big enough and my fairies never small enough, my enchanters, dragons, dungeons and castles never on the really grand scale of his own imaginative needs. I felt dreadfully below the mark. At last he would open his wilful little mouth and yawn in my face, with a dreadfully dry want of conviction. I felt flattered when by chance I had pleased him, for, by a precocious instinct, he knew tinsel from gold. "Look here," he would say, "you are remarkably ugly; what makes you so ugly? Your nose is so big at the end." (You needn't protest; I *was* ugly. Like most very plain women, I have improved with time.) Of course I used to rebuke him for his rudeness; though I was secretly thankful, because it taught me a number of things. Once he said something, I forget what, that made me burst into tears. It was the first time, and the last; for I found that, instead of exciting his pity, tears only moved his contempt, and apparently a kind of cynical, physical disgust. The best way was to turn the tables on him by pretending to be indifferent and superior. In that case he himself would condescend to tears—bitter, wrathful tears. Then you had perhaps gained nothing, but you had lost nothing. In every other case you *had* lost.

II

OF course these close relations lasted but a couple of years. I had made him very much wiser than myself; he was growing tall and boyish and terribly inquisitive. My poor little stories ceased to have any illusion for him, and he would spend hours lying on his face on the carpet, kicking up his neat little legs and poring over the *Arabian Nights*, the *Fairy Queen*, the other prime enchanters of childhood. My advice would have been to pack him off to school; but I might as well have asked his mother to send him to the penitentiary.. He was to be educated *en prince*; he was to have an instructor to himself. I thought sympathetically of the worthy pedagogue who was to minister to Eustace without competition. But such a one was easily found—in fact, he was found three times over. Three private tutors came and went successively. They fell in love, punctually, with Mrs Garnyer. Their love indeed she might have put up with; but unhappily, unlike Viola, they "told" it—by letter—with an offer of their respective hands. Their letters were different, but to Mrs Garnyer their hands were all alike, all very untidy paws. "The horrid creatures!" was her invariable commentary. "I wouldn't speak to them for the world. My dear, you must do it." And I, who had never declined an offer on my own account, went to work in this wholesale manner for my friend! You will say that, young as she was—pretty, independent, lonely—Mrs Garnyer would have looked none the worse for a spice of coquetry. But she never would have forgiven herself a flirtation. Her greatest charm for me was her scorn for this sort of levity, and indeed her general contempt for cheap sentimental effects. It was as if, from having drunk at the crystal head-spring, she had lost her taste for standing water. She was absolutely indifferent to attention; it inspired her, in fact, with a kind of terror. She had not a trace of personal vanity; she was even without visible desire to please. Unfortunately, as you see, she pleased in spite of herself. As regards love, she had an imposing arrays of principles; on this one point she was always very explicit. "It's either a passion," she said, "or it's nothing. You can know it by being willing to give up everything for it—name and fame, past and future, this world and the next. Do you keep back a feather's weight of tenderness or trust? Then you are not in love. You must risk everything, for you get everything—if you are happy. I can't understand a woman trifling with such feelings. They talk about the unpardonable sin; that's it, it seems to me. Do you know the word in the language I most detest?—*Flirtation*. Poh! it makes me ill." When Mrs Garnyer uttered this hint of an esoteric doctrine, her clear blue eyes would become clouded with the gathered mists of memory. In this matter she understood herself and meant what she said.

Impatient as she was of being "made up to," she exposed herself very little to such dangers, and almost never went into the world. She met her few friends but two or three times a year, and was without a single intimate. As time went on she came to care more for me than for any one. When Eustace had outgrown my teaching she insisted on my remaining in any capacity I chose—as housekeeper, companion, seamstress, guest; I might make my own terms. I became a little of each of these, and with the increasing freedom of our intercourse grew to regard her as a younger and weaker sister. I gave her, for what it was worth, my best judgment on all things. Her own confidence always stopped short of a certain point; a little curtain of reticence was always suspended between us. Sometimes it appeared to grow thinner and thinner, becoming almost transparent and revealing the figures behind it. Sometimes it seemed to move and flutter in the murmur of our talk, as if in a moment it might drop away or melt away into air. But it was a magical web; it played a hundred tormenting tricks, and year after year it hung in its place. Of course I had fits of immense curiosity, but I can't say more for the disinterested affection I felt for Mrs Garnyer than that I never pried, never pressed her. I lingered near the door of her Blue-Beard's chamber, but I never peeped through the keyhole. She was a poor lady with a secret; I took her into my heart, secret and all. She insisted that her isolation was her own choice, and pretended to be exceedingly glad that society let her so well alone. She made her widowhood serve as a motive for her monotonous years, and declared that her boy's education amply filled them. She was a widow, however, who never of her own accord mentioned her husband's name, and she wore her weeds very lightly. She was very fond of white, and for six months of the year was rarely seen in a dark dress. Occasionally, on certain fixed days, she would flame forth in some old-fashioned piece of finery from a store which she religiously preserved, and would flash about the house in rose-colour or blue. One day—her boy's birthday— she kept with extraordinary solemnity. It fell in the middle of September. On this occasion she would put on a faded ball-dress, overload herself with jewels and trinkets, dress her hair with flowers. Eustace, too, she would trick out in a suit of crimson velvet, and in this singular guise the pair would walk with prodigious gravity about the garden and up and down the avenue. Every now and then she would stoop and give him a convulsive hug. The child himself seemed to feel the magnitude of this festival, and played his part with pre-cocious effect. He would appear at dusk with the curl still in his hair, his velvet trousers unstained, his ruffles uncrumpled. In the evening the coachman let off rockets in the garden; we feasted on ice-cream and a bottle of champagne was sent to the kitchen. No wonder Master Eustace carried himself like an heir-apparent! Once, I remember, the mother and son were overtaken in their festal promenade by some people who had come to live in the neighbourhood and, who drove up, rather officiously, to leave their cards. They stared, in amazement, from the carriage-window, and were told Mrs Garnyer was not at home. A few days later we heard that Mrs Garnyer was out of her mind; she had been found masquerading in her grounds with her little boy, in the most indecent costume. From time to time she received an invita-tion, and occasionally she accepted one. When she went out she made her mourning more marked, and she always came home in a fret. "It is the last house I will go to," she used to say, as I helped her to undress. "People's neglect I can bear, and thank them for it; but heaven deliver me from their

kindness! I won't be patronised—I won't, I won't! Shall I, my
boy? We will wait till you grow up, shan't we, my darling?
Then his poor little mother shan't be patronised, shall she,
my brave little man?" The child was constantly dangling at
his mother's skirts, and was seldom beyond the reach of some
such passionate appeal.

A preceptor had at last been found of a less inflammable
composition than the others—a worthy, elderly German of
fair attainments, with a stout, sentimental wife—she gave
music-lessons in town—who monopolised his ardour. He
was a mild, patient man: a nose of wax, as the saying is—a
pretty nose it grew to be in Eustace's supple fingers! I will
answer for it that in all those years he never carried a single
point. I believe that, like me, he had begun with tears; but
finding this an altogether losing game, he was content now
to take off his spectacles, drop his head on one side, look
imploringly at his pupil with his weak blue eyes, and then
exhale his renunciation in a plaintive *Lieber Gott!* Under this
discipline the boy bloomed like a flower; but it was to my
sense a kind of hot-house growth. His tastes were sedentary,
and he lived most of the time within doors. He kept a horse,
and took long lonely rides; but there were whole days that
he spent lounging over a book, trifling at the piano, or fretting
over a water-colour sketch which he was sure to throw aside
in disgust. One amusement he pursued with unwearying
constancy; it was a sign of especial good-humour, and I
never knew it to fail him. He would sit for hours lounging in
a chair, with his head thrown back and his legs extended,
staring at vacancy, or what seemed to us so: but a vacancy
filled with the silent revel of his imagination and the scenes
it presented to him. What was the substance of these ecstatic
visions? The broad, happy life on which he would enter some
day, the great world whose far-off murmur caressed his ear—
the joys of prosperous manhood—pleasure, success, popu-
larity—a kind of triumphant and transfigured egotism. His

reveries swarmed with tinted pictures and transcendent delights; his handsome young face, his idle insolent smile, wore the cold reflection of their brightness. His mother, after watching him for a while in these moods, would steal up be-hind him and kiss him softly on the forehead, as if to marry his sweet illusions to sweeter reality. For my part, I wanted to divorce them. It was a sad pity, I thought, that desire and occasion, in the lad's life, played so promptly into each other's hands. I longed to spoil the game, to shuffle the cards afresh and give him a taste of bad luck. I felt as if between them— she by her measureless concessions, he by his consuming arrogance—they were sowing a crop of dragon's teeth. This sultry summer of youth couldn't last for ever, and I knew that the poor lady would be the first to suffer by a change of weather. He would turn some day, in his passionate vanity, and rend the gentle creature who had fed it with the delusive wine of her love. And yet he had a better angel as well as a worse, and it was a marvel to see how this superior spirit (a sort of human conscience) tussled with the fiend and, in spite of bruises and ruffled pinions, returned again and again to the onset. There were days when his generous, boyish gaiety —the natural sunshine of youth and cleverness—warmed our women's hearts and kindled our most trusting smiles. Me, as he grew older, he treated as a licensed old-time friend. I was the prince's jester—I used to tell him his truths, as the French say. He believed them just enough to feel an agreeable irritation in listening; for the rest, doubtless, they seemed as vague and remote as the croaking of the frogs in the pond. There were moments, I think, when the eternal blue sky of his mother's temper wearied his capricious brain. At such times he would come and sprawl on the sofa near my little work-table, clipping my threads, mixing my reels, mislaying my various utensils, and criticising my work without reserve —chattering, gossiping, complaining, boasting. With all his faults, Eustace had one sovereign merit—that merit without which even the virtues he lacked lose half their charm: he was magnificently candid. He was only too transparent. The light of truth played through his interlaced pretensions, and against it they stood relieved in their hard tenacity, like fine young trees against a sunrise. He expressed his passions—expressed them only too loudly; you received ample notice of his revenges. They came as a matter of course; he never took them out in talk; but you were warned.

III

IF these intense meditations of which I have spoken followed exclusively the train of his personal fortunes, his conversation was hardly more disinterested. It was altogether about himself—his ambitions, his ailments, his dreams, his opinions, his intentions. He talked a great deal of his property, and though he had a great aversion to figures he knew the amount of his expectations before he was out of jackets. He had a keen relish for luxury, and, indeed, as he respected pretty things and used them with a degree of tenderness which he by no means lavished upon animate objects, saving, sparing, and preserving them, this seemed to me one of his most human traits, though, I admit, an expensive virtue—and he promised to spend his fortune in books and pictures, in art and travel. His mother was frequently called upon to do the honours of his castles in the air. She would look at him always with her doting smile, and with a little glow of melancholy in her eyes—a faint tribute to some shadowy chance that even her Eustace might reckon without his host. She would shake her head tenderly, or lean it on his shoulder and murmur, "Who knows, who knows? It's perhaps as foolish, my son, to try and anticipate our happiness as to attempt to take the measure of our misery. We know them each when they come. Whatever comes to us, at all events, we shall meet it together." Resting in this delicious contact, with her arm round his neck and her cheek on his hair, she would close her eyes in a sort of mild ecstasy. As I have never had a son myself I can speak of maternity but by hearsay; but I feel as if I knew some of its secrets, as if I had gained from Mrs Garnyer a revelation of maternal passion. The perfect humility of her devotion, indeed, seemed to me to point to some motive deeper than common motherhood. It looked like a kind of penance, a kind of pledge. Had she done him some early wrong? Did she meditate some wrong to come? Did she wish to purchase pardon for the past or impunity for the future? One might have supposed from the lad's calm relish of her incense—as if it were the fumes of some perfumed chibouque palpitating lazily through his own lips—that he had a gratified sense of something to forgive. In fact, he had something to forgive us all—our dulness, our vulgarity, our not guessing his unuttered desires, the want of a pre-established harmony between our wills and his. It seemed to me, however, that there were even moments when he turned dizzy on the edge of this awful gulf of his mother's self-sacrifice. Fixing his eyes, then, an instant, to steady himself, he took comfort in the thought that she had ceased to suffer —her personal ambitions lay dead at the bottom. He could vaguely see them—distant, dim, motionless. It was to be hoped that no adventurous ghost of those shuffled-off passions would climb upward to the light.

A frequent source of complaint, with Eustace, when he had no more handy dissatisfaction, was that he had not known his father. He had formed a mental image of the late Mr Garnyer which I am afraid hardly tallied at all points with the original. The boy knew that he had been a man of pleasure, and he had painted his portrait in ideal hues. What a charming father—a man of pleasure, Eustace thought, as if he had believed that gentlemen of this stamp take their pleasure in the nursery.

What pleasures they might have shared; what rides, what
talks, what games, what adventures—what far other hours
than those he passed in the deserted billiard-room (this had
been one of Mr Garnyer's most marked tastes), clicking the
idle balls in the stillness. He learned to talk very early of
arranging his life to resemble his father's. What he had done
his son would do. A dozen odds and ends which had belonged
to Mr Garnyer he carried to his room, where he paraded them
on his mantel-shelf like relics on a high altar. When he was
seventeen years old he began to smoke an old silver-mounted
pipe which had his father's initials embossed on the bowl.
"It would be a great blessing," he said, as he puffed this pipe
—it made him dismally sick, for he hated tobacco—"to
have some man in the house. It's so fearfully womanish here.
No one but you two and Hauff, and what's he but an old
woman? Mother, why have you always lived in this way?
What's the matter with you? You have no *savoir vivre*. What
are you blushing about? That comes of moping here all your
days—that you blush for nothing. I don't want my mother
to blush for anything or anyone, not even for me. But I give
you notice, I can stand it no longer. Now I'm seventeen it's
time I should see the world. I am going to travel. My father
travelled; he went all over Europe. There's a little French
book upstairs, the poems of Parny—it's awfully French, too
—with 'Henry Garnyer, Paris, 1802,' on the fly-leaf. I must
go to Paris; I shan't go to college. I have never been to school.
I want to be complete—privately educated altogether. Very
few Americans are; it's quite a distinction. Besides, I know all I
want to know. Hauff brought me out some college-catalogues.
They're absurd; he laughs at them. We did all that three
years ago. I know more about books than most young
fellows; what I want is knowledge of the world. My father
had it, and you haven't, mother. But he had plenty of taste,
too. Hauff says that little edition of Parny is very rare. I shall
bring home lots of such things. *Vous allez voir!*" Mrs Garnyer

listened to such effusions of filial emulation in sad, embarrassed silence. I couldn't but pity her. She knew that her husband was no proper model for her child; yet she couldn't in decency turn his heart against his father's memory. She took refuge in that tremulous reserve which committed her neither to condemnation of her husband nor to approval with her son.

She had recourse at this period, as I had known her to do before, to a friend attached to a mercantile house in India—an old friend, she had told me; "in fact," she had added, "my only friend—a man to whom I am under immense obligations." Once in six months there came to her from this distant benefactor a large square letter, heavily sealed and covered with foreign post-marks. I used to believe it to be a kind of bulletin of advice for the coming half-year. Advice about what? Her cares were so few, her habits so simple, that they offered scanty matter for discussion. But now, of course, came a packet of good counsel in regard to these plans of Eustace's. I knew that she dreaded it; but, since her oracle had spoken, she put on a brave face. She was certainly a very faithful believer. She concealed from Eustace the extent of her dependence on this far-away monitor, for the boy would have resented such interference, even though it should fall in with his own projects. She had always read her friend's letters in secret; this was the only practice of her life she failed to share with her son. Me she now for the first time admitted into her confidence. "Mr Cope strongly recommends my letting him go," she said. "He says it will make a man of him. He needs to rub against other men. I suppose, at least," she cried, with her usual sweet fatuity, "it will do other men no harm! Perhaps I don't love him as I ought, and I must lose him awhile to learn to prize him. If I only get him back again! It would be monstrous that I shouldn't! But why are we cursed with these perpetual scruples and fears? It's a weary life!" She would have said more if she had known that it was not his departure but his return that was to be cruel.

The excellent Mr Hauff was too limp and battered to be a bear-leader in distant lands; but a companion was secured in the person of his nephew, an amiable young German, who was represented to know the world as well as he knew books. For a week before he left us Eustace was so friendly and good-humoured that we cried for him in advance. "I give her into your care," he said to me. "If anything happens to her I shall hold you responsible. She is very woe-begone just now, but will cheer up as soon as I am out of sight. But, mother, you are not to be too cheerful, mind. You are not to forget me an instant. If you do I will never forgive you. I insist on being missed. There's little enough merit in loving me when I am here; I wish to be loved in my absence." For many weeks after he left he might have been satisfied. His mother wandered about like a churchyard-ghost keeping watch near a buried treasure. When his letters began to come she read them over a dozen times, and sat for hours, with her eyes closed, holding them in her hand. They were wretchedly meagre and hurried, but their very brevity gratified her. He was prosperous and happy, and could snatch but odd moments from the recreations of his age.

One morning, after he had been away some three months, there came two letters, one from Eustace, the other from India, the latter very much in advance of its time. Mrs Garnyer opened the Indian letter first. I was pouring out tea; I observed her from behind the urn. As her eyes ran over the pages she turned deadly pale; then, raising her glance, she met mine. Immediately her paleness turned to crimson. She rose to her feet and hurried out of the room, leaving Eustace's letter untouched on the table. This little fact was eloquent, and my curiosity was excited. Later in the day it was partially satisfied. She came to me with a singular, conscious look—the look of a sort of oppression of happiness—and announced Mr Cope was coming home. He had obtained release from his engagement in India, and would arrive in a fortnight. She uttered no words of rejoicing, and I could see that her joy was of the unutterable sort. As the days elapsed, however, her emotion betrayed itself in a restless, aimless flutter of movement, so violent as to be painful to behold. She roamed about the house, singing to herself, gazing out of the windows, shifting the chairs and tables, smoothing the curtains, trying vaguely to brighten the faded look of things. Before every mirror she paused and inspected herself, with that frank audacity of pretty women which I have always envied, tucking up a curl of her fair hair or smoothing a crease in those muslins which she always kept so fresh. Of Eustace for the moment she rarely spoke; the boy's prediction had not been so very much amiss. Who was this wonderful Mr Cope, this mighty magician?

I very soon learned. He arrived on the day he had fixed, and took up his residence in the house. From the moment I looked at him I felt that he was a man I should like. I suppose I was flattered by the notice he took of so humble a personage. He had often heard of me, he said; he knew how good a friend I had been to Mrs Garnyer; he hoped very much I would be indulgent to him. I felt as if I were amply repaid for my years of domestic service. But, in spite of this pleasant assurance, I had a sense of being for the moment altogether *de trop*. He was united to his friend by a closer bond than I had suspected. I left them alone with their old memories and references, and confined myself to my own room; though indeed I had noticed between them a sort of sentimental intelligence in which words might pass without audible speech. Mrs Garnyer underwent a singular change; I seemed to know her now for the first time. It was as if she had flung aside a veil which muffled her tones and blurred her features. There was a new decision in her tread, a deeper meaning in her smile; so, at thirty-eight her girlhood had come back to her! She was as full of blushes and random prattle and foolish falterings for very pleasure as a young bride. Upon Mr Cope

the years had set a more ineffaceable seal. He was a man of
forty-five, but you might easily have given him ten years
more. He had that look which I have always liked, of people
who have lived in hot climates; a bronzed complexion and a
cool, deliberate gait, as if he had learned to think twice before
moving. He was tall and lean, yet very powerful, like a large
man somewhat "reduced." His hair was thin and perfectly
white, and he wore a grizzled moustache. He dressed in loose,
light-coloured garments of those fine Eastern stuffs. I had a
singular impression of having seen him before, but I could
never say when or where. He was extremely deaf—so deaf
that I had to force my voice; though I observed that Mrs
Garnyer easily made him hear by speaking slowly and looking at him. He had, peculiarly, that patient, appealing air
which you find in very deaf persons less frequently than in
the blind, but which is more touching when the eye is alive
and sees what the ear loses. He had been obliged to make
good company of himself, and the glimpses that one got of
this resigned fellowship in stillness were of a kind to make one
long to enter into it. But with others, too, he was a charming
talker, though he was obliged to keep the talk in his own
hands. He took your response for granted with a kind of
conciliating brightness, guessed your opinion with a glance,
and phrased it usually better than you would have done.

IV

For ten years I had been pitying Mrs Garnyer; it was odd now
to find myself envying her. Patient waiting is no loss, and at
last her day had come. I had always rather wondered at her
patience; but, after all, it was spiced with private reasons. She
had lived by precept and example, by chapter and verse; for
his sake it was easy to be wise. I say for "his" sake, because,

as matter of course, I now connected her visitor with that element of mystery which had been one of my earliest impressions of Mrs Garnyer. Mr Cope's presence renewed my memory of it. I fitted the key to the lock, but on coming to open the casket I was disappointed to find that the principal part of the secret had evaporated. I made up my mind that Mr Cope had been her first and only love. Her parents had frowned on him and forced her into a marriage with poor dissolute Mr Garnyer—a course the more revolting as he had already spent half his own property and was likely to make sad havoc with his wife's. He had a high social value, which the girl's own family, who were plain enough people to have had certain primitive scruples in larger measure, deemed a compensation for his vices. The discarded lover, thinking she had not resisted as firmly as she might, embarked for India, and there, half in spite, half in despair, married as sadly amiss as herself. He had trifled with his happiness; he lived to repent. His wife lived, as well, to perpetuate his misery; it was my belief that she had only recently died, and that this event was the occasion of his return. When he arrived he wore a weed on his hat; the next day it had disappeared. Reunion had come to the pair in the afternoon of life, when the tricks and graces of passion are no longer becoming; but when these have spent themselves something of passion still is left, and this my companions were free to enjoy. They had begun to enjoy it with the chastened eagerness of which I caught the aroma. Such was my reading of the riddle. Right or not, at least it made sense.

I had promised Eustace to write to him, and one afternoon as I sat alone, well pleased to have a theme, I despatched him a long letter, full of the praises of Mr Cope, and, by implication, of his mother's improved condition. I wished to anticipate his possible suspicions and reconcile him with the altered situation. But after I had posted my letter it seemed to me that I had been too precipitate. I doubted whether, even amid the larger life of the grand tour, he had unlearned the old trick of jealousy. Jealousy surely would have been quite misplaced, for Mr Cope's affection for his hostess embraced the boy, embraced everything that concerned her. He regretted the lad's absence; he manifested the kindliest interest in everything that spoke of him; he turned over his books, he looked at his sketches, he examined and compared the half-dozen portraits which the fond mother had caused to be executed at various stages of his growth. One sultry day, when poor Mr Hauff travelled out from town for news of his pupil, he made a point of being introduced and of shaking his hand. The tutor stayed to dinner, and on Mr Cope's proposition we drank the boy's health in brimming glasses. The old German of course wept profusely; it was Eustace's mission to make people cry. I thought too I saw a tear on Mr Cope's lid. The cup of his contentment was full; at a touch it overflowed. On the whole, however, he took this bliss of reunion more quietly than his friend. He was a melancholy man. He had the air of one for whom the moral of this fable of life has greater charms than the plot, and who has made up his mind to ask no favours of destiny. When he met me he used to smile gently, frankly, saying little; but I had a great liking for his smile. It seemed to say much—to murmur, "Receive my compliments. You and I are a couple of tested souls; we understand each other. We are not in a flutter with the privilege of existence, like charity-children on a picnic. We have had, each of us, to live for years without the thing we once fancied gave life its only value. We have tasted of servitude; and patience, taken up as a means, has grown grateful as an end. It has cured us of eagerness." So wisely it gossiped, the smile of our guest. No wonder I liked it.

One evening, a month after his advent, Mrs Garnyer came to me with a strange, embarrassed air. "I have something to tell you," she said; "something that will surprise you. Do you consider me a *very* old woman? I am old enough to be wiser, you will say. But I have never been so wise as to-day. I am engaged to be married to Mr Cope. There! make the best of it. I have no apologies to make to any one," she went on, almost defiantly. "It's between ourselves. If we suit each other, it's no one's business. I know what I am about. He means to remain in this country; we should be constantly together and extremely intimate. As he says, I am young enough to be—what do they call it?—compromised. Of course, therefore, I am young enough to marry. It will make no difference with you; you will stay with me all the same. Who cares, after all, what I do? No one but Eustace, and he will thank me for giving him such a father. Ah, I shall do well by my boy!" she cried, clasping her hands in ecstasy. "I shall do better than he knows. My property, it appears, is dreadfully entangled. Mr Garnyer did as he pleased with it; I was given to him with my hands tied. Mr Cope has been looking into it, and he tells me that it will be a long affair to put things to rights. I have been living all these years at the mercy of unprincipled agents. But now I have given up everything to Mr Cope. *He* will drive the money-changers from the temple! It's a small reward to marry him. Eustace has no head for money-matters; he only knows how to spend. For years now he needn't think of them—Mr Cope is our providence. Don't be afraid; Eustace won't object, and at last he will have a companion—the best, the wisest, the kindest. You know how he used to long for one—how tired he was of me and you. It will be a new life. Oh, I'm a happy mother—at last—at last! Don't look at me so hard; I am a blushing bride, remember. Smile, laugh, kiss me. There! You are a good creature. I shall make my boy a present— the handsomest that ever was made. Poor Mr Cope—I am happier than he! I have had my boy all these years, and he has had none. He has the heart of a father—he has longed for a son. Do you know," she added, with a strange smile, "that I think he marries me as much for my son's sake as for my own? He marries me at all events—boy and all!" This speech was uttered with a forced and hurried animation which betrayed the effort to cheat herself into pure enthusiasm. The matter was not quite so simple as she tried to believe. Nevertheless, I was exceedingly pleased, and I kissed her in genuine sympathy. The more I thought of it the better I liked the marriage. It relieved me personally of a burdensome sense of ineffectual care, and it filled out solidly a kind of defenceless breach which had always existed on the wordly face of Mrs Garnyer's position. Moreover, it promised to be full of advantages for Eustace. It was a pity indeed that Eustace had but a slender relish for things that were good for him. I venture to hope, however, that his worship of his father's memory had been, at bottom, the expression of a need for some higher authority and of a capacity to be respectful when there was something really to respect. Yet I took the liberty of suggesting to Mrs Garnyer that she perhaps counted too implicitly on her son's concurrence; that he was always in opposition; that a margin should be left for his possible perversity. Of course I was called a suspicious wretch for my pains.

"For what do you take him?" she cried. "I shall just put them face to face. Eustace has delicacy. A word to the wise, says the proverb. I know what I am about."

She knew it, I think, hardly so well as she declared. I had deemed it my duty to make a modest little speech of congratulation to the bridegroom elect. He blushed—somewhat to my surprise—but he answered me with a few proper, grateful words. He was much preoccupied; Mrs Garnyer was of a dozen different minds about her wedding-day. I had taken for granted that they would wait for Eustace's return; but I was somewhat startled on learning that Mr Cope disapproved of further delay. They had waited twenty years! Mrs Garnyer told me that she had not announced the news to Eustace—she wished it to be a "surprise." She seemed, however, not altogether to believe in her surprise. Poor lady! she had made herself a restless couch. One evening, coming into the library, I found Mr Cope pleading his cause. For the first time I saw him excited, and he turned appealingly to me. "You have great influence with this lady," he said. "Argue my case. Are we people to care for Mrs Grundy? Has she been so very civil to us? We don't marry to please her; I don't see why she should arrange the wedding. Mrs Garnyer has no trousseau to buy, no cards to send. Indeed, I think any more airs and graces are rather ridiculous. They don't belong to our years. There's little Master Grundy, I know," he went on, smiling—"a highly honourable youth! But I will take charge of him. I should like immensely, of course, to have him at the wedding; but one of these days I shall make up for the breach of ceremony by punctually attending his own." It was only an hour before this, as it happened, that I had received Eustace's answer to my letter. It was brief and hasty, but he had found time to insert some such words as this: "I don't at all thank you for your news of Mr Cope. I knew that my mother only wanted a chance to forget me and console herself, as they say in France. Demonstrative mothers always do. I am like Hamlet—I don't approve of mothers consoling themselves. Mr Cope may be an excellent fellow—I have no doubt he is; but I do hope he will have finished his visit by the time I get back. The house isn't large enough for both of us. You will find me a bigger man than when I left home, I give you warning. I have got a bristling black moustache, and I am proportionately fiercer." I said nothing about this letter, and a week later my companions were married. The time will always be memorable to me, apart from this matter of my story, for the intense and overwhelming heat which then prevailed. It had lasted several days when the nuptials took place; it bade fair to last all summer. The ceremony was performed by the little old Episcopal clergyman whose ministrations Mrs Garnyer had regularly attended, and who had always given her a vague parochial countenance. His sister, a mature spinster who wore her hair cut short and called herself "strong-minded," and, thus qualified, had made overtures to Mrs Garnyer—this lady and myself were the only witnesses. The marriage had nothing of a festive air; it seemed a solemn sacrifice to the unknown god. Mrs Garnyer was very much oppressed by the heat; in the vestibule, on leaving the church, she fainted. They had arranged to go for a week to the seaside, to a place they had known of old. When she had revived we placed her in the carriage, and they immediately started. I, of course, remained in charge of the empty house, greatly envying them their cooling breezes.

V

On the morning after the wedding, sitting alone in the darkened library, I heard a rapid tread in the hall. My first thought, of course, was of burglars—my second of Eustace. In a moment he came striding into the room. His step, his glance, his whole outline, foretold trouble. He was extraordinarily changed, and all for the better. He seemed taller, older, manlier. He was bronzed by travel and dressed with great splendour. The moustache he had mentioned, though but a slender thing as yet, gave him, to my eye, a formidable foreign look. He gave me no greeting.

"Where's my mother?" he cried.

My heart rose to my throat; his tone seemed to put us horribly in the wrong. "She's away—for a day," I said. "But you"—and I took his hand—"pray where have you dropped from?"

"From New York, from shipboard, from Southampton. Is this the way my mother receives me?"

"Why, she never dreamed you were coming."

"She got no letter? I wrote from New York."

"Your letter never came. She left town yesterday, for a week."

He looked at me hard. "How comes it you are not with her?"

"I am not needed. She has—she has——" But I faltered.

"Say it—say it!" he cried; and he stamped his foot. "She has a companion."

"Mr Cope went with her," I said, in a still small voice. I was ashamed of my trepidation, I was outraged by his imperious manner, but the thought of worse to come unnerved me.

"Mr Cope—ah!" he answered, with an indefinable accent. He looked about the room as if he wanted to pick out some offensive trace of Mr Cope's passage. Then flinging himself into a chair, "What infernal heat!" he went on. "What a horrible climate you have got here! Do bring me a glass of water."

I brought him his glass, and stood before him as he quickly drank it. "Don't think you are not welcome if I ask what has brought you home so suddenly," I ventured to say.

He gave me another hard look over the top of his glass. "A suspicion. It's none too soon. Tell me what is going on between my mother and Mr Cope."

"Eustace," I said, "before I answer you, let me remind you of the respect which, under all circumstances, you owe your mother."

He sprang from his chair. "Respect! I am right then—they mean to marry! Speak!" And as I hesitated, "You needn't speak," he cried, "I see it in your face. Thank God, I'm here!"

His violence roused me. "If you have a will to enforce in the matter, you are indeed none too soon. You are too late —your mother is married." I spoke passionately, but in a moment I repented of my words.

"*Married!*" the poor boy shouted, "MARRIED, you say!" He turned deadly pale, and stood staring at me with his mouth wide open. Then, trembling in all his limbs, he dropped into a chair. For some moments he was silent, gazing at me with a kind of fierce stupefaction, overwhelmed by the treachery of fate. "Married," he went on. "When, where, how? Without me—without notice—without shame! And you stood and watched it, as you stand and tell me now! I called you friend!" he cried, with the bitterest reproach. "But if my mother betrays me, what can I expect of *you?* Married!" he repeated. "Is the devil in it? I'll unmarry her! When—when—when?" And he seized me by the arm.

"Yesterday, Eustace. I entreat you to be calm."

"Calm? Is it a case for calmness? *She* was calm enough—that she couldn't wait for her son?" He flung aside the hand I had laid upon his to soothe him, and began a furious march about the room. "What has come to her? Is she mad? Has she lost her head, her heart, her memory—all that made her mine? You are joking—come, it's a horrible dream!" And he stopped before me, glaring through fiery tears. "Did she hope to keep it a secret? Did she hope to hide away her husband in a cupboard? Her husband! And I—I—I—what has she done with me? Where am I in this devil's game? Standing here crying like a schoolboy for a cut finger—for the bitterest of disappointments! She has blighted my life—she has blasted my rights. She has insulted me—dishonoured me. Am I a man to treat in that fashion? Am I a man to be made light of? Brought up as a flower and trampled as a weed! Wrapped in cotton and then exposed—you needn't speak" —I had tried, for pity, to remonstrate—"you can say nothing that is not idiotic. There's nothing to be said but this—that I'm *insulted*. Do you understand?" He uttered the word with a concentrated rancour of vanity. "I guessed it from the first. I knew it was coming. Mr Cope—Mr Cope—always Mr Cope! It poisoned my journey—it poisoned my pleasure—it poisoned Italy. You don't know what that means. But what matter, so long as it has poisoned my home? I held my tongue—I swallowed my rage; I was patient, I was gentle, I forbore. And for this! I could have damned him with a word! At the seaside, hey? Enjoying the breezes—splashing in the surf—picking up shells. It's idyllic, it's ideal: great heavens, it's fabulous, it's monstrous! It's well she's not here. I don't answer for myself. Yes, you goose, stare, stare—wring your hands! You see an angry man, an outraged man, but a man, mind you! He means to act as one."

This sweeping torrent of unreason I had vainly endeavoured to arrest. He pushed me aside, strode out of the room, and went bounding upstairs to his own chamber, where I heard him close the door with a terrible bang and turn the key. My hope was that his passion would expend itself in this first explosion; I was glad to bear the brunt of it. But I regarded it as my duty to communicate with his mother. I wrote her a hurried line: "Eustace is back—very ill. Come home." This I entrusted to the coachman, with injunctions to carry it in person to the place where she was staying. I believed that if she should start as soon as she received it she might reach home late at night. Those were the days of private conveyances. Meanwhile I did my best to pacify the poor young man. There was something almost insane in his resentment; he seemed absolutely rabid. This was the sweet compliance, the fond assent, on which his mother had counted; this was the "surprise"! I went repeatedly to the door of his room with soft speeches and urgent prayers and offers of luncheon, of wine, of vague womanly comfort. But there came no answer but shouts and imprecations, and finally a sullen silence. Late in the day I heard him, from the window, order the gardener to saddle his horse; and in a short time he came stamping down stairs, booted and spurred, pale, dishevelled, with bloodshot eyes. "Where are you going," I said, "in this awful heat?"

"To ride—ride—ride myself cool!" he cried. "There's nothing so hot as my rage!" And in a moment he was in the saddle and bounding out of the gate. I went up to his room. Its wild disorder told me how he had raved up and down. A dozen things were strewn, broken, on the floor; old letters were lying crumpled and torn; I was sickened by the sight of a pearl necklace, snatched from his gaping valise, and evidently purchased as a present to his mother, ground into fragments on the carpet, as if by his boot-heels. His father's relics were standing in a row, untouched, on the mantel-shelf, save for a couple of pistols, mounted with his intials, in silver, which were tossed upon the table. I made a courage-ous effort to thrust them into a drawer and turn the key, but to my eternal regret I was afraid to touch them. Evening descended and wore away; but neither Eustace nor his mother returned. I sat gloomily enough on the verandah, listening for wheels or hoofs. Towards midnight a carriage rattled over the gravel; my friend descended, with her husband, at the door. She fluttered into my arms with a kind of shrinking eagerness. "Where is he—how is he?" she cried.

I was spared the pain of answering, for at the same moment I heard Eustace's horse clatter into the stable-yard. He had rapidly dismounted, and he passed into the house by one of the lateral windows, which opened from the piazza into the drawing-room. There the lamps were lighted; I led in my companions. Eustace had crossed the threshold of the win-dow; the lamplight fell upon him, relieving him against the darkness. His mother, with a shriek, flung herself toward him, but in an instant, with a deeper cry, she stopped short, pressing her hand to her heart. He had raised his hand, and, with a gesture which had all the spiritual force of a blow, he had cast her off. "Ah, my son, my son!" she cried, with a piteous moan, and looking round at us in wild bewilderment.

"I am not your son!" said the boy, in a voice half stifled with passion "I give you up! You are not my mother!

Don't touch me! You have cheated me—betrayed me—dishonoured me!" In this mad peal of imprecations it was still the note of vanity which rang clearest.

I looked at Mr Cope—he was deadly pale. He had seen the lad's gesture; he was unable to hear his words. He sat down in the nearest chair and eyed him wonderingly. I hurried to his poor wife's relief; she seemed smitten with a sudden tremor, a deadly chill. She clasped her hands, but she could barely find her voice. "Eustace—my boy—my darling —my own—do you know what you say? Listen, listen, Eustace. It's all for you—that you should love me more. I have done my best. I seem to have been hasty, but hasty to do for you—to do for you——" Her strength deserted her; she burst into tears. "He curses me—he denies me!" she cried. "He has killed me!"

"Cry, cry!" Eustace retorted; "cry as I have been crying! But don't be falser than you have been. That you couldn't even wait! And you prate of my happiness! Is my happiness in a ruined home—in a disputed heart—in a bullying stepfather! You have chosen him big and strong! Cry your eyes out—you are no mother of mine."

"He's killing me—he's killing me," groaned his mother. "Oh heavens, if I dared to speak I should kill *him!*" She turned to her husband. "Go to him—go to him?" she cried. He's ill, he's mad—he doesn't know what he says. Take his hand in yours—look at him, soothe him, cure him. It's the hot weather," she rambled on. "Let him feel your touch! Eustace, Eustace, be cured!"

Poor Mr Cope had risen to his feet, passing his handkerchief over his forehead, on which the perspiration stood in great drops. He went slowly towards the young man, bending his eyes on him half in entreaty, half in command. Before him he stopped and frankly held out his hand. Eustace glared at him defiantly, from head to foot, him and his proffered friendship, pressed upon him as it was in the kindest, wisest,

firmest way. Then pushing his hand savagely down, "Hypo-
crite!" he roared close to his face—"can you hear that?"
and marched straight out of the room. Mr Cope shook his
head with a world of tragic meaning, and for an instant
exchanged with his wife a long look, brimming with anguish.
She fell upon his neck with passionate sobs. But soon recovering herself, "Go to him," she repeated, "follow him; say
everything, spare nothing. No matter for me; I have got
my blow."

VI

I HELPED her up to her room; her strength had completely
left her; she only half undressed and let me lay her on her bed.
She was in a state of the intensest excitement; every nerve
in her body was thrilling and quivering. She kept murmuring
to herself, with a kind of heartbreaking incoherency. "Nothing
can hurt me now; I needn't be spared. Nothing can disgrace
me—or grace me. I have got my blow. It's my fault—all,
all, all! I heaped up folly on folly and weakness on weakness.
My heart's broken; it will never be of any use again. You have
been right, my dear—I perverted him, I taught him to
strike. Oh what a blow! He's hard—he's hard. He's cruel.
He has no heart. He is blind with vanity and egotism. But it
matters little now; I shan't live to suffer. I have suffered
enough. I am dying, my friend, I am dying."

In this broken strain the poor lady poured out the bitterness of her grief. I used every art to soothe and console her,
but I felt that the tenderest spot in her gentle nature had
received an irreparable bruise. "I don't want to live," she
murmured. "I have seen something too dreadful. It could
never be patched up; we should never be the same. He has
shown his character—isn't it his character? It's bad!"

In spite of my efforts to restore her to calmness she became, not more excited—for her strength seemed to be ebbing and her voice was low—but more painfully and incoherently talkative. Nevertheless, from her distressing murmur I gathered the glimmer of a meaning. She seemed to wish to make a kind of supreme confession. I sat on the edge of her bed, with her hand in mine. From time to time, above her loud whispers, I heard the sound of the two gentlemen's voices. Adjoining her chamber was a large dressing-room; beyond this was Eustace's apartment. The three rooms opened upon a long, uncovered balcony.

Mr Cope had followed the young man to his own room, and was addressing him in a low, steady voice. Eustace apparently was silent; but there was something sullen and portentious to my ear in this unnatural absence of response.

"What have you thought of me, my friend, all these years?" his mother asked. "Have I seemed to you like other women? I haven't been like others. I have tried to be so—and you see—you see! Let me tell you. It don't matter whether you despise me—I shan't know it. These are my last words; let them be frank."

They were not, however, so frank as she intended. She seemed to lose herself in a dim wilderness of memories; her faculty wandered, faltered, stumbled. Not from her words—they were ambiguous—but from her silence and from the rebound of my own quickened sympathy, as it were, I guessed the truth. It blossomed into being, vivid and distinct; it flashed a long, illuminating glow upon the past—a lurid light upon the present. Strange it seemed now that my suspicions had been so late to bear fruit; but our imagination is always too timid. Now all things were clear! Heaven knows that in this unpitying light I felt no contempt for the poor woman who lay before me, panting with a supreme disappointment.

Poor victims of destiny—if I could only bring them to terms! For the moment, however, the unhappy mother and wife demanded all my attention. I left her and passed along the balcony, intending to make her husband come to her. The light in Eustace's room showed me the young man and his companion. They sat facing each other, silent for the moment. Mr Cope's two hands were on his knees, his eyes were fixed on the carpet, his teeth were set—as if, baffled, irate, desperate, he was preparing to play his last card. Eustace was looking at him hard, with a terribly vicious expression. It made me sick. I was on the point of rushing in and forcing them somehow apart, when suddenly Mr Cope raised his eyes and exchanged with the boy a look with which he seemed to read his very soul. He waved his hand in the air as if to say that he had been patient enough.

"If you were to see yourself as I see you," he said, "you would be immensely surprised; you would know your absurd appearance. Young as you are, you are rotten with arrogance and pride. What would you say if I were to tell you that, least of men, you have reason to be proud? Your stable-boy there has more. There's a leak in your vanity, there's a blot on your scutcheon! You force me to take strong measures. Let me tell you, in the teeth of your monstrous egotism, what you are. You're a——"

I knew what was coming, but I hadn't the heart to hear it. The word, ringing out, overtook my ear as I hurried back to Mrs Cope. It was followed by a loud, incoherent cry, the sound, prolonged for some moments, of a scuffle, and then the report of a pistol. This was lost in the noise of crashing glass. Mrs Cope rose erect in bed and shrieked aloud, "He has killed him—and me!" I caught her in my arms; she drew her last breath. I laid her gently on the bed and made my trembling way, by the balcony, to Eustace's room. The first glance reassured me. Neither of the men were visibly injured; the pistol lay smoking on the floor. Eustace had sunk into a chair, with his head buried in his hands. I saw his face burning red through his fingers.

"It's not murder," Mr Cope said to me as I crossed the threshold, "but it has just missed being suicide. It has been fatal only to the looking-glass." The mirror was shivered.

"It *is* murder," I answered, seizing Eustace by the arm and forcing him to rise. "You have killed your mother. This is your father!"

My friend paused and looked at me with a triumphant air, as if she was very proud of her effect. Of course I had foreseen it half-an-hour ago. "What a dismal tale!" I said. "But it's interesting. Of course Mrs Cope recovered."

She was silent an instant. "You are like me," she answered; "your imagination is timid."

"I confess," I rejoined, "I am rather at a loss how to dispose of our friend Eustace. I don't see how the two could very well shake hands—nor yet how they couldn't."

"They did once—and but once. They were for years, each in his way, lonely men. They were never reconciled. The trench had been dug too deep. Even the poor lady buried there didn't avail to fill it up. Yet the son was forgiven—the father never!"

GUEST'S CONFESSION

I

"Arrive half past eight. Sick. Meet me."

The telegrammatic brevity of my step-brother's missive gave that melancholy turn to my thoughts which was the usual result of his communications. He was to have come on the Friday; what had made him start off on Wednesday? The terms on which we stood were a perpetual source of irritation. We were utterly unlike in temper and taste and opinions, and yet, having a number of common interests, we were obliged, after a fashion, to compromise with each other's idiosyncrasies. In fact, the concessions were all on my side. He was altogether too much my superior in all that makes the man who counts in the world for me not to feel it, and it cost me less to let him take his way than to make a stand, for my dignity. What I did through indolence and in some degree, I confess, through pusillanimity, I had a fancy to make it appear (by dint of much whistling, as it were, and easy thrusting of my hands into my pockets) that I did through a sort of generous condescension. Edgar cared little enough upon what recipe I compounded a salve for my vanity, so long as he held his own course; and I am afraid I played the slumbering giant to altogether empty benches. There had been, indeed, a vague tacit understanding that he was to treat me, in form, as a man with a mind of his own, and there was occasionally something most incisively sarcastic in his observance of the treaty. What made matters the worse for me, and the better for him, was an absurd physical disparity; for Musgrave was like nothing so much as Falstaff's description of Shallow,—a man made after supper of a cheese-paring. He was a miserable invalid, and was perpetually concerned with his stomach, his lungs, and his liver, and as he was both doctor and patient in one, they kept him very busy. His head was grotesquely large for his diminutive figure, his eye fixed and salient, and his complexion liable to flush with an air of indignation and suspicion. He practised a most resolute little strut on a most attenuated pair of little legs. For myself, I was tall, happily; for I was broad enough, if I had been shorter, to have perhaps incurred that invidious monosyllabic epithet which haunted Lord Byron. As compared with Edgar, I was at least fairly good-looking, a stoutish, blondish, indolent, amiable, rather gorgeous young fellow might have served as my personal formula. My patrimony, being double that of my step-brother (for we were related by my mother), was largely lavished on the adornment of this fine person. I dressed in fact, as I recollect, with a sort of barbaric splendor, and I may very well have passed for one of the social pillars of a small watering-place.

L—— was in those days just struggling into fame, and but that it savored overmuch of the fresh paint lately lavished upon the various wooden barracks in which visitors were to be accommodated, it yielded a pleasant mixture of rurality and society. The vile taste and the sovereign virtue of the spring were fairly established, and Edgar was not the man to forego the chance of trying the waters and abusing them. Having heard that the hotel was crowded, he wished to secure a room at least a week beforehand; the upshot of which was, that I came down on the 19th of July with the mission to retain and occupy his apartment till the 26th. I passed, with people in general, and with Edgar in particular, for so very idle a person that it seemed almost a duty to saddle me with some wholesome errand. Edgar had, first and always, his health to attend to, and then that neat little property and those everlasting accounts, which he was never weary of contemplating, verifying, and overhauling. I had made up my mind to make over his room to him, remain a day or two for civility's sake and then leave him to his cups. Meanwhile, on the 24th, it occurred to me that I ought really to see something of the place. The weather had been too hot for going about, and, as yet, I had hardly left the piazza of the hotel. Towards afternoon the clouds gathered, the sun was obscured, and it seemed possible even for a large, lazy man to take a walk. I went along beside the river, under the trees, rejoicing much in the midsummer prettiness of all the land and in the sultry afternoon stillness. I was discomposed and irritated, and all for no better reason than that Edgar was coming. What was Edgar that his comings and goings should affect me? Was I, after all, so excessively his younger brother? I would turn over a new leaf? I almost wished things would come to a crisis between us, and that in the glow of exasperation I might say or do something unpardonable. But there was small chance of my quarrelling with Edgar for vanity's sake. Somehow, I didn't believe in my own egotism, but I had an indefeasible respect for his. I was fatally good-natured, and I should continue to do his desire until I began to do that of some one else. If I might only fall in love and exchange my master for a mistress, for some charming goddess of unreason who would declare that Mr Musgrave was simply intolerable and that was an end of it!

So, meditating vaguely, I arrived at the little Episcopal chapel, which stands on the margin of the village where the latter begins to melt away into the large river-side landscape. The door was slightly ajar; there came through it into the hot outer stillness the low sound of an organ,—the rehearsal, evidently, of the organist or of some gentle amateur. I was warm with walking, and this glimpse of the cool musical dimness within prompted me to enter and rest and listen. The body of the church was empty; but a feeble glow of color was diffused through the little yellow and crimson windows upon the pews and the cushioned pulpit. The organ was erected in a small gallery facing the chancel, into which the ascent was by a short stairway directly from the church. The sound of my tread was apparently covered by the music, for the player continued without heeding me, hidden as she was behind a little blue silk curtain on the edge of the gallery. Yes, that gentle, tentative, unprofessional touch came from a feminine hand. Uncertain as it was, however, it wrought upon my musical sensibilities with a sort of provoking force. The air was familiar, and, before I knew it, I had begun to furnish the vocal accompaniment,—first gently, then boldly. Standing with my face to the organ, I awaited the effect of my venture. The only perceptible result was that, for a moment, the music faltered, and the curtains were stirred. I saw nothing, but I had been seen, and, reassured apparently by my aspect, the organist resumed the chant. Slightly mystified, I felt urged to sing my best, the more so that, as I continued, the player seemed to borrow confidence and emulation from my voice. The notes rolled out bravely, and the little vault resounded. Suddenly there seemed to come to the musician, in the ardor of success, a full accession of vigor and skill. The last chords were struck with a kind of triumphant intensity, and their cadence was marked by a clear soprano voice. Just at the close, however, voice and music were swallowed up in the roll of a huge thunder-clap. At the same instant, the storm-drops began to strike the chapel-windows, and we were sheeted in a summer rain. The rain was a bore; but, at least, I should have a look at the organist, concerning whom my curiosity had suddenly grown great. The thunder-claps followed each other with such violence that it was vain to continue to play. I waited in the confident belief that that charming voice—half a dozen notes had betrayed it—denoted a charming woman. After the lapse of some moments, which seemed to indicate a graceful and appealing hesitancy, a female figure appeared at the top of the little stairway and began to descend. I walked slowly down the aisle. The stormy darkness had rapidly increased, and at this moment, with a huge burst of thunder, following a blinding flash, a momentary midnight fell upon our refuge. When things had become visible again, I beheld the fair musician at the foot of the steps, gazing at me with all the frankness of agitation. The little chapel was rattling to its foundations.

"Do you think there is any danger?" asked my companion.

I made haste to assure her there was none. "The chapel has nothing in the nature of a spire, and even if it had, the fact of our being in a holy place ought to insure us against injury."

She looked at me wonderingly, as if to see whether I was in jest. To satisfy her, I smiled as graciously as I might. Whereupon, gathering confidence, "I think we have each of us," she said, "so little right to be here that we can hardly claim the benefit of sanctuary."

"Are you too an interloper?" I asked.

She hesitated a moment. "I'm not an Episcopalian," she replied; "I'm a good Utinarian."

"Well, I'm a poor Episcopalian. It's six of one and half a dozen of the other." There came another long, many-sheeted flash and an immediate wild reverberation. My companion, as she stood before me, was vividly illumined from head to foot. It was as if some fierce natural power had designed to interpose her image on my soul forever, in this merciless electric glare. As I saw her then, I have never ceased to see her since. I have called her fair, but the word needs explanation. Singularly pleasing as she was, it was with a charm that was all her own, not the charm of beauty, but of a certain intense expressiveness, which seems to have given beauty the go-by in the very interest of grace. Slender, meagre, without redundancy of outline or brilliancy of color, she was a person you might never have noticed, but would certainly never forget. What there was was so charming, what there might be so interesting! There was none of the idleness of conscious beauty in her clear gray eyes; they seemed charged with the impatience of a restless mind. Her glance and smile, her step and gesture, were as light and distinct as a whispered secret. She was nervous, curious, zealous, slightly imperious, and delicately elegant withal; without which, possibly, she might have seemed a trifle too positive. There is a certain sweet unreason in a picturesque toilet. She was dressed in a modish adjustment of muslins and lace, which denoted the woman who may have fancied that even less beauty might yet please. While I drew my conclusions,—they were eminently flattering, —my companion was buttoning her gloves and looking anxiously at the dripping windows. Wishing, as far as I might, to beguile her impatience, I proceeded to apologize for the liberty I had taken in singing to her music. "My best excuse," I said, "is your admirable playing, and my own most sensitive ear!"

"You might have frightened me away," she answered. "But you sang too well for that, better than I played. In fact, I was afraid to stop, I thought you might be one of the—the hierarchy."

"A bishop!"

"A bishop,—a dean,—a deacon,—or something of that sort."

"The sexton, perhaps."

"Before the sexton I should have succumbed. I take it his business would have been to eject me as a meddlesome heretic. I came in for no better reason than that the church door was ajar."

"As a church door ought always to be."

She looked at me a moment. "No; see what comes of it."

"No great harm, it seems to me."

"O, that's very well for us! But a church shouldn't be made a place of convenience."

I wished, in the interest of our growing intimacy, to make

a point. "If it is not a place of convenience," I ventured to propound, deprecating offence with a smile, "what is it?"

It was an observation I afterwards made, that in cases when many women drop their eyes and look prettily silly or prudishly alarmed, this young lady's lucid glance would become more unaffectedly direct and searching. "Indeed," she answered, "you *are* but an indifferent Episcopalian! I came in because the door was open, because I was warm with my walk, and because, I confess, I have an especial fondness for going into churches on week-days. One does it in Europe, you know; and it reminds me of Europe."

I cast a glance over the naked tabernacle, with the counterfeit graining scarcely dry on its beams and planks, and a strong aroma of turpentine and putty representing the odor of sanctity. She followed my glance; our eyes met, and we laughed. From this moment we talked with a freedom tempered less by the sanctity of the spot than by a certain luxury of deference with which I felt prompted to anticipate possible mistrust. The rain continued to descend with such steady good-will that it seemed needful to accept our situation frankly and conjure away the spirit of awkwardness. We spoke of L——, or the people there, of the hot weather, of music. She had as yet seen little of the place, having been confined to her apartments by domestic reasons. I wondered what her domestic reasons were. She had come forth at last to call upon a friend at one of the boarding-houses which adorned this suburb of the village. Her friend being out, but likely soon to return, she had sought entertainment in a stroll along the road, and so had wandered into the chapel. Our interview lasted half an hour. As it drew to a close, I fancied there had grown up between us some delicate bond, begotten of our mutual urbanity. I might have been indiscreet; as it was, I took my pleasure in tracing the gradual evanescence of my companion's sense of peril. As the moments elapsed, she sat down on the bench with an air of perfect equanimity, and looked patiently at the trickling windows. The still small voice of some familiar spirit of the Lord, haunting the dedicated vault, seemed to have audibly blessed our meeting. At last the rain abated and suddenly stopped, and through a great rift in the clouds there leaped a giant sunbeam and smote the trickling windows. Through little gaudy lozenges the chapel was flooded with prismatic light. "The storm is over," said my companion. She spoke without rising, as if she had been cheated of the sense of haste. Was it calculated civility, or was it momentary self-oblivion? Whatever it was, it lasted but a moment. We were on our feet and moving toward the door. As we stood in the porch, honest gallantry demanded its rights.

"I never knew before," I said, "the possible blessings of a summer rain."

She proceeded a few steps before she answered. Then glancing at the shining sky, already blue and free, "In ten minutes," she said, "there will be no trace of it!"

"Does that mean," I frankly demanded, "that we are not to meet again as friends?"

"Are we to meet again at all?"

"I count upon it."

"Certainly, then, not as enemies!" As she walked away, I imprecated those restrictions of modern civilization which forbade me to stand and gaze at her.

Who was she? What was she?—questions the more intense as, in the absence of any further evidence than my rapid personal impression, they were so provokingly vain. They occupied me, however, during the couple of hours which were to elapse before my step-brother's arrival. When his train became due, I went through the form, as usual, of feeling desperately like treating myself to the luxury of neglecting his summons and leaving him to shift for himself; as if I had not the most distinct prevision of the inevitable event,—of my being at the station half an hour too early, of my calling his hack and making his bargain and taking charge of his precious little handbag, full of medicine-bottles, and his ridiculous bundle of umbrellas and canes. Somehow, this evening, I felt unwontedly loath and indocile; but I contented myself with this bold flight of the imagination.

It is hard to describe fairly my poor step-brother's peculiar turn of mind, to give an adequate impression of his want of social charm, to put it mildly, without accusing him of wilful malevolence. He was simply the most consistent and incorruptible of egotists. He was perpetually affirming and defining and insuring himself, insisting upon a personal right or righting a personal wrong. And above all, he was a man of conscience. He asked no odds, and he gave none. He made honesty something unlovely, but he was rigidly honest. He demanded simply his dues, and he collected them to the last farthing. These things gave him a portentous solemnity. He smiled perhaps once a month, and made a joke once in six. There are jokes of his making which, to this day, give me a shiver when I think of them. But I soon perceived, as he descended from the train, that there would be no joke that evening. Something had happened. His face was hard and sombre, and his eye bright and fierce. "A carriage," he said, giving me his hand stiffly. And when we were seated and driving away, "First of all," he demanded, "are there any mosquitoes? A single mosquito would finish me. And is my room habitable, on the shady side, away from the stairs, with a view, with a hair-mattress?" I assured him that mosquitoes were unknown, and that his room was the best, and his mattress the softest in the house. Was he tired? how had he been?

"Don't ask me. I'm in an extremely critical state. Tired? Tired is a word for well people! When I'm tired I shall go to bed and die. Thank God, so long as I have any work to do, I can hold up my head! I haven't slept in a week. It's singular, but I'm never so well disposed for my duties as when I haven't

slept! But be so good, for the present, as to ask me no questions. I shall immediately take a bath and drink some arrow-
root; I have brought a package in my bag, I suppose I can
get them to make it. I'll speak about it at the office. No, I
think on the whole, I'll make it in my room; I have a little
machine for boiling water. I think I shall drink half a glass
of the spring to-night, just to make a beginning."

All this was said with as profound a gravity as if he were
dictating his will. But I saw that he was at a sort of white-
heat exasperation, and I knew that in time I should learn
where the shoe pinched. Meanwhile, I attempted to say something cheerful and frivolous, and offered some information
as to who was at the hotel and who was expected; "No one
you know or care about, I think."

"Very likely not. I'm in no mood for gossip."

"You seem nervous," I ventured to say.

"Nervous? Call it frantic! I'm not blessed with your
apathetic temperament, nor with your elegant indifference
to money-matters. Do you know what's the matter with me?
I've lost twenty thousand dollars."

I, of course, demanded particulars; but, for the present, I
had to content myself with the naked fact. "It's a mighty
serious matter," said Edgar. "I can't talk of it further till I
have bathed and changed my linen. The thermometer has
been at ninety-one in my rooms in town. I've had this pretty
piece of news to keep me cool."

I left him to his bath, his toilet, and his arrow-root and
strolled about pondering the mystery of his disaster. Truly,
if Edgar had lost money, shrewdness was out of tune. Destiny
must have got up early to outwit my step-brother. And yet
his misfortune gave him a sort of unwonted grace, and I
believe I wondered for five minutes whether there was a
chance of his being relaxed and softened by it. I had, indeed,
a momentary vision of lending him money, and taking a
handsome revenge as a good-natured creditor. But Edgar

would never borrow. He would either recover his money or grimly do without it. On going back to his room I found him dressed and refreshed, screwing a little portable kettle upon his gas-burner.

"You can never get them to bring you water that really boils," he said. "They don't know what it means. You're altogether wrong about the mosquitoes; I'm sure I heard one, and by the sound, he's a monster. But I have a net folded up in my trunk, and a hook and ring which I mean to drive into the ceiling."

"I'll put up your net. Meanwhile, tell me about your twenty thousand dollars."

He was silent awhile, but at last he spoke in a voice forcibly attuned to composure. "You're immensely tickled, I suppose, to find me losing money! That comes of worrying too much and handling my funds too often. Yes, I *have* worried too much." He paused, and then, suddenly, he broke out into a kind of fury. "I hate waste, I hate shiftlessness, I hate nasty mismanagement! I hate to see money bring in less than it may. My imagination loves a good investment. I respect my property, I respect other people's. But your own honesty is all you'll find in this world, and it will go no farther than you're there to carry it. You've always thought me hard and suspicious and grasping. No, you never said so; should I have cared if you had? With your means, it's all very well to be a fine gentleman, to skip the items and glance at the total. But, being poor and sick, I have to be close. I wasn't close enough. What do you think of my having been cheated?— cheated under my very nose? I hope I'm genteel enough now!"

"I should like to see the man!" I cried.

"You shall! see him. All the world shall see him. I've been looking into the matter. It has been beautifully done. If I were to be a rascal, I should like to be just such a one."

"Who is your rascal?"

"His name is John Guest."

I had heard the name, but had never seen the man.

"No, you don't know him," Edgar went on. "No one knows him but I. But I know him well. He had things in his hands for a week, while I was debating a transfer of my New Jersey property. In a week this is how he mixed matters."

"Perhaps, if you had given him time," I suggested, "he meant to get them straight again."

"O, I shall give him time. I mean he shall get 'em straight, or I shall twist him so crooked his best friend won't know him."

"Did you never suspect his honesty?"

"Do you suspect mine?"

"But you have legal redress?"

"It's no thanks to him. He had fixed things to a charm, he had done his best to cut me off and cover his escape. But I've got him, and he shall disgorge!"

I hardly know why it was; but the implacable firmness of my brother's position produced in my mind a sort of fantastic reaction in favor of Mr John Guest. I felt a sudden gush of the most inconsequent pity. "Poor man!" I exclaimed. But to repair my weakness, I plunged into a series of sympathetic questions and listened attentively to Edgar's statement of his wrongs. As he set forth the case, I found myself taking a whimsical interest in Mr Guest's own side of it, wondering whether he suspected suspicion, whether he dreaded conviction, whether he had an easy conscience, and how he was getting through the hot weather. I asked Edgar how lately he had discovered his loss and whether he had since communicated with the criminal.

"Three days ago, three nights ago, rather; for I haven't slept a wink since. I have spoken of the matter to no one; for the present I need no one's help, I can help myself. I haven't seen the man more than three or four times; our dealings have generally been by letter. The last person you'd suspect. He's as great a dandy as you yourself, and in better taste, too. I was told ten days ago, at his office, that he had gone out of town. I suppose I'm paying for his champagne at Newport."

II

On my proposing, half an hour later, to relieve him of my society and allow him to prepare for rest, Edgar declared that our talk had put an end to sleep and that he must take a turn in the open air. On descending to the piazza, we found it in the deserted condition into which it usually lapsed about ten o'clock; either from a wholesome desire on the part of our fellow-lodgers to keep classic country hours, or from the soporific influences of excessive leisure. Here and there the warm darkness was relieved by the red tip of a cigar in suggestive proximity to a light corsage. I observed, as we strolled along, a lady of striking appearance, seated in the zone of light projected from a window, in conversation with a gentleman. "Really, I'm afraid you'll take cold," I heard her say as we passed. "Let me tie my handkerchief round your neck." And she gave it a playful twist. She was a pretty woman, of middle age, with great freshness of toilet and complexion, and a picturesque abundance of blond hair, upon which was conquettishly poised a fantastic little hat, decorated with an immense pink rose. Her companion was a seemingly affable man, with a bald head, a white waistcoat, and a rather florid air of distinction. When we passed them a second time, they had risen and the lady was preparing to enter the house. Her companion went with her to the door; she left him with a great deal of coquettish by-play, and he turned back to the piazza. At this moment his glance fell upon my step-brother. He started, I thought, and then, replacing his hat with an odd, nervous decision, came towards him with a smile. "Mr Musgrave!" he said.

Edgar stopped short, and for a moment seemed to lack words to reply. At last he uttered a deep, harsh note: "Mr Guest!"

In an instant I felt that I was in the presence of a "situation." Edgar's words had the sound of the "click" upon the limb of the entrapped fox. A scene was imminent; the actors were only awaiting their cues. Mr Guest made a half-offer of his hand, but, perceiving no response in Eagar's, he gracefully dipped it into his pocket. "You must have just come!" he murmured.

"A couple of hours ago."

Mr Guest glanced at me, as if to include me in the operation of his urbanity, and his glance stirred in my soul an impulse of that kindness which we feel for a man about to be executed. It's no more than human to wish to shake hands with him. "Introduce me, Edgar," I said.

"My step-brother," said Edgar, curtly. "This is Mr Guest, of whom we have been talking."

I put out my hand; he took it with cordiality. "Really," he declared, "this is a most unexpected—a—circumstance."

"Altogether so to me," said Edgar.

"You've come for the waters, I suppose," our friend went on. "I'm sorry your health continues—a—unsatisfactory."

Edgar, I perceived, was in a state of extreme nervous exacerbation, the result partly of mere surprise and partly of keen disappointment. His plans had been checked. He had determined to do thus and so, and he must now extemporize a policy. Well, as poor, pompous Mr Guest wished it, so he should have it! "I shall never be strong," said Edgar.

"Well, well," reponded Mr Guest, "a man of your parts may make a little strength serve a great purpose."

My step-brother was silent a moment, relishing secretly, I think, the beautiful pertinence of this observation. "I suppose I can defend my rights," he rejoined.

"Exactly! What more does a man need?" and he appealed to me with an insinuating smile. His smile was singularly frank and agreeable, and his glance full of a sort of conciliating gallantry. I noted in his face, however, by the gaslight, a haggard, jaded look which lent force to what he went on to say. "I have been feeling lately as if I hadn't even strength for that. The hot weather, an overdose of this abominable water, one thing and another, the inevitable premonitions of—a—mortality, have quite pulled me down. Since my arrival here, ten days ago, I have really been quite—a—the invalid. I've actually been in bed. A most unprecedented occurrence!"

"I hope you're better," I ventured to say.

"Yes, I think I'm myself again,—thanks to capital nursing. I think I'm myself again!" He repeated his words mechanically, with a sort of exaggerated gaiety, and began to wipe his forehead with his handkerchief. Edgar was watching him narrowly with an eye whose keenness it was impossible to veil; and I think Edgar's eye partly caused his disquiet. "The last thing I did, by the way, before my indisposition, was to write you ten lines, Mr Musgrave, on—a little matter of business."

"I got your letter," said Edgar, grimly.

Mr Guest was silent a moment. "And I hope my arrangements have met your approval?"

"We shall talk of that," said Edgar.

At this point, I confess, my interest in the situation had become painful. I felt sick. I'm not a man of ready-made resolution, as my story will abundantly prove. I am discountenanced and bullied by disagreeable things. Poor Mr Guest was so infallibly booked for exposure that I instinctively retreated. Taking advantage of his allusion to business, I turned away and walked to the other end of the piazza. This genial gentleman, then, was embodied fraud! this sayer of civil things was a doer of monstrously shabby ones! that irreproachable white waistcoat carried so sadly spotted a conscience! Whom had he involved in his dishonor? Had he a wife, children, friends? Who was that so prosperously pretty woman, with her flattering solicitude for his health? I stood for some time reflecting how guilt is not the vulgar bugaboo we fancy it,—that it has organs, senses, affections, passions, for all the world like those of innocence. Indeed, from my cursory observation of my friend, I had rarely seen innocence so handsomely featured. Where, then, was the line which severed rectitude from error? Was manhood a baser thing than I had fancied, or was sin a thing less base? As I mused thus, my disgust ebbed away, and the return of the wave brought an immense curiosity to see what it had come to betwixt guilt and justice. Had Edgar launched his thunder? I retraced my steps and rejoined my companions. Edgar's thunder was apparently still in the clouds; but there had been a premonitory flash of lightning. Guest stood before him, paler than before, staring defiantly, and stammering out some fierce denial. "I don't understand you," he said. "If you mean what you seem to mean, you mean rank insult."

"I mean the truth," said Edgar. "It's a pity the truth should be insulting."

Guest glared a moment, like a man intently taking thought for self-defence. But he was piteously unmasked. His genial smile had taken flight and left mere vulgar confusion. "This is between ourselves, sir," he cried, angrily turning to me.

"A thousand pardons," I said, and passed along. I began to be doubtful as to the issue of the quarrel. Edgar had right on his side, but, under the circumstances, he might not have force. Guest was altogether the stouter, bigger, weightier person. I turned and observed them from a distance. Edgar's thunderbolt had fallen and his victim stood stunned. He was leaning against the balustrade of the piazza, with his chin on his breast and his eyes sullenly fixed on his adversary, demoralized and convicted. His hat had dropped upon the floor. Edgar seemed to have made a proposal; with a passionate gesture he repeated it. Guest slowly stooped and picked up his hat, and Edgar led the way toward the house. A series of small sitting-rooms opened by long windows upon the piazza. These were for the most part lighted and empty. Edgar selected one of them, and, stopping before the window, beckoned to me to come to him. Guest, as I advanced, bestowed upon me a scowl of concentrated protest. I felt, for my own part, as if I were horribly indelicate. Between Edgar and him it was a question of morals, but between him and myself it was, of course, but one of manners. "Be so good as to walk in," said Edgar, turning to me with a smile of unprecedented sauvity. I might have resisted his dictation; I couldn't his petition.

"In God's name, what do you mean to do?" demanded Guest.

"My duty!" said Edgar. "Go in."

We passed into the room. The door of the corridor was open; Guest closed it with a passionate kick. Edgar shut the long window and dropped the curtain. In the same fury of mortification, Guest turned out one of the two burners of the chandelier. There was still light enough, however, for me to see him more distinctly than on the piazza. He was tallish and stoutish, and yet sleek and jaunty. His fine blue eye was a trifle weak, perhaps, and his handsome grizzled beard was something too foppishly trimmed; but, on the whole, he was a most comely man. He was dressed with the punctilious elegance of a man who loved luxury and appreciated his own good points. A little moss-rosebud figured in the lappet of his dark-blue coat. His whole person seemed redolent of what are called the "feelings of a gentleman." Confronted and contrasted with him under the lamp, my step-brother seemed wofully mean and grotesque; though for a conflict of forces that lay beneath the surface, he was visibly the better equipped of the two. He seemed to tremble and quiver with inexorable purpose. I felt that he would heed no admonitory word of mine, that I could not in the least hope to blunt the

edge of his resentment, and that I must on the instant decide
either to stand by him or leave him. But while I stood thus
ungraciously gazing at poor Guest, the instant passed.
Curiosity and a mingled sympathy with each—to say nothing
of a touch of that relish for a fight inherent in the truly
masculine bosom—sealed my lips and arrested my steps.
And yet my heart paid this graceful culprit the compliment
of beating very violently on his behalf.

"I wish you to repeat before my brother," said Edgar,
"the three succinct denials to which you have just treated
me."

Guest looked at the ceiling with a trembling lip. Then
dropping upon the sofa, he began to inspect his handsome
finger-nails mechanically, in the manner of one who hears in
some horrible hush of all nature the nearing footsteps of
doom. "Come, repeat them!" cried Edgar. "It's really delicious. You never wrote to Stevens that you had my assent
in writing to the sale of the bonds. You never showed Stevens
my telegram from Boston and, assured him that my 'Do as
you think best' was a permission to raise money on them.
If it's not forgery sir, it's next door to it, and a very flimsy
partition between."

Guest leaned back on the sofa, with his hands grasping
his knees. "You might have let things stand a week or so,"
he said, with unnatural mildness. "You might have had
common patience. Good God, there's a gentlemanly way of
doing things! A man doesn't begin to roar for a pinch. I
would have got things square again."

"O, it would have been a pity to spoil them! It was such
a pretty piece of knavery! Give the devil his due!"

"I would have rearranged matters," Guest went on. "It
was just a temporary convenience. I supposed I was dealing
with a man of common courtesy. But what are you to say to
a gentleman who says, 'Sir, I trust you,' and then looks
through the keyhole?"

"Upon my word, when I hear you scuttling through the window," cried Edgar, "I think it's time I should break down the door. For God's sake, don't nauseate me with any more lies! You know as well as you sit there, that you had neither chance nor means nor desire to redeem your fraud. You'd cut the bridge behind you! You thought you'd been knowing enough to eat your cake and have it, to lose your virtue and keep your reputation, to sink half my property through a trap-door and then stand whistling and looking t'other way while I scratched my head and wondered what the devil was in it! Sit down there and write me your note for twenty thousand dollars at twenty days."

Guest was silent a moment. "Propose something reasonable," he said, with the same tragic gentleness.

"I shall let the law reason about it."

Guest gave a little start and fixed his eyes on the ground. "The law wouldn't help you," he answered, without looking up.

"Indeed! do you think it would help *you?* Stoddard and Hale will help me. I spoke to them this morning."

Guest sprang to his feet. "Good heavens! I hope you mentioned no names."

"Only one!" said Edgar.

Guest wiped his forehead and actually tried to smile. "That was your own, of course! Well, sir, I hope they advised you to—a—temper justice with mercy."

"They are not parsons, Mr Guest; they are lawyers. They accept the case."

Guest dropped on the sofa, buried his face in his hands, and burst into tears. "O my soul!" he cried. His soul, poor man! was a rough term for name and fame and comfort and all that made his universe. It was a pitiful sight.

"Look here, Edgar," I said. "Don't press things too hard. "I'm not a parson either—"

"No, you've not that excuse for your sentimentality!"

Edgar broke out. "Here it is, of course! Here come folly and fear and ignorance maundering against the primary laws of life! Is rascality alone of all things in the world to be handled without gloves? Didn't he press me hard? He's danced his dance,—let him pay the piper! Am I a child, a woman, a fool, to stand and haggle with a swindler? Am I to go to the wall to make room for impudent fraud? Not while I have eyes to know black from white! I'm a decent man. I'm this or I'm nothing. For twenty years I've done my best for order and thrift and honesty. I've never yielded an inch to the detestable sharp practice that meets one nowadays at every turn. I've hated fraud as I hate all bad economy; I've no more patience with it than a bull with a red rag. Fraud is fraud; it's waste, it's wantonness, it's chaos; and I shall never give it the go-by. When I catch it, I shall hold it fast, and call all honest men to see how vile and drivelling a thing it is!"

Guest sat rigidly fixed, with his eyes on the carpet. "Do you expect to get your money?" he finally demanded.

"My money be hanged! I expect to let people know how they may be served if they intrust their affairs to you! A man's property, sir, is a man's person. It's as if you had given me a blow in the chest!"

Guest came towards him and took him by the button-hole. "Now see here," he said, with the same desperate calmness. "You call yourself a practical man. Don't go on like one of those d—d long-haired reformers. You're off the track. Don't attempt too much. Don't make me confoundedly uncomfortable out of pure fantasticality. Come, sir, you're a man of the world." And he patted him gently on the shoulder. "Give me a chance. I confess to not having been quite square. There! My very dear sir, let me get on my legs again."

"O, you confess!" cried Edgar. "That's a vast comfort. You'll never do it again! Not if I know it. But other people, eh? Suppose I had been a decent widow with six children, and not a penny but that! You'd confess again, I suppose. Would your confession butter their bread! Let your confession be public!"

"My confession *is* public!" and Guest, with averted eyes, jerked his head towards me.

"O, my step-brother! Why, he's the most private creature in the world. Cheat him and he'll thank you! David, I retain you as a witness that Mr Guest has confessed."

"Nothing will serve you then? You mean to prosecute?"

"I mean to prosecute."

The poor man's face flushed crimson, and the great sweat-drops trickled from his temples. "O you blundering brute!" he cried. "Do you know what you mean when you say that? Do we live in a civilized world?"

"Not altogether," said Edgar. "But I shall help it along."

"Have you lived among decent people? Have you known women whom it was an honor to please? Have you cared for name and fame and love? Have you had a dear daughter?"

"If I had a dear daughter," cried Edgar, flinching the least bit at this outbreak, "I trust my dear daughter would have kept me honest! Not the sin, then, but the detection unfits a man for ladies' society!—Did you kiss your daughter the day you juggled away my bonds?"

"If it will avail with you, I didn't. Consider her feelings. My fault has been that I have been too tender a father,—that I have loved the poor girl better than my own literal integrity. I became embarrassed because I hadn't the heart to tell her that she must spend less money. As if to the wisest, sweetest girl in the world a whisper wouldn't have sufficed! As if five minutes of her divine advice wouldn't have set me straight again! But the stress of my embarrassment was such—"

"Embarrassment!" Edgar broke in. "That may mean any-thing. In the case of an honest man it may be a motive for leniency; in that of a knave it's a ground for increased sus-picion."

Guest, I felt, was a good-natured sinner. Just as he lacked

rectitude of purpose, he lacked rigidity of temper, and he found in the mysteries of his own heart no clue to my step-brother's monstrous implacability. Looking at him from head to foot with a certain dignity,—a reminiscence of his former pomposity—"I do you the honor, sir," he said, "to believe you are insane."

"Stuff and nonsense! you believe nothing of the sort," cried Edgar.

I saw that Guest's opposition was acting upon him as a lively irritant. "Isn't it possible," I asked, "to adopt some compromise? You're not as forgiving a man under the circumstances as I should be."

"In these things," retorted Edgar, without ceremony, "a forgiving man is a fool."

"Well, take a fool's suggestion. You can perhaps get satisfaction without taking your victim into court.—Let Mr Guest write his confession."

Guest had not directly looked at me since we entered the room. At these words he slowly turned and gave me a sombre stare by which the brilliancy of my suggestion seemed somewhat obscured. But my interference was kindly meant, and his reception of it seemed rather ungrateful. At best, however, I could be but a thorn in his side. I had done nothing to earn my sport. Edgar hereupon flourished his hand as if to indicate the superfluity of my advice. "All in good time, if you please. If I'm insane, there's a method in my madness!" He paused, and his eyes glittered with an intensity which might indeed, for the moment, have seemed to be that of a disordered brain. I wondered what was coming. "Do me the favor to get down on your knees." Guest jerked himself up as if he had received a galvanic shock. "Yes, I know what I say,—on your knees. Did you never say your prayers? You can't get out of a tight place without being squeezed. I won't take less. I shan't feel like an honest man till I've seen you there at my feet."

There was in the contrast between the inflated self-complacency of Edgar's face as he made this speech, and the blank horror of the other's as he received it, something so poignantly grotesque that it acted upon my nerves like a mistimed joke, and I burst into irrepressible laughter. Guest walked away to the window with some muttered imprecation, pushed aside the curtain, and stood looking out. Then, with a sudden turn, he marched back and stood before my brother. He was drenched with perspiration. "A moment," said Edgar. "You're very hot. Take off your coat." Guest, to my amazement, took it off and fling it upon the floor. "Your shirt-sleeves will serve as a kind of sackcloth and ashes. Fold your hands, so. Now, beg my pardon."

It was a revolting sight,—this man of ripe maturity and massive comeliness on his two knees, his pale face bent upon his breast, his body trembling with the effort to keep his shameful balance; and above him Edgar, with his hands behind his back, solemn and ugly as a miniature idol, with his glittering eyes fixed in a sort of rapture on the opposite wall. I walked away to the window. There was a perfect stillness, broken only by Guest's hard breathing. I have no notion how long it lasted; when I turned back into the room he was still speechless and fixed, as if he were ashamed to rise. Edgar pointed to a blotting-book and inkstand which stood on a small table against the wall. "See if there is pen and paper!" I obeyed and made a clatter at the table, to cover our companion's retreat. When I had laid out a sheet of paper he was on his feet again. "Sit down and write," Edgar went on. Guest picked up his coat and busied himself mechanically with brushing off the particles of dust. Then he put it on and sat down at the table.

"I dictate," Edgar began. "I hereby, at the command of Edgar Musgrave, Esq., whom I have grossly wronged, declare myself a swindler." At these words, Guest laid down the pen and sank back in his chair, emitting long groans, like a man with a violent toothache. But he had taken that first step which costs, and after a moment's rest he started afresh. "I have on my bended knees, in the presence of Mr Musgrave, and his step-brother, expressed my contrition; in consideration of which Mr Musgrave forfeits his incontestable right to publish his injury in a court of justice. Furthermore, I solemnly declare myself his debtor in the sum of twenty thousand dollars; which, on his remission of the interest, and under pain of exposure in a contrary event, I pledge myself to repay at the earliest possible moment. I thank Mr Musgrave for his generosity."

Edgar spoke very slowly, and the scratching of Guest's pen kept pace with his words. "Now sign and date," he said; and the other, with a great heroic dash, consummated this amazing document. He then pushed it away, and rose and bestowed upon us a look which I long remembered. An outraged human soul was abroad in the world, with which henceforth I felt I should have somehow to reckon.

Edgar possessed himself of the paper and read it coolly to the end, without blushing. Happy Edgar! Guest watched him fold it and put it into his great morocco pocket-book. "I suppose," said Guest, "that this is the end of your generosity."

"I have nothing further to remark," said Edgar.

"Have *you*, by chance, anything to remark, Mr Stepbrother?" Guest demanded, turning to me, with a fierceness which showed how my presence galled him.

I had been, to my own sense, so abjectly passive during the whole scene that, to reinstate myself as a responsible creature, I attempted to utter an original sentiment. "I pity you," I said.

But I had not been happy in my choice. "Faugh, you great hulking brute!" Guest roared, for an answer.

The scene at this point might have passed into another phase, had it not been interrupted by the opening of the door from the corridor. "A lady!" announced a servant, flinging it back.

The lady revealed herself as the friend with whom Guest had been in conversation on the piazza. She was apparently, of his nature, not a person to mind the trifle of her friend's being accompanied by two unknown gentlemen, and she advanced, shawled as if for departure, and smiling, reproachfully. "Ah, you ungrateful creature," she cried. "you've lost my rosebud!"

Guest came up smiling, as they say. "Your own hands fastened it!—Where is my daughter?"

"She's coming. We've been looking for you, high and low. What on earth have you been doing here? Business? You've no business with business. You came here to rest. Excuse me, gentlemen! My carriage has been waiting this ten minutes. Give me your arm."

It seemed to me time we should disembarrass the poor man of our presence. I opened the window and stepped out upon the piazza. Just as Edgar had followed me, a young lady hastily entered the room.

"My dearest father!" she exclaimed.

Looking at her unseen from without, I recognized with amazement my charming friend of the Episcopal chapel, the woman to whom—I felt it now with a sort of convulsion—I had dedicated a sentiment.

III

My discovery gave me that night much to think of, and I thought of it more than I slept. My foremost feeling was one of blank dismay as if Misfortune, whom I had been used to regard as a good-natured sort of goddess, who came on with an easy stride, letting off signals of warning to those who stood in her path, should have blinded her lantern and muffled her steps in order to steal a march on poor me,—of all men in the world! It seemed a hideous practical joke. "If I had known,—if I had only known!" I kept restlessly repeating. But towards morning, "Say I had known," I asked myself, "could I have acted otherwise? I might have protested by my absence; but would I not thus have surrendered poor Guest to the vengeance of a very Shylock? Had not that suggestion of mine divested the current of Edgar's wrath and saved his adversary from the last dishonor? Without it, Edgar would have held his course and demanded his pound of flesh!" Say what I would, however, I stood confronted with this acutely uncomfortable fact, that by lending a hand at that revolting interview, I had struck a roundabout blow at the woman to whom I owed a signally sweet impression. Well, my blow would never reach her, and I would devise some kindness that should! So I consoled myself, and in the midst of my regret I found a still further compensation in the thought that chance, rough-handed though it had been, had forged between us a stouter bond than any I had ventured to dream of as I walked sentimental a few hours before. Her father's being a rascal threw her image into more eloquent relief. If she suspected it, she had all the interest of sorrow; if not, she wore the tender grace of danger.

The result of my meditations was that I determined to defer indefinitely my departure from L——. Edgar informed me, in the course of the following day, that Guest had gone by the early train to New York, and that his daughter had left the hotel (where my not having met her before was apparently the result of her constant attendance on her father during his illness) and taken up her residence with the lady in whose company we had seen her. Mrs Beck, Edgar had learned this lady's name to be; and I fancied it was upon her that Miss Guest had made her morning call. To begin with, therefore, I knew where to look for her. "That's the charming girl,"

I said to Edgar, "whom you might have plunged into disgrace."

"How do you know she's charming?" he asked.

"I judge by her face."

"Humph! Judge her father by his face and *he's* charming."

I was on the point of assuring my step-brother that no such thing could be said of him; but in fact he had suddenly assumed a singularly fresh and jovial air. "I don't what it is," he said, "but I feel like a trump; I haven't stood so firm on my legs in a twelvemonth. I wonder whether the waters have already begun to act. Really, I'm elated. Suppose, in the afternoon of my life, I were to turn out a sound man. It winds me up, sir. I shall take another glass before dinner."

To do Miss Guest a kindness, I reflected, I must see her again. How to compass an interview and irradiate my benevolence, it was not easy to determine. Sooner or later, of course, the chances of watering-place life would serve me. Meanwhile, I felt most agreeably that here was something more finely romantic than that feverish dream of my youth, treating Edgar some fine day to the snub direct. Assuredly, I was not in love; I had cherished a youthful passion, and I knew the signs and symptoms; but I was in a state of mind that really gave something of the same zest to consciousness. For a couple of days I watched and waited for my friend in those few public resorts in which the little world of L——used most to congregate,—the drive, the walk, the post-office, and the vicinage of the spring. At last, as she was nowhere visible, I betook myself to the little Episcopal chapel, and strolled along the road, past a scattered cluster of decent boarding-houses, in one of which I imagined her hidden. But most of them had a shady strip of garden stretching toward the river, and thitherward, of course, rather than upon the public road, their inmates were likely to turn their faces. A happy accident at last came to my aid. After three or four days at the hotel, Edgar began to complain that the music in the evening kept him awake and to wonder whether he might find tolerable private lodgings. He was more and more interested in the waters. I offered, with alacrity, to make inquiries for him, and as a first step, I returned to the little colony of riverside boarding-houses. I began with one I had made especial note of,—the smallest, neatest, and most secluded. The mistress of the establishment was at a neighbor's, and I was requested to await her return. I stepped out of the long parlor window, and began hopefully to explore the garden. My hopes were brightly rewarded. In a shady summer-house, on a sort of rustic embankment, overlooking the stream, I encountered Miss Guest and her coquettish duenna. She looked at me for a moment with a dubious air, as if to satisfy herself that she was distinctly expected to recognize me, and then, as I stood proclaiming my hopes in an appealing smile, she bade me a frank good-morning. We talked, I lingered, and at last, when the proper moment came for my going my way again, I sat down and paid a call in form.

"I see you know my name," Miss Guest said, with the peculiar—the almost boyish—directness which seemed to be her most striking feature; "I can't imagine how you learned it, but if you'll be so good as to tell me your own, I'll introduce you to Mrs Beck. You must learn that she's my deputed chaperon, my she-dragon, and that I'm not to know you unless she knows you first and approves."

Mrs Beck poised a gold eye-glass upon her pretty *retroussé* nose—not sorry, I think, to hold it there a moment with a plump white hand and acquit herself of one of her most effective manœuvres,—and glanced at me with mock severity. "He's a harmless-looking young man, my dear," she declared, "and I don't think your father would object." And with this odd sanction I became intimate with Miss Guest,—intimate as, by the soft operation of summer and rural juxtaposition, an American youth is free to become with an American maid. I had told my friends, of course, the purpose of my visit, and learned, with complete satisfaction, that there was no chance for Mr Musgrave, as they occupied the only three comfortable rooms in the house,—two as bedrooms, the third as a common parlor. Heaven forbid that I should introduce Edgar *dans cette galère*. I inquired elsewhere, but saw nothing I could recommend, and, on making my report to him, found him quite out of conceit of his project. A lady had just been telling him horrors of the local dietary and making him feel that he was vastly well off with the heavy bread and cold gravy of the hotel. It was then, too I think, he first mentioned the symptoms of that relapse which subsequently occurred. He would run no risks.

I had prepared Miss Guest, I fancy, to regard another visit as a matter of course. I paid several in rapid succession; for, under the circumstances, it would have been a pity to be shy. Her father, she told me, expected to be occupied for three or four weeks in New York, so that for the present I was at ease on that score. If I was to please, I must go bravely to work. So I burned my ships behind me, and blundered into gallantry with an ardor over which, in my absence, the two ladies must have mingled their smiles. I don't suppose I passed for an especially knowing fellow; but I kept my friends from wearying of each other (for such other chance acquaintances as the place afforded they seemed to have little inclination), and by my services as a retailer of the local gossip, a reader of light literature, an explorer and suggester of drives and strolls, and, more particularly, as an oarsman in certain happy rowing-parties on the placid river whose slow, safe current made such a pretty affectation of Mrs Beck's little shrieks and shudders, I very fairly earned my welcome. That detestable scene at the hotel used to seem a sort of horrid fable as I sat in the sacred rural stillness, in that peaceful streamside nook, learning what a divinely honest girl she was, this daughter of the man whose dishonesty I had so complacently attested. I wasted many an hour in wondering on what terms she stood with her father's rankling secret, with his poor pompous peccability in general, if not with Edgar's particular grievance. I used to fancy that certain momentary snatches of revery in the midst of our gayety, and even more, certain effusions of wilful and excessive gayety at our duller moments, portended some vague torment in her filial heart. She would quit her place and wander apart for a while, leaving me to gossip it out with Mrs Beck, as if she was oppressed by the constant need of seeming interested in us. But she would come back with a face that told so few tales that I always ended by keeping my compassion in the case for myself, and being reminded afresh, by my lively indisposition to be thus grossly lumped, as it were, with the duenna, of how much I was interested in the damsel. In truth, the romance of the matter apart, Miss Guest was a lovely girl. I had read her dimly in the little chapel, but I had read her aright. Felicity in freedom, that was her great charm. I have never known a woman so simply and sincerely original, so finely framed to enlist the imagination and hold expectation in suspense, and yet leave the judgment to such blissful quietude. She had a genius for frankness; this was her only coquetry and her only cleverness, and a woman could not have acquitted herself more naturally of the trying and ungracious *rôle* of being expected to be startling. It was the pure personal accent of Miss Guest's walk and conversation that gave them this charm; everything she did and said was gilded by a ray of conviction; and to a respectful admirer who had not penetrated to the sources of spiritual motive in her being, this sweet, natural, various emphasis of conduct was ineffably provoking. Her creed, as I guessed it, might have been resumed in the simple notion that a man should do his best; and nature had treated her, I fancied, to some brighter vision of uttermost manhood than illumined most honest fellows' conciences. Frank as she was, I imagined she had a remote reserve of holiest contempt. She made me feel deplorably ignorant and idle and unambitious, a foolish, boyish, spendthrift of time and strength and means; and I speedily came to believe that to win her perfect favor was a matter of something more than undoing a stupid wrong,—doing, namely, some very pretty piece of right. And she was poor Mr Guest's daughter, withal! Truly, fate was a master of irony.

I ought in justice to say that I had Mrs Beck more particularly to thank for my welcome, and for the easy terms on which I had become an *habitué* of the little summer-house by the river. How could I know how much or how little the younger lady meant by her smiles and hand-shakes, by laughing at my jokes and consenting to be rowed about in my boat? Mrs Beck made no secret of her relish for the society of a decently agreeable man, or of her deeming some such pastime the indispensable spice of life; and in Mr Guest's absence, I was graciously admitted to competition. The precise nature of their mutual sentiments—Mr Guest's and hers—I was slightly puzzled to divine, and in so far as my conjectures seemed plausible, I confess they served as but a scanty offset to my knowledge of the gentleman's foibles. This lady was, to my sense, a very artificial charmer, and I think that a goodly portion of my admiration for Miss Guest rested upon a little private theory that for her father's sake she thus heroically accepted a companion whom she must have relished but little. Mrs Beck's great point was her "preservation." It was rather too great a point for my taste, and partook too much of the nature of a physiological curiosity. Her age really mattered little, for with as many years as you pleased one way or the other, she was still a triumph of juvenility. Plump, rosy, dimpled, frizzled, with rings on her fingers and rosettes on her toes, she used to seem to me a sort of fantastic vagary or humorous experiment of time. Or, she might have been fancied a strayed shepherdess from some rococo Arcadia, which had melted into tradition during some profane excursion of her own, so that she found herself saddled in our prosy modern world with this absurdly perpetual prime. All this was true, at least of her pretty face and figure; but there was another Mrs Beck, visible chiefly to the moral eye, who seemed to me excessively wrinkled and faded and world-wise, and whom I used to fancy I could hear shaking about in this enamelled envelope, like a dried nut in its shell. Mrs Beck's morality was not Arcadian; or if it was, it was that of a shepherdess with a keen eye to the state of the wool and the mutton market, and a lively perception of the possible advant-ages of judicious partnership. She had no design, I suppose, of proposing to me a consolidation of our sentimental and pecuniary interests, but she performed her duties of duenna with such conscientious precision that she shared my society most impartially with Miss Guest. I never had the good for-tune of finding myself alone with this young lady. She might have managed it, I fancied, if she had wished, and the little care she took about it was a sign of that indifference which stirs the susceptible heart to effort. "It's really detestable," I at last ventured to seize the chance to declare, "that you and I should never be alone."

Miss Guest looked at me with an air of surprise. "Your remark is startling," she said, "unless you have some excellent reason for demanding this interesting seclusion."

My reason was not ready just yet, but it speedily ripened. A happy incident combined at once to bring it to maturity and to operate a diversion for Mrs Beck. One morning there appeared a certain Mr Crawford out of the West, a worthy bachelor who introduced himself to Mrs Beck and claimed cousinship. I was present at the moment, and I could not but admire the skill with which the lady gauged her aspiring kinsman before saying yea or nay to his claims. I think the large diamond in his shirt-front decided her; what he may have lacked in elegant culture was supplied by this massive ornament. Better and brighter than his diamond, however, was his frank Western *bonhomie*, his simple friendliness, and

a certain half-boyish modesty which made him give a humorous twist to any expression of the finer sentiments. He was
a tall, lean gentleman, on the right side of forty, yellow-haired,
with a somewhat arid complexion, an irrepressible tendency
to cock back his hat and chew his toothpick, and a spasmodic liability, spasmodically repressed when in a sedentary
posture, to a centrifugal movement of the heels. He had a
clear blue eye, in which simplicity and shrewdness contended
and mingled on so lively a fashion that his glance was the
oddest dramatic twinkle. He was a genial sceptic. If he disbelieved much that he saw, he believed everything he fancied,
and for a man who had seen much of the rougher and baser
side of life, he was able to fancy some very gracious things
of men, to say nothing of women. He took his place as a very
convenient fourth in our little party, and without obtruding
his eccentricities, or being too often reminded of a story, like
many cooler humorists, he treated us to a hundred anecdotes of his adventurous ascent of the ladder of fortune. The
upshot of his history was that he was now owner of a silver
mine in Arizona, and that he proposed in his own words to
"lay off and choose." Of the nature of his choice he modestly
waived specification; it of course had reference to the sex of
which Mrs Beck was an ornament. He lounged about meanwhile with his hands in his pockets, watching the flies buzz
with that air of ecstatically suspended resolve proper to a man
who has sunk his shaft deep into the very stuff that dreams
are made of. But in spite of shyness he exhaled an atmosphere
of regretful celibacy which might have relaxed the conjugal
piety of a more tenderly mourning widow than Mrs Beck. His
bachelor days were evidently numbered, and unless I was
vastly mistaken, it lay in this lady's discretion to determine
the residuary figure. The two were just nearly enough akin
to save a deal of time in courtship.

Crawford had never beheld so finished a piece of ladyhood,
and it pleased and puzzled him and quickened his honest

grin very much as a remarkably neat mechanical toy might have done. Plain people who have lived close to frank nature often think more of a fine crisp muslin rose than of a group of dewy petals of garden growth. Before ten days were past, he had begun to fumble tenderly with the stem of this unfading flower. Mr Crawford's *petits soins* had something too much of the ring of the small change of the Arizona silvermine, consisting largely as they did of rather rudimentary nosegays compounded by amateur florists from the local front-yards, of huge bundles of "New York candy" from the village store, and of an infinite variety of birch-bark and bead-work trinkets. He was no simpleton, and it occurred to me, indeed, that if these offerings were not the tokens and pledges of a sentiment, they were the offset and substitute of a sentiment; but if they were profuse for that, they were scanty for this. Mrs Beck, for her part, seemed minded to spin the thread of decision excessively fine. A silver-mine was all very well, but a lover fresh from the diggings was to be put on probation. Crawford lodged at the hotel, and our comings and goings were often made together. He indulged in many a dry compliment to his cousin, and, indeed, declared that she was a magnificent little woman. It was with surprise, therefore, that I learned that his admiration was divided. "I've never seen one just like her," he said; "one so out and out a woman,—smiles and tears and everything else! But Clara comes out with her notions, and a man may know what to expect. I guess I can afford a wife with a notion or so! Short of the moon, I can give her what she wants." And I seemed to hear his hands producing in his pockets that Arizonian tinkle which served with him as the prelude to renewed utterance. He went on, "And tells me I mustn't make love to my grandmother. That's a very pretty way of confessing to thirty-five. She's a bit of coquette, is Clara!" I handled the honest fellow's illusions as tenderly as I could, and at last he eyed me askance with a knowing air. "You praise my cousin," he said, "because you think I want you to. On the contrary, I want you to say something against her. If there is anything, I want to know it." I declared I knew nothing in the world; whereupon Crawford, after a silence, heaved an impatient sigh.

"Really," said I, laughing, "one would think you were disappointed."

"I wanted to draw you out," he cried; "but you're too confoundedly polite. I suppose Mrs Beck's to be my fate; it's borne in on me. I'm being roped in fast. But I only want a little backing to hang off awhile. Look here," he added suddenly, "let's be frank!" and he stopped and laid his hand on my arm. "That other young lady isn't so pretty as Mrs Beck, but it seems to me I'd kind of trust her further. You didn't know I'd noticed her. Well, I've taken her in little by little, just as she gives herself out. Jerusalem! there's a woman. But you know it, sir, if I'm not mistaken; and that's where the shoe pinches. First come, first served. I want to act on the square. Before I settle down to Mrs Beck, I want to know distinctly whether you put in a claim to Miss Guest."

The question was unexpected and found me but half prepared. "A claim?" I said. "Well, yes, call it a claim!"

"Anyway," he rejoined, "I've no chance. She'd never look at me. But I want to have her put out of my own head; so that I can concentrate on Mrs B. If you're not in love with her, my boy, let me tell you you ought to be! If you are, I've nothing to do but to wish you success. If you're not, upon my word, I don't know but what I would go in! She could but refuse me. Modesty is all very well; but after all, it's the handsomest thing you can do by a woman to offer yourself. As a compliment alone, it would serve. And really, a compliment with a round million isn't so bad as gallantry goes hereabouts. You're young and smart and good-looking, and Mrs Beck tells me you're rich. If you succeed, you'll have more than your share of good things. But Fortune has her favorites, and they're not always such nice young men. If you're in love, well and good! If you're not,—by Jove, I am!"

This admonition was peremptory. My companion's face in the clear starlight betrayed his sagacious sincerity. I felt a sudden satisfaction in being summoned to take my stand. I performed a rapid operation in sentimental arithmetic, combined my factors, and established my total. It exceeded expectation. "Your frankness does you honor," I said, "and I'm sorry I can't make a kinder return. But—I'm madly in love!"

IV

My situation, as I defined it to Crawford, was not purely delightful. Close upon my perception of the state of my heart followed an oppressive sense of the vanity of my pretensions. I had cut the ground from under my feet; to offer myself to Miss Guest would be to add insult to injury. I may truly say, therefore, that, for a couple of days, this manifest passion of mine rather saddened than exalted me. For a dismal forty-eight hours I left the two ladies unvisited. I even thought of paying a supreme tribute to delicacy and taking a summary departure. Some day, possibly, Miss Guest would learn with grief and scorn what her father had to thank me for; and then later, as resentment melted into milder conjecture, she would read the riddle of my present conduct and do me justice,— guess that I had loved her, and that, to punish myself, I had renounced her forever. This fantastic magnanimity was followed by a wholesome reaction. I was punished enough, surely, in my regret and shame; and I wished now not to suffer, but to act. Viewing the matter reasonably, she need never learn my secret; if by some cruel accident she should, the favor I had earned would cover that I had forfeited. I stayed, then, and tried to earn this precious favor; but I encountered an obstacle more serious, I fancied, than even her passionate contempt would have been,—her serene and benevolent indifference. Looking back at these momentous days, I get an impression of a period of vague sentimental ferment and trouble, rather than of definite utterance and action; though I believe that by a singular law governing human conduct in certain cases, the very modesty and humility of my passion expressed itself in a sort of florid and hyperbolical gallantry; so that, in so far as my claims were inadmissible, they might pass, partly as a kind of compensatory homage, and partly as a jest. Miss Guest refused to pay me the compliment of even being discomposed, and pretended to accept my addresses as an elaborate device for her amusement. There was a perpetual assurance in her tone of her not regarding me as a serious, much less as a dangerous man. She could not have contrived a more effective irritant to my resolution; and I confess there were certain impatient moods when I took a brutal glee in the thought that it was not so very long since, on a notable occasion, my presence had told. In so far as I *was* serious, Miss Guest frankly offered to accept me as a friend, and laughingly intimated, indeed, that with a little matronly tuition of her dispensing, I might put myself into condition to please some simple maiden in her flower. I was an excellent honest fellow; but I was excessively young and—as she really wished to befriend me, she would risk the admonition—I was decidedly frivolous. I lacked "character." I was fairly clever, but I was more clever than wise. I liked overmuch to listen to my own tongue. I had done nothing; I was idle; I had, by my own confession, never made an effort; I was too rich and too indolent; in my very good-nature there was nothing moral, no hint of principle; in short, I was—boyish. I must forgive a woman upon whom life had forced the fatal habit of discrimination. I suffered this genial scepticism to expend itself freely, for her candor was an enchantment. It was all true enough. I had been indolent and unambitious; I had made no effort; I had lived in vulgar ignorance and ease; I had in a certain frivolous fashion tried life at first hand, but my shallow gains had been in proportion to my small hazards. But I was neither so young nor so idle as she chose to fancy, and I could at any rate prove I was constant. Like a legendary suitor of old, I might even slay my dragon. A monstrous accident stood between us, and to dissipate its evil influence would be a fairly heroic feat.

Mr Guest's absence was prolonged from day to day, and Laura's tone of allusion to her father tended indeed to make a sort of invincible chimera of her possible discovery of the truth. This fond filial reference only brought out the more brightly her unlikeness to him. I could as little fancy her doing an act she would need to conceal as I could fancy her arresting exposure by a concession to dishonor. If I was a friend, I insisted on being a familiar one; and while Mrs Beck and her cousin floated away on perilous waters, we dabbled in the placid shallows of disinterested sentiment. For myself, I sent many a longing glance toward the open sea, but Laura remained firm in her preference for the shore. I encouraged her to speak of her father, for I wished to hear all the good that could be told of him. It sometimes seemed to me that she talked of him with a kind of vehement tenderness designed to obscure, as it were, her inner vision. Better—had she said to herself?—that she should talk fond nonsense about him than that she should harbor untender suspicions. I could easily believe that the poor man was a most lovable fellow, and could imagine how, as Laura judged him in spite of herself, the sweet allowances of a mother had grown up within the daughter. One afternoon Mrs Beck brought forth her photograph-book, to show to her cousin. Suddenly, as he was turning it over, she stayed his hand and snatched one of the pictures from its place. He tried to recover it and a little tussle followed, in the course of which she escaped, ran to Miss Guest, and thrust the photograph into her hand. "You keep it," she cried; "he's not to see it." There was a great crying out from Crawford about Mrs Beck's inconstancy and his *right* to see the picture, which was cut short by Laura's saying with some gravity that it was too childish a romp for a man of forty and a woman of—thirty! Mrs Beck allowed us no time to relish the irony of this attributive figure; she caused herself to be pursued to the other end of the garden, where the amorous frolic was resumed over the following pages of the album. "Who is it?" I asked. Miss Guest, after a pause, handed me the card.

"Your father!" I cried precipitately.

"Ah, you've seen him?" she asked.

"I know him by his likeness to you."

"You prevent me asking you, as I meant, if he doesn't look like a dear good man. I do wish he'd drop his stupid business and come back."

I took occasion hereupon to ascertain whether she suspected his embarrassments. She confessed to a painful impression that something was wrong. He had been out of spirits for many days before his return to town; nothing indeed but mental distress could have affected his health, for he had a perfect constitution. "If it comes to that," she went on, after a long silence, and looking at me with an almost intimate confidence, "I wish he would give up business altogether. All the business in the world, for a man of his open, joyous temper, doesn't pay for an hour's depression. I can't bear to sit by and see him imbittered and spoiled by this muddle of stocks and shares. Nature made him a happy man; I insist on keeping him so. We are quite rich enough, and we need nothing more. He tries to persuade me that I have expensive tastes, but I've never spent money but to please him. I have a lovely little dream which I mean to lay before him when he comes back; it's very cheap, like all dreams, and more practicable than most. He's to give up business and take me abroad. We're to settle down quietly somewhere in Germany, in

Italy, I don't care where, and I'm to study music seriously. I'm never going to marry; but as he grows to be an old man, he's to sit by a window, with his cigar, looking out on the Arno or the Rhine, while I play Beethoven and Rossini."

"It's a very pretty programme," I answered, "though I can't subscribe to certain details. But do you know," I added, touched by a forcible appeal to sympathy in her tone, "although you refuse to believe me anything better than an ingenuous fool, this liberal concession to my interest in your situation is almost a proof of respect."

She blushed a little, to my great satisfaction. "I surely respect you," she said, "if you come to that! Otherwise we should hardly be sitting here so simply. And I think, too," she went on, "that I speak to you of my father with peculiar freedom, because—because, somehow, you remind me of him." She looked at me as she spoke with such penetrating candor that it was my turn to blush. "You are genial, and gentle, and essentially honest, like him; and like him," she added with a half-smile, "you're addicted to saying a little more than it would be fair to expect you to stand to. You ought to be very good friends. You'll find he has your own *jeunesse de cœur*."

I murmured what I might about the happiness of making his acquaintance; and then, to give the conversation a turn, and really to test the force of this sympathetic movement of hers, I boldly mentioned my fancy that he was an admirer of Mrs Beck. She gave me a silent glance, almost of gratitude, as if she needed to unburden her heart. But she did so in few words. "He does admire her," she said. "It's my duty, it's my pleasure, to respect his illusions. But I confess to you that I hope this one will fade." She rose from her seat and we joined our companions; but I fancied, for a week afterwards, that she treated me with a certain gracious implication of deference. Had I ceased to seem boyish? I struck a truce with urgency and almost relished the idea of being patient.

A day or two later, Mr Guest's "illusions" were put before me in a pathetic light. It was a Sunday; the ladies were at church, and Crawford and I sat smoking on the piazza. "I don't know how things are going with you," he said; "you're either perfectly successful or desperately resigned. But unless it's rather plainer sailing than in my case, I don't envy you. I don't know where I am, anyway! She will and she won't. She may take back her word once too often, I can tell her that! You see, she has two strings to her bow. She likes my money, but she doesn't like *me*. Now, it's all very well for a woman to relish a fortune, but I'm not prepared to have my wife despise —my *person!*" said Crawford with feeling. "The alternative, you know, is Mr Guest, that girl's father. I suppose he's handsome, and a wit, and a dandy; though I must say an old dandy, to my taste, is an old fool. She tells me a dozen times an hour that he's a fascinating man. I suppose if I were to leave her alone for a week, I might seem a fascinating man. I wish to heaven she wasn't so confoundedly taking. I can't give her up; she amuses me too much. There was once a little actress in Galveston, but Clara beats that girl! If I could only have gone in for some simple wholesome girl who doesn't need to count on her fingers to know the state of her heart!"

That evening as we were gathered in the garden, poor Crawford approached Laura Guest with an air of desperate gallantry, as if from a desire to rest from the petty torment of Mrs Beck's sentimental mutations. Laura liked him, and her manner to him had always been admirable in its almost sisterly frankness and absence of provoking arts; yet I found myself almost wondering, as they now strolled about the gardens together, whether there was any danger of this sturdy architect of his own fortunes putting out my pipe. Mrs Beck, however, left me no chance for selfish meditation. Her artless and pointless prattle never lacked a purpose; before you knew it she was, in vulgar parlance, "pumping" you, trying to pick your pocket of your poor little receipt for prosperity.

She took an intense delight in imaginatively bettering her condition, and one was forced to carry bricks for her castles in the air.

"You needn't be afraid of my cousin," she said, laughing, as I followed his red cigar-tip along the garden-paths. "He admires Laura altogether too much to make love to her. There's modesty! Don't you think it's rather touching in a man with a million of dollars? I don't mind telling you that he has made love to me, that being no case for modesty. I suppose you'll say that my speaking of it is. But what's the use of being an aged widow, if one can't tell the truth?"

"There's comfort in being an aged widow," I answered gallantly, "when one has two offers in a month."

"I don't know what you know about my offers; but even two swallows don't make a summer! However, since you've mentioned the subject, tell me frankly what you think of poor Crawford. Is he at all presentable? You see I like him, I esteem him, and I'm afraid of being blinded by my feelings. Is he so dreadfully rough? You see I like downright simple manliness and all that; but a little polish does no harm, even on fine gold. I do wish you'd take hold of my poor cousin and teach him a few of the amenities of life. I'm very fond of the amenities of life; it's very frivolous and wicked, I suppose, but I can't help it. I have the misfortune to be sensitive to ugly things. Can one really accept a man who wears a green cravat? Of course you can make him take it off; but you'll be knowing all the while that he pines for it, that he would put it on if he could. Now that's a symbol of that dear, kind, simple fellow—a heart of gold, but a green cravat! I've never, heard a word of wisdom about that matter yet. People talk about the sympathy of souls being the foundation of happiness in marriage. It's pure nonsense. It's not the great things, but the little, that we dispute about, and the chances are terribly against the people who have a different taste in colors."

It seemed to me that, thus ardently invoked, I might hazard the observation, "Mr Guest would never wear a green cravat."

"What do you know about Mr Guest's cravats?"

"I've seen his photograph, you know."

"Well, you do him justice. You should see him in the life. He looks like a duke. I never saw a duke, but that's my notion of a duke. Distinction, you know; perfect manners and tact and wit. If I'm right about it's being perfection in small things that assures one's happiness, I might—well, in two words, I might be very happy with Mr Guest!"

"It's Crawford and soul, then," I proposed, smiling, "or Guest and manners!"

She looked at me a moment, and then with a toss of her head and a tap of her fan, "You wretch!" she cried, "you want to make me say something very ridiculous. I'll not pretend I'm not worldly. I'm excessively worldly. I always make a point of letting people know it. Of course I know very well my cousin's rich, and that so long as he's good he's none the worse for that. But in my quiet little way I'm a critic, and I look at things from a high ground. I compare a rich man who is simply a good fellow to a perfect gentleman who has simply a nice little fortune. Mr Guest has a nice property, a very nice property. I shouldn't have to make over my old bonnets. You may ask me if I'm not afraid of Laura. But you'll marry Laura and carry her off!"

I found nothing to reply for some moments to this little essay in "criticism"; and suddenly Mrs Beck, fancying perhaps that she was indiscreetly committing herself, put an end to our interview. "I'm really very kind," she cried, "to be talking so graciously about a lover who leaves me alone for a month and never even drops me a line. It's not such good manners after all. If you're not jealous of Mr Crawford, I am of Miss Guest. We'll go down and separate them."

Miss Guest's repose and dignity were decidedly overshadowed. I brought her the next afternoon a letter from the post-office, superscribed in a hand I knew, and wandered away while she sat in the garden and read it. When I came back she looked strangely sad. I sat down near her and drew figures in the ground with the end of her parasol, hoping that she would do me the honor to communicate her trouble. At last she rose in silence, as if to return to the house. I begged her to remain. "You're in distress," I said, speaking as calmly and coldly as I could, "and I hoped it might occur to you that there is infinite sympathy close at hand. Instead of going to your own room to cry, why not stay here and talk of it with me?"

She gave me a brilliant, searching gaze; I met it steadily and felt that I was turning pale with the effort not to obey the passionate impulse of self-denunciation. She began slowly to walk away from the house, and I felt that a point was gained. "It's your father, of course," I said. It was all I could say. She silently handed me the unfolded letter. It ran as follows:

MY DEAREST DAUGHTER: I have sold the house and everything in it, except your piano and books, of course at a painful sacrifice. But I needed ready money. Forgive your poor blundering, cruel father. My old luck has left me; but only *trust me*, and we shall be happy again.

Her eyes, fortunately, were wandering while I read; for I felt myself blushing to my ears.

"It's not the loss of the house," she said at last; "though of course we were fond of it. I grew up there,—my mother died there. It's the trouble it indicates. Poor dear father! Why does he talk of 'luck'? I detest the word! Why does he talk of forgiving him and trusting him? There's a wretched tone about it all. If he would only come back and let me look at him!"

"Nothing is more common in business," I answered, "than a temporary embarrassment demanding ready money.

Of course it must be met at a sacrifice. One throws a little something overboard to lighten the ship, and the ship sails ahead. As for the loss of the house, nothing could be better for going to Italy, you know. You've no excuse left for staying here. If your father will forgive me the interest I take in his affairs, I strongly recommend his leaving business and its sordid cares. Let him go abroad and forget it all."

Laura walked along in silence, and I led the way out of the garden into the road. We followed it slowly till we reached the little chapel. The sexton was just leaving it, shouldering the broom with which he had been sweeping it for the morrow's services. I hailed him and gained his permission to go in and try the organ, assuring him that we were experts. Laura said that she felt in no mood for music; but she entered and sat down in one of the pews. I climbed into the gallery and attacked the little instrument. We had had no music since our first meeting, and I felt an irresistible need to recall the circumstances of that meeting. I played in a simple fashion, respectably enough, and fancied, at all events, that by my harmonious fingers I could best express myself. I played for an hour, in silence, choosing what I would, without comment or response from my companion. The summer twilight overtook us; when it was getting too dark to see the keys, I rejoined Miss Guest. She rose and came into the aisle. "You play very well," she said, simply; "better than I supposed."

Her praise was sweet; but sweeter still was a fancy of mine that I perceived in the light gloom just the glimmer of a tear. "In this place," I said, "your playing once moved me greatly. Try and remember the scene distinctly."

"It's easily remembered," she answered, with an air of surprise.

"Believe, then, that when we parted, I was already in love with you."

She turned away abruptly. "Ah, my poor music!"

The next day, on my arrival, I was met by Mrs Beck, whose pretty forehead seemed clouded with annoyance. With her own fair hand she button-holed me. "You apparently," she said, "have the happiness to be in Miss Guest's confidence. What on earth is going on in New York? Laura received an hour ago a letter from her father. I found her sitting with it in her hand as cheerful as a Quakeress in meeting. 'Something's wrong, my dear,' I said; 'I don't know what. In any case, be assured of my sympathy.' She gave me the most extraordinary stare. 'You'll be interested to know,' she said, 'that my father has lost half his property.' Interested to know! I verily believe the child meant an impertinence. What is Mr Guest's property to me? Has he been speculating? Stupid man?" she cried, with vehemence.

I made a brief answer. I discovered Miss Guest sitting by the river, in pale contemplation of household disaster. I asked no questions. She told me of her own accord that her father was to return immediately, "to make up a month's sleep," she added, glancing at his letter. We spoke of other matters, but before I left her, I returned to this one. "I wish you to tell your father this," I said. "That there is a certain gentleman here, who is idle, indolent, ignorant, frivolous, selfish. That he has certain funds for which he is without present use. That he places them at Mr Guest's absolute disposal in the hope that they may partially relieve his embarrassment." I looked at Laura as I spoke and watched her startled blush deepen to crimson. She was about to reply; but before she could speak, "Don't forget to add," I went on, "that he hopes his personal faults will not prejudice Mr Guest's acceptance of his offer, for it is prompted by the love he bears his daughter."

"You must excuse me," Laura said, after a pause. "I had rather not tell him this. He would not accept your offer."

"Are you sure of that?"

"I shouldn't allow him."

"And why not, pray? Don't you, after all, like me well enough to suffer me to do you so small a service?"

She hesitated; then gave me her hand with magnificent frankness. "I like you too well to suffer you to do me just that service. We take that, from *les indifférents*."

V

BEFORE the month was out. Edgar had quarrelled with the healing waters of L——. His improvement had been most illusory; his old symptoms had returned in force, and though he now railed bitterly at the perfidious spring and roundly denounced the place, he was too ill to be moved away. He was altogether confined to his room. I made a conscience of offering him my company and assistance, but he would accept no nursing of mine. He would be tended by no one whom he could not pay for his trouble and enjoy a legal right to grumble at. "I expect a nurse to *be* a nurse," he said, "and not a fine gentleman, waiting on me in gloves. It would be fine work for me, lying here, to have to think twice whether I might bid you not to breathe so hard." Nothing had passed between us about John Guest, though the motive for silence was different on each side. For Edgar, I fancied, our interview with him was a matter too solemn for frequent allusion; for me it was a detestable thought. But wishing now to assure myself that, as I supposed, to had paid his ugly debt. I asked Edgar, on the evening I had extorted from Miss Guest those last recorded words of happy omen, whether he had heard from our friend in New York. It was a very hot night; poor Edgar lay sweltering under a sheet, with open windows. He looked pitifully ill, and yet somehow more intensely himself than ever. He drew a letter from under his pillow. "This

came to-day," he said. "Stevens writes me that Guest yesterday paid down the twenty thousand dollars in full. It's quick
work. I hope he's not robbed Peter to pay Paul."

"Mr Guest has a conscience," I said; and I thought bitterly
of the reverse of the picture. "I'm afraid he has half-ruined
himself to do it."

"Well, ruin for ruin, I prefer his. I've no doubt his affairs
have gone to the dogs. The affairs of such a man must, sooner
or later! I believe, by the way, you've been cultivating the
young lady. What does the papa say to that?"

"Of course," I said, without heeding his question, "you've
already enclosed him the—the little paper."

Edgar turned in his bed. "Of course I've done no such
thing!"

"You mean to keep it?" I cried.

"Of course I mean to keep it. Where else would be his
punishment?"

There was something vastly grotesque in the sight of this
sickly little mortal erecting himself among his pillows as a
dispenser of justice, an appraiser of the wages of sin; but I confess that his attitude struck me as more cruel even than
ludicrous. I was disappointed. I had certainly not expected
Edgar to be generous, but I had expected him to be just, and
in the heat of his present irritation he was neither. He was
angry with Guest for his excessive promptitude, which had
given a sinister twist to his own conduct. "Upon my word,"
I cried, "you're a veritable Shylock!"

"And you're a veritable fool! Is it set down in the bond
that I'm to give it up to him? The thing's mine, to have and
to hold forever. The scoundrel would be easily let off indeed!
This bit of paper in my hands is to keep him in order and
prevent his being too happy. The thought will be wholesome
company,—a *memento mori* to his vanity."

"He's to go through life, then, with possible exposure
staring him in the face?"

Edgar's great protuberant eyes expanded without blinking. "He has committed his fate to Providence."

I was revolted. "You may have the providential qualities, but you have not the gentlemanly ones. I formally protest. But, after a decent delay, he'll of course demand the document."

"Demand it? He shall have it then, with a vengeance!"

"Well, I wash my hands of further complicity! I shall inform Mr Guest that I count for nothing in this base negation of his right."

Edgar paused a moment to stare at me in my unprecedented wrath. Then making me a little ironical gesture of congratulation, "Inform him of what you please. I hope you'll have a pleasant talk over it! You made rather a bad beginning, but who knows, if you put your heads together to abuse me, you may end as bosom friends! I've watched you, sir!" he suddenly added, propping himself forward among his pillows; "you're in love!" I may wrong the poor fellow, but it seemed to me that in these words he discharged the bitterness of a lifetime. He too would have hoped to please, and he had lived in acrid assent to the instinct which told him such hope was vain. In one way or another a man pays his tax to manhood. "Yes, sir, you're grossly in love! What do I know about love, you ask? I know a drivelling lover when I see him. You've made a clever choice. Do you expect John Guest to give the girl away? He's a good-natured man, I know; but really, considering your high standard of gentlemanly conduct, you ask a good deal."

Edgar had been guilty on this occasion of a kind of reckless moral self-exposure, which seemed to betray a sense that he should never need his reputation again. I felt as if I were standing by something very like a death-bed, and forbearingly without rejoinder, I withdrew. He had simply expressed more brutally, however, my own oppressive belief that the father's aversion stood darkly massed in the rear of the daughter's indifference. I had, indeed, for the present, the consolation of believing that with Laura the day of pure indifference was over; and I tried hard to flatter myself that my position was tenable in spite of Mr Guest. The next day as I was wandering on the hotel piazza, communing thus sadly with my hopes, I met Crawford, who, with his hands in his pockets and his hat on the bridge of his nose, seemed equally a sullen probationer of fate.

"I'm going down to join our friends," I said; "I expected to find you with them."

He gave a gloomy grin. "My nose is out of joint," he said; "Mr Guest has come back." I turned pale, but he was too much engaged with his own trouble to observe it. "What do you suppose my cousin is up to? She had agreed to drive with me and I had determined to come home, once for all, engaged or rejected. As soon as she heard of Guest's arrival, she threw me overboard and tripped off to her room, to touch up her curls. Go down there now and you'll find her shaking them at Mr Guest. By the Lord, sir, she can whistle for me now! If there was a decently good-looking woman in this house, I'd march straight up to her and offer myself. You're a happy man, my boy, not to have a d—d fool to interfere with you, and not to be in love with a d—d fool either."

I had no present leisure to smooth the turbid waters of poor Crawford's passion; but I remembered a clever remark in a French book, to the effect that even the best men—and Crawford was one of the best—are subject to a momentary need not to respect what they love. I repaired alone to the house by the river, and found Laura in the little parlor which she shared with Mrs Beck. The room was flooded with the glow of a crimson sunset, and she was looking out of the long window at two persons in the garden. In my great desire to obtain some firm assurance from her before her father's interference should become a certainty, I lost no time. "I've been able to think of nothing," I said, "but your reply to that poor offer of mine. I've been flattering myself that it really means something,—means, possibly, that if I were to speak—here—now—all that I long to speak, you would listen to me more kindly. Laura," I cried, passionately, "I repent of all my follies and I love you!"

She looked at me from head to foot with a gaze almost strange in its intensity. It betrayed trouble, but, I fancied, a grateful trouble. Then, with a smile, "My father has come," she said. The words set my heart a beating, and I had a horrible fancy that they were maliciously uttered. But as she went on I was reassured. "I want him to see you, though he knows nothing of your offer."

Somehow, by her tone, my mind was suddenly illumined with a delicious apprehension of her motive. She had heard the only murmur of that sentiment whose tender essence resents compulsion. "Let me feel then," I said, "that I am not to stand or fall by *his* choice."

"He's sure to like you," she answered; "don't you remember my telling you so? He judges better of men than of women," she added sadly, turning away from the window.

Mr Guest had been advancing toward the house, side by side with Mrs Beck. Before they reached it the latter was met by two ladies who had been ushered into the garden from the front gate, and with whom, with an air of smothered petulance, perceptible even at a distance, she retraced her steps toward the summer-house. Her companion entered our little parlor alone from the piazza. He stepped jauntily and looked surprisingly little altered by his month's ordeal. Mrs Beck might still have taken him for a duke, or, at least, for an earl. His daughter immediately introduced me. "Happy to make your acquaintance, sir," he exclaimed, in a voice which I was almost shocked to find how well I knew. He offered his hand. I met it with my own, and the next moment we were fairly face to face. I was prepared for anything. Recognition faltered for a mere instant in his eyes; then I felt it suddenly leap forth

in the tremendous wrench of his hand, "Ah, you—*you*—
YOU!"

"Why, you know him!" exclaimed Laura.

Guest continued to wring my hand, and I felt to my cost
that he was shocked. He panted a moment for breath, and
then burst into a monstrous laugh. I looked askance at Laura;
her eyes with filled with wonder. I felt that for the moment
anger had made her father reckless, and anything was better
than that between us the edge of our secret should peep out.
"We have been introduced," I said, trying to smile. Guest
dropped my hand as if it burned him, and walked the length
of the room.

"You should have told me!" Laura added, in a tone of
almost familiar reproach.

"Miss Guest," I answered, hardly knowing what I said,
"the world is so wide—"

"Upon my soul, I think it's damnably narrow!" cried
Guest, who had turned very pale.

I determined then that he should know the worst. "I'm here
with a purpose, Mr Guest," I said; "I love your daughter."

He stopped short, fairly glaring at me. Laura stepped toward him and laid her two hands on his arm. "Something is
wrong," she said, "very wrong! It's your horrible money
matters! Weren't you really then so generous?" and she
turned to me.

Guest laid his other hand on hers as they rested on his arm
and patted them gently. "My daughter," he said solemnly,
"do your poor father a favor. Dismiss him forever. Turn
him out of the house," he added, fiercely.

"You wrong your daughter," I cried, "by asking her to
act so blindly and cruelly."

"My child," Guest went on, "I expect you to obey!"

There was a silence. At last Laura turned to me, excessively
pale. "Will you do me the very great favor," she said, with
a trembling voice, "to leave us?"

I reflected a moment. "I appreciate your generosity; but in the interest of your own happiness, I beg you not to listen to your father until I have had a word with him alone."

She hesitated and looked, as if for assent, at her father. "Great heavens, girl!" he cried, "you don't mean you love him!" She blushed to her hair and rapidly left the room.

Guest took up his hat and removed a speck of dust from the ribbon by a fillip of his finger-nail. "Young man," he said, "you waste words!"

"Not, I hope, when, with my hand on my heart, I beg your pardon."

"Now that you have something to gain. If you respect me, you should have protested before. If you don't, you've nothing to do with me or mine."

"I allow for your natural resentment, but you might keep it within bounds. I religiously forget, ignore, efface the past. Meet me half-way! When we met a month ago, I already loved your daughter. If I had dreamed of your being ever so remotely connected with her, I would have arrested that detestable scene even by force, brother of mine though your adversary was!"

Guest put on his hat with a gesture of implacable contempt. "That's all very well! You don't know me, sir, or you'd not waste your breath on *ifs!* The thing's done. Such as I stand here, I've been *dishonored!*" And two hot tears sprang into his eyes. "Such as I stand here, I carry in my poor, sore heart the vision of your great, brutal, staring, cruel presence. And now you ask me to accept that presence as perpetual! Upon my soul, I'm a precious fool to talk about it."

I made an immense effort to remain calm and courteous. "Is there nothing I can do to secure your good-will? I'll make any sacrifice."

"Nothing but to leave me at once and forever. Fancy my living with you for an hour! Fancy, whenever I met your eyes, my seeing in them the reflection of—of that piece of business! And your walking about looking wise and chuckling! My precious young man," he went on with a scorching smile, "if you knew how I hated you, you'd give me a wide berth."

I was silent for some moments, teaching myself the great patience which I foresaw I should need. "This is after all but the question of our personal relations, which we might fairly leave to time. Not only am I willing to pledge myself to the most explicit respect—"

"Explicit respect!" he broke out. "I should relish that vastly! Heaven deliver me from your explicit respect!"

"I can quite believe," I quietly continued, "that I should get to like you. Your daughter has done me the honor to say that she believed you would like me."

"Perfect! You've talked it all over with her?"

"At any rate," I declared roundly, "I love her, and I have reason to hope that I may render myself acceptable to her. I can only add, Mr Guest, that much as I should value your approval of my suit, if you withhold it I shall try my fortune without it!"

"Gently, impetuous youth!" And Guest laid his hand on my arm and lowered his voice. "Do you dream that if my daughter ever so faintly suspected the truth, she would even look at you again?"

"The truth? Heaven forbid she should dream of it! I wonder that in your position you should allude to it so freely."

"I was prudent once; I shall treat myself to a little freedom now. Give it up, I advise you. She may have thought you a pretty young fellow; I took you for one myself at first; but she'll keep her affection for a man with the bowels of compassion. She'll never love a coward, sir. Upon my soul, I'd sooner she married your beautiful brother. *He*, at least, had a grievance. Don't talk to me about my own child. She and I have an older love than yours! and if she were to learn that I've been weak—Heaven help me!—she would only love me the more. She would feel only that I've been outraged."

I confess that privately I flinched, but I stood to it bravely. "Miss Guest, doubtless, is as perfect a daughter as she would be a wife. But allow me to say that a woman's heart is not so simple a mechanism. Your daughter is a person of a very fine sense of honor, and I can imagine nothing that would give her greater pain than to be reduced to an attitude of mere compassion for her father. She likes to believe that men are strong. The sense of respect is necessary to her happiness. We both wish to assure that happiness. Let us join hands to preserve her illusions."

I saw in his eye no concession except to angry perplexity. "I don't know what you mean," he cried, "and I don't want to know. If you wish to intimate that my daughter is so very superior a person that she'll despise me, you're mistaken! She's beyond any compliment you can pay her. You can't frighten me now; I don't care for things." He walked away a moment and then turned about with flushed face and trembling lip. "I'm broken, I'm ruined! I don't want my daughter's respect, nor any other woman's. It's a burden, a mockery, a snare! What's a woman worth who can be kind only while she believes? Ah, ah!" and he began to rub his hands with a sudden air of helpless senility, "I should never be so kissed and coddled and nursed. I can tell her what I please; I shan't mind what I say now. I've ceased to care—all in a month! Reputation's a farce; a pair of tight boots, worn for vanity. I used to have a good foot, but I shall end my days in my slippers. I don't care for anything!"

This mood was piteous, but it was also formidable, for I was scantily disposed to face the imputation of having reduced an amiable gentleman, in however strictly just a cause, to this state of plaintive cynicism. I could only hope that time would repair both his vanity and his charity, seriously damaged as they were. "Well," I said, taking my hat, "a man in love, you know, is obstinate. Confess, yourself, that you'd not think the better of me for accepting dismissal philosophically. A single word of caution, keep cool; don't lose your head; don't speak recklessly to Laura. I protest that, for myself, I'd rather my mistress shouldn't doubt of her father."

Guest had seated himself on the sofa with his hat on, and remained staring absently at the carpet, as if he were deaf to my words. As I turned away, Mrs Beck crossed the piazza and stood on the threshold of the long window. Her shadow fell at Mr Guest's feet; she sent a searching glance from his face to mine. He started, stared, rose, stiffened himself up, and removed his hat. Suddenly he coloured to the temples, and after a second's delay there issued from behind this ruby curtain a wondrous imitation of a smile. I turned away, reassured. "My case is not hopeless," I said to myself. "You *do* care for something, yet." Even had I deemed it hopeless, I might have made my farewell. Laura met me near the gate and I remember thinking that trouble was vastly becoming to her.

"Is your quarrel too bad to speak of?" she asked.

"Allow me to make an urgent request. Your father forbids me to think of you, and you, of course, to think of me. You see," I said, mustering a smile, "we're in a delightfully romantic position, persecuted by a stern parent. He will say hard things of me; I say nothing about your believing them, I leave that to your own discretion. But don't contradict them. Let him call me cruel, pusillanimous, false, whatever he will. Ask no questions; they will bring you no comfort. Be patient, be a good daughter, and—wait!"

Her brow contracted painfully over her intensely lucid eyes, and she shook her head impatiently. "Let me understand. Have you really done wrong?"

I felt that it was but a slender sacrifice to generosity to say Yes, and to add that I had repented. I even felt gratefully that whatever it might be to have a crime to confess to, it was not "boyish."

For a moment, I think, Laura was on the point of asking me a supreme question about her father, but she suppressed it and abruptly left me.

My step-brother's feeble remnant of health was now so cruelly reduced that the end of his troubles seemed near. He was in constant pain, and was kept alive only by stupefying drugs. As his last hour might strike at any moment, I was careful to remain within call, and for several days saw nothing of father or daughter. I learned from Crawford that they had determined to prolong their stay into the autumn, for Mr Guest's "health." "I don't know what's the matter with his health," Crawford grumbled. "For a sick man he seems uncommonly hearty, able to sit out of doors till midnight with Mrs B., and always as spick and span as a bridegroom. I'm the invalid of the lot," he declared; "the climate don't agree with me." Mrs Beck, it appeared, was too fickle for patience; he would be made a fool of no more. If she wanted him, she must come and fetch him; and if she valued her chance, she must do it without delay. He departed for New York to try the virtue of missing and being missed.

On the evening he left us, the doctor told me that Edgar could not outlast the night. At midnight, I relieved the watcher and took my place by his bed. Edgar's soundless and motionless sleep was horribly like death. Sitting watchful by his pillow, I passed an oppressively solemn night. It seemed to me that a part of myself was dying, and that I was sitting in cold survival of youthful innocence and of the lavish self-surrender of youth. There is a certain comfort in an ancient grievance, and as I thought of having heard for the last time the strenuous quaver of Edgar's voice, I could have wept as for the effacement of some revered horizon-line of life. I heard his voice again, however; he was not even to die without approving the matter. With the first flash of dawn and the earliest broken bird-note, he opened his eyes and began to murmur disconnectedly. At length he recognized me, and, with me, his situation. "Don't go on tiptoe, and hold your breath, and pull a long face," he said; "speak up like a man. I'm doing the biggest job I ever did yet, you'll not interrupt me; I'm dying. One—two, three—four; I can almost count the ebbing waves. And to think that all these years they've been breaking on the strand of the universe! It's only when the world's din is shut out, at the last, that we hear them. I'll not pretend to say I'm not sorry; I've been a man of this world. It's a great one; there's a vast deal to do in it, for a man of sense. I've not been a fool, either. Write that for my epitaph, *He was no fool!*— except when he went to L. I'm not satisfied yet. I might have got better, and richer. I wanted to try galvanism, and to transfer that Pennsylvania stock. Well, I'm to be transferred myself. If dying's the end of it all, it's as well to die worse as to die better. At any rate, while time was mine, I didn't waste it. I went over my will, pen in hand, for the last time, only a week ago, crossed the *t*'s and dotted the *i*'s. I've left you— nothing. You need nothing for comfort, and of course you expect nothing for sentiment. I've left twenty thousand dollars to found an infirmary for twenty indigent persons suffering from tumor in the stomach. *There's* sentiment! There will be no trouble about it, for my affairs are in perfect shape. Twenty snug little beds in my own little house in Philadelphia. They can get five into the dining-room." He was silent awhile, as if with a kind of ecstatic vision of the five little beds in a row. "I don't know that there is anything else," he said, at last, "except a few old papers to be burned. I hate leaving rubbish behind me; it's enough to leave one's mouldering carcass!"

At his direction I brought a large tin box from a closet and placed it on a chair by his bedside, where I drew from it a dozen useless papers and burned them one by one in the candle. At last, when but three or four were left, I laid my hand on a small sealed document labelled *Guest's Confession.*

My hand trembled as I held it up to him, and as he recognized it a faint flush overspread his cadaverous pallor. He frowned, as if painfully confused. "How did it come there? I sent it back, I sent it back," he said. Then suddenly with a strangely erroneous recollection of our recent dispute, "I told you so the other day, you remember; and you said I was too generous. And what did you tell me about the daughter? You're in love with her? Ah yes! What a muddle!"

I respected his confusion. "You say you've left me nothing," I answered. "Leave me this."

For all reply, he turned over with a groan, and relapsed into stupor. The nurse shortly afterwards came to relieve me; but though I lay down, I was unable to sleep. The personal possession of this little scrap of paper acted altogether too potently on my nerves and my imagination. In due contravention of the doctor, Edgar outlasted the night and lived into another day. But as high noon was clashing out from the village church, and I stood with the doctor by his bedside, the latter, who had lifted his wrist a little to test his pulse, released it, not with the tenderness we render to suffering, but with a more summary reverence. Suffering was over.

By the close of the day I had finished my preparations for attending my step-brother's remains to burial in Philadelphia, among those of his own people; but before my departure, I measured once more that well-trodden road to the house by the river, and requested a moment's conversation with Mr Guest. In spite of my attention being otherwise engaged, I had felt strangely all day that I carried a sort of magic talisman, a mystic key to fortune. I was constantly fumbling in my waist-coat pocket to see whether the talisman was really there. I wondered that, as yet, Guest should not have demanded a surrender of his note; but I attributed his silence to shame, scorn, and defiance, and promised myself a sort of golden advantage by anticipating his claim with the cogent frankness of justice. But as soon as he entered the room

I foresaw that Justice must show her sword as well as her scales. His resentment had deepened into a kind of preposterous arrogance, of a temper quite insensible to logic. He had more than recovered his native buoyancy and splendour; there was an air of feverish impudence in his stare, his light swagger, in the very hue and fashion of his crimson necktie. He had an evil genius with blond curls and innumerable flounces.

"I feel it to be a sort of duty," I said, "to inform you that my brother died this morning."

"Your brother? What's your brother to me? He's been dead to me these three days. Is that all you have to say?"

I was irritated by the man's stupid implacability, and my purpose received a check. "No," I answered, "I've several things more to touch upon."

"In so far as they concern my daughter, you may leave them unsaid. She tells me of your offer to—*buy off* my opposition. Am I to understand that it was seriously made? You're a coarser young man than I fancied!"

"She told you of my offer?" I cried.

"Oh, you needn't build upon that. She hasn't mentioned your name since."

I was silent, thinking my own thoughts. I won't answer for it, that, in spite of his caution, I did *not* lay an immaterial brick or two. "You're still irreconcilable?" I contented myself with asking.

He assumed an expression of absolutely jovial contempt. "My dear sir, I detest the sight of you!"

"Have you no question to ask, no demand to make?"

He looked at me a moment in silence, with just the least little twitch and tremor of mouth and eye. His vanity, I guessed on the instant, was determined stoutly to ignore that I held him at an advantage and to refuse me the satisfaction of extorting from him the least allusion to the evidence of his disgrace. He had known bitter compulsion once; he would not do it the honor to concede that it had not spent itself. "No demand but that you will excuse my further attendance."

My own vanity took a hand in the game. Justice herself was bound to go no more than half-way. If he was not afraid of his little paper, he might try a week or two more of bravery. I bowed to him in silence and let him depart. As I turned to go I found myself face to face with Mrs Beck, whose pretty visage was flushed with curiosity. "You and Mr Guest have quarrelled," she said roundly.

"As you see, madam."

"As I see, madam! But what is it all about?"

"About—his daughter."

"His daughter and his ducats! You're a very deep young man, in spite of those boyish looks of yours. Why did you never tell me you knew him? You've quarrelled about money matters."

"As you say," I answered, "I'm very deep. Don't tempt me to further subterfuge."

"He has lost money, I know. Is it much? Tell me that!"

"It's an enormous sum!" I said, with mock solemnity.

"Provoking man!" And she gave a little stamp of disgust.

"He's in trouble," I said. "To a woman of your tender sympathies he ought to be more interesting than ever."

She mused a moment, fixing me with her keen blue eye. "It's a sad responsibility to have a heart!" she murmured.

"In that," I said, "we perfectly agree."

VI

It was a singular fact that Edgar's affairs turned out to be in by no means the exemplary order in which he had flattered himself he placed them. They were very much at sixes and

sevens. The discovery, to me, was almost a shock. I might
have drawn from it a pertinent lesson on the fallacy of human
pretensions. The gentleman whom Edgar had supremely
honored (as he seemed to assume in his will) by appointing
his executor, responded to my innocent surprise by tapping
his forehead with a peculiar smile. It was partly from curiosity
as to the value of this explanation, that I helped him to look
into the dense confusion which prevailed in my step-brother's
estate. It revealed certainly an odd compound of madness
and method. I learned with real regret that the twenty
eleemosynary beds at Philadelphia must remain a superb conception. I was horrified at every step by the broad license with
which his will had to be interpreted. All profitless as I was in
the case, when I thought of the comfortable credit in which he
had died, I felt like some greedy kinsman of tragedy making
impious havoc with a sacred bequest. These matters detained
me for a week in New York, where I had joined my brother's
executor. At my earliest moment of leisure, I called upon
Crawford at the office of a friend to whom he had addressed
me, and learned that after three or four dismally restless days
in town, he had taken a summary departure for L. A couple
of days later, I was struck with a certain dramatic connection
between his return and the following note from Mr Guest,
which I give verbally, in its pregnant brevity:

SIR:—I possess a claim on your late brother's estate which it is
needless to specify. You will either satisfy it by return of mail or
forfeit forever the common respect of gentlemen.

J.G.

Things had happened with the poor man rather as I hoped
than as I expected. He had borrowed his recent exaggerated
defiance from the transient smiles of Mrs Beck. They had gone
to his head like the fumes of wine, and he had dreamed for a
day that he could afford to snap his fingers at the past. What
he really desired and hoped of Mrs Beck I was puzzled to say.

In this woful disrepair of his fortunes he could hardly have meant to hold her to a pledge of matrimony extorted in brighter hours. He was infatuated, I believed, partly by a weak, spasmodic optimism which represented his troubles as momentary, and enjoined him to hold firm till something turned up, and partly by a reckless and frivolous susceptibility to the lady's unscrupulous blandishments. While they prevailed, he lost all notion of the wholesome truth of things, and would have been capable of any egregious folly. Mrs Beck was in love with him, in so far as she was capable of being in love; his gallantry, of all gallantries, suited her to a charm; but she reproached herself angrily with this amiable weakness, and prudence every day won back an inch of ground. Poor Guest indeed had clumsily snuffed out his candle. He had slept in the arms of Delilah, and he had waked to find that Delilah had guessed, if not his secret, something uncomfortably like it. Crawford's return had found Mrs Beck with but a scanty remnant of sentiment and a large accession of prudence, which was graciously placed at his service. Guest, hereupon, as I conjectured, utterly disillusioned by the cynical frankness of her defection, had seen his horizon grow ominously dark, and begun to fancy, as I remained silent, that there was thunder in the air. His pompous waiving, in his note, of allusion both to our last meeting, and to my own present claim, seemed to me equally characteristic of his weakness and of his distress. The bitter after-taste of Mrs Beck's coquetry had, at all events, brought him back to reality. For myself, the real fact in the matter was the image of Laura Guest, sitting pensive, like an exiled princess.

I sent him nothing by return of mail. On my arrival in New York, I had enclosed the precious document in an envelope, addressed it, and stamped it, and put it back in my pocket. I could not rid myself of a belief that by that sign I should conquer. Several times I drew it forth and laid it on the table before me, reflecting that I had but a word to say

to have it dropped into the post. Cowardly, was it, to keep it?
But what was it to give up one's mistress without a battle?
Which was the uglier, my harshness or Guest's? In a holy
cause,—and holy, you may be sure, I had dubbed mine,—
were not all arms sanctified? Possession meant peril, and
peril to a manly sense, of soul and conscience, as much as of
person and fortune. Mine, at any rate, should share the danger.
It was a sinister-looking talisman, certainly; but when it had
failed, it would be time enough to give it up.

In these thoughts I went back to L. I had taken the morning
train; I arrived at noon, and with small delay proceeded to
the quiet little house which harbored such world-vexed
spirits. It was one of the first days of September, and the
breath of autumn was in the air. Summer still met the casual
glance; but the infinite light of summer had found its term;
it was as if there were a leak in the crystal vault of the firma-
ment through which the luminous ether of June was slowly
stealing away.

Mr Guest, I learned from the servant, had started on a walk,
—to the mill, she thought, three miles away. I sent in my card
to Laura, and went into the garden to await her appearance—
or her answer. At the end of five minutes, I saw her descend
from the piazza and advance down the long path. Her light
black dress swept the little box-borders, and over her head she
balanced a white parasol. I met her, and she stopped, silent
and grave. "I've come to learn," I said, "that absence has
not been fatal to me."

"You've hardly been absent. You left a—an influence
behind,—a very painful one. In Heaven's name!" she cried,
with vehemence, "what horrible wrong have you done?"

"I have done no horrible wrong. Do you believe me?"
She scanned my face searchingly for a moment; then she gave
a long, gentle, irrepressible sigh of relief. "Do you fancy
that if I had, I could meet your eyes, feel the folds of your
dress? I've done that which I have bitterly wished undone;

I did it in ignorance, weakness, and folly; I've repented in passion and truth. Can a man do more?"

"I was never afraid of the truth," she answered slowly; "I don't see that I need fear it now. I'm not a child. Tell me the absolute truth!"

"The absolute truth," I said, "is that your father once saw me in a very undignified position. It made such an impression on him that he's unable to think of me in any other. You see I was rather cynically indifferent to his observation, for I didn't know him then as your father."

She gazed at me with the same adventurous candor, and blushed a little as I became silent, then turned away and strolled along the path. "It seems a miserable thing," she said, "that two gentle spirits like yours should have an irreparable difference. When good men hate each other, what are they to do to the bad men? You must excuse my want of romance, but I cannot listen to a suitor of whom my father complains. Make peace!"

"Shall peace with him be peace with you?"

"Let me see you frankly shake hands," she said, not directly answering. "Be very kind! You don't know what he has suffered here lately." She paused, as if to conceal a tremor in her voice.

Had she read between the lines of that brilliant improvisation of mine, or was she moved chiefly with pity for his recent sentimental tribulations,—pitying them the more that she respected them the less? "He has walked to the mill," I said; "I shall meet him, and we'll come back arm in arm." I turned away, so that I may not see her face, pleading for a clemency which would make me too delicate. I went down beside the river and followed the old towing-path, now grassy with disuse. Reaching the shabby wooden bridge below the mill, I stopped midway across it and leaned against the railing. Below, the yellow water swirled past the crooked piers. I took my little sealed paper out of my pocket-book and held it over the stream, almost courting the temptation to drop it; but the temptation never came. I had just put it back in my pocket when I heard a footstep on the planks behind me. Turning round, I beheld Mr Guest. He looked tired and dusty with his walk, and had the air of a man who had been trying by violent exercise to shake off a moral incubus. Judging by his haggard brow and heavy eyes, he had hardly succeeded. As he recognized me, he started just perceptibly, as if he were too weary to be irritated. He was about to pass on without speaking, but I intercepted him. My movement provoked a flash in his sullen pupil. "I came on purpose to meet you," I said. "I have just left your daughter, and I feel more than ever how passionately I love her. Once more, I demand that you withdraw your opposition."

"Is that your answer to my letter?" he asked, eyeing me from under his brows.

"Your letter puts me in a position to make my demand with force. I refuse to submit to this absurd verdict of accident. I have just seen your daughter, and I have authority to bring you to reason."

"My daughter has received you?" he cried, flushing.

"Most kindly."

"You scoundrel!"

"Gently, gently. Shake hands with me here where we stand, and let me keep my promise to Laura of our coming back to her arm in arm, at peace, reconciled, mutually forgiving and forgetting, or I walk straight back and put a certain little paper into her hands."

He turned deadly pale, and a fierce oath broke from his lips. He had been beguiled, I think, by my neglect of his letter, into the belief that Edgar had not died without destroying his signature,—a belief rendered possible by an indefeasible faith he must have had in my step-brother's probity. "You've kept that thing!" he cried. "The Lord be praised! I'm as honest a man as either of you!"

"Say but two words,—'Take her!'—and we shall be honest together again. The paper's yours." He turned away and leaned against the railing of the bridge, with his head in his hands, watching the river.

"Take your time," I continued; "I give you two hours. Go home, look at your daughter, and choose. An hour hence I'll join you. If I find you've removed your veto, I undertake to make you forget you ever offered it: if I find you've maintained it, I expose you."

"In either case you lose your mistress. Whatever Laura may think of me, there can be no doubt as to what she will think of you."

"I shall be forgiven. Leave that to me! That's my last word. In a couple of hours I shall take the liberty of coming to learn yours."

"O Laura, Laura!" cried the poor man in his bitter trouble. But I left him and walked away. I turned as I reached the farther end of the bridge, and saw him slowly resume his course. I marched along the road to the mill, so excited with having uttered this brave *ultimatum* that I hardly knew whither I went. But at last I bethought me of a certain shady streamside nook just hereabouts, which a little exploration soon discovered. A shallow cove, screened from the road by dense clumps of willows, stayed the current a moment in its grassy bend. I had noted it while boating, as a spot where a couple of lovers might aptly disembark and moor their idle skiff; and I was now tempted to try its influence in ardent solitude. I flung myself on the ground, and as I listened to the light gurgle of the tarrying stream and to the softer rustle of the cool gray leafage around me, I suddenly felt that I was exhausted and sickened. I lay motionless, watching the sky and resting from my anger. Little by little it melted away and left me horribly ashamed. How long I lay there I know not, nor what was the logic of my meditations, but an ineffable change stole over my spirit. There are fathomless depths in spiritual mood and motive. Opposite me, on the farther side of the stream, winding along a path through the bushes, three or four cows had come down to drink. I sat up and watched them. A young man followed them, in a red shirt, with his trousers in his boots. While they were comfortably nosing the water into ripples, he sat down on a stone and began to light his pipe. In a moment I fancied I saw the little blue thread of smoke curl up from the bowl. From beyond, just droning through the air, came the liquid rumble of the mill. There seemed to me something in this vision ineffably pastoral, peaceful, and innocent; it smote me to my heart of hearts. I felt a nameless wave of impulse start somewhere in the innermost vitals of conscience and fill me with passionate shame. I fell back on the grass and burst into tears.

The sun was low and the breeze had risen when I rose to my feet. I scrambled back to the road, crossed the bridge, and hurried home by the towing-path. My heart, however, beat faster than my footfalls. I passed into the garden and advanced to the house; as I stepped upon the piazza, I was met by Mrs Beck. "Answer me a simple question," she cried, laying her hand on my arm.

"I should like to hear you ask one!" I retorted, impatiently.

"Has Mr Guest lost his mind?"

"For an hour! I've brought it back to him."

"You've a pretty quarrel between you. He comes up an hour ago, as I was sitting in the garden with—with Mr Crawford, requests a moment's interview, leads me apart and —offers himself. 'If you'll have me, take me now; you won't an hour hence,' he cried. 'Neither now nor an hour hence, thank you,' said I. 'My affections are fixed—elsewhere.'"

"You've not lost your head, at any rate," said I; and, releasing myself, I went into the parlor. I had a horrible fear of being too late. The candles stood lighted on the piano, and tea had been brought in, but the kettle was singing unheeded. On the divan facing the window sat Guest, lounging back on the cushions, his hat and stick flung down beside him, his hands grasping his knees, his head thrown back, and his eyes closed. That he should have remained so for an hour, unbrushed and unfurbished, spoke volumes as to his mental state. Near him sat Laura, looking at him askance in mute anxiety. What had passed between them? Laura's urgent glance as I entered was full of trouble, but I fancied without reproach. He had apparently chosen neither way; he had simply fallen there, weary, desperate, and dumb.

"I'm disappointed!" Laura said to me gravely.

Her father opened his eyes, stared at me a moment, and then closed them. I answered nothing; but after a moment's hesitation went and took my seat beside Guest. I laid my hand on his own with a grasp of which he felt, first the force, then, I think, the kindness; for, after a momentary spasm of repulsion, he remained coldly passive. He must have begun to wonder. "Be so good," I said to Laura, "as to bring me one of the candles." She looked surprised; but she complied and came toward me, holding the taper, like some pale priestess expecting a portent. I drew out the note and held it to the flame. "Your father and I have had a secret," I said, "which has been a burden to both of us. Here it goes." Laura's hand trembled as she held the candle, and mine as I held the paper; but between us the vile thing blazed and was consumed. I glanced askance at Guest; he was staring wide-eyed at the dropping cinders. When the last had dropped, I took the candle, rose, and carried it back to the paino. Laura dropped on her knees before her father, and, while my back was turned, something passed between them with which I was concerned only in its consequences.

When I looked round, Guest had risen and was passing his fingers through his hair. "Daughter," he said, "when I came in, what was it I said to you?"

She stood for an instant with her eyes on the floor. Then, "I've forgotten!" she said, simply.

Mrs Beck had passed in by the window in time to hear these last words. "Do you know what you said to me when you came in?" she cried, mirthfully shaking a finger at Guest. He laughed nervously, picked up his hat, and stood looking, with an air of odd solemnity, at his boots. Suddenly it seemed to occur to him that he was dusty and dishevelled. He settled his shirt-collar and levelled a glance at the mirror, in which he caught my eye. He tried hard to look insensible; but it was the glance of a man who felt more comfortable than he had done in a month. He marched stiffly to the door.

"Are you going to dress?" said Mrs Beck.

"From head to foot!" he cried, with violence.

"Be so good, then, if you see Mr Crawford in the hall, as to ask him to come in and have a cup of tea."

Laura had passed out to the piazza, where I immediately joined her. "Your father accepts me," I said; "there is nothing left but for you—"

Five minutes later, I looked back through the window to see if we were being observed. But Mrs Beck was busy adding another lump of sugar to Crawford's cup of tea. His eye met mine, however, and I fancied he looked sheepish.

A NOTE ON THE TEXT

In preparing these tales for publication, the editor had to choose between James's original magazine texts, those published in book form soon afterwards and those revised and rewritten for the New York Edition. The obvious choice, it seemed to him, was the original book form of the story where there was one. In that form it had the benefit of revision from magazine to volume; and in that form it was best known to James's generation. It seemed to the editor that in a chronological edition of James's shorter fictions, the New York Edition texts had no relevance. They belong exclusively to the edition for which they were designed; particularly since the revisions were often made several decades after the original publication.

The original magazine publications of the tales in this volume were as follows:

"Osborne's Revenge," *Galaxy*, July 1868.

"A Light Man," *Galaxy*, July 1868.

"Gabrielle de Bergerac," *Atlantic Monthly*, July–September 1869.

"Travelling Companions," *Atlantic Monthly*, November–December 1870.

"A Passionate Pilgrim," *Atlantic Monthly*, March–April 1871.

"At Isella," *Galaxy*, August 1871.

"Master Eustace," *Galaxy*, November 1871.

"Guest's Confession," *Atlantic Monthly*, October–November 1872.

James made "A Passionate Pilgrim" the title-story of his first book in 1875. "A Light Man" was reprinted in *Stories by American Authors* in 1884. These two tales and "Master

Eustace" were included in *Stories Revived*, 1885. The text used here is that of the first book publication. The rest of the tales follow the original magazine texts, which have never before appeared in England. "Master Eustace" has not appeared in the United States in this revised form.

For the complete bibliography of the tales the reader is referred to *A Bibliography of the Writings of Henry James* by Leon Edel and Dan H. Laurence (second edition, revised, London, 1961) in the Soho Bibliographies published by Rupert Hart-Davis.